Dinosaur Lake IV

Dinosaur Wars

(4th and final book of the Dinosaur Lake series)

By Kathryn Meyer Griffith

Dinosaur Lake IV

Dinosaur Wars
(4th and final book of the Dinosaur Lake series)
by Kathryn Meyer Griffith

Cover art by: Dawné Dominique

** This book is not meant to be based on scientific facts of any kind...it is purely a fictional, made up story about make-believe dinosaurs.*

Other books by Kathryn Meyer Griffith:
Evil Stalks the Night
The Heart of the Rose
Blood Forged
Vampire Blood
The Last Vampire (2012 Epics EBook Awards Finalist)
Witches
The Calling
Scraps of Paper
All Things Slip Away
Ghosts Beneath Us
Egyptian Heart
Winter's Journey
The Ice Bridge
Don't Look Back, Agnes
A Time of Demons and Angels
The Woman in Crimson
Four Spooky Short Stories
Human No Longer
Dinosaur Lake (2014 Epic EBook Awards Finalist)
Dinosaur Lake II: Dinosaurs Arising
Dinosaur Lake III: Infestation

***All Kathryn Meyer Griffith's books can be found here:**
http://tinyurl.com/ld4jlow
***All her Audible.com audio books here:**
http://tinyurl.com/oz7c4or

For my beloved brother Jim Meyer...who was the best musician and songwriter I've ever known, and always my best friend. My life wouldn't have been half as rich without you having been in it. I love you, brother! Here's his music:
https://www.youtube.com/playlist?list=PLEypYatBBgrWxOzQGsLOs3IItVVUywSsV

Chapter 1

The winter had been a bitter one, with more ice and snow than any other year since Chief Park Ranger Henry Shore and his wife, Ann, had moved into Crater Lake National Park fourteen years earlier; harsher even than the year before which itself had been record breaking. Thanksgiving and Christmas, bare of material gifts but full of comradery and thrown together meals, were almost happy times because no one had seen a dinosaur in months and it was hard for any of them to believe they still existed beyond the strong walls of their sanctuary ranger headquarters. For a while they lived in ignorant bliss as life felt almost normal again, except for all of them living locked up in a barracks-like settlement. Some of the residents began to hope the war was over, but Henry knew better. It was only the frigid weather that kept the beasts away. New Year's came and went. People talked and visited among themselves, played guitar with Steven, or card games with each other, read books or their Kindles…and prepared…just in case the dinosaurs rematerialized. The snow fell, drifted, and covered every sign of man and beast right through to mid-April and only then did it begin to subside.

Yet the inclement weather persistently fended off the prehistoric prowlers. The respite had given Henry, his family, his rangers and Captain McDowell's soldiers a chance to rest and strategize the moves they would make in the spring when they might have to continue the fight.

Finally, at long last, the spring thaw had arrived…and with it, Henry feared, the dinosaurs would surely return. When the snow had melted enough during a winter's lull for patrols to resume, Henry and his son-in-law, paleontologist Doctor Justin Maltin, along with some of Captain Sherman McDowell's soldiers, once again ventured out into the park in their M1A2 Abrams battle tanks to flush the remaining monsters out and exterminate them.

At first they found none. They journeyed across the park's lands, into the back woods, over hills, into the valleys and up to the crater's rim. They scanned the lake with high-powered binoculars. The soldiers threw a decayed deer carcass they'd found earlier out in the woods over the rim and watched it splash into the lake a thousand feet below. No sea monsters rose to devour it. It sank into the icy water and disappeared. Wherever they toured there were no signs of dinosaurs, not a cry, not a glimpse of a claw, fang or tail.

And as the days went by the snow and ice slowly began to melt. The temperature rose in tiny increments each day.

"It could be it's too cold yet for them. They're still hiding out somewhere," Justin remarked to Henry one morning as the scientist stood feet away from their tank and gazed out over the caldera. The water was rimmed in ice and the color wasn't the usual brilliant blue, but a pale imitation, reflecting the overcast and cloudy skies. Patches of snow and ice clung to the hard ground around the rim itself. Justin believed, as Henry did, there might be more snow coming. There was that frosty smell in the air. Justin was dressed in borrowed army fatigues, one of his baseball caps covering his long hair. The faint sunlight glinted off his gold-rimmed glasses. "Though they are warm-blooded, they don't like the cold any better than we do."

Henry nodded. "Maybe."

"Or maybe," Captain McDowell interjected hopefully in her softer voice, "they've left the vicinity? Vamoosed. Or are all dead? The violent winter killed them off. It was a bone-freezer." She was lurking behind the scientist. Henry was on his right and one of her soldiers on his left. All of them had rifles slung over their shoulders and high-powered handguns on their hips. They always left one man in the Abrams because they never knew when they'd need to perform a hasty attack or retreat. Since they'd moved into Fort Headquarters, as some of the soldiers liked to refer to it, the year before, and after the years of battles they'd endured, they had become seasoned dinosaur hunters. They never took chances and were heavily armed wherever they went.

"I wouldn't bet on that," Justin replied. "They're out there all right. I feel it. They are skulking in caves or snug in their nests, waiting for the weather to get a tad warmer. There were too many of them left after the final siege last fall for that not to be the case.

"Then there will be the new crop hatching out, of course." His eyes lifted to the sky. There were no birds above them and nothing, not anything alive, moved in the woods around the humans. There was a dead calm now. Very eerie. The wildlife, large and small, had been decimated months ago. It was assumed the dinosaurs had eaten them.

"Great. Baby dinosaurs. More dinosaurs," McDowell grumbled. "Just what we need."

"Uh, yup." Henry swung away from the view and headed back to their ride. "Let's call it a day, people. We'll get an early start tomorrow and do this all over again. We can search the other side of the caldera. Ann mentioned this morning the weather report is predicting snow, just as we thought, later today, any time now really; it shouldn't accumulate more than a couple of inches, but it is better if we're safe and warm indoors."

"I agree," Justin responded, eyes still on the sky.

The others followed him to the Abrams and climbed in. The tank, and a second one behind it, rolled towards park headquarters and through the gates as an icy snow began to fall.

The whole way there Henry had the uncomfortable feeling there were eyes on them. Lots of eyes. And, he'd bet, none of them were the usual park inhabitants or human. That's when the bad feeling began to shadow him and for the rest of the night he couldn't shake it. It just got stronger.

*****

The next morning was the warmest one so far. The white stuff, as it often did in April, had raged half the night and then swiftly began to melt when the bright sun came out. That was early spring in Crater Lake. It snowed one day and melted the next, though it could just as easily snow and the snow, feet of it, stick.

Henry exited his and Ann's room fully dressed and ready for the day's patrol, Ann behind him, and met Justin, their granddaughter Phoebe, Laura with the baby, and Steven outside its door. Ann's eyes lit up when she saw her daughter holding little Timothy and she pushed by her husband to get to them. The boy, with the soft blond hair and expressive blue eyes, was big for his age and already walking. He had most of the rangers and soldiers wrapped around his chubby little fingers. Over the long hard winter, voluntarily imprisoned inside the fort, the rangers and soldiers had become Phoebe's and Timothy's family, their protectors, too.

Ann opened her arms to the younger child. "Give me that sweet little boy." And Laura handed the baby over. The boy grabbed at Henry as he went past him in the air between the two women and Henry gave his plump face a quick kiss. The boy laughed and Henry couldn't help but smile. The children had brought nothing but joy and having them among them had given them new hope. This was what they were fighting for. The children. The next generation and the generation after that. The future. The dinosaurs couldn't be allowed to take over the earth because it belonged to man and his descendants.

Phoebe was nine years old, she'd grown tall and slender, and she took on chores around headquarters as if she were an adult. She had the same chestnut colored hair and blue eyes as her mother, and as her mother, she'd be a pretty woman someday, too. She helped her mother feed the troops and keep their spirits up. Justin had taught her how to shoot a gun, a rifle, so she'd be able to protect herself. She was a clever child, brave, and a quick learner. Laura had begun home schooling the girl and did the best she could, being a nurse and not a teacher; but Ann helped and between the two they believed they were doing an adequate job.

Justin smiled at his daughter and his son, pulling his wife up against him. She kissed him on the cheek. They were well aware in these times any separation could be their last and any patrol could end in deaths. It had brought them closer.

Henry and Ann's marriage, their relationship, too, had never been better, except for the dinosaur situation and her weakening health. Lately she rarely helped prepare meals for the men or took her turn doing any of the other housekeeping chores. She was too weak. The winter had been hard on her. She hadn't complained or said anything to Henry, she never would, but the cancer must be winning. Her face was gaunt, frame emaciated, skin a sallow yellow and her eyes lacked the luster he was used to. She was having trouble walking and often standing; wobbling when she moved from room to room. Someone had to help her. She slept a lot and, at times, coughed incessantly and had trouble breathing. She was getting worse and was trying to hide it from him, but he'd seen. He saw everything when it came to Ann. He'd already made the decision as soon as the weather allowed, and the path out of the park was clear of snow and prehistoric creatures, he would do whatever he had to do to get her to a hospital and real treatment. He only prayed there was a medical facility still open somewhere with doctors, nurses, and the life-saving and chemotherapy equipment she'd probably need. The thought there might not be one near enough to get to, and still operating, worried him constantly.

So it was crucial the dinosaurs be dealt with as soon as possible. The park, and the surrounding areas, had to be free of them. It had to be safe so he could take care of Ann and get her what she needed, so they could all stop fighting and life could return to normal. Henry prayed for that every day.

"We ready to move out?" Henry faced Justin, Steven, and his rangers. "Who's coming with me today?"

"I am," Justin announced as he did almost every day. He was after all the expert on the ancient creatures they hunted and his counsel was as always welcomed. "Steven's staying here today. He's on fence duty." Fence duty was the ongoing upkeep of the wooden barricade that surrounded them and kept the dinosaurs from overrunning the compound. It was constantly being shored up, reinforced; built higher and stronger. The week before, because the weather had gotten better, they'd begun stringing barbed wire along the top and bottom of it. It was heavy duty strength with thick and wickedly sharp barbs because it was only a matter of time now before the spring offensive would begin and their defenses had to be ready.

Captain McDowell stepped forward. So did two of her soldiers. "I'm with you, Chief Ranger. Sergeant Gilbert, Private Harmon and I. You and Maltin will make five. The other tank crew will consist of Sergeant Brinker and a team of his men." Her smile covered most of her face. She loved going on patrol, getting out of headquarters, and hated being cooped up. Four or five men could comfortably fit in a tank and the patrols usually consisted of at least two of the machines. There was safety in numbers and how well they'd learned that since the dinosaur troubles and sieges had begun.

"All right. Let's go then." Henry led the group out the door and into the sunshine. His eyes immediately went to the formidable fence that encircled them. The barbed wire twisted along the top glinted silver in the sun. Laura, Phoebe and Ann trailed a little behind, cooing over the baby Laura now held in her arms. Ann's waning strength wouldn't let her carry the child for long. He'd gotten too heavy.

Once outside Henry turned to Captain McDowell. "You hear anything from your boyfriend lately? I tried calling him once more last night and, again, no answer. I just keep leaving these messages and he just keeps ignoring them." Her boyfriend being Henry's friend and long-time consultant to the FBI, Scott Patterson. Patterson had spent precious little time with them over the last couple months because he was extremely busy helping to coordinate the agency's response to the growing worldwide dinosaur threat. He was constantly flying off here or there for meetings or for heaven knew what. He didn't tell Henry everything that was occurring around the globe during the developing crisis but enough for Henry to know people were fighting and dealing with dinosaurs everywhere now. China. Russia. Japan. Australia. England. It'd become a war for the planet, for the humans' very existence and lately it was becoming fiercer. But this time Patterson had been gone for weeks and Henry was anxious to hear whatever news he might have.

McDowell flashed him a smug look. "I talked to him the other night…oh, I guess it was three days ago now. He's up to his boot straps in top-secret dinosaur crap." She shrugged, a faint smile playing on her lips. "He couldn't say much–all that top-secret malarkey, you know–but I gathered he was in England again conferring with some higher up muckety-muck scientists and defense officials on how best to defeat these prehistoric intruders of ours. He did ask me to tell you he's sorry he hasn't gotten back to you as much as he'd like but his superiors are keeping him hopping. He did say he'll be seeing us soon. Real soon." She smiled again. "He misses me."

Henry couldn't wait for that visit. Patterson was one of their most dependable links to the outside world. The Internet connections, at best, were sporadic. Some days the Worldwide Web could be tapped into and some days, more and more as time had gone by, it couldn't. The computers, iPhones, iPads and tablets sat silent most of the time. Pieces of useless junk from a by-gone era. And when they could raise the Internet or watch television broadcasts the hard news had been taken over by sensationalistic reports and videos of dinosaurs and dinosaur attacks; end of civilization propaganda which only increased the chaos and fear. There was so much disinformation and craziness in the world. Heck, it had been bad before the dinosaurs had come, with political upheaval, rising crime and murder rates, but it was even worse now. Henry thought the whole world had gone nuts. Cell phone reception didn't always work, either, especially in the park. It was so frustrating. He depended on Patterson to let them know what was happening beyond the park. But lately Patterson had gone to silent running. Something really big must be going on.

"I hope it's soon. Being cut off from what's going on out there is driving me up the wall."

"Me, too. But I know he'll get here when he can. He did say something to me you'll find interesting."

"What?"

"There's talk of a major conference of leading scientists from across the globe convening together in England or perhaps New York sometime this month, very soon in fact, to discuss better ways to rid us of these unwanted dragons of ours. Apparently, shooting and blowing them up isn't doing the trick fast enough. They've been proliferating far too quickly for what we've been doing. We need a better plan. The governments of the world are looking for solutions."

Now we're calling them dragons, huh? Cute. Justin would be interested in knowing about the conference. He'd probably want to join it. "Sounds like a good idea to me."

As he spoke to McDowell, Henry was watching his granddaughter conversing with a young soldier. She was giggling at something the Private had said.

The girl was friends with everyone and everyone liked her. Henry smiled. Then his eyes went to his daughter, Laura, as she playfully swung her son around in her arms in the open area. The boy wanted down to play out in the sunlight and the fresh air. As for all of them the long winter, and being locked up all the time, had made him crave being outside. The bright sunshine and the patches of snow on the ground called to him. With an excited squeal, the boy wiggled out of Laura's arms, plopped to the ground and started toddling away from her, his fat little legs wobbling beneath him. Laura laughed and set out after him with her arms outstretched in case he fell. Ann was smiling at both of them and following behind. The boy could really move on his little legs. In a few seconds he was halfway across the compound, giggling and thrashing his arms in childhood joy. He was outside! Sun on his face. Happy.

Henry frowned and instinctively began to move towards the miniature escapee. It was too dangerous for the child to be out running around in the open like that. Though they hadn't seen any dinosaurs recently, of the stomping or of the flying variety, he, of all people, knew they were out there somewhere lurking and waiting for an opportunity to prey on them.

He glanced over at his son-in-law, who was also in pursuit of his runaway son, and suddenly he caught something moving in the upper corner of his eye. A dark, fast moving blob on the horizon. An object gliding high above them and now swiftly coming down towards the earth…and headed towards Timothy. Two, three of them now…rocketing towards the humans in the unprotected enclosure.

Everyone had seen the danger.

Phoebe, her attention wrenched away from the soldier, pointing up at the sky, screamed, "Look out! Flying dinosaurs!"

There were more than one.

"*Gargoyles!*" Henry shouted, bringing his rifle off his shoulder and lifting it to aim. He was nearly to his grandson, reaching out for him, when the child, looking up and seeing what was above him, cried out and dashed the other way. Laura was a heartbeat behind her son by then and screaming herself now. There was terror on her face. Her hands were extended and inches away from the boy. Justin was feet beyond her and was also shooting at the gargoyle zeroing in on the child, desperately trying to bring it down.

Yelling and gunfire filled the compound as the gargoyle, hit, screeched in pain and soared off into the sky; another one plummeted to the ground about fifteen feet away from Henry. Wounded or dead.

In horror, Henry watched the smallest and closest of the flying dinosaurs, about twice the size of a man, stretch out its claws for the little boy and–

In the very moment the creature had locked onto the child and started to rise with him, Laura reached them and in a frantic tug-of-war, wrenched the boy away from the monster.

The world grew silent and stopped.

What happened next Henry wouldn't ever forget as the image would never stop haunting him for the rest of his life. Laura fought for her child. Slapping and cursing at the creature as she pulled her son back to safety and the gargoyle spun around in the air and took her instead. As she kicked and screamed, hanging from its talons, it lifted into the sky, flew away over the barbed wire of the fence and then straight up.

"No!" Henry bellowed and shot at the thing over and over, stumbling and running along the fence trying to keep the creature in his sights as long as he could as they moved in the direction of the gates. "*Let her go! Let her go, you S.O.B!*" He'd hit it, he was sure he'd hit it. By then everyone in the yard was shooting at it. *Someone* would hit it.

The creature was sixty…a hundred feet rising swiftly in the air, struggling with its heavy human load because Laura was fighting with everything she had.

With a howl of pain, the monster dropped her into the trees outside the compound and plunged to the earth. Someone's aim had been true.

The rest of the recovery mission was a blur. Henry and his men didn't waste time loading into a tank. The gates were thrown open and everyone, soldiers and rangers alike, rushed into the woods searching for his daughter. Their weapons close and their eyes peeled for any more flying predators.

They found her in the snow, in a clearing not far outside the gates, a lifeless bloodied ragdoll. Either her wounds or the fall had killed her. It made no difference. She was dead.

Henry picked up her broken body and silently, tears running down his face, handed her to Justin, whose own expression was numb with shock. The heartache in the young man's eyes was awful to see as he took Laura from Henry's arms and carried her back into the compound where he laid her at her mother's feet.

He'd also never forget the expression of grief in his sick wife's eyes as she knelt in the snow, her arms protectively around a weeping Phoebe and Timothy, when her dead daughter was brought to her. Ann's face was whiter than the snow around her. Her crying was muffled because she didn't want to frighten her grandchildren any more than they already were. But the children knew something was terribly wrong and cried anyway. Justin took his son into his arms and the boy held on to him tightly. Phoebe ran to Henry and threw her arms around him, buried her head in his side.

"I'm sorry." Henry could barely get the words out. "I'm so sorry, Ann. Phoebe. Justin. I couldn't save her. We couldn't save her."

Justin said nothing, but Ann looked up at Henry, her eyes brimming with tears. "I know you tried," she whispered and lowered her head. "It was those damn dinosaurs. I wish every last one of them would go to hell where they belong."

Then Ann, as if she were in a trance, gazed down at her lifeless daughter. Ann's body heaved. "Oh no…our child is dead, Henry. *Our child is dead.*" With a gasp of heart-wrenching grief, she gathered her motionless daughter tighter into her arms and the tears streamed down her face and dropped to the ground. And all Henry could do was hold Phoebe and watch as the grief washed over him in huge waves. His only child was dead; nothing would ever be the same again. Ever.

*****

The remainder of the day was a continuation of the nightmare. Justin was inconsolable and Ann, after they wrapped Laura's body and placed her in one of the unheated storage sheds–until they could have the funeral service–ended up in bed, unable to do anything but cry and sleep. Henry scrounged up a few sleeping pills and later that evening made Ann take them. She was so distraught, he knew only rest, time, might help…if anything would ever help. How does one get over losing a child?

Captain McDowell and her soldiers went out on patrol alone that day. Now that they knew the dinosaurs were awake and on the move again they were eager to go out and hunt them down. She left behind guards posted inside the fort because after what had happened the humans would have to be extremely cautious when they exited the buildings and moved between them. There wasn't a fence high enough to keep out the airborne varieties so Henry proposed a coverage of thick wire netting laid across the openings between the buildings, twelve feet or so above the ground and bolstered up by thick wooden posts pounded deep into the earth. So their world, again, became even smaller.

He telephoned Patterson but received no answer. He didn't leave a message. The news he had to impart wasn't meant for a message machine.

*****

That night Henry couldn't sleep because the only thing on his mind beside his sorrow was the hatred he had for the dinosaurs that had invaded and destroyed his park, his family, his life, and now had killed his daughter. In the dark he got up from the bed and wandered towards the windows.

Outside the wind wailed and whipped around the compound. The temperature was somewhere below freezing and not a night for any human to be out in an unheated structure. He went in search of Justin and, and as he'd feared, found him in the shed with his wife's body. The young man, his face blank and frozen white, was bundled in a coat and cap, gloves on his hands, shivering, on a folding chair.

"Son," he tugged the man up from the chair, "you're going to die of pneumonia if you stay out here." He kept his voice gentle. "It's way too cold. You've stood sentry over her body long enough. Come on inside, please?"

Justin wouldn't meet his eyes. "I can't leave her here by herself," he muttered, "you know how she hates to be alone."

"Justin, it's okay. You can come inside for a while and warm up. She won't mind." Henry forced himself to glance at the canvas wrapped lump on the floor but quickly looked away. He couldn't bear to think his daughter was inside it. Cold flesh. Her spirit no longer there. That she was gone…forever. Dead. Suddenly he felt very, very old and weary.

"I can't leave her."

Henry sighed. "She wouldn't want you to get sick out here. What about Phoebe and Timothy? They need you now more than ever and they need you to be healthy. Come inside."

Justin didn't respond. He'd tried to sit back down

again but Henry held him up and refused to let go.

Henry switched tactics. “I have one of the last bottles of whiskey inside and I was going to have a glass or two. I hate to drink alone. So join me.”

The younger man, staring down, shook his head. “I can’t.” His voice was tinged with anguish. “Can’t leave her.”

“Truth is, Justin, I need someone to talk to. She was my daughter. I loved her, too.”

That’s when his son-in-law met his gaze. He must have seen his own grief reflected in Henry’s eyes because he finally shook his head in the affirmative and allowed the older man to steer him out into the cold night and towards the main building.

The two were joined by Steven who was also awake and they found sitting at the table in the conference room when they came in. He wanted to be there for his friend because he’d experienced the same sort of grief when he’d lost his own wife and knew what it was like. The three of them sat up most of the night, sipping whiskey and reminiscing about Laura the wife and mother, Laura the daughter and friend. Justin finally wept and so did Henry. Steven brought out his guitar and softly sang some songs of his Laura had loved. Every so often, Henry would check on Ann as she slept, Timothy, Phoebe and the cat tucked in the bed beside her to make sure they were all right.

Once Ann woke up and, half asleep from the pills, inquired in a teary voice, “Is it true, is she really dead, Henry? Is our baby really dead?” Tears glistened on her puffy face and Henry’s heart broke all over again.

"Shh, don't fret about it now. Go back to sleep, sweetheart. Go back to sleep."

He kissed her on her forehead as she drifted away, snuggling their grandson up close. Phoebe restlessly shifted beneath the covers and moaned. The cat purred. Ann released one final sob as he left the room to rejoin Justin.

A short time later, he had Steven help him get Justin to a cot. The young man had drank himself into a stupor and Henry was relieved he had. There was no way he was going to let him sleep out in the shed with Laura's body.

Henry laid down but still couldn't sleep so he rose from the bed and watched the sun come up behind the window. Outside the world appeared normal as the pre-light arrived and the sun inched up in the sky just as any other day. The adjacent buildings looked the same, the trees and the sky…but the wire-encrusted fence encircling the encampment let him know nothing was normal any longer. The war wasn't over.

For a moment, as the shadows of night ebbed and crept away, he could have sworn he'd seen something…*something*…skulking outside the window. Two sinister eyes glittered in at him. Scrutinizing him. But the eyes were different than any other dinosaur's he'd seen so far. They actually looked as if there were thoughtful intelligence behind them. Which was crazy. He looked again and nothing was there. *After what happened yesterday*, he thought, *I'm just seeing things that aren't real. I'm seeing monsters everywhere.*

Because how could one of those creatures have snuck into their heavily protected camp without being seen or stopped? Impossible. Unless it was one of the gargoyles? No, the silhouette hadn't been a gargoyle's because there had been no wings on it. If anything had even been there at all. In the end Henry convinced himself it'd been the shadows and he'd conjured it up from his fears and grief. There had been nothing there.

As the sun's rays filled the world he saw there wasn't anything hulking outside the window. So it *had* been his imagination.

When Timothy woke, Henry let Ann and Phoebe sleep, and scooping his grandson into his arms, carried the boy into the main room to give him breakfast and reunite him with his father.

Henry, though, couldn't wait until he resumed patrolling. More than anything he wanted to slaughter as many dinosaurs as he could. They'd taken something precious from him, and not for the first time, and all he could think about was revenge. Perhaps it would alleviate a fraction of the emptiness Laura's death had created in him.

It turned out his revenge had to wait because after that Ann's misery overwhelmed her and he didn't dare leave her side for days; not until her wave of grief released her. She needed him. Justin, Phoebe and Timothy needed him. So he stayed with them and sent McDowell out to do the hunting.

Chapter 2

A week later Henry thought it was at last safe to leave Ann alone. At least she wasn't crying all the time, but her distress had weakened her further. She was a shadow of herself and he was increasingly worried. He had to find a doctor for her. Soon. He was afraid the cancer was no longer in remission and unless she got help he wouldn't have her long and he couldn't live in the world without both Laura and Ann.

In that week they'd fought the hard frozen ground and buried Laura inside the fence behind the main building and had her memorial service. The day had been warmer and a cold rain had fallen as they'd stood over her grave. Henry had to drag Justin away from it as the rain had turned to icy snow and night had come. The man was so distressed. "*Should have protected her,*" he kept saying. "*Should have saved her, but didn't. What kind of husband can't save his wife's life? Coward, coward, coward.*"

Captain McDowell had gone out each day with her crew and hunted for dinosaurs. So far they hadn't found any. There'd been no more marauders, flying or otherwise, trying to get inside their stockade and none were sighted anywhere. That in itself was strange. Where were they? What were the dinosaurs up to? Most likely no damn good.

Henry waited one more day after the funeral and resumed patrolling.

"You sure you want to go out today, Henry?"

Captain McDowell pressed as they prepared to climb into the tank. The day was overcast and there was a strong scent of rain in the air. A storm was coming. "Everyone would understand if you wanted to take more time off."

Henry shook his head. "I've taken enough time off. Ann is stable now, she's out of bed and almost herself again or as much herself as she can be these days. She's determined to be there for Timothy, Phoebe and Justin and under the circumstances I'm relieved she feels that way. It's better than the weeping zombie she's been since Laura died. Having her granddaughter and grandson to care about gives her a reason to go on. She's become their substitute mother." His brief smile was at once relieved and sad.

"All right, Chief Ranger, we're going dinosaur hunting." The woman soldier nodded her head, her manner serious. As most of them had she'd lost weight over the winter and her face sported more lines than the fall before. She looked fifty years old instead of the forty she was. "Where do we look today? Which section of the park?"

"Today, Sherman, we're not searching for or fighting dinosaurs."

"We're not?" The woman's eyes showed mild surprise.

"We're not. Today we're going on another mission entirely. Are you familiar with the town of Nampa? It's about a half day away from here by car but in a tank it'll probably take longer."

"I know where Nampa is. I had a friend who lived there once. That was years ago, though, and she's probably long gone along with half the population that fled months ago from the dinosaurs. They were strongly attacked early on. What's in Nampa?"

"A doctor for Ann. Her name is Emily Macon and she's working in a small hospital in the heart of town, or she was a few months ago. She's been there since the beginning of the dinosaur troubles and refuses to leave. Her patients need her, she claims."

"How do you know of her?"

"Last year when Ann underwent chemo treatment when she was staying with Justin and Laura she was given Emily Macon's name as a physician she could see when she returned here. Macon was recommended because she's an expert on the kind of cancer Ann has, familiar with Ann's case because a fax of Ann's files were sent to her last year, and she lives fairly close in Nampa. My wife has her address, telephone number and email.

"One day last week when the Internet was actually not acting up too much Ann got through to Doctor Macon and found out she was still at the hospital fighting the good fight. The doctor says, as with us, the dinosaurs that had been persecuting their town haven't been prevalent over the winter. Now, while it's still fairly cold, would be the time to travel there and bring her back to examine and treat Ann. Since Ann is too weak to take the trip herself, Doctor Macon has agreed to visit her here. If we promise to get her back to her hospital when she's done attending to Ann."

"So we're going to collect a doctor and bring her

back, huh?"

"That's about it. And I also figured if she did a house call then anyone else who is having any physical or other health problems can see her as well. There are a few I know of who need to see a doctor for one reason or another, for meds or a diagnosis. It has been a long, hard winter."

"That it has," McDowell acknowledged. "Having a doctor house visit is a good idea in so many ways. I'm in."

"Also, taking this journey will let us see how the area around us is faring. See how many, if any, dinosaurs we come across. And, along the way, I thought we'd offer sanctuary to anyone who needs or wants it. We'd lead them back here with us if they want to come."

"Two missions, then, Chief. So let's saddle up and get on our way to Nampa."

"You got it. Saddle up and let's ride."

Henry, Ranger Gillian, Captain McDowell and one of her soldiers climbed into the first tank and Sergeant Gilbert, Private Harmon and two other soldiers got into the other. As usual they took at least two tanks when traveling across dinosaur lands because they never knew what they'd run into. He would have preferred to have Justin along with them but the young man was still reeling from his wife's death and needed more time. Henry was giving it to him. Whereas Henry had no choice but to set aside his sorrow and go in search of help for Ann. Love. It made him stuff the grief down and carry on.

The trip through the Oregon landscape to Nampa

was uneventful. They didn't see any people, which didn't surprise Henry because they didn't veer off the highway. Yet on the other hand they did not see one dinosaur of any variety either, on the highway or in the bordering wilderness. Again, Henry wondered where they were.

They were about an hour outside of Nampa when a man, sprinting out of the woods on the side of the road in front of them, wildly waving one of his hands in the air while the other held a rifle, brought them to a screeching stop. It was miracle they didn't flatten him like a pancake. Tanks aren't easy to halt quickly.

Henry volunteered to talk to the man and popped his head out of the top. He didn't have a chance to ask anything before the guy, dressed in a frayed but heavy plaid coat and wearing thick glasses, began to speak.

"Where are you coming from and did you see any of those prehistoric terrors on your way?"

"We're coming from Crater Lake National Park Headquarters. I'm Chief Park Ranger Henry Shore. And no, we haven't seen any dinosaurs yet…today." The smile he offered the man was meant to be friendly and the fellow smiled back. He seemed really happy to see them.

"That's good. I mean no dinosaur sightings and all. You have a lot of the critters up your way?"

"We did. Lots. We killed most of them and we're waiting for more to show themselves as the weather becomes warmer," Henry said. "You seen any recently?"

"No, we haven't seen any lately–not live ones

anyway. You're from Crater Lake, huh?"

"We are. We spent the winter hunkered down behind fortified wooden walls awaiting the spring. What do you mean by *not live ones anyway*?"

The man shaded his eyes with his hand. The sun was shining directly in his face. "My son, Grant, and I discovered a whole mess of dead giant critters deep in the woods behind our house the other day. Every last one of them was stiff as a rock. Looked like they'd been dead a while."

Henry wanted to speak to the man face to face and exited the tank. He wasn't surprised when Captain McDowell followed after him.

She introduced herself to the man.

"Nice to meet you, too, Captain. I'm Noah Winters," the man informed them, shaking hands with both of them. He was a short guy, but stocky. His wiry gray hair was captured beneath a sock cap. "I live about a quarter mile over the ridge there with my son and my wife, Gertrude." He stuck a thumb in the direction behind him. "I heard your tanks rumbling miles away and came running. I wanted any news you had about what's going on out in the world these days. Our television stopped working weeks ago, power goes in and out, and we haven't had Internet since summer because our computer blew a fuse or something and I'm not good with the things. I can use them easy enough, but I can't fix them no how."

As briefly as he could, Henry revealed what he knew about the world's situation, which wasn't much more than the man himself already knew. Dinosaurs had overrun their planet and caused havoc everywhere and the human race was fighting back. Communication at times could be spotty and unreliable. But Winters seemed glad to get what he was given. "Now, Mr. Winters, could you show us where you and your son found those dead dinosaurs?"

"Sure. Follow me to the house so I can let my wife and son know what I'm doing. They'll be worried otherwise and might even come out searching for me. I don't want that. Though the dinosaurs haven't been showing their ugly selves much lately, I still don't trust them. I don't allow my family to meander around out in the woods much."

"And you're wise to think like that," Henry stated. "Is it all right if the tanks cut through this field here and accompany us?"

"I see no problem. The ground's so frozen their weight won't hurt it. Where we're going is a straight shot up that hill and through a sparse woods." The man pointed a hand in a northern direction. "They shouldn't have any trouble making the trip."

Henry took a minute or two to alert the others in the tanks of what they were doing by his personal intercom radio attached to his shoulder and then, along with McDowell, fell in beside Mr. Winters as they hiked up towards his house. The tanks shadowed along behind them at a close but safe distance.

They came across no living dinosaurs. Not even one of those pesky diminutive ones that bounced around like kangaroos. It'd been like that the entire expedition since they'd left the ranger station. They hadn't seen any dinosaurs anywhere. Like Winters, Henry didn't trust the lull in hostilities one bit. He never took his eyes off the surrounding land as they made their way to Winters' house. They came up to a natural fence of tall trees encircling the house and walked through them.

The house surprised Henry. It was a modern, glass-covered mansion, all sharp angles and steel, sprawling on the next hill top like one of those millionaire residences a person saw in the old Rich and Famous shows.

Winters caught Henry's expression and grinned. "Yeah, I'm filthy rich. I created and built a start-up Internet company a couple years ago–before the dinosaur threat, thank goodness–and unloaded it for a lot of money. I was lucky. It's worth a hell of a lot less now, I imagine. What with the Internet so unpredictable these days."

Henry stared at the man and again at his house as they moved up the sidewalk and entered it.

The tanks roared up the hill through a break in the trees and parked in the enormous driveway; cutting their engines and bringing back the silence. Sergeant Gilbert and Ranger Gillian lifted their heads out of the tanks and Henry waved at them. "We won't be long," he shouted.

Henry, returning his attention to Winters, was mulling over two things: Wasn't it strange how one could never tell a millionaire by the way he looked and dressed? And, glancing up at the house before him…boy, one of those big dinosaurs would have a field day smashing all those beautiful windows. The humans inside wouldn't stand a chance. He shuddered, just thinking about it. But Henry didn't let the house's owner know what he was thinking. Why scare him?

Then another surprise. "I know what you're thinking, Chief Park Ranger," Winters commented as he led them inside. "All these glass windows with the big-footed dinosaurs rampaging about and all? Not real safe. But my family and I know how to defend ourselves. We all got our carry licenses last year; took classes and everything. If any of those monsters get anywhere near our home we'll shoot them to pieces." He raised his rifle and shook it gently. "And I'm a crack shot. So is my son and wife."

"Sometimes," Henry said, studying the beautiful room he found himself in, "rifles aren't enough. Even three of them."

"Well, here's the thing," Winters laid his rifle down carefully on an elaborately carved mahogany coffee table and met Henry's gaze, "as strange as it sounds we haven't had any prehistoric visitors around here at all. Not a one. It's like there's an invisible protective shield around my land and this house. My son and I have run into some of those voracious critters from another time out there." He waved his hand at the window. "We've fought them out there, but not a one has come past that line of trees since the wars began."

"The wars?" McDowell, who had walked past them and further into the house to see it better, asked. She was gawking at the lovely possessions the house was filled with. There was money here. A lot of money and good taste.

"You know," Winters supplied, "the dinosaur wars. That's what I'm calling all this trouble we're having with those creepy throw-back monsters."

"Huh," McDowell muttered. "Good a name as any for what's happening, I guess." She reached out and touched the smooth shiny nose of a life size black leopard statue. It was stunningly realistic, exquisite, and probably ludicrously expensive.

In fact…. Henry was looking around now. There were animal statues everywhere. Marble, stone or wood. They were intricately carved and were beautifully made. Winters must be an animal lover. There was even a dinosaur statue, a small T-Rex about the size of a man, in one corner of the room by the windows. Maybe that was why the real dinosaurs stayed away? Henry almost laughed, but he didn't. Nothing to do with dinosaurs ever made him laugh anymore.

Henry and McDowell were introduced to the man's wife and son and the man told his family why they were there. "I'm going to lead them to that place you found the other day, Grant, down in the hollow. The one covered in dead dinosaurs?" Winters explained to them and his son bobbed his head in understanding.

The boy looked to be about nineteen, tall and lanky with a head of bright red hair and a cynical smile. He'd gotten up from a plush couch and shook hands with Henry and McDowell. He didn't say much other than hello. The quiet sort.

Winters' wife, on the other hand, was a friendly middle-aged woman with hair down to her waist and very white skin. She was pretty for her age and with eyes the same olive hue as her son's, though she was a great deal more talkative. Her name was Shelia. She seemed happy to meet them and offered them refreshments of sandwiches, potato chips and something to drink.

"I just baked a humongous ham last night and we have plenty," she addressed McDowell. "You must be hungry. Could I make you both one or more sandwiches?"

McDowell slid a glance sideways at Henry. They'd been on the road since morning and food sounded good. He nodded.

"We have more men outside in the tanks–" McDowell didn't get to finish her sentence before Shelia completed it.

"That's okay. I can make you a bag of sandwiches and chips to take to them when you return from your little expedition with my husband, so they'll have some food, too."

"That's too much to ask of you," Henry said, touched she would even offer.

"Oh, no, Chief Ranger, I'd be honored. We humans have to stick together now more than ever."

And Henry had to agree on that. "That would be so kind of you. But if it's all right we'll have those sandwiches after our little trek into the woods. It's getting late and we still have a far piece to go before the day is through."

"They'll be ready when you get back," Shelia spoke. "Should I put mustard or mayo on them?"

"It doesn't matter. We, and our men, will eat just about anything. Fresh baked ham will be a treat enough in itself," McDowell told her.

"We ready to go then?" Winters had given his wife a kiss and picked up his rifle again.

"Can I come along, Dad?" his son asked. "I know a short cut you don't to that place. I can get us there and back faster." The boy showed interest for the first time.

Winters appeared to think about it and looking out the window at the waiting tanks, he decided, "That's fine, son. I guess the sooner we get there and back, the better, for all of us. We haven't seen any dinosaurs out and about for months but there's no reason not to be cautious. Go get your rifle and put on a warm coat, but hurry."

Within minutes the four of them were outside, joined by Gillian and Harmon, and in the woods moving briskly between the trees. Because Winters claimed the route was too congested for them to roll through, the tanks would wait for them at the house. The sun was on the downslide of its daily path and Henry was impatient to get there, see what had to be seen, gather samples, and get back on the road to Nampa. He wished Justin was with them, but he wasn't so he'd just have to make do. He'd take photos with his cell phone and gather flesh samples for the paleontologist to examine later.

It was quiet in the woods. No signs or sounds of dinosaurs. But there was also no other animal noises either. The eerie stillness still unnerved Henry.

About two miles into the brush they came upon the valley Winters has spoken of. It wasn't really a valley as much as an indentation in the ground about fifty feet across. No way of telling how deep it was because it was filled with dinosaur corpses. There had to be at least fifteen or twenty dead ones in front of them stacked up like decayed cordwood in the hollow. Henry walked to the edge of it and stared. Good thing it was as cold as it was or he imagined the stink would be overpowering.

It made him uneasy to be at the burial ground with the dead things before him. It reminded him of the day they rescued Ellie Stanton from the dinosaur nest. And that brought the sad memories of Stanton and Kiley's death the year before back to him. Memories he didn't want to revisit at the moment.

The overcast day had, as anticipated, developed into a rainy one. At first it had been simply a drizzle but Henry suspected soon it could become heavier and eventually turn into snow after the sun went down. He needed to get the samples and leave. He leaned over a small dinosaur body, a gargoyle by the looks of it, but it was so decomposed he wasn't sure. Holding fingers over his nose, he sliced off a piece of its flesh and tucked it into the plastic baggie Winters' wife had given him for that purpose. It only took a minute. He couldn't wait to get away from the place, as if it were cursed or something, or a trap. He kept expecting live dinosaurs to appear and swoop in for the kill. But none did. The forest was empty of everything but scrub, snow patched grass, winter trees and gray skies above.

"It's something, isn't it?" Winters made the observation of the place while everyone gawked at the pieces of decomposing dinosaur remnants.

"Yeah, something."

"They don't look sick or anything, just dead. What do you think they died of?" Winters' boy asked.

"I don't know." Henry had put the sample in the baggie and the baggie into his coat pocket. "That's what we need to find out. Hopefully my son-in-law, a paleontologist, will figure it out. He's a smart man."

The rain, falling harder now, slapped against the men standing over the dinosaur graveyard.

"You've seen what you needed to see? Got what you needed to get, Chief Ranger?" Winters inquired, his face shaded and protected from the rain beneath his cap.

"Yep. Let's vacate this place. It gives me the willies." Too many dead dinosaurs. Ghosts probably floating around everywhere. Human and dinosaur. "Let's go."

And they did.

At the mansion Shelia had a bag of food and drinks, cans of soda, ready. Before they left Henry said to the three of them, "You know, if the dinosaurs show up again and resume their attacks, you're welcome to come and stay with us at the Ranger's Station at Crater Lake. We have quite a settlement there now. It's enormously fortified. Got a huge stockade fence around it. We have soldiers and tanks. Big guns. It's safe."

"I appreciate the offer, Chief Ranger, but I believe the threat is over, or at least around these parts. We haven't seen any prehistoric attackers for months. I'll take my chances here protecting what's mine."

"Have it your way, Winters, but remember we're there if you need us. Just call if you have any dinosaur troubles and we'll come. If you can't reach any of those numbers, keep trying. Eventually you'll get through." Henry had already given the man the Ranger Station's and his own cell phone numbers.

After saying their goodbyes, Henry, McDowell and their men climbed into the tanks and resumed their journey to Nampa.

"That was a strange side road we took, Henry," McDowell mentioned once they were within the tank and moving. The men were busy gulping down the sandwiches and snacks and grateful to have them. They were sick of army rations. "Do you believe, as Winters does, that it's over? The dinosaurs are gone for good or almost gone? That they're dying out for some reason? Somehow God or fate has intervened and solved our problem for us?"

"No, I don't. Not by a long shot," Henry replied, feeling a heavy sadness that had become an all too familiar friend the last few years. "Mark my words, our enemy is still out there, scheming and planning their next attack. Somewhere. I don't know what happened to those dead ones in the meadow back there…an illness of some kind. Maybe Justin will be able to tell us. We've seen something like it before, haven't we? A mysterious ailment in the dinosaur population when we went to save Ellie Stanton?" And McDowell nodded in agreement remembering what he was referring to. "But, as we unfortunately know after what befell my daughter, the dinosaurs aren't gone. The ones left will, no doubt, show themselves here soon enough. I'd bet a year's pay on it."

McDowell sighed. "I hope the Winters make it then. They seem like a nice family."

"They do. I lent Mr. Winters one of my MP7A1 rifles, until we know if the dinosaurs are gone or not. It'd do a hell of a lot more damage to any unwanted intruders that show up than any of the weapons he has."

"Lent it, huh? That's not really legal, is it?"

"These days what's legal? Survival is more important and I don't think the Winters are as safe as they believe they are."

"We'll have to check up on them once and a while and make sure they're still alive," McDowell commented cynically. "With spring coming there could be all sorts of things awakening and roaming around. It could be a brand new ballgame."

"That's what I'm afraid of."

*****

The town of Nampa was a pleasant revelation to Henry. In the rain it looked so normal. There were people driving on the streets and going into and out of the open shops. It was like going back two years in time. For a brief moment Henry felt a wave of relief and hope. Perhaps it was over…perhaps the dinosaur threat was fading. Life would be as it once was. If only.

It felt funny trundling down the roads in line with cars and trucks. People stared at them, some waved, some smiled or scowled.

Instead of comforting Henry, the normalcy only

made him itchy. These people were living in a fantasy world, he brooded. They were going about their lives as if the dinosaur menace didn't exist. Poor people. Just wait.

They had no problem finding the hospital. Doctor Macon was waiting for them in her office exactly where she'd told Ann she'd be. She was prettier and younger than he had imagined, probably in her late thirties or early forties; of willowy build and medium height. Her short dark hair was soft around her heart-shaped face and her blue eyes were intense. She wasted little time in pleasantries. Putting her hand out to Henry, and smiling at McDowell, she confirmed, "So you're my ride to Crater Lake, huh?"

"Yep, that's us…and we're taking you first class in an Abrams tank. Nothing is too good for our visiting doctor." Henry shook her hand. She had a strong grasp.

He introduced himself and McDowell.

"I've never been in a tank before," she imparted seriously. "I guess it'll be a new experience for me. I like new experiences."

"The ride's rough but it gets us where we want to go," McDowell interjected. "And if we run into anything dangerous it'll protect us and blow the threat to kingdom come."

"I bet," the woman physician said with another smile. "But I was prepared and knew I'd be transported by an armored vehicle. Ann told me what to expect.

"How was Ann when you left her?" she now asked Henry.

Henry knew his wife had been in constant contact with the doctor for over a week and most likely had glossed over her true condition. That was Ann.

"She's really weak, Doctor Macon, no matter what she's told you. She never wants to worry anyone. I'll be so relieved once you see and examine her."

The woman didn't say anything to that, merely nodded. Standing by the door, she seemed anxious to start her journey.

"So, Doctor, are you ready to go?" Henry wanted to get her to his wife as soon as he could.

"I'm ready." Doctor Macon snatched up her overstuffed weekend bags and gestured at a mound of boxes sitting on the floor beside her desk. "Do we have room for my equipment and medical supplies? I'm coming prepared. You did say no one at your compound had seen a doctor in nearly a year? I have flu and pneumonia shots and anything else I thought we might be needing."

"That's right, no one's seen a doctor for a long time." Henry sized up the woman and her supplies. "It'll be a tight fit but we will get everything squeezed into the tanks, I assure you, even if we have to tie and secure the supplies on top." But Henry didn't believe they'd have to resort to that. They'd find the room.

"Is it still really bad up your way…with the dinosaurs, I mean?"

"It has been. A full out war. We've lost people." Henry held his fresh misery inside and tried not to show it. "But we're in a lull right now. We were able to sneak out and I know we'll be able to sneak in again–as long as this cold weather holds. It's mostly kept the creatures away."

Doctor Macon met his gaze and couldn't hide the pain in hers. Henry assumed Ann had confided in her about Laura's death. "Like you, some of us think the cold weather is the reason for the lull, as well, while others think the danger is over. Strange, isn't it? That for months and months, all summer and into the fall, it was a daily battle with the creatures as if we were in a nightmare sci-fi movie or something. Now, or at least since full winter settled in, we haven't seen a dinosaur in months. It makes you think they never existed to begin with and it was all in our fevered minds." She whispered under her breath but Henry heard her, "*But I know better.*"

Then she went on in her regular voice, "Most of the townspeople have let down their guard as if the dinosaurs are gone forever. They're going about their daily lives as if nothing is wrong."

"They shouldn't." Henry's voice was grave. "I fear it isn't over. Not by a long shot. My son-in-law, a respected paleontologist, believes the same thing. They'll be back."

The doctor shook her head in agreement. "I'm with you and your son-in-law, Chief Ranger Shore. I've had just about enough of those monsters but I suspect in the spring, sadly, we'll see them again." A soft sigh was released. "Yet how I want the old world back. I'd do anything to see that, to have that."

"We all would, Doctor."

Then Henry said to everyone, "Let's move out, people. Time's a wasting." He scooped up two boxes, McDowell did the same, Doctor Macon hoisting her overnight bags, and the three of them left the building. There weren't any people in the hallways, though it wasn't that late in the day, and the building seemed empty. Their footsteps echoed in the silence.

"Are you alone here, Doctor Macon?" Henry inquired as they hurried through the main lobby towards the exit doors.

"No, during the earlier part of the day there are other doctors and nurses. Most of the ones still on duty are downstairs now tending to our patients, what we have of them. It's a small hospital and it was packed, believe me, until recently with dinosaur casualties. Bad weather always lessens our intake. Without dinosaur attacks just the usual patients come in. It's why I'm able to travel back to your compound with you. Right now I can be spared for a couple days."

"Lucky for us then I'd say."

Outside, in the rain that had turned into sleet, shivers, and not from the cold, forced Henry to warily look around. There was nothing out of the ordinary to be seen. Only a town going about its usual business in the frozen rain and the Abrams waiting for them on the parking lot. No dinosaurs anywhere. He'd been on high alert because of the monsters for so long it had become second nature to be that way at all times. Still, he'd be glad to be within the safety of the tanks and on their way.

They'd loaded Doctor Macon's supplies in the

second tank and squeezed her in the first one with Gillian, McDowell and him.

Everything and everyone fit, barely, and they rumbled out of town as the sleet transformed into snow and the day darkened.

The return trip to Crater Lake sped by faster than the way out and Henry got to know the doctor better. She was more talkative, curious about their lives at the ranger station and what they'd gone through the last year, and sociable, than he would have thought. He realized after only a short time of speaking with her, for whatever reason, she was lonely. He warmed up to her right off. She was an amiable and curious person. Smart. Of course she would be, she was a doctor.

"So you built a solid wooden fence with barbed wire along the top around the entire ranger station and you're stretching a mesh cover between the buildings?" the doctor questioned when they were scarcely out of town. She was sitting between McDowell and him and took turns asking them each questions about their lives and the place she was headed for.

"We did and we are." As he conversed with the doctor Henry was also attempting to call Ann on his cell but she wasn't picking up, so he left a message saying they were on their way back with the doctor and all was well. He tried not to get too worried. Ann could be sleeping or doing something with the children.

"The fence has kept most of the dinosaurs out, except for the flying variety," he responded and tried again not to dwell on Laura's death. It was difficult because it was still too fresh in his mind. The way she'd screamed and fought as the gargoyle had taken her off. The way her body had plummeted from the sky and the horror of seeing her dead and broken on the ground. *No, don't think about it.* Don't. Think. About. It.

"Did you have many of the creatures attacking you in the fall?" The doctor was studying Henry's face as if she was trying to read his thoughts. He noticed how her left eyebrow kept raising when she asked a question.

"An endless herd of them. We thought they'd never stop coming. We've pretty much cleaned them out since then though, I hope." He knew it was a lie the second he uttered it, but couldn't help himself.

"But you still go on patrols every day to hunt for more?"

"We have to be sure the park is clear. Safe."

The doctor wasn't fooled. "You still have a dinosaur problem, don't you?"

Henry exhaled and shot a look at McDowell. "A lot of us think we do."

McDowell lowered her voice and spoke to the doctor about the latest gargoyle attack the week before and what had exactly occurred. The way the doctor paid attention tipped Henry off that perhaps Ann hadn't told her everything about the circumstances surrounding Laura's death. Henry busied himself with what was happening on the outside of their vehicle and tried not to listen. Afterwards the doctor was silent for a time, then she turned to Henry. "I'm so sorry for you and your wife's loss."

"Thank you." Henry fought to stay in the moment because he had a job to do.

"And I imagine it hasn't helped your wife's condition, either, that loss?"

"It hasn't. She's mostly been in bed, distressed and apathetic, since it happened. If it weren't for our grandchildren she wouldn't leave it. They've become her lifeline."

"The love of a child can heal many sorrows."

It was time to change the subject.

"How was it in Nampa, Doctor, with the dinosaurs, I mean? Did you have a lot of them stomping through your town?"

"We had some," the doctor's voice had tensed. "The townspeople fought them off with help from the National Guard, but there was this one, a brute of a monster–fifty feet tall or more–that stalked the town for months in the summer. It was diabolically clever. It seemed to know by instinct where and when it could strike and not be caught. It terrorized and butchered so many people. It killed my husband, Charles. He was a doctor, too. We worked together."

"I'm so sorry for you, as well, then. How long has it been?" Henry hardly knew what else to say. Everyone had lost someone; was there anyone who hadn't? It was commonplace to hear the stories and a person only had so much grief they could soak in.

"Ten months ago now."

McDowell was the one to delve deeper. "If you don't mind me asking, what happened?"

"No, Captain McDowell, I don't mind.

Sometimes it almost helps talking about it. Charles went out with our neighbors one day to track down that monster I was just talking about. It had demolished another house on the outskirts of town and murdered the family living there. There'd been six children. They all perished. By then the town had had enough so the men went out to find and deal with it. They tracked it for days, cornered it in the woods where its lair was, lured it out and kept shooting at it until it died. Before it did, though, it killed three more of the men hunting it. Charles was one of them."

Henry couldn't bear to meet her eyes. He didn't need to know any more details. He didn't want to know.

"So, Ranger Shore," Doctor Macon broke the uncomfortable silence, "tell me about your wife's present condition? What are her symptoms and her general state of mind? Is she having trouble sleeping or sleeping too much? Don't leave anything out, no matter how trivial. As you said, your daughter's death has hit her hard, in her fragile state, and it could complicate her illness. The more I know the better I will be able to treat her condition." The doctor's voice was once more professional as was her demeanor.

Henry described Ann's symptoms as best he could and the doctor took in what he had to say with only a question here and there. When he was done she seemed satisfied with what she'd learned.

The remainder of the trip they discussed less sensitive subjects, everyday things, and by the time they drove through the compound's gates Henry thought he knew why Ann had developed an email friendship with her. They had a lot in common and the doctor seemed truly concerned about Ann's well-being.

As Henry helped the doctor from the tank and escorted her into the station he couldn't wait to see Ann.

But along the way Justin caught up to him. His son-in-law held his sleeping son in his arms and Henry took a second to ruffle the boy's hair and stroke his cheek, but gently so he wouldn't wake up.

"I'm glad you're back, Henry. I have something to tell you…and we have a problem." Justin's pale face was grave, his shoulders slumped. The young man looked worse than when Henry had left. "I'm putting Timothy to bed now, but after I do, we need to talk."

Henry introduced Justin to Doctor Macon and then added, "All right. After you tuck your son in, Justin, meet me in the conference room and I'll join you as soon as I get the doctor here to Ann. I have something to tell you, too, and something to show you."

"I'll be waiting for you."

Henry watched his son-in-law walk away and continued moving to where he believed Ann was. In their bedroom. In her bed.

Chapter 3

Ann hadn't planned on sleeping as long as she did. Henry had left hardly an hour before on his jaunt to Nampa and she'd fed her grandson breakfast and ate a little bit herself. She'd been forcing herself to eat every day, but most of the time she had no appetite. Afterwards the child had fallen asleep in a corner of her bed cuddled up with a drowsy Sasha. The boy loved the cat and the cat loved the boy. It made Ann smile to see the two together. She was happy to have the child and the feline with her in her prison because it helped to break up the monotony.

She had sat down at her computer thinking she'd see if the Internet was up or not–it wasn't–to check her emails. Well, no emails for now. Perhaps later. Suddenly, looking down at the sleeping child, she'd laid down beside him; took him in her arms and had drifted off to sleep so quickly she didn't even remember doing it.

Sleep slid off her shoulders like a silk shawl, soft and swift. She'd switched the lights off when she'd laid down and there were creeping shadows in the room. Sasha was no longer in the bed with them. The feline was in the corner of the room chasing a small red ball with tiny bells inside. They jingled as the ball rolled from corner to corner. Sasha was full grown now and fatter than a cat should be. She was the compound's mascot, their pet, and everyone snuck her portions of their food rations. So she was a chubby cat. Basically white, she had black batman-tipped ears, an ebony tail and one inky spot on her back. Ann considered her distinctive markings uncommon for a black and white feline. Henry compared the cat to Peanut's Snoopy, saying they were marked alike–except Sasha wasn't a dog. She was a curious, contented, cat even if she had to be locked up inside headquarters and was never allowed outside. These days she was oblivious to the dinosaur menace beyond the windows and Ann wanted her to remain that way. Ann couldn't lose her as they'd lost Ellie's pet, Miss Kitty Cat, who'd somehow managed to steal out of the building months before. Miss Kitty Cat had escaped through the barricade somehow and vanished into the dinosaur infested woods, probably searching for her dead mistress. And Ellie's cat had never returned. That couldn't happen to Sasha. She was better medicine, along with the children, Ann thought, than any old pill or chemo treatment.

"Here kitty, here kitty," Ann cooed as she slipped out of bed and, getting down on her hands and knees, crawled over to where the cat was playing with the ball. For a moment, the new dizziness she'd almost become used to engulfed her and the world spun around her. The coughing, she tried so hard to hide from others, especially her husband, followed and it was a bad spell; the worst she'd had in weeks. It left her weak and disoriented as she lay on the floor. Sasha ran to her, purring as loudly as an airplane engine, rubbed up against her and licked her hand. Ann smiled. It was as if the cat knew when she wasn't feeling well and wanted to cheer her up. The feline knocked the ball in Ann's direction, staring at her with her huge cat eyes. So darn cute. She wanted Ann to play with her. It was a game they often shared.

Ann flicked the ball and it careened across the floor with the cat hot on its trail. Sasha's sharp claws caught the ball, flipped it up in the air like a juggler would have, and batted it back to her owner.

Ann chuckled softly, though tears for her daughter were trickling down her face, and fought off another bout of coughing. She and the cat played like that for a while until a strange noise stopped Ann in mid-throw. The noise was similar to a weird animal snort.

What is that?

Frozen, Ann listened. For a while nothing. It could have been the wind or a tree branch rubbing against the window.

Then another strange sound. *What is it?*

The cat rubbed up against her. Its subtle way of reminding her they were in the middle of playing. Ann sent the ball bouncing across the floor and it stopped below the window.

The cat crept up to the ball, stopped, looked up and then ran off, hissing, eyes down and tail between its legs.

"Sasha, what are you doing? Where are you going?" The cat was hiding beneath the bed on the other side of the room.

Another odd sound. This time it was near the window.

Ann rose to a crouch and moved towards it. There was something there, something looking in at them. *Something….*

Oh, my God it was a dinosaur. A damn dinosaur-

at-the-window…inside the compound…again! It occurred to her it had been watching her–for heaven knows how long–and the cat play.

Ann stared at the creature staring back at her through the glass. It wasn't a large specimen. Man size possibly. Hard to tell because she couldn't see all of it. It could be smaller if it was standing on something. No, it had to be man size because there was nothing for it to stand on. It didn't look like any of the other dinosaurs she'd seen so far. It was a brownish color. Small ears. Its front arms were held out loosely in front of it, its claws, more like paws, hovered close to its mouth. A mouth full of sharp teeth. Tilting its head at her, it appeared to grin. Its gaze fell on her and then on the bed where the cat was hiding. It had an ape-like quality about it. Its movements anyway reminded her of a simian like an ape or a monkey…a monkey-dinosaur.

She was about to scream when something about the creature's expression, its eyes, stopped her. They were so *human*. Their expression seemed to say: *Don't be afraid of me. I won't hurt you.* The animal behaved as if it were trying to communicate with her. Its behavior puzzled her, but the creature wasn't doing anything scary or aggressive. It simply stared in at her, watching. It pointed first at her with a paw and then at the cat.

She stood up, too quickly. The room spun again.

What was it trying to tell her?

Wait…a dinosaur was trying to communicate with her, a human? That was ridiculous. Was she hallucinating now, too? Her illness so far gone she was seeing intelligent monsters where there were none? Or perhaps she had never awakened and was dreaming? That was it, she was still dreaming.

But she had no time to gawk or fret further because the world went black around her and she felt it slipping away as she slid to the floor.

When she came to, by the clock an hour had passed, Timothy was softly whimpering in the bed, the cat's tongue was leaving a wet trail on her face as she lay on the floor–and there was nothing framed in the window. Had the sentient dinosaur with the monkey face and expressive eyes only been in her fevered mind and not real at all? Wait until she told Henry about her hallucination. He'd be amused. Or worried. Maybe she wouldn't tell him about it at all. Well, maybe she would tell him. She'd decide later.

After she drug herself up from the floor, coughing, her body weaker than ever, she bent down and picked Timothy up in her arms to comfort him. She nearly dropped him so she slipped down to the bed holding him. "It's going be fine, honey. Hush, hush. How about some lunch? Some of those ravioli with the cheese inside you like so much. What do you say?" It was only canned ravioli but the child loved it.

The boy had ceased crying and, bobbing his head, offered her a tear-stained smile. Ann took him out of the room in search of food. And, for her, a hot cup of tea with honey in it which might help her cough. It sometimes did.

The cat tailed them out of the room, and with one last perplexed glance at the window Ann closed the door.

Chapter 4

When Henry returned to their room that night, Ann was taking a nap. He opened the door and seeing her sleeping so peacefully he hated to wake her, but he did.

"Ann, honey." He perched on the edge of their bed and took her hand in his. It was very warm. "Wake up. I'm back from Nampa and I have Doctor Macon with me. See, she's right here standing beside me. She wants to talk to you so can you wake up please? Honey?"

His wife's eyes opened. "Oh, good, you're back, Henry. And you brought the doctor. Otherwise, how did it go? Any problems? Did you run into any dinosaurs on the way?"

She sat up, rubbing her eyes and smiled at the doctor. The doctor smiled back.

"No. It was an uneventful trip on that account…I mean no dinosaurs sightings." Or not live ones anyway. "Ann, this is Doctor Emily Macon." Henry stood up from the bed so Ann could see the doctor better.

"It's nice to finally meet you in person, Doctor Emily Macon." Ann dropped her legs over the side of the bed and put her hand out to shake the doctor's.

"And it's good to finally meet you, Ann, after all the emails we've exchanged over the last few months. You know, I also knew your old doctor in Klamath Falls, Doctor Edna Williams. We met once at a medical symposium in Portland. I was so sorry to hear she'd died in one of the earlier dinosaur attacks. She was a kind person and an exceptional doctor. But her files were somehow saved and knowing I was coming here I was lucky to make contact with someone who used to work with her, knew where they were, and he sent me your earlier records going back to when your cancer was first diagnosed. So I have your full medical history now to compare with and aid me in your case."

"Doctor Williams was a great doctor and an exceptional human being. I will miss her," Ann replied. "I hadn't heard she had died, but I sort of guessed it. Her office was destroyed and there was no sign of her anywhere after that."

"Now, how have you been feeling? Tell me everything." The doctor sat on the edge of the bed Henry had vacated. Her eyes were firmly on Ann's face as if she were trying to gauge how sick she was by examining it.

The two women took it from there and after Henry thought it was all right to go he excused himself saying, "I'll leave you women to it. And if you need me for anything I'll be in the conference room and you can send for me. I have to meet Justin there now. I ran into him on the way in and he said he wanted to talk to me as soon as I could get away. You have any idea what's up, Ann?"

"No. Justin's been gone most of the day. I've been in here. After you and Captain McDowell left this morning there was an emergency somewhere and his friend Steven came looking for him. Justin actually got out of his funk and drove off with his friend and some of the other soldiers. I didn't see him leave, didn't talk to him before he left. I guess I was sleeping then, too. Ranger Williamson stopped by later and told me he'd gone. It's been a strange day." His wife flashed him a look he knew well. Something unusual had happened and she'd tell him about it later.

Henry gave her a quick hug and kiss on his way out. "See both you ladies later."

"Henry," Ann said as he was at the door, "there's left over stew from last night in the fridge. If you're hungry, get a bowl of it."

"I will. Don't you worry about me. I can take care of myself. Now you take care of yourself and let the doctor examine you. And tell her everything, sweetheart, you hear? Everything. All your symptoms. How you're feeling." He tried to make his expression serious. As if anything he could do or say would make his wife do as he asked. She always did only what she wanted to do. That was his Ann.

"I will. Now go. Justin is probably waiting for you. You can tell me all about it and your day when you come back."

Henry quietly shut the door behind him and, relieved Ann was finally getting medical help, strolled into the conference room. There Justin along with Ranger Williamson, Cutters and Justin's musician friend, Steven, were sitting at the table discussing something in lowered voices. When his son-in-law looked up and grimaced at him, Henry knew something was wrong. Now what?

"I hear you found and brought the doctor back with you?"

"I did."

"The doctor is with Ann now, huh?" Justin asked.

"She is."

"I'm glad Ann is getting help," Justin's voice was soft. "She's been so sick for so long and I've been worried."

Henry nodded. "Me, too."

Everyone was suddenly silent and no one was meeting his eyes. Oh, oh.

"Hey, guys, what's up," he wanted to know. "You all look as if you have something to tell me but don't want to."

"You could say that," Justin hedged, "we have had an exciting time of it, but don't worry, you're going to hear all about it. We've been waiting to talk about it until you got here."

"So I see. Well, people, I need coffee after the day I've had and some of that stew in the refrigerator Ann mentioned we had, if there's any left. So let me get something to eat and I'll be right back. You can tell me everything then. And I also have news for you, as well."

Henry returned with a cup and a bowl in his hands. He plopped down next to Justin and began shoveling the warm meat and vegetables into his mouth. He'd better eat before any bad news arrived. It tended to ruin his appetite. "Okay, Justin and company, what's wrong?"

Ranger Williamson and Steven exchanged looks with Justin. Henry would bet that no matter what Justin had said, these two already knew what was going on.

"You tell him Justin." The ranger was drinking a

cup of something, probably coffee, and set it on the table. There was steam coming off of it. Williamson liked his coffee so hot Henry didn't know how he could drink it.

"First I'll give you the good news, Chief, or I think it's good," his son-in-law began the conversation. "I've been invited to be a participating paleontologist at an important government symposium in New York the day after tomorrow…on how to deal with the dinosaur conundrum. The best and the brightest scientists from all across the world, a think-tank of experts if you will, are being assembled to tackle the prehistoric epidemic and uncover a final solution for it. It's a great honor to be asked to attend and be on the panel." There was actually a little of the old excitement in his voice. Henry was glad to hear it.

"I imagine it is and I'm proud of you, kid. About how many paleontologists will be there?"

"I don't know, but I'll find out."

"And it's scheduled for the day after tomorrow, huh?"

"That's when it starts. Our friend Patterson called me before you arrived back here tonight and presented me with the invitation. He was sorry to have missed you. He said he called you earlier but you never answered your cell phone."

"Hmm, I might have been busy. Skulking around in the woods, checking out a mound of dead dinosaurs or roaming around the hospital looking for the doctor and bringing her back."

Justin flashed him a questioning look when he mentioned the mound of dinosaurs, but had to tack on, "Patterson mentioned he'd call you again later tonight if nothing gets in the way first. He's been as busy as us, more by what he told me, but he wants to talk to you."

"Good. It's been a while since he last checked in and we compared notes."

"Anyway, the military is sending a helicopter for me first thing tomorrow morning and I'll be transferred at the army base to a plane that'll be headed for New York," Justin went on. "They're picking up some of the attendees in this area up by Portland and making a sweep of it. I wanted to ask if you and Ann could keep Phoebe and Timothy for me while I'm gone? It could be days, weeks or longer. Patterson says the conference will last as long as it takes to come up with solutions."

"You know we'll care for the children as long as you need us to. They're family. You just go and do what needs to be done and don't burden yourself about anything here or about Phoebe or Timothy. The symposium will be darn lucky to get you. I have faith in you." Henry was relieved to see any signs of life in his son-in-law after Laura's death. If this was what it took to get the man living again, and perhaps rid them once and for all of the dreaded monsters that had taken over their world, so be it. He'd be a babysitter for as long as Justin needed him to be.

"So the government finally believes we have a problem? I mean we haven't seen any of the creatures since last fall, other than those flying ones, but all of us here at this table know it's only a matter of time before they resume their assaults."

Henry was careful to glide over the connection between the gargoyles and their recent tragedy as quickly as he could. Even the very word gargoyle now meant something so much darker than before. Henry hated uttering it. "And having just gotten back from Nampa I can attest somewhat to the truth of that. Though we didn't see one live dinosaur anywhere there or back and the people we spoke to reported the same thing, there were signs they're still out there…waiting for warmer weather. I can *feel* it. But most of the folks we talked to along our journey are fooling themselves by believing the creatures have somehow spontaneously disappeared."

Justin shook his head. "They haven't–but yes, the government finally accepts we have a big problem, about time, and I agree, especially after recent events." Justin glanced at the dark window above their heads.

The wind had picked up and Henry could hear its wailing on the other side of the glass. He shivered, relieved they'd made it back before full dark. It had turned bone-chilling cold outside and night had brought the sleet, as predicted, and it was rapidly evolving into a heavy snow. The white particles tapped at the glass and the sound filled the room. Ah, spring in Oregon. One minute almost warm and the next freezing.

"Henry, like you I know the dinosaurs are hiding, biding their time. They're up to something."

"More organizing, huh? All those brainy dinosaurs planning more troubles for us, huh?"

"We can hope not, but I'm not that optimistic,"

Justin huffed. "I can't wait to hear from other paleontologists across the country, the world, as to what they've experienced, seen, and what they think about the current situation. With enough of us we might finally fit all the pieces of the puzzle together."

"So," Henry nudged him, "if that's the good news, what's the bad?"

Now it was Justin and Steven's turn to exchange looks and Henry prepared himself for whatever would come. Ranger Williamson sat back in his chair and inhaled a deep breath. All of a sudden no one was speaking. That wasn't good.

"Okay, lay it on me." Henry sighed. "Spit it out."

Justin, with a forlorn expression, was the one to answer. "You know after you left this morning Sergeant Gilbert and some of his soldiers and I resolved to go out on patrol anyway. I needed to get out. We all did. This place was feeling like a prison. So we took two tanks and searched the areas we hadn't been to for a while, like up there where you live. And…." Justin's words stopped.

"And?" Henry prompted.

"And…sorry, Henry, but your cabin is gone. We drove past it today and discovered it smashed to smithereens. Something really big, or a herd of them, stomped it to splinters. There's nothing left but a pile of wood, glass and stones. I'm sorry."

Henry experienced a sharp stab in his gut. The cabin he and Ann had lavished such love, care and personal sweat on, their home with all their worldly possessions inside, was gone? Gone! His groan was one of frustration and acceptance in the same breath. Half of Klamath Falls had been destroyed the fall before and so many other people had lost their homes, some their very lives, so why should Ann and he escape the same fate? Well, they hadn't.

Then his next thought was: *Oh, no...how was he going to tell Ann?* After all that had happened that week this would be more than she could bear. For her, losing a daughter and learning she'd lost her home in the same month would be too much.

"Ann doesn't know yet, does she?" Henry asked.

Justin shook his head. Steven, Ranger Cutters and Williamson were eying him with pity. They knew how much Ann and he had loved their home.

"And there's nothing to be salvaged, huh?"

"I don't think so," Cutters replied and hesitated.

Oh, oh, there was something else.

"What else happened today, Ranger?" Henry was trying to let the news sink in but he was having a hard time of it. Ann and he had always thought when all the dinosaurs were taken care of they'd be able to return to their home. Now that would never happen.

But Ranger Cutters and the others acquiesced to Justin again and he answered, "You know how you reported McDowell and you didn't come across any live dinosaurs today on your round trip into Nampa?"

"I remember." Henry waited. Oh, oh, no doubt more unsettling news.

"We did." Justin's fingers nervously drummed on the tabletop. "After we found your wrecked cabin we followed the tracks into the backwoods on the northern side of the lake and as we were going in we spied a vast herd of dinosaurs traveling away from us. They were literally stampeding as if devils were on their backs. It was as if they'd been warned of our coming and were high-tailing it out of there."

Cutters was shaking his head. "There were more of them than we could count, Chief. All different breeds in different sizes. Some were giants and some weren't any bigger than dogs. And they were all running together. Friendly like with each other and, I swear, communicating somehow between themselves, their heads tilted near each other before they ran this way or that way. It was almost spooky."

"Yeah, you could call it spooky," Ranger Williamson chimed in. "I called it downright scary. We hardly see any of the critters all winter and within days we see gargoyles and a giant herd of all the rest of them. I concur with the doc here. They're up to something *big*."

"They knew you were coming as if something had warned them? Organized consultation between the beasts? You're kidding." Yet Henry wasn't as surprised as he could have been. They'd already suspected the dinosaurs were collaborating with each other. But that news along with the cabin's destruction suddenly made Henry feel older than he'd ever felt. Had the creatures destroyed the cabin because they knew it was his? Whoa, now that was another creepy notion. It was all too much. "Crap. This day just keeps getting better and better. Now, at least, we know our enemies have been hiding from us. Anywhere but around us. Just what I thought. They aren't gone at all."

"Exactly. We didn't kill all of them last fall…they've only learned exceedingly well how to conceal themselves from us." Justin's tone was solemn.

"It makes me wonder if on our trip to Nampa and back, they were doing the same thing. Letting their friends know we were coming so they could hide."

"It's possible," Justin said. "I think our war has just ramped up."

The men remained at the table, drinking coffee, and spoke about what to do next. There'd be more patrols with more tanks in each convoy and a higher level of attention to the fort's overall security and protection. Now that they knew for sure the park, and perhaps beyond it, was still teeming with their enemy.

Before they called it a night, Henry brought Justin up to date about his day trip and the pile of dead dinosaurs Noah Winters had shown them. He gave the scientist the bagged slice of flesh he'd procured from one of them. Justin was extremely grateful to get it. "I'll take it along with me to New York and see if I or any of my colleagues can figure out what might have killed it. If there's some illness deflating their numbers it could be extremely important for us to identify it. Maybe even try to strengthen and duplicate it. It could help us find a way to eventually defeat them."

"You do that. I sure hope you and your colleagues find the answers we need. I sure do."

"You and I both. I'm counting on it. After seeing those dinosaurs fleeing from us today I'm really concerned about what will come next."

Henry didn't need to answer that. He grasped what was ahead of them if they didn't find answers. Soon. It was disheartening to realize after the last exhaustingly fevered year of fighting and decimating the monsters in droves and believing they had obliterated most of them, that they hadn't.

A short time later the meeting broke up and Henry said goodnight to the others. He was exhausted and wanted to see his wife. "I'll introduce everyone to Doctor Macon first thing tomorrow at our usual morning meeting. I think she's planning on staying a day or two to give anyone who needs her services a chance to see her. So if any of you need a doctor, for anything, be here in the morning."

"That's good," Steven spoke up. "I'm going to have her do a general physical on me and make sure I'm as healthy as I can be. Never know when I'll have the chance again the way the world is going. It looks like I'll be needing my full strength to fight more dinosaurs soon enough."

"We all should have the doctor check us out before she leaves. As you said, we might not have a chance again for a while. She has a hospital to run."

Henry exited the room and with heavy steps returned to Ann and the doctor. He was almost afraid to open the door to their make-shift bedroom, scared to hear what the doctor would have to say about Ann's condition. He was so afraid the cancer had returned and didn't know how he or Ann would handle that. And how was he going to tell Ann about the cabin?

He took a deep fortifying breath before he

entered the room. A person had to face everything sooner or later and he'd always held the belief it was better to do it sooner. Some things couldn't be run from.

He opened the door and went in.

Chapter 5

The first thing Henry saw was his wife laying on the bed, a transparent tube coming from her arm to a bottle full of some clear liquid hanging from a make-shift holder, which was normally the wooden coat tree that resided in a corner. The coats were in a pile on the floor beside the doctor's over-stuffed black bag. Henry thought it was an inspired use of the coat tree.

Ann glanced up and the hesitant smile on her face dissolved some of the fears he'd been holding inside. There was hope in her eyes. The first he'd seen in weeks. Moving closer to the bed he took her hand and faced the doctor. "What's all this, Doctor?" He waved his hand at the contraption hanging beside the bed.

The physician fiddled with something at the bottom of the bottle and peering over her shoulder at him, her lips reflected Ann's smile. "I'm giving your wife a concentrated dose of antibiotics, Chief Ranger. I did my preliminary examination–though I'll still take her blood sample back to the hospital for more extensive testing, I'm fairly sure of my diagnosis–and what your wife is suffering from seems to be a virulent strain of influenza bordering on pneumonia. Because of her earlier fight with cancer her weakened immune system made her an easy target. Which would explain her symptoms of intense fatigue, shortness of breath and dizziness. The antibiotics, rest and the medicines I'm going to leave her should help her fight off the respiratory infection." The doctor's eyes were stern as she added, "But she must rest. No more stress for a while, either, if you want her to fully recover."

Yeah, no stress. How could he keep her calm with crazy dinosaurs proliferating in every nook and cranny of the country and plotting to take over the world; with people, like the daughter they'd loved, still dying?

"You mean the cancer hasn't returned...she might still be in remission?" Henry felt a great rush of relief. His Ann was sick but she wasn't dying. It wasn't the cancer again. Thank the Lord. He sat down beside his wife, careful not to crowd her too much or disturb the tube snaking from her arm to the bottle.

"As far as I can tell, yes, Ranger Shore, she's still in remission. But with her medical history pneumonia caused by this influenza is nothing to play around with."

"This influenza," Henry spoke, "how contagious is it?"

The doctor was watching the window and the snow, her face thoughtful. She appeared world weary to Henry. Perhaps, as all of them, she'd had too much loss and, as a doctor, she was trying to care for too many patients. One medicine woman could only do so much. "I wouldn't be too worried about anyone else here catching it, unless they've been weakened by another illness or a chronic condition. Your wife was an exception. But I did bring along a generous supply of flu shots for anyone who will want one. I'd advise it. This strain of influenza, as bad as it is, is fairly common and the shot will protect most people."

"Thank you. I'll spread the word about the shots. The last thing we want around here is a flu epidemic. We have enough trouble with dinosaurs."

Henry was about to ask the doctor another question when a knock came at the door.

Ann gave him a nod and Henry opened it. It was Justin, Phoebe and Steven. Justin was holding his sleeping son in his arms.

"Henry," Justin started out with, "I know it's late but we had to see how Ann was doing. And since I'm leaving early tomorrow morning I wasn't sure I'd have a chance to see her before I left." He looked over at Ann with an apologetic smile. "So how are you, Ann?"

The two men and the girl moved into the room and surrounded the bed.

"Don't any of you get too close to her," Henry warned. "What she has is catching. Better to be safe than sorry."

Justin fell back a few feet not wanting the baby to be too close.

But Phoebe ran up to her grandmother and, not heeding the warning, took her hand. "If I haven't gotten what she has so far, I most likely won't get it. I've been with her every day and I'm still as healthy as can be.

"Grandma, how are you feeling?" The girl leaned over and laid a kiss on Ann's flushed cheek. Phoebe and her grandmother had always been close, but the last year locked up together and her mother's death had made them even closer.

But it was Doctor Macon who spoke up and summarized Ann's condition and what she was doing about it.

Both Justin and Steven seemed relieved after the doctor had finished talking. Steven asked her specific questions about Ann's treatment and the doctor explained her answers. She mentioned the flu vaccine and that everyone should take it. "I brought enough doses for everyone. I hope. I guess I should have asked how many people were staying here, but I think I have enough."

Henry caught Steven smiling shyly at the doctor as they spoke and he caught the instant spark which ignited between them. The doctor stood straighter, smiled brighter at him than at the others in the room, and her fingers kept lightly brushing her hair away from her face. He could have sworn she was blushing. Ann might be the matchmaker of the family, but Henry could recognize instant attraction or love at first sight when he saw it.

Hmm. Interesting.

"I'll take one of those shots," Steven volunteered a little too enthusiastically. "I always get one each year but I never had the chance to last year. I was too busy fighting dinosaurs." He grinned like a shy teenager.

Oh yeah, love.

"Then roll up your sleeve, big bad dinosaur hunter," Doctor Macon mouthed in a teasing voice, pulling a small plastic package from her medical bag and tearing it open to reveal the wrapped hypodermic needle. "And I'll give it to you right now. You, too, Chief Ranger. Doctor Maltin. The children as well."

"I hate shots," Justin mumbled, "but going where

I'm going I'd better get one so I don't give the flu to everyone at the conference." He rolled his sleeve down and offered his arm after the doctor was done with Steven. Then he helped the doctor give a shot to his son. Timothy didn't like the needle much and ended up crying, but his father soothed him, rocking him in his arms. The crying didn't last long.

With her father reassuring her, Phoebe stepped forward and, closing her eyes for courage, received her vaccination. "I ain't afraid of no shot," she sing-songed the modified Ghost Buster's jingle.

"Now you, too, Chief Ranger." Doctor Macon whipped out another packaged needle.

Henry didn't protest and moments later was rolling down his sleeve again, task accomplished. "Tomorrow morning, Doctor," he said to the physician, "I'll set you up in the conference room so you can give out the rest of those shots and meet with anyone else who may have other health concerns. I know many here have been waiting patiently for your visit and they're glad you're here."

"That will do fine," she replied, yawning, her eyes never leaving Steven for more than a minute or two at a time. Her smile kept reemerging as well, often aimed in his direction. "I'm happy to be able to help. I can't imagine what it's been like for you trapped behind these walls for so long. The fight you've had to survive. You've been so brave. I admire that."

"We've only done what we had to do." Steven smiled at the woman. Henry noticed the musician had maneuvered closer to the doctor since he'd come in. Now he was standing beside her, their bodies practically touching. She didn't move away.

The people in the room traded conversation for a while until Henry, seeing how exhausted everyone was, called it a night. "Doctor Macon we have a modest cubicle prepared for you for the night or for as long as you remain with us. It's not much, a comfortable cot and a table for your things surrounded by heavy canvas curtains, but we're short of space here as you can see and it's the best we can do. At least you'll have some privacy. Here, follow me and I'll see you settled in. Oh, and there's some homemade stew left in the kitchen if you're hungry?"

"Now that sounds good. I am exhausted but I'm also hungry. It's been a full day." She gathered up her medicine bag and overnight bag. She glanced at Ann, who was half-asleep on the bed, patted her patient's shoulder. "I'll see you in the morning, Ann."

"In the morning, Emily," Ann's voice was faint, her eyes already closed. The doctor had also given her a sedative to help her sleep.

"Henry," Steven stepped forward, "I can take the doctor to the kitchen, help her get some supper, and then lead her to her sleeping quarters. You stay with Ann. You've been gone all day and you look as if you're going to keel over any minute."

"Is that all right with you, Doctor?" Henry asked.

"That would be fine." The doctor was smiling at Steven again and her cheeks were slightly flushed. So cute. A blossoming romance in the midst of the apocalyptic madness. Henry wished he could appreciate it but after the day he'd had, he was just too tired.

He didn't argue, but caught the grin Justin flashed him. "Thanks Steven." All he wanted now was to be with his wife and to rest. Let Steven take over, it was fine with him.

Justin, with a sleeping Timothy cradled in his arms, and Phoebe left with Steven and the doctor and Henry shut the door behind them.

It was good to be alone finally with his wife. He wanted to tell Ann about his day, his great relief at her diagnosis and the obvious instant attraction between Steven and the doctor, she'd get a kick out of it, but she was already in dream land and he didn't want to disturb her. As the doctor had said, she needed her sleep.

Then again he'd also have to wait to find out what Ann had wanted to tell him. He was curious but the morning was soon enough to hear about it, whatever it was. It was probably some funny antic Sasha had done that day or something endearing Timothy had done.

After he changed his clothes for comfortable pants and an old sweatshirt because he didn't sleep in pajamas–he never knew when he'd have to make a mad dash out of bed for some emergency or other–he dropped into the chair beside his wife, groaning and rubbing his eyes. Every bone in his body was as tired as his brain, but their cat jumped into his arms and the room was filled with her purring. As he petted the feline, he stared out the window at the snow and let the fatigue take over. He contemplated the change of events with Justin leaving for New York and what it might mean–something good he prayed–and how he was going to tell his wife about their ruined cabin. He worried about what the spring would bring. Yet within minutes he was asleep in the chair. He never made it to the bed.

Chapter 6

The dinosaur outside the window gawked in at the strange creatures inside. They were such silly things. They walked on two appendages and were so frail and thin. They were like walking *sticks*. Yes, *sticks*. And that was what it was going to call them. The *Sticks*. They squawked out a bizarre series of sounds to each other, very noisy, and the dinosaur wished it could decipher them. The sticks all had pasty skin as pale as the frozen liquid falling around it but they draped their frames in strange coverings. It was so funny, too, how they needed to cover themselves the way they did. Shaking its head, it wondered why they did that? *It* didn't need to carry around bulky coverings as its own skin was thick, tough and a beautiful shade similar to the stuff which blanketed the ground beneath the green material in the warmer seasons.

There'd been a room full of the funny creatures but now there weren't as many…and a tiny furry thing the creatures seemed to dote on. The dinosaur licked what would have been its lips, if it would have had any. It was reminded it was hungry. Soon it would have to go in search of food. The furry mouthful yawned in the larger stick creature's lap and its eyes glowed in the dimness, like the objects in the night sky, as it looked around. Could it be one of their offspring? It could be…yet it didn't look like any of them. No, it couldn't be one of theirs. So why were they caring for it and protecting it? Again, very strange.

The dinosaur thrust its head up against the glass

to get a clearer view. It was curious about these creatures. Why did they reside within a cave with holes like this in it and that were surrounded in branchless trees so close together it had to climb over them instead of through them to get near? It didn't mind the darkness, the snow or cold. It was used to all of them. But it didn't want the creatures to see it. Somehow it knew it was important to remain invisible to them though it wasn't sure exactly why. Only that they seemed to get really upset when they saw any of his kind. It had witnessed their frightened or angry reactions when one of its brethren showed itself to them. It never ended well.

The creatures also had these dark rods that made a lot of racket. They hurt its ears. When they pointed them at his comrades sometimes his comrades fell to the ground and stopped moving…forever. What was inside his comrades, flowing or more solid parts of them, sometimes spilled out. It didn't really understand what death was, but it did know once one of those creatures pointed those dark rods at any of them it was final. One less of them escaping back to their lairs. One less of them to romp the woods or tend to their young. It didn't feel sadness so seeing the dead ones like itself around it didn't bother it much. They were just gone. Many things disappeared and never returned in its world. It made no difference to it.

Its attention returned to the sticks in their cave. It was fascinated by them for some reason.

Then there were those huge growling, rumbling ground eating monsters that sometimes ate the strange pale creatures and came chasing after it and its herd. More strange creatures. Their skin was so hard it couldn't even bite into it. It knew that because it had tried many times. No matter how hard it bit, it couldn't taste the creature's blood or break its skin. What *were* those things?

All in all the creatures beyond the window were a mystery to it. One it wanted badly to solve. It liked observing them. They came in all different sizes. Hmmm. Cocking its head, it watched. It thought: it didn't hate the creatures. It wanted to understand them. Perhaps if it could understand them, they could all live together in peace. No more dark rods making noise and growling ground eaters taking his brethren from the herd.

The cold stuff floating in the air increased until it could barely see through the hole into the cave; could barely see the funny creatures, now not moving at all in their dim cave, within. Moving in closer, it peered in trying to see them.

Suddenly the tiny furry thing was right in front of it, glaring at it through the hard barrier between them. It couldn't hear the sounds the thing was making but saw its mouth open wide, teeth barred, face scrunched up and its body contorted as if it were trying to look bigger. Glaring back at it *as if the furry creature really saw it on the other side.* Ugly little thing. Ugh. If the dinosaur could have smiled, it would have. That tiny furry thing wasn't scary at all. It would be barely a bite it was so small. And it speculated if it would taste good. Maybe. But all that fur, and it looked to be all skin and bones beneath that fur….ugh.

Oh oh, the stick creatures were stirring in their cave so the dinosaur spun around and scurried away, scrambled over the tall close-knit trees and bounded into the night woods to return to its lair with the rest of its herd. It was careful as it went over the top for there were sharp needles that bit into its skin and it had to place its claws just so. But it knew it'd be back because it had realized that understanding these pale stick creatures was important to the survival of it and its kind. Understanding them was important.

Besides they interested it. Such strange creatures.

He wondered if they tasted good.

Chapter 7

Henry woke, still in the chair, as the sun crept into the room. So it was no wonder his body felt stiff and achy. He stretched his legs out and raised his arms to shake the numbness away. Ann was sleeping. Good. She needed the rest. The clear bag hanging over her head was empty, though. The cat was curled at the end of the bed. It lifted its head and meowed. The cat was probably hungry. It was always hungry.

Henry came to his feet, stretched again and walked to the window. Outside the snow was no longer falling but there had to be at least a foot of it on the ground. He pushed his nose to the glass and looked through the bars they'd put on the window months ago. Outside there were weird tracks going away from the window through the snow's blanket. Critter tracks. But the tracks were small. Something had gotten into the compound again and that wasn't good. How had it gotten over the barbed wire fortified stockade fence? He had no clue. And there were tracks on the outside window ledge. A frown reshaped Henry's mouth. He'd have to get his men to check it out. This was the second time in a month that dinosaurs–or something–had crept through their guarded perimeter and gained access to their compound. Simply the thought that some animal had been surreptitiously observing them during the night made his skin crawl. It might have been a wild animal, if there were any of them left, or it might have been a dinosaur. But why would one of them be eavesdropping in on them? He couldn't help but think again: *what the heck are they up to?*

"Henry?" Ann's voice behind him was hesitant. "Don't tell me you spent the whole night in that chair? You know what that does to your back."

Henry put a smile on his face before he swung around. He didn't want to frighten her with his suspicions. "I know. But my back is fine. I slept fairly well in fact." He crossed the room and stood above her with a smile on his face. Ann did look better this morning. Her skin was no longer pasty and there was pink in her cheeks. "How are you feeling, sweetheart?"

"Actually better, I think. Leastways I feel rested for the first time in weeks." She sat up in bed and gave him a hopeful smile.

There was a knock at the door.

It was the doctor. Henry let her in and she went to Ann. She disconnected the antibiotic feed from Ann's arm, took her vitals and asked her patient a series of questions. Ann must have given the right answers because the doctor seemed more than satisfied.

"Ah, good," the doctor murmured, "I believe you're doing better this morning."

"I guess I am," Ann responded, sending a cheerful look Henry's way. "I actually do feel better. The room's no longer spinning."

"Even so, I want you to stay in bed for another day or two. Total bed rest. No leaving it or this room, you understand?"

Reluctantly, Ann replied, "I understand, Doctor. I'll obey orders."

"I'll have someone bring you some breakfast,

honey," Henry promised as he dropped a kiss on her forehead.

"Make it soon…I'm starved."

"Another good sign," the doctor asserted. "Her appetite has returned." The women conferred further about Ann's recovery and afterwards discussed other things. The doctor seemed curiously interested, in Henry's opinion, in how Ann's life in headquarters had been during and since the fall siege. But the two women seemed to be developing a true friendship so perhaps it wasn't all that curious. It occurred to Henry the doctor thought Ann's life was exciting. If she only knew. Excitement wasn't the word. Terror and loss were.

Henry was about to escort the doctor out of the room when his wife said, "Henry, before you go, I need to tell you something."

Henry halted and swung around to face the doctor. "Go on ahead to the conference room, Doctor Macon, you know where it is. I'll meet you there. I left orders for some breakfast to be waiting for you, knowing you were setting up your temporary clinic there. Scrambled eggs and toast, I think. If it's cold you can reheat it in the microwave. There's one in the rear of the room against the wall near the refrigerator. There should be a pot of coffee brewing, too. Help yourself."

"Thanks, Chief Ranger. I'll see you there." The door closed quietly behind her.

"All right, honey. What do you want to tell me?" Henry moved towards the bed, and pulling the chair closer sat down in it. By the ambiguous look on her face he could see something else was on her mind but she wasn't sure she should reveal it. He'd seen that look many times over their long marriage so he knew she'd tell him in the end.

"Well, late yesterday before you came home," Ann began falteringly, a worried expression shadowing her features, "something strange happened. I would have spoken to you about it last night but it was so late and I wasn't…myself." She reached out and he took her hands. They were trembling.

Henry's senses were on high alert. *Oh, oh.* "Go on."

"I saw something at that window last night…." She nodded her head at the window and Henry glanced at it.

"What?"

She finished explaining about the strange sighting of the creature she thought she'd had. He sat there and listened, trying not to let her see his growing concern.

"So you say it was a dinosaur…a small one…but one like you've never seen before? And it appeared as if it were trying to communicate with you? Really?"

"Really. At first I thought I dreamed it in my fevered state of mind. I wish I had. But now I'm not so sure. So I figured I had to tell you." She gave him a more detailed version of what she'd seen and Henry listened with a growing uneasiness.

When Ann was done Henry stood up, exhaling a deep breath. If what Ann had divulged was true then the dinosaurs were now sending advance emissaries to spy on them. Which was crazy, wasn't it?

"But Henry, I could have imagined it. I can't be sure."

"Ann, if you did it's understandable. You've been ill. So I don't want you to fret anymore about it. I'm glad you told me, but to be truthful…I'm not sure what you saw was real, either. But just in case, I'll have some of my men fortify those windows a little more."

"More bars, huh?"

"More bars."

She nodded her head and resettled it on her pillow. She was rubbing the spot where the intravenous needle had recently been.

"But right now," he said, "I'm going to go get you some breakfast, sweetheart."

"Thanks honey. Don't forget the coffee. If we have any left."

"We have enough left and, no, I won't forget. After I bring the food I'll be seeing Justin off. The snow has stopped so the helicopter should be here soon to take him away. I want to be there."

"Say goodbye for me, would you, and wish him luck."

"You know I will. Now rest as you're supposed to and I'll be back."

"Don't worry, Henry, I'm not going to get up and run any marathons."

Henry smiled at that. "Not today anyway."

"No, not today."

*****

Henry was at the conference room, his hand on the door, but paused to watch the scene unfolding inside. Phoebe, yawning, and looking as if she'd just dragged herself from bed, was by her father, holding his hand, while he spoke to Ranger Gillian. The girl's eyes were anxious because he was leaving. Timothy was waddling around in circles holding on to his father's legs so he wouldn't fall.

Steven was in the corner at the microwave conversing with Doctor Macon. No, he was openly flirting with her and the doctor, laughing, was flirting back, or that's the way it looked. Their affectionate banter made Henry smile. So he hadn't been wrong the night before when he'd caught first sight of their attraction. Good for Steven. Good for the doctor. Hmm, a doctor and a musician. It was an unlikely pairing, but in their strange new world, who could say it wouldn't work.

Henry made his way to Justin and the scientist broke away from Ranger Gillian to greet him. Timothy, overjoyed at seeing his grandpa, launched his chubby body into Henry's arms. Laughing, Henry swung the boy around and deposited him safely on the ground again at his sister's side. He had to make sure Ann got her breakfast but he needed time to speak with Justin before he flew away to New York. He had to tell him about Ann's intelligent, imaginary or not, little dinosaur window friend. See what Justin thought about it.

So Henry asked Ranger Gillian to take the breakfast into Ann. "Tell her I'll be in later after Justin leaves."

"Sure, Chief. I was going in to see how she was doing anyway. We're all worried about our mama bear." That's what the men had taken to calling Ann because, before she had become so ill, she took care of everyone.

"Thanks Gillian. She's getting treatment and feeling better today. The doctor knows her job." He lowered his voice. "She has pre-pneumonia but hopefully it's under control now. It isn't the cancer again."

Relief flickered across the other ranger's face. "Thank heaven," a whisper.

"Be sure to take her coffee with that breakfast. You know how she has to have it."

The ranger grinned at his boss. "And with lots of cream and sugar. I remember. I'll take her two cups. I'm so happy she's eating again and feeling better."

"As am I. Oh, also, after you get that food to Ann could you grab Williamson and check the bars on our bedroom windows? Make sure they're secure, would you? I'm afraid there's a chance we might be having uninvited visitors staring in at us from the outside."

"Dinosaurs?" Gillian's eyes reflected surprise.

"We don't know, but it's better to be safe than sorry."

"Okey-dokey, you got it, boss." Gillian took off to complete his assigned tasks.

As the ranger left the room, Henry tagged on, "When you're done, Gillian, come back here and get a flu shot. The doctor is giving them out free today."

"Oh, goodie. I hate shots, but hate the flu more, so I'll return later for it," Ranger Gillian's voice drifted back.

Henry gave his attention to his son-in-law. "You ready to fly away into the wild blue yonder to the big city and hobnob with the brightest and best in your field?" Timothy had grabbed his hand and was pulling at him again, wanting attention; wanting to play. Henry hugged the boy but continued talking to Justin. He noticed the sorrow that never seemed to leave the young man's eyes and a stab of fresh grief hit him again. *My daughter is dead…my daughter is dead.* It can't be true…oh, Lord, he wished it'd been a bad dream. No, it was real. He shook the sadness away. He had other people to care for and protect so he needed to focus.

"I'm more than ready. I'm excited. I've followed some of these paleontologists and their careers, their discoveries, for years. They are the elite of my profession. Possibly with their collaboration we can solve our dinosaur problems once and for all."

"And I bet you have some theories of your own to present to them on how to do that, right?"

"I could have some." Justin was being humble as he always was.

"Before you go you might be interested in something Ann just told me."

In the corner the doctor laughed softly at something Steven had said and when Henry glanced their way Steven grinned at him. There was definitely something happening between them. Their heads were bowed and they were whispering about something that made Steven chuckle. Every few seconds, though, the musician would peer over at Justin as if he were afraid to openly show any happiness when his friend was going through his own sadness.

Timothy released Henry's hand, grabbed his

father's and pressed his face against his leg, clinging to him. The child must sense he was leaving.

"Then you better tell me about it quickly. They're picking me up in," Justin glanced at his wristwatch, "about fifteen minutes."

Henry repeated what Ann had told him.

"Oh, my, just what I feared," Justin's tone was incredulous. "They're developing increasing intelligence, utilizing primitive weapons, strategizing, and genetically adapting–and now they are even spying on us. This is *not* good."

"Just what I said. If Ann really saw what she says she did."

Justin didn't have time to respond before Henry caught the sound of an incoming helicopter. "I think your ride is here, kiddo."

"I think you're right." Justin put on his coat and picked up his travel bag and with his free hand swept his son up against him. The boy hugged his father tightly and began to cry as they moved towards and out the door. The child had already lost his mother and now he was afraid he was losing his father. Phoebe, too, was hanging on to Justin, trying to be a big girl and not let the tears come.

Henry slipped on his coat and collected the boy from Justin's arms as Steven fell in behind them. Doctor Macon had already hurried off to check on Ann again but would return later to give out flu shots and consultations.

"Hush, Timothy," Henry soothed the child, speaking to him as if he could understand what he was saying. "Your father won't be gone long and he'll be back, I promise. He's going to a special meeting with other scientists and they're going to get rid of the dinosaurs. And your Grandma Ann and I will take care of you. If you're a good boy, no more tears, I think there's a Hersey bar in it for you." That quieted the child a bit. As young as he was he knew what a Hersey bar was. Like his grandma, he loved chocolate. Henry handed the boy over to his older sister who would watch him until after he saw Justin off.

"You stay inside, sweetie, with your brother," Henry said to his granddaughter, "and help take care of your grandma. She needs you." He didn't want her or Timothy going outside the gates. It was too dangerous. The soldiers hadn't finished putting up the hanging mesh blanket yet. "Take Timothy with you. Your grandma is probably waiting for you to visit her. You can go see her now."

"Okay grandpa." Then she gave her father one more hug, a wave and a smile as she left the room with her brother squirming in her arms. The boy was crying louder now and his cries could be heard going down the corridor. Poor kids.

Justin and Steven had already gone out the door and Henry ran to catch up with them.

*****

The snow on the ground was so glaringly white Henry had to slip his sunglasses on when he stepped outside. The sun was shining but the air was glacial.

The helicopter had landed outside the gates and soldiers and rangers were converging on it, eyes alert and weapons ready. Henry and his rangers had cleared the temporary landing pad the year before when the dinosaur attacks had amped up. It had proved very convenient and much safer than where the aircrafts used to land a few miles away.

They got Justin and his bags loaded on the chopper, though, with no dinosaur sightings and no trouble.

Henry and Steven flapped their arms in goodbye gestures as the helicopter rose into the sky, Justin waving in return.

"Well," Steven muttered aside to Henry as they, along with the other humans, trekked through the snow to the gates, "I'm going to miss him, but this trip could do him a world of good…getting away and all after what's happened. He needs it."

"I agree. And I pray he and his colleagues find something we can use against our nemeses before they begin another major all-out attack."

"Amen. I have the same prayer." Steven's eyes were on the compound as the gates swung open to receive them. The chopper was above them now and it had cleared the tops of the trees.

"Talking about good things for people…I couldn't help but see how well you and the visiting doctor are getting along. You two make such a nice couple."

Steven's grin was reticent. "I'm only being friendly, that's all. Since her husband died she admitted she's been lonely. She's an interesting woman, not to mention if I get sick she can heal me. Give me drugs." Another grin.

Henry flashed him a knowing look. "Uh, huh. It looks like a case of new love to me. I've never seen you so helpful, so charming, in fact." They'd reached the gate and it was opening.

Steven didn't answer Henry because he was gawking at the sky above them.

The expression of horror on Steven's face made Henry look up, too.

Justin's helicopter was being attacked by two very large gargoyles. It was using evasive tactics, dropping up and down like a yoyo; jerking to the left and then the right as it attempted to stay away from the gargoyles' talons. The soldiers inside the aircraft were shooting at the monsters, but the creatures were too fast and the bullets didn't hit flesh. The flying monsters were determined and wouldn't give up. They continued to chase the chopper.

Henry, as the other rangers with him, had brought up his high-powered rifle and was trying to bring the assailants down but they and the helicopter had moved too far away, were too high in the sky.

This can't be happening, Henry thought frantically as he sprinted away from the gates and plunged into the woods. *The damn gargoyles can't get both his daughter and Justin in the same month. They can't! He wouldn't let them.*

One of the gargoyles, finally taking bullets from the soldiers inside the helicopter, screeched like a wounded banshee and soared off towards Mount Scott. The other one, after a final run at its target and being slammed away by the helicopter's tail, was also shrieking, but reluctantly joined its companion. Both monsters vanished into the horizon.

Some of the humans raised their weapons and cheered. The helicopter was in one piece and still in the air.

For a minute Henry wondered if the chopper was going to return, but it didn't. It swung around and headed in the direction it had originally been going, apparently no worse for the hostile confrontation.

"God, that was close," Steven exclaimed, catching up to where Henry had come to a full stop in the woods. He was clutching the Bushmaster rifle Henry had given him earlier, yet his gaze was uneasy and he kept examining the trees and sky around them.

"Way too close," Henry snapped. "But it appears as if Justin is safe, for the moment, and on his way to his conference. I pray he makes it. There's a lot of sky between here and New York and it looks like our enemies are at long last all waking from their winter's slumber."

"Looks like it, doesn't it? But Justin will get there. I know he will. It's destiny that he does, and he will find a way to kill those monsters."

Henry gave Steven a cynical glance. Gosh, the man was such an optimist. After what had happened recently, he wasn't as sure. Yet there wasn't anything he could do about it. The helicopter with Justin inside was gone.

The rangers from the compound had caught up with them. They voiced their shock at what had occurred and their relief the scientist and the men in the chopper had escaped the ambush.

"It's over. And I get the feeling we shouldn't linger out in the open as we are any longer. Let's get out of these woods and behind our walls before more of the gargoyles' fiendish friends decide to make an appearance." Henry gestured at his men to follow and started ploughing through the snow the way they'd come.

They didn't quite make it to headquarters.

From among the underbrush and trees a mob of eerie looking creatures had stealthily emerged to ogle the humans. The closest were about a hundred feet away. Some were the size of large dogs and some the size of ponies. They stood on two strong hind legs and had front ones extremely human looking. Their expressions and movements also seemed to mimic human beings. They were a dull brownish color with roundish faces. For some reason they reminded Henry of furless simians. And there was something about their mannerisms and the empathetic depths of their large liquid-looking eyes which unnerved him. These were not dumb dinosaurs. He'd bet these were exceptionally intelligent.

"Well, these are new ones, aren't they?" Steven whispered, unmoving, and staring back at the curious creatures now surrounding them. "I've never seen any of their ilk before."

Neither had Henry.

One of the dinosaurs, the largest, grinned at them, showing a mouth of razor sharp spiked teeth. It motioned to the rangers. *Come here. Come…here.* Then its eyes turned hungry. Desperately hungry. Its tongue, nothing like a human's because it was forked and long, flicked out and slid across its scaly snout. It took a step forward as if it were ready to pounce. The others around it did the same. There were more of them now flooding out of the woods. There was an army of them.

Oh, oh, time to go, Henry thought. "Time to go! Intelligent or not, I think these beasts are starving and I don't want to be on their menu."

"Should we shoot them, Chief?" Ranger Williamson muttered under his breath just loud enough for Henry to hear.

"No, too many of them," he whispered back. But it was more than that which made Henry resist shooting the creatures. Shooting at them would declare open war and for some reason he didn't want to do that. Yet. "*Just...RUN!*"

He didn't have to tell his men again to skedaddle. Every human took off through the snowy forest towards headquarters like snow bunnies, hopping and stumbling through the snow between the trees.

The monkey-like monsters were right behind them, stampeding now on all four limbs and making the oddest human-like cries of pursuit Henry had ever heard…from a dinosaur. The creatures gave Henry the creeps, but they didn't like the deep snow, though, and seemed to be having trouble advancing in it. Which was probably the reason the dinosaurs didn't catch up to them.

The gates were wide open and Henry and his men rocketed through them with barely seconds to spare before the horde behind them caught up. The gates swung shut and they could hear the hard dull thuds of monkey-monster bodies hitting it on the other side.

Henry growled, "That was *way* too close."

“Wow, and what a way to start the day,” Steven moaned, leaning against the gate beside Henry and wiping his sweaty face.

“Feels almost normal to me.” Henry’s grin was morose. Then he shouted to the rangers and soldiers who had come running out into the yard at the commotion, “Don’t shoot our uninvited guests unless they get inside! That’s an order!”

Weapons were lowered. The thuds could still be heard but gradually tapered off until there was silence. An unnatural silence.

A few minutes later, one of the soldiers yelled out, “They’re gone, Sir. Every last one of them is gone. There’s nothing out there.”

Henry marched through the compound and went inside. He suddenly had the urge to see his wife and grandchildren, hold them near, because he had the feeling things were about to get bad again.

The warmer weather had brought the dinosaurs out in force and they were ravenous and restless. Well, so much for hoping and praying most of the creatures had died off or gone away over the brutal winter. They hadn’t. And now there was another new unknown species to contend with. Oh, whoopee. Would the fun ever stop?

Chapter 8

Henry was in the meeting room a half hour later getting something to eat when his cell phone rang. There was no one else with him yet and he'd left the doctor, Ann, Phoebe and Timothy in the room. Ann was feeling so much better she'd requested if the children could spend more time with her. Henry had agreed. The children made her happy and Phoebe had proven to be quite the little nurse. He had conveniently neglected to mention the attack on Justin's helicopter or the monkey horde pursuing them to headquarters. Ann didn't need any of that extra stress. Besides nothing had actually happened and no one had been hurt or killed. In the scheme of things, being chased and escaping unscathed in both instances wasn't all that bad. In the last seven years running from the dinosaurs had become commonplace. So all was well that ended well. He'd enlighten Ann about the incidents when she was stronger and Justin was in New York, safe and sound.

Henry grumbled into his cell phone, "Well, Scott, it's good to finally hear from you. I was beginning to think you'd gone to another planet or something–" Henry glanced up as he was chatting and spied Zeke hobbling through the door. Henry gestured at the old man to take a seat. "I'll be with you as soon as I'm done chatting with Patterson. He's been the devil to catch lately," Henry whispered to Zeke, muting his cell phone for a moment. "Get yourself a cup of coffee."

The elderly man, appearing older and wearier

than Henry had ever seen him, cocked his head in affirmation, got his coffee, and settled into a chair. Now days his body seemed shrunken, his hair was pure white and his eyes were dull. His fingers shook holding his cup. He was no longer the tenacious and competent man who'd been publisher of the Klamath Falls Journal newspaper for all those years when Ann worked for him. Time and circumstances had caught up with him.

The winter at the settlement had been hard on him and his girlfriend Wilma. Wilma had weakened physically with each passing month. She was nearly eighty-five after all, two years older than Zeke. The whole dinosaurs-are-everywhere-trying-to-kill-them lifestyle had aged her more. At first she'd been grateful to be hidden behind the walls and stockade protected from the monsters, but lately she no longer seemed to care one way or another. Henry feared she was in the early stages of dementia but he didn't have the courage to broach the subject to Zeke and what it might mean to them; not when Zeke had been showing more signs of physical and memory frailties himself over the last year. The man was trying so hard to take care of his friend when he himself wasn't well. It broke Henry's heart to think what the future might hold for the old ones. But then they could be any old couple, for everyone aged. A person either died or aged…for humans there was no choice in the matter. He and Ann could be them, with diminishing cognizance and debilitating infirmities, one day. Watching his own parents age and die a decade past had shown Henry in excruciating detail old age wasn't for sissies. For many people the golden years weren't so golden. At least Zeke and Wilma had good friends around them and were grateful for that.

Henry transferred his attention again to the man on the other end of the phone.

"I meant to call last night as soon as I heard the awful news. I'm so sorry about your daughter, Henry."

The bitterness of his grief hit Henry again and he winced. "Thank you." He didn't have any other words to offer. The wound was still too painful.

"I know you wanted to be the one to tell me, in person and all, but when I talked to Sherman on the phone last I knew immediately something was very wrong. She can't hide anything from me. It's always in her voice. I made her tell me. I'm sorry."

Henry released a sigh. Nothing could change the fact Laura was gone. Nothing. Then it hit him he didn't mind Scott already knew…it saved him saying it out loud again.

"How are you and Ann holding up? Justin? Oh my, I was the one who recommended him for that conference in New York. But it was before I knew about Laura. I had no idea he'd just lost her."

"It's okay. Leaving, getting away, and having a greater purpose was what he needed. It gave him something else to focus on. I should thank you," Henry stated.

"I can't talk long," Patterson said. "I only wanted to tell you I was coming for a visit the day after tomorrow. I have something I need to speak to you about…and I wanted to give you and Ann my condolences in person. See how things are there with all of you. Catch up. I haven't visited in a while."

Henry was glad to hear his friend Scott was coming. With Justin on his way to the big city he needed all the extra friends around him he could muster. "I'll be happy to see you. I guess you aren't going to even give me a hint as to what your, er, mission is?"

"No. I'll see you day after tomorrow and confess all. Take care, friend." Then Patterson hung up. Henry had wanted to talk to him about Justin's close call with the gargoyles and the new breed of dinosaur they'd run into but it'd have to wait until he saw him.

Just like Patterson. He always worked hard at being enigmatic.

Henry clipped his cell phone on his belt and swung around to Zeke. "Hi Zeke. What can I do for you?"

Zeke was at the coffee machine pouring another cup of coffee. Henry joined him.

"How's Ann doing today?" Zeke inquired, concern in his gravelly voice. "I heard from one of the rangers the new woman doctor has really been helping her."

"She is. Ann's much better this morning. We also got good news…the doctor doesn't believe Ann's cancer has returned. She has pneumonia, which is bad enough but treatable, and she's on an intravenous antibiotics drip. Just with that IV overnight she's doing better. The grandkids are with her now."

"That's great news, I guess, but it'd be better if

she wasn't sick at all. Pneumonia is nothing to fool with. When can I see her?"

"Could you wait until later today, like after supper? She has plenty of company now and we don't want to tire her too much. She's still weak and the doctor wants her to have as much rest as possible. The kids are handful enough now."

"I'll do that. Let her know I'm thinking of her and will see her later."

"I will."

Zeke took a breath. "That was a really close call with Justin's helicopter and those flying monkeys this morning." Unlike Henry who had always called them gargoyles, the old man called the flying dinosaurs *flying monkeys* after the creepy but smaller evil witch's creatures in The Wizard of Oz. "I was watching the show from the yard and when it started I climbed up to the guard tower. I feared for a time Justin and the crew were goners. In my mind it was a true miracle they escaped. I prayed the whole time and my prayers were answered. I hope he gave that pilot a big hug because the guy showed how well he could fly by evading those critters the way he did. What a pilot. I knew a few, fighter pilots that is, who could maneuver and dodge the enemy like that in the skies in my service days." Zeke shook his head, his fingers thumping the table top. "I hope all of them in the helicopter made it to New York. From what I hear that think tank of top scientists might be just what the world needs to get a handle on this dinosaur epidemic we're having. I have high hopes for the boy finding a solution for us."

"We can only pray," Henry said. "I was scared for Justin and the others on that helicopter, too. I was so relieved when they made it away safely."

Over his cup the older man leveled his gaze at Henry. "And after that helicopter spectacle I also saw you and your men's hasty retreat and hot-footed entrance through the gates. I saw what happened. You all just made it in time."

"We did. Those dinosaurs, a pack of them, were behaving crazy."

"My eyes aren't as good as they once were so I couldn't tell precisely what they looked like…just running blurs chasing running blurs." He smiled at his little joke. "What did they look like?"

"To me they looked like big monkeys."

"Did they fly?" Zeke probed with a sly look.

"No, but they could really travel on those monkey claws of theirs and we barely got ahead of them and inside the settlement before they threw themselves at the gates like giant kamikaze mosquitos. So here we are at square one again as spring looms. Us against the dinosaurs. And it appears they haven't been wasting their time. They've been multiplying. There's a heck of a lot of them and new strains to boot."

Henry plunked down beside Zeke and took a sip of coffee. He wondered what the old man had been doing out in the yard that early in the morning to see what he'd seen but didn't ask. Eventually Zeke would tell him. But the elderly man often did peculiar things and Henry was reminded of Ann's recent concern that Zeke's mental state was getting worse. "So what brings you here right now?"

"I heard the doc's holding court today in here to give out flu shots. I figured I'd sneak in early and see if she'd make a quick visit to Wilma before the crowd arrives."

"Is she sick? Something wrong?" Henry studied the man's face and saw the discomfort in it. His back must be acting up again. Some days he could barely walk without pain, but all Zeke cared about was Wilma's health and well-being. The two were more like old married folks instead of boyfriend and girlfriend. Which was good because they needed each other. Everyone needed someone.

With a dip of his thin shoulders, Zeke acknowledged, "She's slipping fast is all I can say. Yesterday she forgot who I was for a while. *Me.* This morning when you and your men came rushing into the settlement she was so frightened she ran willy-nilly out towards the gates–screaming she was going to escape the monsters by hiding in the woods where they could never find her–and I had to hurry after her to stop her. She forgot who I was and slapped me before she remembered. She thought I was some dirty old man trying to accost her or something. Who knows. She gets such nutty notions sometimes." Zeke cradled his cup and stared into it as if it held the answers he sought. "I fell in the damn snow scuttling after her and think I might have sprained something." He reached down and massaged his left ankle. "Oooh," he moaned under his breath. "That hurts."

"Maybe you should let the doctor check you out first?"

"I might do that." The other man looked up at

Henry. "But I'm more worried about Wilma. Besides her forgetfulness she's also been obsessed lately with returning to her house in town. Heaven knows if it's even standing, after the dinosaurs stormed through last fall, but she's adamant she has to go and see it again and make sure it's okay. She even talks about living there again. No way am I going to take her to Klamath Falls to find out if it is still there much less see her living there, with or without me. Yet I can't have her shambling off into the woods every time she gets a hair-brained idea. Perhaps the doctor could give her some medicine or something, you know, to calm her down some? Help her to sleep?"

Henry felt sorry for his friend. He didn't think there was a cure for old age, dementia or flattened houses. "The doctor might be able to prescribe something to help her." The remark about Wilma's house reminded Henry he hadn't told Ann about their destroyed cabin yet. He'd have to confess soon before someone else did. Another thing he didn't want to do. Oh, well.

Steven strolled into the room. "Hi Henry. Hi Zeke."

"Hi music man," Zeke greeted him, leaning in his chair and smiling, for a moment the old twinkle in his eyes.

"Hi," Henry echoed. "Ah, I thought I'd be seeing you in here sooner or later. Looking for Doctor Emily?" Henry used the doctor's title and first name and decided he liked the way it sounded. Doctor Emily. More personal.

"How did you know?" Steven visited the coffee

counter and grabbed himself a cup.

"A lucky guess." Henry grinned at Steven and noticed the time on the wall clock. "She should be here any minute. I left her with Ann and she said she wouldn't be long. She knows soon there'll be patients in here clamoring for their flu shots." He chuckled.

A grin spread across Steven's face. Plopping down next to Henry and Zeke, he declared, "That was an awful mess out there in the woods, wasn't it? I was terrified for Justin and the crew up in that helicopter. Wow, what a close call. And then those damn weirdo bouncing dinos attacking us. Man, what a morning!"

"You can say that. You gonna put that in your dinosaur book? You are still writing it, aren't you?"

"Sort of. I mean I put everything that's happened to us the last year and what occurs around here in my notes or my journal, and it is getting pretty fat. But the book, it's on hold. I mean with the world in the dire state it's in these days and the fight we are in for our species basic existence, a book seems a trivial pursuit. Besides, I wanted to self-publish it as an eBook on the Internet at Amazon, iTunes, Barnes & Noble and everywhere and we all know how unreliable those platforms are these days. Is anyone even buying books anymore? Does anyone even care? According to the social media experts few people are because they're too busying looking for, watching, hunting or running away from dinosaurs. So I think I'll postpone it for now."

Henry nodded. "Smart move. There'll be plenty

of time to publish it after the war is over."

Steven's expression mirrored Henry's assessment. "Yes, after the war is over and we win."

Doctor Emily came into the room smiling. Her hair was down, brushed and very becoming. She was wearing more make-up than the day before and looked especially pretty in a flower-patterned blouse. Her eyes went right to Steven as she brushed past him on her way to the coffee. She was making herself at home.

"Did you sleep okay?" Steven asked as he got up to shadow her, meeting her smile with one of his own.

Henry smiled, too, when he saw how Steven laid his hand softly on her back in passing and then got her coffee for her.

"I was so tired I was asleep before I knew it." She sent a look at Henry and spoke, "Thank you, Chief Ranger for the comfortable accommodations. I appreciate them."

"You're welcome, Doctor. We try to please all our visiting physicians by providing them the comforts of home away from home," he replied warmly.

"Ah, I'm the first one, right?"

"Yep," Steven interjected. "And we're overjoyed to have you with us."

"How did you find Ann this morning, Doctor?" Henry slid in his query.

"She's really much better. The antibiotics are doing their job. Another few days in bed and she might even be herself again."

"Thank you, Doctor." Henry was so relieved.

The news was better than he could ever have expected. It lifted a huge weight from his shoulders. Now he could concentrate on getting rid of the dinosaurs in the park.

Zeke introduced himself to the doctor and asked her if she'd look in on Wilma and she agreed.

"We're just on the other end of the building, Doctor, by the south door. We have a nice comfy nest. It isn't far."

With her coffee in one hand, and her black bag in the other, she ordered Zeke, "Lead on. Take me to her and I'll follow." To Henry she added, "I will try to be back as soon as I can. Anyone comes in here to see me, ask them to wait if they can."

"I'll do that, Doctor." Henry walked her and Zeke to the door. He fully expected Steven to follow them but the young man didn't, though he caught the look the two lovebirds exchanged and guessed Steven would be waiting for her when she returned.

When Zeke and the doctor were gone Henry faced Steven. "Is there anything I can do for you, friend?"

"I only wanted to ask if I could go on the next park patrol. With Justin gone I feel at loose ends. I could use something to do."

"You got it if you want it. I don't know how long the doctor is going to be with us but I imagine it won't be but a couple days. She has a hospital full of patients she's still responsible for and needs to get back to them. Are you sure you want to run off on a patrol while she's still here?"

"I assume any patrol we go on would only last

until sundown. She'll be busy with patients all day so I can't be with her while she's working." Then he grinned at Henry. "We have a prearranged date for later tonight after she's seen everyone who needs to see her."

"Ah, I see. Well then, after I slip in to see my wife one last time McDowell and I are saddling up for a tank ride around the park. There's something Justin wanted me to look into. We leave in thirty minutes. Can you be ready?"

"I can."

The two exited the conference room. Steven heading off to pack for the reconnaissance tour and Henry to visit Ann. It did his heart good to see his wife smiling at their grandchildren and playing with the cat. Her color was good and she admitted she felt better than she had in weeks. He explained what he had to do, that he had to go out on patrol. Then, after asking Phoebe to take Timothy to the other side of the room while he had a private conversation with Ann, he sat on the edge of her bed and confessed to her about their destroyed cabin. He owed her the truth. She didn't bemoan what had happened or get angry, she calmly accepted it.

"I'm so sorry, Ann. I know how much you loved that place. How hard you worked on it."

"Don't feel bad on my account, sweetheart. We'll always have our memories. It was only a house. Four walls, lumber and stone. When these dinosaur troubles are over, when it's safe, we can rebuild. We can make it better than before. You'll see. All that matters is that we're alive and we have each other." Her eyes went to their grandchildren.

"And our grandchildren. Our friends. Everything else is just a bonus. It is what it is."

That was his Ann, always looking at the positive side of everything. He was proud of her. So much had been thrown at her the last seven years–loss of her job and her business, cancer, dinosaurs and the death of their only child–and she never lost faith that it would get better, never stopped believing or trying. It took courage.

"On patrol today we'll be stopping by what remains of our cabin. I hope to salvage some of our keepsakes if any are left and not in pieces. Is there anything you can think of that I should look for and retrieve if possible?"

"Our family pictures, especially any of Laura, our wedding photos and anything you think is important and irreplaceable…if they are, as you said, not in pieces, and you can gather them up."

"I'll do my best, sweetheart. I'll recover everything precious I can dig out from what's left and bring it to you."

"And Henry, more than anything, be careful. There are a new breed of dinosaurs out there and I have the feeling they're a lot smarter than any kind we've encountered so far. We don't know if they're dangerous or not or what they want. But I want you back here with me, alive and well, before night falls. I can't lose you too," she whispered and squeezed his hand.

"I promise I'll be careful. The monsters haven't gotten me yet and they never will."

He kissed her lovingly before he left this time. He was anxious to see where their enemy was gathering, calculate their numbers, see what they were up to and to see what had become of their home. Justin had told him where to search for the dinosaurs so they'd do the reconnaissance first.

Steven, McDowell, two of her soldiers, and Henry met up in the yard. The second and third tank had been staffed with crews consisting of McDowell and Henry's men and waited for them. They were convoying three Abrams because of what Justin had warned them of. If they came across the same large numbers they would need all three. They climbed in the first tank and the machines went through the open gates and into the snow-covered woods.

For the first time in months Henry was nervous about what they'd find.

*****

"The temperature is rising and the snow's melting. It's about time," Captain McDowell remarked over the headsets as their tank rolled down the road towards the caldera's rim beneath a bright warming sun. The ground crunched beneath the treads. "The dinosaurs will begin coming out like ants at a summer picnic again in no time."

"As far as I'm concerned they already have." Henry's tone was sullen.

"Sorry, Chief." McDowell realized too late what she'd said and had reminded him of. His daughter's demise.

"It's okay. I'm dealing with my loss the best I can as so many others have since the attacks began." Henry, driving the tank because he'd asked to and was getting very proficient at it, was taking in the scenery through the window as it zipped past outside and trying not to let his anguish sabotage him.

They were coming up to the lake's rim. The tanks roared along the road and stopped near the top. Henry, McDowell and Steven exited and, stooping low so they wouldn't be seen, they moved through the snow towards the edge overlooking Cleetwood Cove where the tourist boats would normally have been docked, but were no longer. The lake was empty of any human or human trappings. There hadn't been any prehistoric monsters in it just two weeks before, but were there now?

It was worse than Justin had reported, worse than what Henry had imagined. The water below, kissed with a thin rim of frosty snow, was now teeming with movement below the white caps and waves. Every once and a while a lumpy shape emerged from the surface and quickly submerged again. There were eerie, unearthly silhouettes below the water and they filled the caldera. On the shore there were also alien-looking creatures stumbling around. Some were fighting among themselves and Henry could hear their roars and shrieks from as far away as he was. Trouble in paradise, he mused. Either that or the dinosaurs' hunger was making them turn on each other. He had no doubt with their growing numbers they'd exhausted the park's native wildlife and there was nothing left for them to feed on but each other. How in the world had they multiplied so much in such a short span of time?

"Look at that, would you?" Steven mumbled,

clutching his rifle against his side. He was shivering and Henry wasn't sure it was from the cold or fear. "There must be hundreds of the creatures down there swimming and crawling about. Some of them are *huge*. My God, have they been proliferating. I had hoped, as you Henry, with the severe winter and lack of prey they'd be dying off, not reproducing like termites. Oh my."

"No such luck," Henry replied softly. He knew from experience some of the dinosaurs had extraordinary hearing so he kept his voice down.

McDowell said nothing but her eyes never left the scene below them.

The noises from the lake exploded into an ear-screeching pandemonium. One of the larger dinosaurs on the shore had killed another one and the other spectators had scrambled in for the feast. Henry could almost smell the blood and guts.

One of them, a mutant T-Rex by the looks of it, suddenly peered up at where Henry and his team were hiding. It looked straight at them, frozen in its meal eating. Had it spotted them?

"I've seen enough," Henry said, scooting back from the edge and leaving a drag trail behind him in the snow. "Let's get out of here before they see or smell us. I don't feel safe out in the open like this. I want tank walls around us and the big guns in front of us."

The others listened without argument and trudged behind him to the waiting tank.

When they were tucked safely in the Abrams McDowell spoke over the headsets. "I expected our prehistoric pests to still be around but I didn't expect so many. Doctor Maltin wasn't exaggerating as I hoped he was. I will be reporting to my superiors at Kingsley Field about this new development. I'm going to request more back-up. We're going to need it."

"I concur, Captain. Also ask your boss to send more tanks and weapons if he can spare them."

"I'll do that."

Henry rubbed his eyes. Even with sunglasses the snow had strained them or perhaps it was what he'd glimpsed in the lake. The farther away they traveled from the water the better he'd feel. He prayed they hadn't been seen or were being followed.

"Now what Chief Ranger?" McDowell asked.

"I want to go by our cabin, or what's left of it, and see if I can salvage anything. I promised Ann."

Ten minutes later the tanks were pulling up to where Henry and Ann's home had once been. He'd been preparing himself for seeing what he knew he would see. And there it was: remnants of the beautiful cabin he and Ann had lived in and so lovingly cared for. Now it was a pile of rubble glittering with patches of snow. Whatever, or however many whatevers, had destroyed their home must have been gigantic. There was nothing recognizable of their house remaining.

How would he ever find anything in that wreckage? He'd have to try, though, for his wife's sake as well as his.

The tanks thundered to a stop and, their eyes peeled for any dinosaur interlopers once they'd disembarked, Henry, McDowell and Steven sifted through the cabin's ruins. The other tank crews hovered nearby watching over them as they searched. They hadn't seen any dinosaurs on their journey from the rim but Henry knew they were there somewhere around them, watching. Waiting. He could feel their beady eyes on him. It made his skin prickle. What were they waiting for? An invitation?

Henry was lucky and uncovered a couple of their old photo albums in a corner of what had once been his and Ann's bedroom. One was full of Laura's and Phoebe's pictures and the other was family photos of him and Ann. No wedding pictures, though. Among the debris he did find other mementos his wife would be happy to see again. Their coffeepot, practically and surprisingly untouched, and in a muddy box some precious figurines her mother had given her over the years. A stuffed bear Phoebe had left behind at some time. Ann's jewelry box filled with special pieces he'd given her for birthdays and anniversaries. A quilt Ann's grandmother had made for her as a wedding present, stained now but possibly savable. A pink flowered blanket Ann had crocheted by hand when she'd been pregnant with Laura. Steven uncovered a file of Ann's old newspaper articles and the dinosaur book she'd written and had saved. McDowell rescued their smashed metal box of important documents, containing birth certificates and life insurance policies paperwork, they'd hadn't been able to find quick enough to take with them when they'd last fled.

In the distance they could hear dinosaur's trumpeting and screeching. It was growing louder.

Coming closer. Maybe that T-Rex *had* seen them and alerted his companions. Now the whole bunch of them were coming after them.

"Time we get out of here," he announced to Steven and McDowell. "I think something is coming."

"We're not going to fight them?" Steven demanded, his hands full of what he'd salvaged from the cabin's ruins.

"I don't think so…we need more tanks and guns. By the way the earth is shaking and the sounds, worse than I've ever felt and heard, we're probably outnumbered. There's a massive horde of them coming this way. We'll be safer at the fort and we'll fight them from there. Better safe than sorry. Let's go."

With the precious items they'd recovered in their arms, the humans sprinted back to the tank, scrambled in, and the convoy moved out. The ground shook harder as they ramped the tanks' speed up as fast as they would go, rocketing away from the mob that was surely behind them and knew what was in front of them. Food.

At one point on the rise of a hill, Henry swung the window around and stole a fleeting look at what was behind them and he was *so glad* they hadn't decided to stand and fight. There was a sea of charging starving dinosaurs filling the valley below. "I've never seen so many in one place," he reported to his tank mates. "And all coming this way after us. No, Justin didn't exaggerate at all. It's an army all right."

They were fortunate and somehow kept ahead

of the stampede, rattling through the compound's gates as the day began to wane.

Henry was relieved to be behind the strong walls, all of them were, because soon after the gates were slammed shut everyone could hear the enemy howling outside as the moon rose. The dinosaurs, mysteriously though, did not attack. Henry didn't understand why they were waiting, but they were. For more reinforcements? For orders? Perhaps.

But the hiatus in the fighting was definitely over.

Chapter 9

From behind a copse of trees the small dinosaur watching the skinny stick beings was transfixed by them as they stomped around in a messy nest of wood and stones looking for what it had no idea. Silly creatures. Always going here or there, bouncing around and squawking like his offspring babies. It had tracked them from the land by the water after they had climbed into those gigantic growling monster-things. It'd had a hard time keeping up because the growling monster-things ran through the forest so swiftly.

But here in such an unlikely place they had stopped and the stick beings were busy exploring what must have been one of their empty nests. One of its larger cousins had stomped around on the structure a few moons ago and flattened the thing. What were they doing scratching around in it? There were no stick beings living in it anymore that he could tell. Hmmm. Curious.

The dinosaur hissed a warning at one of its offspring who had begun fighting with another one of its siblings. They'd followed him from the water and were being troublesome. The babies were always squabbling among themselves, chasing each other around and play-biting, and making a racket. And that could be a considerable amount of noise because the dinosaur had a very large brood this time. There were as many of the little stinkers as the trees rooted around them. It slapped at another baby as it flew past and launched itself at a bigger one. They scuffled in the snow and left their bright colored inner liquid staining it. Humph, the runt was feisty and always picked fights with the larger ones. He was showing off. The dinosaur snarled at both of them, knocked them apart, but couldn't stay mad at his babies, though. He was too proud to have them all. They were strong and growing. They were all clever, too, especially the runt. But they did tend to shadow him everywhere he went and they couldn't stay quiet or still. It made it difficult to sneak through the woods and spy on the stick beings.

It would take the babies back to its mate in their lair and order them to stay while it would travel to the stick beings home with the tall to-close-together trees around it. It wasn't sure why but it got a kick out of spying on them.

Their females were of special interest to it. The one in their wooden cave behind the opening blocked with hard sticks was amusing, though it sensed she was ill. It could tell by her scent. She had this smaller fuzzy creature, not anything like it or even her kind, which amused him. It wondered why the female didn't eat the tiny furry creature. It would have. The furry thing looked like a tasty morsel. The dinosaur's tongue flicked out just thinking about food. But the female stick seemed to care for the furry thing, even seemed fond of it. Again, so strange.

The female stick had young, as well. Not many, though. The stick beings didn't seem to have large broods. Which was why their numbers weren't expanding as rapidly as his brethren's. And, oh, were his kind breeding and multiplying. As were the others. Yet the greater of his species weren't like it was, small, agile and clever. They were lumbering, taller than trees, but dumb as the hard ground they tread upon. They wanted to fight the stick beings. They wanted to crush them beneath their weight; tear at them and eat them.

Not it. It and its descendants were different. They did not want to battle the sticks. It had taken a bite out of a stick being before the white stuff covered the ground and it hadn't cared much for their flavor. The meat was too stringy and had a bitter aftertaste. Yuck. And it surprised itself when the realization, like the ball of fire in the sky that brought light and warmth, came to it: *It wanted to live in peace with all the creatures around it in this wondrous place of caves, lushness and serenity. It wanted to understand all others sharing their beautiful world. Not battle them.*

Its attention was brought back to what was happening in front of it. The stick beings were abandoning the ruined nest and climbing into the growling monsters. The monsters started roaring and moving away and the dinosaur knew where they were going. Their fortified larger home nest. They always returned there before the light faded and the light was going as it did after so much time.

It corralled its offspring and herded them to the cave to leave them with its mate. Before it left, though, it checked on the nursery in another part of its cave lair. The eggs were plentiful these days and they filled the whole rear section. They were almost ready to hatch. Then his brood would be immense. If it could have smiled, it would have. It felt pride, though, at all its coming offspring. It would need more numbers because the others of its species were quickly reproducing as well and some of them, mainly the larger ones, were too angry and war-thirsty. It couldn't let them win. So it had to have more of its kind to protect itself.

It didn't want to keep fighting the stick beings.

After its rounds of the lair, making sure the eggs were safe, it spent time with its mate, communicating where it had been and what it was doing and going to do, and then it exited their cave and bounded through the woods towards the sticks home nest. It wanted to see what they were up to. It wanted to watch the stick female, her offspring and the tiny furry creature. But it had to be sure it wasn't seen or the sticks would come after it with their booming rods that could make his kind stop moving forever. It had seen that too many times. It made sure it was never in front of one of them.

All the way there it thought about how to communicate with them. How would it make them understand it didn't want to be their enemy…but their friend? It didn't know the answer but it would find it sooner or later. Somehow.

Chapter 10

Justin felt as if he were in another world, a world of shiny steel, stone and glittering glass buildings that rose to the sky, as they ushered him from the helicopter after it had landed on the five-star hotel's roof. He was at least thirty stories up. Wow, what a view. One of the first things that hit him were the sounds. The place was so noisy. There were planes roaring above his head, cars and taxis with squealing tires and blaring horns, and a cacophony of human voices, mingling below in the streets. He'd been flown into the city by jet and picked up by another helicopter at the airport thirty minutes before. Now, suitcase and briefcase in hand, he was heading towards the room they'd reserved for him so he could get ready for the conference tomorrow morning. For the first time in years he felt important, privileged. He was being treated as a respected scientist again and it felt good. His opinion, research and proposals meant something.

It also got his mind off Laura's death and that helped assuage some of his sorrow. Pushing thoughts of his dead wife away, he thought: *Not today. Not here. He had work to do. Laura would want him to do what he was doing...find a cure for the dinosaur plague. She'd be proud.*

One more time he attempted to telephone Henry and let him know he'd arrived in New York okay, no more dinosaur attacks, but he couldn't get through. It didn't surprise him because reception in the park and to the park was always iffy. He'd try again later. He had asked the helicopter pilot to put in a call to the army base in Klamath Falls after he'd dropped him off on the roof, though, to let Crater Lake and Henry know he got to his destination safely. That was something at least.

He was excited about the coming symposium and what it might achieve. He was excited to see what his colleagues thought about his findings and if they'd agree with him on his proposed solutions. And he needed their help, too, because he didn't have all the answers. Yet.

The hums of the city assailed his ears and nose and it made him feel more alive than he'd felt since his wife's death. Taking a deep breath of the city smells, he smiled for the first time in days. A more temperate climate than Oregon in May, there was no snow here. It was warm, near seventy degrees and sunny–or it was with the sun out. Evening was coming. He soaked in the gorgeous sunset bathing the skyscrapers and sidewalks below in shadows of tawny gold and pale crimson. It'd been a while since he'd been in New York or any big city for that matter; a while since he'd experienced this level of civilization. It was a bit of a shock to see there was still a thriving metropolis untouched by the dinosaur epidemic. A place where a person could go out to a nice restaurant and have an expensive and tasty meal. A place where life was as normal as if the dinosaurs had never existed. It was like a miracle and he was determined to take the hiatus it offered him to recharge his heart, soul and mind. He was going to go out to dinner in a fancy restaurant, get new clothes, gifts for his children, and a haircut. All the things he'd been missing the last year.

Patterson had updated him that the military and the National Guard had kept the city clear of any berserking dinosaurs…so far. It hadn't been easy. The armed forces kept a tight perimeter around the city and destroyed any primeval intruders that came near. Most of the infestation was still occurring in the wilderness and primitive places of the earth like state and national parks and isolated forest lands. But the epidemic was spreading every day and those in power in the governments across the world finally knew and accepted something had to be done. Thank Goodness. About time.

Gazing down on the bustling humanity and the gleaming buildings beneath him it looked as if there were no dinosaur wars anywhere. Everything looked so normal. He shook his head in amazed gratitude. It was, after all, a relief to get away from a continuous war zone and be able to walk streets without a MP7 or a M4 Carbine hanging from his shoulder. Though he did feel a little naked without weapons. He hadn't brought any. Patterson had told him they'd be provided if needed.

He was escorted by two soldiers–friendly enough but mostly professional–to a room on the fifteenth floor. One of them, the taller, handed him a hotel entry card and watched as he used it to let himself into his room before both soldiers left him. Then Justin was alone in a lushly decorated and accessorized room. There was a bar stocked with liquor, a plush sofa, a giant soft bed and a television that–another miracle–actually worked. Ah, civilization.

On the table setting in the middle of a thick rug there was a bottle of chilled champagne and a large basket of fruit, crackers, expensive looking candy and other snacks. The tag on the gift welcomed him as a participant of the dinosaur conference and said they hoped his stay would be comfortable.

Whoa, that was nice of them. Whoever had sent the basket and champagne anyway. He tore off the cellophane and snatched a yellow apple off the top and bit into it. He was hungry and since he was going to clean up before he went in search of his supper, he munched the apple, a couple pieces of silver-wrapped chocolate, some crackers and cheese, before he went into the luxurious bathroom and took a long hot shower. That felt great, too. Hot water had been in short supply at Crater Lake with all the people using it.

An hour later he was closing the room's outer door and strolling down the hallway to the elevators in search of the barbershop he'd been informed was on the third floor. Laura had always liked his long hair but for some reason now she was gone he'd have it cut shorter. It was time. He was a grown man with responsibilities, two children, and shoulder-length hair was no longer appropriate or so he believed. The barbershop wasn't crowded, no waiting, and a half-hour later he was on his way to the hotel's clothing store with his hair cut inches shorter and styled. He bought a new suit and two shirts, new jeans and everything else he'd need for the following days. New clothes had also been in short supply at Crater Lake. Everything was being paid for by the people staging the conference so he didn't hesitate to spend the money. If they were going to offer it, why not?

In the mirror he appeared a new man, thinner, more haggard; only his gold rimmed glasses remained the same. But he looked good. It had been a long time since he'd spiffed himself up like this. He had the old clothes he'd been wearing sent to his room and wore some of his new ones, blue jeans and an olive green shirt. Oh, if only his Laura could see him now she'd be so proud of him.

He located the five-star restaurant on the first floor and settled in at a table by the window so he could enjoy the view. Night had arrived and the streets around him twinkled with lights from the taxis and the shop windows. Voices of people going about their errands or hurrying home from work came to his ears. Suddenly it all seemed unreal, where he was and what he was doing, as if he were watching himself from a far distance, sitting at a lovely table in a city that didn't actually exist, getting ready to order a steak dinner with all the fixings. It'd been such a long time since he'd had such a meal. No bone-crunching dinosaurs anywhere. So far.

He ordered his supper and while he waited he opened the briefcase he'd brought and began to sift through the papers, photos and documents. When the conference commenced tomorrow he must be completely prepared. He didn't want to look the fool in front of his peers.

He was finishing his steak and considering which scrumptious-looking dessert he wanted when someone spoke to him.

"Doctor Maltin? Justin? Is that you?"

Justin's eyes moved up from his papers and met those of an attractive young woman, with blond hair and intense emerald hued eyes, poised above him.

It took him a minute to recognize her because she'd changed so much since he'd last seen her.

"I can't believe it. Delores…Delores Taylor?"

"That's me. But, as yourself, it's doctor now. Doctor Delores Taylor. After you graduated I finished getting my degree as well. I've been working here in New York ever since because my family lives here and the foundation I work for."

"Doctor it is then."

"But because we're old friends you can call me Delores." She grinned that old familiar grin at him he remembered so well, with always a touch of mischief in it.

"How have you been Delores? Here, sit down." He was genuinely happy to see her. They'd been friends and classmates while attending The Department of Earth and Planetary Science, University of California, Berkeley when he'd been studying to be a paleontologist over a decade before. It seemed like a lifetime ago.

"If you don't mind me interrupting your dinner, I will." She smiled again and sat down across from him. "I almost didn't know you Justin. You look so different." She tempered her remarks with a soft voice, her smile never wavering. "But you look good, don't get me wrong. Just different. I miss the long hair, though. Short hair gives you a truly different look."

"Strangely enough I just had it cut off in the

hotel's barbershop. It was down to my shoulders until an hour or so ago."

"Really?"

"Really." His grin was subdued. "I thought it was time I grew up."

"My, my, is that the Justin I knew saying that? I thought you'd wear your hair long until it turned gray." She laughed.

"A father with two children and a wife needs to look as mature as he actually is, not like some hippie." The words *and a wife* slipped out before he could catch them and he didn't take them back. He still felt married and perhaps he always would. He saw Delores looking at the wedding ring he hadn't taken off.

"Married with two children, huh? Congratulations," she said. "What ages are they?"

Switching to talking about his kids was easier. "A boy, Timothy, who's about a year old and a daughter, Phoebe, who's almost ten."

"You lucky dog."

"What, you don't have any children, Delores?" He found he was enjoying the conversation and the company. But again, it all seemed unreal. Too good to be true. He kept glancing out the windows expecting to see an attacking giant dinosaur clomping down the sidewalks, tearing things up and grabbing screaming people for appetizers. He shook his head and silently told himself: *stop that!*

"No, no kids. Truth is I never got married. Not so far." She flashed him a strange look which swiftly faded from her face.

There was an uncomfortable second or two

between them and then it evaporated. It was just so good to see her. Oh, he'd known all those years ago in college she'd had a big crush on him, but he hadn't felt the same for her. Not then anyway. So they'd settled on being good friends. They'd helped each other through the difficult school years, studied together and had each other's backs. In the end, he'd thought of her like a sister. But now…she seemed different. Older, of course, and more self-assured and professional.

"So you're here for the big dino conference, huh?" she finally asked.

"I am. You, too?"

"Me, too. Fantastic. I've been asked to sit on the main panel. We have to come up with some answers to how to get rid of these diabolical prehistoric creatures who have invaded our world. They don't belong in it."

"Of that I fully agree. We have got to find a way to exterminate them. All of them. Ha, I never thought I'd say such a thing–imagine me wanting to destroy a live, breathing dinosaur–or feel that way, but after seeing the destruction they leave in their path, the humans they've killed, I can't think any other way." He couldn't help but stare at her. Dressed in a demure navy blue suit and skirt, white silk blouse, she was so much more attractive than she'd been in college. Her hair was swept up in a loose, wispy knot at the back of her head. She looked so…grown-up. Had he realized she was so pretty all those years ago? He couldn't recall.

The waitress came by and Justin asked his table mate, "Have you eaten your supper yet?"

"I have." She nodded to her left. "I was at that table in the corner behind you while I was eating and I kept staring at you. I thought it was you but I wasn't sure. I finally got up the courage to see if it was."

"And it was."

"Yes, it was. Though I've had my supper," she went on, "I could be talked into another cup of coffee so we can catch up on the years we've missed? I don't have anyone or anything waiting for me in my room." She put out a hand and lightly touched the paperwork scattered on his side of the table. "And all my homework is finished. I'm free for the night."

He was happy to oblige. He had about finished going over his notes anyway. What he had left to do could be done in the morning when he got up. "I'd like that. I'm was about to have some dessert. A humongous hot fudge sundae with whipped cream, nuts and cherries on top. You can watch me eat it." He looked at the waitress and ordered one.

"Make that two," she addressed the waitress. "Coffee, as well, and put it on the National Dinosaur Conference's tab." Her smile was devilish.

Aside she whispered to Justin as the waitress bustled off, "I love free desserts. Free food, room and board. This has been like a vacation for me. I'm going to milk it for all I can."

"Me, too," he whispered back.

And over their ice cream and coffee they talked, caught up on each other's accomplishments and lives. For the first time in a long time, sitting in a fancy restaurant eating ice cream and drinking the best coffee he'd ever had in his life, with an old friend across the table from him, Justin felt a touch of happiness. He liked it.

Justin didn't tell her about Laura's death. He didn't know why, but he couldn't. He pretended his wife was still alive or skimmed over mentioning her. Instead he spoke of what the last seven years had been like for him and his friends at Crater Lake, their life-and-death battles with the dinosaurs and how they'd survived. He spoke of what he'd seen and done.

In turn she confided her story. "When the outbreaks first began, or when I first heard of them, oh about three years ago, I was living here in the city, working at the American Museum of Natural History in the Paleontology Department setting up the displays and doing research. I was dating my long-time boyfriend and live-in, Daryl, and living in a tiny apartment with him. He's a New York police officer. We aren't together any longer…my job took too much of my time and he got tired of it. Anyway, I heard the rumors and saw the pictures and videos coming from your neck of the woods but I didn't believe they were real, true, not for a New York second. Then as time went by there were more sightings, more attacks across the country, the world, and eventually all that became irrefutable proof even I couldn't ignore.

"My job sent me out to California last year to see for myself. I toured a few of the National Park hot spots where dinosaurs had been sighted and finally I saw a herd of the creatures myself. Then I believed. I've been on a mission to contain, control or destroy them ever since. Lately, though, I've been leaning heavily towards destroying them because of all the human fatalities. The last few months I've been traveling over the world following the reports of sightings and documenting them when I saw they were true. I actually tried to visit Crater Lake but was warned off because my boss thought it was too dangerous. My boss," she smiled, "is so protective. Apparently, your Crater Lake was and is ground zero and the epicenter to all the dinosaur disturbances."

"You're telling me. I've been there fighting the good fight now since almost the beginning and that was over seven years ago now."

"Seven years?" Her surprise was instant. "That was way before any of us knew what was going on. Tell me about it. Tell me everything from the beginning."

And he did.

They talked late into the night and when they said goodbye they arranged to meet the next morning early before the conference began to share breakfast together and continue their discussions.

As Justin clicked in his room card and slipped inside, he had to admit it'd been nice to share a meal and conversation with an old friend and such a lovely one at that. As he settled into his unbelievably soft bed his thoughts returned to the compound at Crater Lake. He missed his kids, prayed everything was okay there and made a mental note to try calling Henry once more first thing in the morning. It was way too late to try again that night. As he drifted into sleep his thoughts were on his wife Laura and she followed him into his dreams. In them she was alive and they were back in their house with Phoebe before the dinosaur troubles had become all involving. They were happy. Laura had come home from her job at the hospital and they were having a family dinner together. She was smiling, laughing. They were making plans for the weekend…they were going to visit a nature preserve where there'd be wild animals, buffalo, elk and wild birds, to see and ooh and aah over. Phoebe was so excited because she loved animals. It was heaven.

He almost didn't want to wake up the next morning, but he did. He had an old friend to have breakfast with, seminars to attend and others of his ilk to talk things over with and impress, and solutions to come up with. Hallelujah. He was more than ready for it.

Again he tried to call Henry, but yet again the call didn't go through. Interference of some sort. He'd try later. At least he was fairly sure Henry had gotten the message he had arrived safely. He didn't like not knowing, though, what was going on at Crater Lake. It made him uneasy. No help for that.

Taking a quick shower, he was up, dressed in his new suit, out the door, all in under an hour and waiting for Delores at the same table they'd occupied the night before. He'd had another idea about solving the dinosaur problem and couldn't wait to pass it by her. Excited, he also couldn't wait for the conference to begin.

He smiled at her when he saw her walking

towards him in the morning light. She was also in formal clothes: a tailored beige suit, skirt and heels. Her hair tied up in a sophisticated bun. She looked even prettier than the night before.

"Coffee?" he politely asked her. He was already on his third cup, he couldn't get enough. For a moment he felt a bit guilty because at Crater Lake they were rationing their coffee intake.

"Yes, coffee," she echoed. "Lots of it." It was then he remembered how she had loved coffee. She'd drink cup after cup even late into the night. He'd never understood how she did it. It never ruined her sleep.

And the day began.

*****

It was distracting, practically annoying, at first to be sitting in a hotel auditorium surrounded by chattering, boisterous men and women. Most of them were strangers but Justin did spot some old familiar faces in the crowd. There were scientists he'd read about in scientific journals, seen at other conferences or met in his travels to foreign digs. Acquaintances. Fellow working associates. Some he considered friends. A table of them found each other and soon he and Delores were deep in conversations with people like them. All of them had their briefcases, stacks of messy papers and strong opinions on how to defeat the scourge that was upon them.

"Justin, I heard about your wife," one of them said, a guy named Avery Willet he'd met four years past at another paleontological gathering. "So sorry. She was such a sweet woman. How are you bearing up?"

How had Avery found out about Laura's death? Justin didn't want to ask. How many others sitting around him knew? Probably the whole place.

"Thank you. I'm doing the best I can," he answered and let it drop at that. He didn't want to talk about it. Not that minute, not there.

Delores, who'd been speaking to another woman on her right, looked at him. Her expression was one of kind empathy. She knew. Turning away from the woman she'd been talking to, she leaned over close to him. "Why didn't you tell me about Laura?" she murmured.

So many feelings warred in Justin in that moment but all he could think to say was, "I didn't want to lay that on you last night. I'm sorry. I would have told you sooner or later."

"What happened to Laura?"

In as few words as he could use he told her.

After he was done, she softly patted his hand. Her eyes were in one moment full of anger at the dinosaur that had killed his wife and in the next tinged with sadness for him and his loss. "It's all right. I understand. We can talk about it later if you want. Or not."

Someone had come to the middle of the head table and approached the microphone. The conference was beginning. The man introduced himself and started the dialogue in the room with a bang. "Okay, all you smart scientists out there…how exactly are we going to get to the bottom of this dinosaur dilemma? Let's begin the debate and find an answer. The world is waiting."

Everyone in the room applauded.

The man at the microphone continued after the noise died down. "I'm going to call a list of names now–listen closely–and I'd like each one of you to come up here and give us your expertise, your findings. These are, in the committee's illustrious judgement, the top paleontologists in the field today and they're going to be our main speakers, our leaders."

Both Justin's and Delores names were called out. Delores didn't seem to be surprised, but when his name was called, Justin was. What an honor. Of all the award-winning scientists in the room they wanted his take, his opinion, on what could stop the dinosaurs. All he could figure was it was because of his personal experiences at Crater Lake, on the front lines, with the dinosaurs and what he'd published over the years about it. His face was red as he made his way to the chair they offered him. Delores made sure she was seated beside him.

Two paleontologists spoke into the microphone first. Both of them trying to soften the seriousness of the situation. The dinosaurs weren't that bad. They could be handled. All they had to do was keep them away from the human populations. How about building a fence around New York? Hire big game hunters to go off and shoot them and offer lots of money for the dead dinosaurs. Or why not learn to live with them…share the planet. Blah, blah, blah. And other silly useless solutions that would never work. Justin just shook his head in disbelief during their speeches. Cowards.

Justin was the third paleontologist asked to

present his information and he spoke about Crater Lake and what he'd experienced there since the beginning of the dinosaur incidents. He spoke of the lake leviathan that began the nightmare, Hugo, the gargoyles and finally the mutant herds now roaming the lands around them. How the rangers, soldiers and he now lived behind wooden walls and fought the dinosaurs in the park and surrounding land and towns to survive.

He finished with the statement: "But here's the biggest discovery I've made so far…the dinosaurs aren't just rapidly increasing in numbers but I believe their basic learning capacities–their innate intelligence–is *growing*. They are becoming sentient. I've seen some of them actually use primitive weapons, rocks or anything they can grab up and throw, against us. I've seen them scheme and plan their next moves. What's worse is they are coming together, no matter the variety of dinosaurs they are, and they are *organizing*.

"If we don't do something soon–kill every last one of them–their strength and numbers will rival humanity's. And this time, believe me, we won't be the winning species who inherits the planet. They will."

Everyone in the room had been mesmerized by his story until his final statement then total chaos erupted.

Chapter 11

Scott Patterson appeared fifteen years older than when Henry had seen him last. Stress, worry and extended physical activity could do that to a person; he knew that from personal experience. The man, as usual, was dropped off in the clearing on the landing pad in front of the gates via military helicopter.

The day had dawned so much warmer than the days before and the snow coverage was melting incredibly fast. Henry, though, was just relieved beyond measure the dinosaur army that had chased them and surrounded headquarters the day before had mysteriously diffused when the sun had come up. He didn't have a clue as to why they hadn't attacked and had left in such a hurry, evaporating like mist in the dawning light, but he didn't question it. Who questions a gift from heaven? Not he.

"Well, it's so damn good to see you, Henry!" Patterson grinned as he shook the Chief Ranger's hand. Standing there, a large bag hanging from his shoulders, he regarded the clearing around them intently. But it was quiet, empty of everything but the snow, trees and sky. He seemed to breathe a sigh of relief and his gaze returned to his friend.

Henry didn't know what was worse, though, the dead calm or the calls of distant dinosaurs. Either one could mean trouble coming. "It's good to see you, too, Agent."

"I told you, I'm no longer working for the FBI. No longer an agent."

Henry flashed him a skeptical look. "If you say

so."

"I heard there was an army of slavering dinosaurs outside your place dreaming of having all of you for supper last night. You were expecting a knock down and drag out battle." Patterson didn't smile when he made the remarks as they walked side by side.

"How did you know that?" As always Henry was astounded at what information his old friend always seemed to know right after it happened.

"I can't tell you that." Patterson flashed him an evasively sly smile.

"You slay me, Patterson." Henry shook his head and slapped the other man's back in a friendly manner. "You really do."

"Good. Keeps me interesting, doesn't it?"

"You could say that. Good to have you back, friend."

"Good to be back. I miss you all but I miss my girl Sherman more. It's the real reason why I'm here." Patterson's smile was bigger now but still playful.

"So we're second best, huh? Hey, I'll take that. I have a significant other, too. They do come first."

The men hiked towards the gates as the helicopter lifted off and flew away into space. This time there were no gargoyles waiting to soar in and ram it and for that Henry was tremendously thankful.

"Henry," Patterson faced him once they were through the gates, "I'm so sorry about Laura. I really wanted to come for her funeral but I couldn't get away–I'll tell you why over a cup of coffee–and

I tried."

"It's all right. The service, before Justin flew off to New York, was swift. I couldn't let her remain unburied with the way Justin was behaving. He wouldn't have gone as long as her body was in that shed. So my men found a way to dig in the frozen ground and we put her to rest inside the compound behind the main building. I'll show you her grave whenever you'd like to see it." Henry couldn't go on, couldn't let the grief return to slice him up, and his words stopped.

"I'd like that." Patterson seemed to understand and didn't press him further. He'd known Laura for years and had cared for her, too. He truly was sorry over her passing and would also miss her.

Henry led him to the conference room first so he could talk to him undisturbed.

Patterson slid the well-worn bag off his shoulder and setting it down on the table, produced four hefty cans of coffee and a folded piece of paper from it. "I brought you and Ann a present. I was told you were running low on java so I packed a few for you."

"Thanks buddy. Just in time. We were getting low and you know how we love our coffee. Ann will be so happy. She hates to face a day without her coffee. Again, how did you know that?" Yet Henry had the suspicion it had been Justin's doing. His son-in-law had wanted to do something nice for them and he had probably told Patterson they needed some.

"I'll never tell." He changed the subject. "How is Ann doing? Is she feeling better?"

"She is. The visiting doctor, Emily Macon, has

been treating her and her recovery is nothing short of a miracle. I am so relieved. After Laura I couldn't have taken any more bad news."

Patterson's smile had returned. "I'm so glad she's feeling better. I can't wait to see her…but I need to tell you some things first."

"And what's this?" Curious, Henry couldn't wait, and tapped the paper on the table with his finger.

"Let me make us both a cup of this coffee I filched, we'll sit down and I'll show you. It's another reason I'm here."

Henry waited while the other man made the coffee, placed a cup in front of him, and sat down again.

"Have you heard from Justin yet?" Patterson asked as he unfolded the paper and spread it out. It was a map of some sort with lots of big red dots on it.

"No, not yet. We don't always get such great cell reception here as you should remember."

"Oh, how well I do. I hope everything is going well there. It's our last, best hope. Those scientists have got to find a final remedy for us or we will all be thrown back to prehistoric times, except we'll be the dinosaurs' everyday edibles instead of other little creatures in the forest. It won't be pretty."

"You're not telling me anything I don't already know." Henry was scrutinizing the United States map and when he realized what the crimson dots represented dread crept through his bones and chilled his blood. He met Patterson's eyes and a silent acknowledgement passed between the two.

"You know what this shows, don't you?" Patterson prompted.

"I do…and I can't believe it. *Really?*"

"Really."

"Oh my God, the red dots show where our anachronistic predators have been seen or where they've attacked? They've spread this much in just two years?" Henry's voice wasn't all that steady. There were so many dots.

"Afraid so. All these have been sightings as well as encounters, but the time line covers more like the last seven years or even longer. I suspect, and so does Justin, they've been breeding surreptitiously in certain isolated places long before our first sighting and confrontation with Godzilla here in the park. Their population has been exploding but they were clever, sneaky, enough to hide themselves until their numbers were larger. Very strategic. I believed it seven years ago and I still believe it…our new age dinosaurs are a hell of a lot smarter than we ever thought and unbelievably smarter than their ancient ancestors."

Henry leaned back and rubbed his neck. His head hurt and his stomach churned. Until he'd seen the map he'd truly thought they were winning the war, had a chance, but now he wasn't sure. He wasn't sure at all. "It looks like our enemy is advancing towards the big cities. They're right on top of Los Angeles. Are they?"

"They are and more. Yesterday morning an enormous army of the creatures, of all different sorts and sizes, and working together, broke through the military's barricades and rioted through the city.

The military couldn't stop them, there were too many. The damage to businesses, homes, and the human fatalities were terribly high. It was a bloodbath. People panicked and fled Los Angeles. The resulting chaos was almost as destructive. People were slamming into each other's vehicles, attacking and shooting each other trying to get out of the city."

"I haven't heard anything about this."

"The military has squashed the news, but not for long because you can't contain something this big. They're afraid of the outright panic it would bring. And rightly so. Los Angeles has been flattened, devastated. And that's not all. Not the worst of it. We've been alerted in the last few days other dinosaur armies are coordinating violent strikes on other highly populated cities across the country."

"Coordinating? Other cities?" Henry repeated, the ache in his head getting worse.

"Anaheim. San Francisco. Redding. They're moving their way across the state and up into Oregon and Nevada. There has also been reports they've been seen advancing on the fringes of east coast cities as well. Boston. New York. I don't know how long the military is going to be able to keep the dinosaurs out or keep this from the American people."

"How about the rest of the world? How is it faring?"

"Not much better. More and more cities are seeing what we're seeing here. The dinosaurs are closing in. Everywhere."

This doesn't seem possible, doesn't seem real.

How could this happen to humans? Weren't they the dominant, strongest, smartest beings on the planet? How could out-of-time beasts who shouldn't even exist threaten their civilization? Henry's eyes went to the door. On the other side of the glass, his rangers were watching and waiting for the news Patterson had brought. How could he tell them?

"Anyway, I'm on my way to Los Angeles now to help clear the monsters out of the city and aid in any way I can. I can't stay here long, but I had to stop and see all of you. Let you know what was happening in the outside world, as appalling as it is." Patterson had noticed the rangers outside the room staring in and he smiled and waved at the ones he knew, Ranger Williamson, Gillian, Cutters and Collins, from earlier adventures.

"I sure pray Justin and his esteemed colleagues can come up with some ways of defeating these dinosaurs before the human race becomes the extinct one."

"Me, too. What do you think our old friend Agent Dylan Greer would think of this situation we've gotten ourselves into?"

Now Patterson's smile was softer as he remembered his old FBI partner and friend. The one who had fought and died on their first battle with the dinosaur-in-the-lake Henry had named Godzilla. "He would have told us to suck it in and keep fighting. Get bigger guns. Don't give the fiends an inch. Pound them back into extinction." He laughed.

"He would have, wouldn't he?" Henry allowed himself a small laugh. "I wish he was here to help us."

"So do I, so do I. He was the best agent I've ever worked with. He was fearless. I miss him.

"Now," Patterson stood up, "let me go see Ann and the kids before I have to fly out." He glanced at his watch. "I have three hours left and I had better spend at least two hours of it with Sherman or I won't have a girlfriend any longer."

Henry nodded and came to his feet. "Ann will be so happy to see you. An old friend is just what she needs now. She's had a difficult couple of weeks, but she is doing a lot better."

The men left the room and headed to see Ann and the children. Henry's steps dragged, his mind so full of turmoil and plans, yet he plastered on a fake smile for his wife's benefit. He didn't want to burden her any further. For her to recover, she needed to be protected from news that might upset her. News like Patterson had brought them.

*****

"Ann, I never thought you were the kind of woman to loll around in bed and have people wait on you," Patterson said teasingly after he'd given Ann a hug.

"I'm not," Ann retorted with a bit of her old fire. "But Henry and the doc here are making me stay in bed. I've told them I'm feeling so much better but they are still keeping me prisoner." Ann pouted for a moment. All for show.

"Doctor Emily," she said, "this is our old friend Scott Patterson. He's a top-secret FBI Agent…but you won't get that out of him." She put her fingers to her lips in a gesture of hush-hush. "Scott, this is Doctor Emily Macon."

The two exchanged hellos.

"Doctor, how is the patient doing?" Patterson inquired of the woman guarding Ann's bed.

Henry's grandchildren had come up to gather around the newcomer. Phoebe gave Patterson a hug, smiling, happy to see him again. Timothy, shy, hid behind his sister and stared at the tall man. But Patterson bent down and gave the boy a hug as well. Timothy giggled.

In the meantime both Captain McDowell and Steven had slipped into the room. McDowell took her place by her man and Steven got close to the doctor. The doctor and Steven smiled at each other and clasped each other's hands behind their backs. As if no one could see. So sweet.

"The patient is doing excellently. She should be able to leave her prison bed as soon as tomorrow…if she follows doctor's orders today, that is." So the doctor had a sense of humor, who knew?

"I can't wait," Ann stated petulantly. "I hate just laying around. I feel so useless."

"Yep, I'd say she was getting better," Henry commented drily. "Back to her old crabby self." But he smiled when he said it.

In a gentle rebuke, Ann lightly slapped his hand she was holding.

The doctor took that moment to excuse herself, telling everyone there were probably patients waiting to see her in the conference room and telling Ann she'd return later. She went out of the room and Steven trailed after her.

"Honey," Ann spoke to Phoebe, "can you take

Timothy and get him something to snack on in the kitchen? He hasn't had breakfast yet."

"Sure, Grandma." Without protesting, Phoebe took her brother's hand and followed after Steven and the doctor.

McDowell made herself comfortable on the edge of Ann's bed, but remained silent.

"Well, now that the kids are gone," Ann said to Patterson, who was now standing behind McDowell, his hands lightly on her shoulders, "what's going on out in the world? I know you're here for more than giving us your condolences in person and seeing how I was doing. What's happened?"

Ann's old reporter senses were still sharp, Henry thought.

"First Ann, I want to say how sorry I am about Laura. I hated to hear about it. She was a special woman. I could say so much more about how beautiful and generous she was, how loved, but you know all that." One of his hands left his girlfriend's shoulder and softly grasped one of Ann's. "I'm just so sorry."

Ann bowed her head to hide the tears she couldn't stop. The loss was too new, too tender. "Thank you, Scott. She thought a lot of you, too."

She wiped her eyes and looked up at Patterson. "Now…tell me everything. What's happened?"

Henry started to object, "Maybe we should wait to tell her–"

"No! I'm better now. I want to know." Ann's eyes drilled into Henry's. He knew that look. No way out of it now. She'd have the news or he'd be in for a fight. He shrugged his shoulders and gave Patterson the go ahead. "All right, tell her."

As briefly as he could Patterson revealed what he'd told Henry earlier.

McDowell listened and took it all in, as well, her eyes somber. She didn't seem surprised. Apparently, she already knew everything. Patterson must have spoken to her about it before arriving or her rank had allowed her to know.

When Patterson was finished, all Ann muttered was, "Oh my God. Los Angeles? Other huge cities? Overrun? And here I thought things were getting better."

No one responded. What could they say? They merely looked at her with gloomy faces.

"I can't stay long, Ann," Patterson said. "I'm expected in Los Angeles pretty quick here. They're picking me up in a couple hours."

Ann accepted that and the friends talked together for a little longer, catching up on things which didn't touch on Laura's death, the dinosaur threat or Patterson's secret missions. Timothy's and Sasha's antics were the main topics.

At one point, when Patterson was saying something to McDowell, Henry said aside to Ann, "I meant to ask before, but forgot. What did the doctor say about Wilma's condition? She's seen her, hasn't she?"

"She has," Ann answered in a conspiratorial whisper.

Henry leaned over to hear his wife's words better. "Did she say anything to you about what might be wrong with the old lady? I'm really anxious about Zeke. He's taking his girlfriend's recent ill health so hard. And her behavior, he claims, is getting worse. If she isn't forgetting things she's running away. It's driving him crazy."

"It's not good news, I'm afraid. Doctor Emily can't be positive without a complete battery of medical tests, but she suspects Wilma is probably in the early stages of Alzheimer's. The old woman has all the symptoms. And, according to Wilma, her mother and grandmother had the disease. That pretty much settles it."

"Oh no. Poor Wilma. Poor Zeke. With the situation we're having I have no idea how he or we are going to cope with such an illness long term."

"We do the best we can, Henry. That's all we can do. But I imagine we're all going to have to keep an eye on the old woman a little better from now on, though the doctor believes we have time. Years, really, before the disease becomes truly full blown."

Henry was still brooding over Zeke and Wilma's dilemma when Ranger Gillian burst into the room. "Chief, we have a problem!" His expression was frantic. As chilly as it was he was sweating. "We're under attack! It's the dinosaurs again…but this time more of those monkey things, as you so appropriately baptized them. They have us surrounded and are howling at the gates. I have no idea why or what they want. Can't you hear them, Chief?"

Henry listened. Yes, now he could hear something from outside the walls and it was getting louder. It sounded like a rising chorus of guttural animal noises, calls, as if a large group of the same kind of animals were all crying out in unison, yet all out of tune and tone deaf. Why? What did they want?

"Are they actually attacking us?" Henry demanded of his ranger.

"Well, yes…no…I don't know what the hell they're doing…you have to see it to believe it. The creatures are behaving so strangely. They're hopping around and screeching like rabid little monsters." The ranger threw up his hands in exasperation. "I've never seen anything like it."

Henry shot a glance at Patterson. "Scott, looks like your departure might be delayed somewhat."

"Looks that way, doesn't it? What difference does it make? I'm either fighting dinosaurs here or in Los Angeles. I don't see much difference."

Henry didn't either.

Then both of them and Captain McDowell were running out the door towards whatever awaited them beyond it.

"Let me know what's happening, would you, Henry, when you know?" Ann called out after them.

"I will," Henry yelled back. "Soon as I know. You stay put, you hear? I'll send the children into you."

The door slammed shut.

*****

Henry peered out at the menagerie of critters capering and howling around the outside of the gates in the sunlight. There had to be hundreds, of all sizes, of them swarming around headquarters. Gillian had been right. They were the same breed as the ones that had waylaid them the morning of Justin's close call with the gargoyles. But they weren't exactly attacking the compound, they seemed to be trying to tell them something. Oh, that was ridiculous. How could they know enough to be trying to communicate with humans? Henry shook his head. *And what would they say: We want to be friends? Let's friend each other on Facebook? Let's Twitter together. Let's pinterest. Nah.* The soldiers and rangers had come running, were armed and waiting for what came next. Except Henry didn't know what would come next.

After sizing up the situation, he gave the order not to shoot at the dinosaurs until they made the first aggressive move–which they hadn't so far. They were just hanging around outside making a god-awful racket. More of the creatures were arriving every second. Somehow, though, they were avoiding the sharpened wooden stakes planted around the perimeter, they were weaving in and out around them or sitting between them. They were clever little devils.

"Lordy, do you think they think they're singing?" Steven had come up behind Henry, Patterson and McDowell out in the yard and was peeking through a crack in the fence at the gyrating dinosaurs.

"Beats me," Henry snapped. "I just wish they'd shut up and go away." He'd been through so much, seen so much during his dinosaur adventures but this was beyond his understanding. He really wished Justin was there with them. Most likely he'd know what was going on and what the critters were trying to tell them, if anything. "I just wish I knew what they wanted."

"A string and piano orchestra accompaniment?"

Henry didn't laugh, though the comment was funny.

The day was the warmest one yet and it occurred to Henry that was probably why the dinosaurs were becoming so active. It could also possibly explain the peculiar behavior of the ones outside. Well, it was a thought.

A group of the beasts suddenly surged up against the gates and pushed. The gates creaked and shook but held. Henry, Patterson and McDowell, as well as the rest of the rangers and soldiers around them, moved back a little. Weapons came up and into position. They were ready to fight if they had to.

"What do we do, Chief?" Ranger Gillian, rifle ready at his side, hissed. "Should we shoot them?"

Henry was about to say, *if they start scuttling up the fence, yes*. Then the racket–the singing–abruptly ceased. "No–"

He watched what was happening through the holes in the fence slats. He could have climbed up to the walking path inside and around the fence but he didn't want to miss anything. The dinosaurs were still out there but their demeanor had changed. They'd shut up and were scattering as if something had really scared them. They were escaping into the woods.

"Henry, look!" Patterson screamed, pointing upward. "Gargoyles! Lots of them!"

And there were. A flock of the monsters were

swooping in at them, screeching and trumpeting as they tried to breech the compound's defenses while others went after the fleeing monkey-dinosaurs. The hanging metal mesh blanket over the spaces between buildings hadn't been completely finished. There were still areas unprotected. So the danger the gargoyles presented was still great.

The soldiers and rangers began running everywhere, shooting at the monsters in the sky.

Outside there came the booming, ear-shattering cries of giant dinosaurs.

"And there's more dinosaurs coming, too," Steven, who'd been gazing out at the melee outside the gates until the last possible second, yelled. "They're the big ones! And they're not serenading us. They want in."

As if to emphasize his words something extremely big shrieked outside the wall and its cries were echoed by others just as loudly, and something hit the gates and made the fence shudder. Once, twice, and then a bombardment of dinosaur bodies were slamming against their fortifications. Some of the primevals were lobbing rocks and hunks of earth at the stockade. For a horrifying second, between the missiles and the bodies, Henry feared the wood would give and the creatures would gain access to their sanctuary. Hadn't the sharp wooden stakes planted all around stopped any of them? Henry didn't know.

His survival instincts kicked in and he yelled out orders to his men as Captain McDowell did the same with her soldiers.

Up in the sky a helicopter whizzed over them

employing extremely skillful evasive tactics as it was being chased by gargoyles. It flew out of their view.

Patterson's ride. Henry prayed they'd get away. He glanced at Patterson and saw he'd seen the helicopter, too.

"They came early and I bet they're sorry they did," Patterson muttered.

After that they were too busy staying alive for much of anything else.

The force rioting at the gates against them turned out to be composed of what Ranger Gillian called *the big monsters* on the scale of Tyrannosaurus, Allosaurus and Giganotosaurus. Henry hadn't see so many in one place since the year before. The severe winter hadn't killed them off. No such luck.

The soldiers and rangers scrambled to the top of the fence platforms and fired into the zoo. As soon as enough of the creatures had fallen and cleared a path, McDowell, along with Patterson, led her men out in the tanks and continued the fight up close.

The battle raged the remainder of the day and as night descended the dinosaurs eventually slithered back into the woods leaving behind a field of bloody carnage. The humans had won the day. Again. Barely.

The tanks rumbled through the gates into the compound.

"We pursued and fought them as long as we could…until the light was gone and we hurried back," McDowell reported to Henry when she and Patterson were before him again that night in the conference room. "How many men did we lose today?"

"Not as many as we could have." Henry sighed. "Seven wounded. Three didn't make it." He couldn't shake the images of the wounded and dead that haunted him now along with all the other victims over the years. He shoved the images away. It was war after all and in war people were hurt and people died. "But, considering all they threw at us, we're really lucky. We're also lucky we have a real doctor in camp and she has been taking care of the wounded for us, primitively, but without her more would have died."

"It's been a hard day," Henry conceded, seeing the darkness framed in the window above them. The night was finally silent. His body ached and his eyes were blurry. He needed a shower. "I say we get some rest. Meet first thing in the morning to go over what we do next. I can't even think any longer."

McDowell and the others who had crowded into the room, all of them as exhausted as Henry, disbanded a few minutes later. The doctor and Steven left together. The doctor had been shaken by the violence and scale of the attacks and the large numbers of wounded. Her night was just beginning. Steven had volunteered to help her.

Patterson, though, stayed and faced Henry. "There is something that puzzles me," his voice soft and serious. "We did take the day, or I think we did. We killed so many of them and they not many of us…but…I don't know why they retreated the way they did. And they did retreat. All at once. As if a signal had been sent. It's bothering me. A lot. They might have finished us off with just an another full assault. Why didn't they?"

Henry had thought the same thing but had been afraid to admit it. "So you believe something made them abandon the fight when they were winning? And they could have overwhelmed us if they'd wanted to?" Henry moaned. "You really believe that?"

"I believe that."

"Great, another conundrum we need to fret over. Not tonight, my friend. I'm too tired to worry a moment more and I have to go check on Ann and the kids. I sent her word earlier about what was happening by Ranger Williamson but I need to see her and make sure she's okay."

"I understand," Patterson replied. "And Sherman is waiting for me, as well." He paused. "I hope that helicopter sent to pick me up got away. Have you heard anything?"

Henry hated having to tell him. "No. Nothing. I'm sorry. But I'm sure they're safe somewhere. I'd bet on it." A lie. He knew no such thing. "Maybe they'll get word to you tomorrow."

"Maybe," Patterson said. "Goodnight Henry. I'll see you here first thing in the morning."

And the two men left together, turning out the lights behind them.

Neither one of them saw the small monkey-like creature gaping in at them through the bars of the window. Its eyes glowing and its movements stealthy.

*****

The creature at the window lurked in the dark after the stick beings left their cave, taking the light with them. Why hadn't they heeded the warning he and his kind had attempted to give them. *The giants are coming! Get ready! Hide or flee! Hide or flee!*

It'd tried so hard to make them understand…chattering in front of their caves and the strange woods. But the sticks hadn't listened. They hadn't understood.

The sticks had waited too long and fought the giants instead. But they hadn't won. Not really. The giants would return with more of their hungry kind. Hungry, always hungry. The giants would eat anything–the sticks, their own kind or even its kind. The giants didn't care. Big stupid walking, stomping, screeching creatures. Didn't they know that war with other creatures wasn't the way? Didn't they want peace? Peace to nestle in their caves and watch their eggs hatch? Peace so they could frolic with their little ones, be with their mates, and learn more about what exists around them? This place they lived in. It was beautiful. Yet all they wanted to do was kill…kill…kill.

It squinted its beady eyes and tried to see into the darkness on the other side of the opening. Nothing moved inside, so it jumped down and scurried around to another hole that looked into their caves. This one it could see into. There was the female with her offspring, her mate, and that tiny furry creature. They were such funny, strange beings. They communicated with squawks and clicks. It wondered what they were communicating to each other. Did they want to keep killing and fighting the giants? Would they be the strongest? Would they win? It didn't know.

It observed them for a time and when the hole went dark, too, it hopped off into the night woods. It avoided the dead giants' carcasses littered around the sticks' cave even though it was hungry. Dead things were nothing strange to it. The forest was full of dead things.

By the time it reached its own cave it had forgotten about what it had seen. It was more concerned with finding food for it and its family, being with its own; briefly hibernating. So it did.

Chapter 12

The helicopter Patterson had been waiting for hadn't made it back to Kingsley ANG Base in Klamath Falls. Patterson had been contacted by phone on the situation by the base commander in the middle of the night. Patterson told Henry the news the following morning as they sat drinking coffee and eating breakfast at the conference table while discussing the battle of the day before and their next move.

"We'll use the Abrams and commence searching for them this morning as soon as things here have settled down a little more," Henry promised his friend. "Right after McDowell and her men can clear a path through what's been left behind in the dinosaur battlefield. There are mountains of dead carcasses that have to be moved and they're already hard at work accomplishing that."

"I know. I saw Sherman off at dawn. I've requested a short leave-of-absence so I can help you look for the helicopter. Los Angeles can wait. I was afraid my superiors wouldn't let me remain, but they have reluctantly given me permission. They'll send another helicopter when I let them know I'm ready."

Henry admired the man for caring about the missing soldiers but staying to help with the search could be a problem. "The park is huge and we might find the helicopter in days…or never. You do know that?"

"Ah, and how well I know that. But I have to try. All three soldiers were friends of mine from the base, two have wives and children waiting for them at home, and I can't fly off to fight another battle without first knowing what has happened to them. I owe them that much."

Henry understood and nodded. They drank their coffee and consumed their toast quickly and went out to look for the downed helicopter. They rolled out in their Abrams and the search began. McDowell had left the clean-up to her men, had joined them, and commanded one of the tanks while Patterson ran another crew that Henry and Steven were part of.

"Did the base have any idea where the helicopter might have crashed?" Henry asked before they entered the woods.

Their eyes vigilantly kept watch for any signs of dinosaurs on the way but for the first day the land they trundled across was free of all their enemies and of all life itself. The park was hollowed out and empty. There were no signs of any of the local native inhabitants or dinosaurs. Henry missed the normal animal noises. They'd been absent for a long time now–at least a year. Again he questioned what the dinosaurs were living on. They were devouring each other, if the humans were lucky. And wouldn't that be convenient if they all ate each other to death? Problem solved.

"Did the commander at the base say where the helicopter's homing beacon was last heard? Any location we could zero in on or come close to?"

Henry grilled Patterson over the intercom as they had moved out of the gates and into the park snug in the belly of their tank. Henry was driving again. He'd gotten good at it.

"He said they lost the signal in the vicinity somewhere over the East Rim road. That's all he could give me. Then the signal died completely."

"Well, then, we head towards the east side of the lake. It'll be slow going, though, because that side of the lake's roads are still deep in snow. We'll have to push our way through."

All of them had been mystified as to why the dinosaurs hadn't attacked again after the first assault the day before. "I can't figure out what their game is, Henry," Steven remarked as the tanks grew near to the rim of Crater Lake. "Why would they attack the way they did–all out–and then simply…stop?"

"Because they're up to something, as Justin is always saying. You can't trust them." Yet Henry was grateful the raids hadn't continued. It gave them time to catch their breath, repair the damage the dinosaurs had caused, and look for the missing helicopter.

"I keep thinking we'll bounce over this next hill and what's left of the dinosaur army will be waiting for us."

"They could be," Patterson admitted.

But the dinosaur army never materialized.

Over the next hill and the next and the next there was nothing. Just snow and silent trees against the gray sky. The lake was a blanket of dense mist and Wizard Island was barely visible. That often happened in the early spring. The lake, its islands and roads were hidden by fog. It made their journey and their search harder, slower.

The search continued for that day and the next along the eastern side of the lake. Each night they'd return to the compound to rest and the following day would begin the search again. Some of the time they'd have a third tank roll out with them, or soldiers from the base would arrive to help in the search, and they'd cover more ground. No matter where they looked they couldn't find the helicopter. By the third day, Henry was beginning to be discouraged. If the copter had crashed anywhere in the deep snowy woods and there were any survivors he couldn't imagine they would survive very long. Though it was gradually warming up each day, it dropped down to below freezing at night.

After four days of searching Henry had begun to doubt they'd find the helicopter or its crew.

"You want to keep looking?" Henry asked Patterson later that night as they sat chatting and drinking hot chocolate in the conference room. The other members of the search team had already called it a night and retired to their cots or cubicles. Both men were exhausted. Outside it was snowing. Not a heavy snowfall, but a light cascade of small flakes. Henry hoped it wouldn't stick.

"I would but there were orders waiting for me when we came in tonight. They said they'd give me just one more day on the search here. They want me to report in to Los Angeles no later than Friday morning. The situation has gotten worse there and they need me."

"That's the day after tomorrow."

"I know. So tomorrow is the final day I'll be participating in the search. But you'll have the contingent from Kingsley to bolster your numbers, the ones out there bunking with the other soldiers. You'll be fine. Hopefully you'll find that helicopter. I'm counting on you."

"Sure. We'll keep looking for your lost soldiers as long as we can. We'll find the helicopter." Henry was grateful for the extra help but doubted if it would make much difference. The park was immense and finding anything in it without coordinates was nearly an impossible task.

Patterson went on to another subject. "I haven't heard anything from Justin since he flew to New York. I wonder how the paleontological summit is progressing. Have you heard from him?"

"He called Ann earlier, when we were out, to see how she and the children were and to let us know how the conference was going. It seems cell reception was unusually good this morning. She summarized the call when I checked in on her. Justin apparently created anarchy with his doomsday theories and predictions. He says many of the scientists don't agree with his ideas of how to go about defeating our prehistoric enemies or that the situation is as dire as it really is. Our time is running out to turn the tide. He believes an especially virulent strain of a mysterious virus he discovered in that flesh sample I gave him, with chemical bulking up, could further decimate their population enough so humanity can take care of what's left. He's working on making that virus even stronger. He wants his fellow scientists' help to create and introduce it into more of the creatures and speed the extinction process along. His esteemed colleagues strongly disagreed. They think more guns, soldiers and bombs can do the trick. Right now he's dealing with a lot of infighting. Most of the great scientific minds there are ego fueled, he says, and each one wants to solve the problem and gain the glory for saving the human race, but haven't a clue how to do it. They don't want to listen to what Justin proposes. It's been a circus."

"Typical," Patterson grumbled. "I've dealt with some of those scientific minds and they are arrogant, to say the least. So…so far there's no concurrence or plans as of yet at the summit?"

"Doesn't appear to be."

"It sort of sounds like our governmental problems. The parties involved can't agree on anything so nothing gets accomplished. All they want to do is fight among themselves, name call and point fingers."

"You got it." Henry grinned. "But Justin is nothing if not obstinately determined. He'll get his point across somehow and he'll perfect that dinosaur-killing virus one way or another. I have faith in him."

"I hope so. He is right about one thing. We don't have much time. At the rate these predators are intensifying the war we'd better come up with some solution soon or it'll be too late, we'll be past the tipping point." Patterson yawned and his gaze went past Henry to someone standing outside the room's glass door.

Outside McDowell was waiting.

"Go on Scott," Henry said. "Spend some time with your fiancée. Ann's waiting for me, too. And all of us need some sleep. I'll see you in the morning and we'll take another run at finding our missing brothers-in-arms."

"Before I retire I have to ask how is Ann tonight?"

"Oh, she's better every day. She had the grandkids with her when I stopped by before I met you and the others here. She's out of bed and pretty much her old self. She said you had better come visit her tomorrow or else."

"I will…and positively before I leave. Thank goodness she's recovering so splendidly. That's one thing turning out well."

"And am I grateful," Henry said. "With their mother gone, Justin absent, and me out on the hunt every day the kids need her more than ever." Again when speaking of his daughter he couldn't bring himself to say the word *dead*. It was easier that way.

"In the morning then." Patterson rose from the chair and went to join McDowell outside the room. The two, arm in arm, moved down the hall together and out of sight.

Henry grabbed a folder from the table and left. His mind was busy planning where they'd try looking tomorrow and a hundred other what-to-do-tomorrow or the next day details. As weary as he was he couldn't turn his thoughts off.

When he entered his and Ann's makeshift bedroom she was in bed and the room was dim because she'd switched off most of the lights, but she was still awake.

"The grandchildren are in bed, huh?" Henry took off his clothes. He was so tired he could have dropped onto the bed and just slept, clothes and all, but he knew better than to try that with Ann. She'd make him get undressed.

"About an hour ago. Gillian took them to their room for me. They were beat."

"Good. I'll see them tomorrow morning before we head out again."

"You better, they were asking about you tonight. They miss you. How did the meeting go?" she requested in a drowsy voice.

"Well as could be expected. Patterson has been ordered to Los Angeles by Friday. He'll be leaving day after tomorrow."

"Oh, my. And without you finding that helicopter or its survivors. That'll be hard on him–and Sherman. She's loved having him here even under the sad circumstances."

"Yeah, if only we could locate that helicopter and be sure if there are survivors or not. Not knowing weighs heavily on Patterson's mind."

Ann didn't have to say: *if there are any survivors and if the helicopter will ever be found*. Both of them knew that was now a long shot. The dinosaurs could have killed the crew, dragged the remains of the chopper off somewhere and destroyed or hid it. Henry wouldn't put it past them.

Henry had undressed and was heading for the bed when a movement at the darkened window caught his eye. There was something there on the other side of the bars and glass. He edged closer. There *was* something there.

"What the..." He switched off the last light so he could see it better.

"What is it, Henry?" Ann murmured, the bed rustling as she rolled over.

"I'm not sure. There appears to be something on our windowsill. Outside. Wait a minute. I'll see if I can get to it." He squeezed his fingers through two of the bars and after much pulling and yanking got the window to open behind them a little. Just enough so he could grab and maneuver the two items inside that had been propped on the outside window ledge.

Ann had sat up in the bed by then, fully awake, and snapped on the night table light beside her.

Henry painstakingly drug the items inside and by carefully turning them he tugged them through the bars and into the room. Scooping them up in his hands, he carried them to Ann.

"They're pieces of something." Henry perched on the edge of the bed and laid the two objects down on the blanket. "This one, if I'm not wrong, looks to be a piece of metal. There are numbers on it. It looks like–"

Ann supplied the answer before he could say it. "It looks like a piece of an...aircraft."

"Yes." Henry switched on the other light on his side of the bed and stared at the thing in his hands. "Good lord, I think it's part of that lost helicopter."

"And this," Ann picked up the other object, "if I'm not wrong, looks like a partial section of the sign that's usually nailed above the Rim Village

Visitor's Center. I can make out the top of the letters *Visitor* and the *C* in Center. I'd recognize that sign anywhere. I've seen it enough walking beneath it and into their building. What does this mean?"

Henry glanced at the window. "It means someone or something has perhaps left us a message."

"To where the helicopter crashed, right? Somewhere around the Rim Village's Visitor Center? That's the connection I get with these two pieces. That's so close."

"It is. And one place, now that I think on it, where we haven't yet searched," Henry whispered. "But I can't believe it. What put these two objects together, somehow snuck into our highly guarded compound and left them there on the windowsill for us to see? And why?"

"I think I know," Ann's voice was thoughtful. "Remember that weird simian-looking creature I thought I'd caught peering in at me here in our room some time ago? The one I thought was an hallucination because I was so sick?"

"I remember. I thought you'd imagined it as well, though I didn't tell you that." Yet now reflecting on it and recalling the monkey-looking dinosaurs that had collected at the gates days before en masse and made an awful commotion, he wasn't so sure Ann had imagined anything. The monkey-dinosaurs did exist and perhaps one had paid them a couple of night visits.

"Maybe I didn't. It was and is real. Could be that creature paid us another visit and left these."

"One of the dinosaurs left us these objects?"

"It has to be. It wanted us to know where the helicopter was," Ann finished as they continued looking down at the two pieces.

"You mean it actually made the connection between us looking for the helicopter and telling us where it was? My gosh, that would take real intelligence. It did that? But why?"

"It wanted to help us?"

"Again, but why?"

Ann shrugged. "I had the feeling when I saw it that time it was trying to communicate with me. It wanted to tell me something."

Henry took that moment to at last confess about the collection of rabid ape-like dinosaurs that had behaved so strangely at the gates before the last big attack had happened. He still hadn't confided about Justin's helicopter's close call with the gargoyles. Why worry her for nothing. Justin had made it safely to New York and that was all that mattered. Right?

"You've got to be kidding? Why didn't you tell me about the monkey chorus?"

"I didn't want to worry you further. You were so sick at the time." A strange realization came to him. Had the monkey dinosaurs been trying to warn them of the eminent attack they suffered later in the day from the larger ones? Could that be true?

"*They wanted to help us. It wants to help us.* Oh, my goodness," Henry exclaimed softly, his fingers brushing across the slab of sign, "if that's true we have a friend, a spy, in the enemy camp. And one that's really damn clever. It's almost too unbelievable." He shook his head and mumbled something beneath his breath, his eyes going to the dark window.

"Well, believe it. What else could have put these two things outside our window? What else could they mean? The link is obvious. It's the only answer." Ann leaned against her pillow and smiled. "Now if you go look tomorrow around the Rim's Visitor Center and find the aircraft, we'll know for sure what this strange message meant."

"It'll be the first place we go tomorrow morning, you can be sure of that."

Henry was mumbling to himself and shaking his head as he put the objects on the night stand and then crawled into bed.

But sleep was impossible to claim with everything on his mind.

Wait until he told Patterson. He'd think he'd gone over the bend and past Oz for sure.

Ha, a dinosaur pointing them possibly to the location where the helicopter had gone down or been dragged to? It was so bizarre.

Dawn couldn't come soon enough. Truth was, he didn't sleep much that night and even before the sun's rays lightened the night sky he was up again, dressed and out the door.

*****

They found the helicopter, or what was left of it, in deep forest a short distance behind the Rim's Visitor's Center. The aircraft, as Henry had feared, hadn't made it. It was in jagged broken pieces and scattered over the scorched patch of woods. There was no sign of the crew; not a body, leg, or scrap of clothing. Nada. The dinosaurs had gotten its human cargo or the soldiers were out there somewhere hiding in the forest waiting for rescue. Henry didn't think that last was likely. The wreckage was too extensive. There was lots of blood on it.

It was easy to see the chopper had somehow been forced from the sky and had crashed.

No human could have walked away from the grisly scene in one piece. If there had been bodies left among the ruins the dinosaurs had gotten them.

Henry hated discovering the crash site. Until they'd seen it he'd had a tiny bit of hope for survivors. Now that hope was dashed.

"I'm sorry, Scott, about your friends," he relayed to Patterson as they stood over the remnants. Henry should be used to the deaths by now, but it never got easier.

"Of course, we'll keep searching the woods for any survivors after you've gone," Henry half-heartedly offered when they finished rooting through the debris and found nothing but more blood. There wasn't a trace of the men who'd occupied it. "One or more of them could have gotten away and they might be out there somewhere trying to get to headquarters."

Patterson exchanged dismal glances with McDowell and shook his head. "I don't believe so, Henry. It doesn't look good for any of them."

"We can keep searching, at least, for the rest of the day," McDowell offered sympathetically.

"We can." It was all Patterson said, it was all he could say, because the next morning he'd be California bound.

"At least," Henry repeated.

The men, weapons at their sides and eyes scanning their surroundings for skulking predators, fanned out on foot with the three tanks trailing behind them at a safe distance and scoured the area for survivors. There was nothing and no one but them.

Snow was everywhere on the rim and around Rim Village. That high up it would be like that for another month or more. Anyone escaping the crash would have left tracks and there were none leading away…except dinosaur prints and those were everywhere. The search team spent the rest of the daylight circling away from the crash site but discovered nothing that might have given them hope for survivors.

For Henry it was eerie being in Rim Village. It was a ghost town full of memories and echoes of laughter, but it was empty. A couple of the buildings, the Café and the Annie Creek Restaurant had both been flattened and were just piles of wood and concrete. Henry and Ann had had many a nice lunch at Annie's so it made him sad to see the state it was in. Other outlying buildings had been damaged but not as extensively.

As the evening shadows crept in McDowell gave the signal to everyone it was time to leave and they climbed into their Abrams.

Coming down from the rim towards home base the tanks slowed down. The snow wasn't as deep, was beginning to melt, the ground soggy beneath their treads and they had to be careful where they traveled. There were sometimes hidden gullies or deep sink holes and the soldiers driving the tanks kept their speed down so as to avoid them. The last thing any of them wanted was to be stuck in a sink hole somewhere and cut off from the safety of home base as night fell.

They weren't far from headquarters when they became aware they were no longer alone.

"We have company, Captain," Sergeant Gilbert, who was, that day, driving Henry and Patterson's tank, announced to McDowell. "A herd of the big dinosaurs are coming up quickly behind us. They came out of nowhere and they're closing in."

McDowell canted her head to study the monitor. "How close?"

"Almost on us," Gilbert reported, his voice brusque.

"You think we could stop and engage them in combat?"

"I don't believe so, Captain. Even with three tanks there's too damn many of them. I'd estimate in the hundreds or more."

"Okay then, sergeant, increase our speed to the max. We're close to headquarters so we'll try to outrun them."

"Yes, Ma'am." And the tank surged forward with the others close behind.

Where had they all come from so quickly? Had they been lying in wait to ambush them? Henry studied the monitor. There was a solid sea of creatures behind them filling it. Even with the tank beneath and around him he could feel the ground shaking under them. He could hear their cries through the metal. "There must be a mess of them."

"There are, Sir," the sergeant concurred.

They weren't that far from headquarters. Henry prayed they'd make it. He was getting *really sick* of running from the monsters.

In front of them all of a sudden there were more of the beasts, another wall of writhing, snarling, tongue-smacking dinosaurs, blocking their way.

"Oh my." Patterson also seemed spooked by what he was seeing on the monitor. "What are we going to do?" He looked at Henry. Everyone was looking at Henry. Why did everyone always think he had all the answers? Well, he didn't.

"What can we do…we can't go back…so we stick together and blast through them."

McDowell barely nodded agreement before she opened the com and ordered the other two tanks behind them to move into a tight V formation, start shooting, and don't stop until they made it to and through headquarters' gates.

She asked Henry to alert home base. "*Ranger Gillian,*" he keyed in headquarters and announced loudly, "*we're coming in hot…got a rapacious mob of the big dinos on our tail and now another throng in front of us trying to cut us off…and if we make it through those…swing open the gates the second we get to them!*"

"Understood, Chief," a voice came back at him. "The gates will be open! God speed!"

"Raise the guns," McDowell commanded over her headset to the three soldiers manning the weapons, "and begin firing. Now! Give 'em all you got, boys!"

It was a strange sensation to feel the tank buck and butt against a wall of dinosaur flesh, halt and plunge forward again every few seconds, hear the roaring and shrieking of wounded, angry dinosaurs as they were ploughed through, knocked aside or mashed beneath the treads. Most scurried out of the way but some didn't make it. Some were brought down by the guns and the tanks rolled over, around or through them as if they were moving through thick dough. Henry didn't know he was holding his breath until he was gasping for air. The dinosaurs howled. Their death cries filled the world. It was slow going, but after what felt like an eternity the tank plowed through the miasma of bloody shattered bodies and broke away. They were full speed ahead and aimed for home.

"Lieutenant Becker you still with us?" she yelled out.

"Present! We're still in one piece and behind you!"

"Sergeant Cassons, all of you all right? Still with us?" McDowell shouted out again.

"Still here!" Cassons responded over the com. "We've fallen back a little, though."

"We're slowing down until you catch up."

A minute, two, three went by and Cassons came on the line again. "Okay, we're directly behind you and Lieutenant Becker."

"Full speed ahead, men," McDowell ordered.

Henry was amazed when he viewed the monitor and saw the dinosaurs had fallen behind them and they were putting distance between them. The tanks were the fastest, strongest, best armed, he'd ever seen and because of that they'd escaped again.

And then the fort was in front of them and the

gates were swinging open. The tanks burst through the opening and the gates closed behind them.

"Wow, that was so damn close," Patterson groaned, wiping sweat from his forehead.

"Really close," Henry affirmed. "But we made it."

"Yes, we made it. Out there and back in alive. Again. Henry, you're like my good luck charm. In the underwater caves seven years ago chasing that Godzilla in the lake, going after the gargoyles in the helicopters last year and now this. As long as I'm with you I always seem to get away. It's almost magical." Patterson laughed.

McDowell smiled at both of them.

"Yep, magical." Henry humphed, and then everyone in the tank grinned at each other.

"Let's get out of here." Henry released another held in breath. "I need fresh air."

No one disagreed.

*****

Unfortunately everyone's good cheer was short lived.

As they exited the tank inside the gates Henry saw nothing but devastation. There was blood and chunks of flesh–dinosaur and human–everywhere. There were people moving across the ground cleaning up and aiding wounded victims. Some of the smaller outer buildings appeared damaged.

He spotted Doctor Emily and Steven across the yard and strode towards them, Patterson and McDowell following behind him.

"What's happened here?" he demanded of Steven when the man swung around to him. The doctor was kneeling down beside him attending to a soldier's bleeding arm. She glanced up and nodded her head curtly at Henry and the others, but was clearly too busy to talk.

"We were attacked by a gang of the big dinosaurs. I have no idea what kind they were, just that they were big. Sort of similar to the tyrannosaurs but with smaller heads and longer forearms. They reminded me of the brutes that chased Justin and me from Klamath Falls last fall, except their hides were spotted. Most of them had to have been fifteen feet tall or more. It was hard to gauge exactly when they were trying to maim or devour me." Steven's clothes were splashed with blood and his bruised face was the face of someone who'd just narrowly escaped death. Ghost white and twitchy.

"You were attacked," Henry stared around at the chaos, "*inside* the compound?"

Instantly, Henry's thoughts went to his wife and grandchildren. "Are Ann and the kids okay?"

At those words the doctor's face tilted up towards him. "They're okay."

Thank God, Henry thought.

As she continued wrapping her patient's injury, the doctor went on, "Your family were inside the main building when the strike occurred and they stayed there. Ranger Gillian made sure of that. None of the dinosaurs made it past the sidewalks. Your rangers and the soldiers stopped them cold, forced them back out through the entrance and shut the gates."

Henry's attention returned to Steven. "How in

the world did the dinosaurs get inside in the first place?"

Doctor Emily had finished with the soldier's triage. The man was picked up and carried away to the make-shift hospital she said was temporarily in headquarters' main hall. She came to her feet, wiped her bloody hands on her jeans, and faced Henry and the others with him. Steven took her hand, blood and all. "They sent in an advance force of smaller dinosaurs that somehow scaled the fence and unlatched the gates so the other larger dinosaurs could come flooding in."

"Damn, but Justin was right. They're actually communicating and working together. We're going to have to tighten up our fortifications, our security, and find another way to secure those gates a hell of a lot better. This cannot happen again."

"We had barely minutes," Steven jumped in, "to get a defense mounted or for the soldiers to bring in the tanks. It happened so quickly. I have to confess, I feared we were done for, but your men and the soldiers were right there fighting from the get go. They forced most of the intruders back through the gates, shut and relocked them and then dealt with the ones still inside."

"Some of us," the doctor stated, "think the dinosaurs that weren't expelled abruptly turned tail and ran away in the middle of the battle, because they heard your tanks returning. You just missed them."

Patterson and McDowell had broken away and were dealing with other problems.

Henry was still in shock that what he'd believed

were impenetrable defenses had been breached. He didn't realize he was moving, but he was, towards the main building, Ann and the children. Steven and the doctor kept a brisk pace with him.

"How many dead, doctor?" Henry asked.

"We were extremely lucky…two," the doctor answered. "And five wounded. Four soldiers and one of your rangers, Ranger Todd, I think someone said his name is. He's got a pretty bad laceration wound across his chest. He's inside. I've treated him already but I'll check in on him and the others right now. It could have been far worse if you and your team hadn't returned when you did."

"Good thing we did." Henry wanted to see for himself that Ann and the kids were okay. After he did, he would collect as many men as he could find and reinforce the gates. It didn't make any difference night was falling, it had to be done immediately.

Ann was so happy to see him, grateful the surprise attack had failed and he was all right, too, she threw herself into his arms and didn't want to let go. Phoebe and Timothy, young as he was, did the same. It was a group hug. Ann was shaken, but, as the children, she seemed to be okay. She'd been getting around more, helping more, and was stronger every day.

"I guess you know what's been happening here?" Ann stopped hugging and looked at him.

"Steven and Doctor Emily caught me up on it. Good thing we returned when we did. The doctor believes we chased them off."

"So that's why they ran away. Thanks."

Phoebe then had to tell him all about the danger they'd been in and how they'd hidden in the bathroom and locked the doors. Henry could see both children were still upset. The baby had been crying; his cheeks were stained with tears and his eyes were red. He did his best to comfort and reassure them as his wife looked on.

When the kids had settled down, Ann finally asked, "Did you find the helicopter?"

"We did." The tone of his voice must have tipped her off.

"Crashed? No survivors?"

"Crashed and no survivors." He described what they'd found, not in too much detail because Phoebe was right there listening, and watched Ann's face fill with sadness.

"The losses must have hit Patterson hard, then, huh? He knew all of them."

"It did."

"Was the crash location by the Rim's Visitor Center?"

"It was."

Now Ann's expression was startled. "Well, I'll be. Our mysterious friend at the window gave us accurate advice. The mystery continues."

"That it does. I only wish it would have also warned us about the attacks today."

"You can't have everything, Henry," she spoke softly. "Maybe it didn't know."

"Maybe it didn't." They were speaking about the monkey-dinosaur as if it was an intelligent being of some sort, as if it were an ally and not one of the enemy. The whole thing was ludicrous. But Henry was too tired and frustrated at the moment to dwell further on the puzzle.

Henry spent a brief time with his family and after went to see how the wounded were faring.

"Sorry, I have to leave again," he told his wife, kissing her before he left, "but I have work to do. I have to find a way to reinforce the main gates so what happened today doesn't happen again. So, I'm afraid, it could be a long night. Don't wait up for me."

"I won't. Just be careful Henry." She kissed him back.

"Always." And Henry went out into the night to do what had to be done.

Chapter 13

Justin was exasperated beyond words with the in-fighting, back-stabbing and ego-posturing his fellow paleontologists were doing. Each one coveted the glory of providing the world with the answer to destroying the dinosaurs, saving the human race and having their names engraved in history. So they wouldn't listen; wouldn't work together. All they wanted to do was throw insults and names at each other and feud among themselves. It was like working with a bunch of children. Worse. Childish brats. If these were the best and brightest the world had to offer, than the world was in deep trouble. He'd been attending meetings and sitting on panels for over a week and, so far, nothing had been decided or accomplished. He was fed up but didn't know what to do about it.

After the exhausting day he'd had he needed to escape and gather his thoughts and he remembered the rooftop he'd been dropped off on. He was surprised to find the door at the top of the steps unlocked and he walked out onto the surface.

The night was warm. There was a stiff breeze swirling around him and it cooled things off. He gazed up at the sky and the stars. There was a full moon and everything around him was touched by a soft silver glow. The great city below him was alive with noise and movement. Every once and a while he caught wisps of peoples' conversations or a taxi revving up. He'd almost gotten used to the myriad smells of the city yet he missed the scents of the deep woods. He still couldn't get used to the fact he was in the Big Apple. He couldn't stop feeling like a deprived child on a fantasy vacation bequeathed on him by a fairy godfather. He'd had gourmet meals, room service whenever he'd desired it, tons of fresh coffee and danish, and a soft bed in an elegant room. It felt like a dream. Even with all the headaches the conference was giving him he was grateful for the comforts, for the taste of civilization he had almost forgotten.

He tried not to think about Laura, but it was hard to continuously ward off the sorrow. He missed Phoebe and Timothy more than he thought he could have. Cell reception was so poor at Crater Lake he'd only been able to speak with any of them, usually Ann, a few times. Henry he could never reach because he was either busy or out on patrol.

Part of him wanted to run back to Crater Lake every night to make sure his children, his friends, were okay but he couldn't leave New York until he had gotten what he needed. He wasn't returning to Oregon without a way to eradicate the monsters that had invaded his world.

If only his fellow scientists would listen and adopt his plan. He needed their backing and the funding that would accompany it. He needed a state-of-the-art lab and lab assistants to help him perfect and produce the dinosaur-killing virus. He was absolutely sure he was on to something. He knew it. The dead dinosaur's flesh slice provided by Henry held the key to making an even more lethal strain which would, if he could find a way to deliver it to the targets, make the other dinosaurs ill and eventually kill them. The work needed to begin now, should have begun yesterday. The dinosaurs were encroaching further into the humans' domain and soon they'd be at the main cities' front doors. Time was running out. Why didn't his colleagues see that?

The door to the roof opened and Delores came out. She joined him as he looked out over the night city.

"You couldn't take any more of their nonsensical blather, either, huh?" he asked, smiling over at her.

"I needed some clean fresh air, yeah." Her hands made a twirling gesture into the air. "Those idiots who call themselves scientists were getting on my nerves. When I left they were yelling like mad clowns at each other again. I think they were throwing things, too. Peanuts and cream pies. It's like being at the circus. They gave me a headache."

Justin laughed.

She was dressed more causally, as most of the participants were now, than at the beginning of the conference in a silky red blouse and comfortable blue jeans. Her hair was no longer tied up but down loose around her face. It made her look younger. Her face inclined slightly away from him, her hair softly blowing in the wind, hurt his heart. She reminded him of Laura. He looked away.

But with her he had a friend in the trenches. A friend who was on his side. The years since college seemed few now. She hadn't changed much over the years. She was still easy to talk to and he appreciated her no nonsense attitude, her solid intelligence and common sense.

Delores lifted her head up to take in the sky. “It is beautiful out here. Peaceful. Let’s never go back to Ringling Brothers down there, what do you say?”

He sighed. “I wish we could walk away…but we need them. If they’d only listen.”

Delores was silent for a moment, then said, “That’s the thing, Justin, we don’t need them. I’m going to tell you a little secret I’ve kept from you. I’m not here to work with any of them. Because of their entitled, insufferable attitudes, they’re the dregs of our profession, in my humble opinion.”

“You’re not here to work with any of them? What are you here for?” Now she had his curiosity running. “What’s you secret?” He had settled down cross-legged on the rooftop because he’d become tired of standing and she plunked down next to him.

“I came here to recruit.”

“Recruit who, for what?”

“I’ll tell you in a minute. I have something important to relate that can’t wait. Right after you came up here we had news. Our friends the dinosaurs have invaded Los Angeles. They’ve made a mess of the city and the death toll is high on our side. The residents weren’t prepared, thought it could never happen to them and their city, and it was a slaughter.”

Justin was stunned. He could hardly believe it. Los Angeles. He had known it was only a matter of time before something catastrophic would happen, but he wasn’t prepared for this. “What’s the situation now?”

"Grim. The governor has called in national and state troops to clear the monsters out of the city, yet it's a slow bloody process because, regrettably, more dinosaurs keep flowing in, like a damn's broken or something. There's fierce fighting going on as we speak."

Justin's anger got the best of him. He jumped to his feet. "I knew we were running out of time, but this…*this*! This is unacceptable. As long as the monsters stayed in the isolated backwoods and smaller towns it was dangerous enough, but if they're invading our largest urban cities, it's gone too far. I've got to get my colleagues to do what has to be done. Now. We're not running out of time–we've already run out of time! I need that lab, the funding, for my experiments. I need to perfect that virus from the flesh samples I showed you. I need assistants to aid me in perfecting, developing and producing the virus I *know* will kill these creatures. Oh, I need–I need–" He stopped ranting and lowered his face into his hands, shaking his head.

"I warned them," he groaned, "but they didn't listen…*I warned them!*"

"You have everything you need. I can give it to you. Right now. That's the secret I told you about."

Justin thought he'd heard wrong and looked down at her. "What are you talking about?"

She stood up too. "I was going to speak to you tonight about it over a late night supper, but now's as good a time as any. I am not just here to attend the summit but to recruit a team of the best and brightest for a private consortium of paleontologists who can actually solve this dinosaur problem. I was given the job of hand-picking them.

"I have the lab you need, the backer, the money and the able assistants. And after a week with our forum colleagues I have picked you as the one who has the best solution and chance of exterminating this dinosaur scourge. If you agree I'm to fly you and two other scientists to a secret location where you'll be able to proceed with your work uninterrupted, without limits of any kind. And…if your dinosaur-killing virus really works my benefactor–a reclusive but philanthropic billionaire who doesn't want to be named at this point–as a bonus will write you a check for a million dollars, to do with as you please."

"This isn't a joke, is it? I mean, I desperately need some humor after the week we've endured, but please…don't tempt me with something I can't have when I want it so badly."

Now it was her turn to laugh. "No. I'm as serious as a judge. Really. I promise. My people have everything you need. All you have to do is come with me. Now."

Justin stared at her. He didn't have to think further about it. "All right. I'm in. Let's go." Taking the hand she offered, he was so relieved an answer to his prayers had been handed to him he found himself smiling.

The smile didn't last long.

Above them a familiar sound taunted his ears and his heart somersaulted in his chest. A wave of clamminess brought a cold sweat out on his skin. The sound of gigantic wings and a familiar cry of a prehistoric anachronism that shouldn't exist but did filled the night. He knew in a heartbeat what he was hearing and what it meant. Danger. Death.

In the moonlight two shadowy creatures with huge wings swooped down low over the building, circled and were soaring in for a closer look at the two humans scrambling to get off the dinner plate.

Gargoyles! What...had they followed him from Crater Lake? Killing his Laura wasn't enough? Damn, they were out to get him. Why wouldn't they leave him alone? Devils!

"We have to get off the roof immediately," Justin shouted, practically dragging Delores towards the door hiding the stairs. "Those are the gargoyles I was telling you about and they're not being friendly, trust me. They're hungry. We're dinner."

The humans sprinted for the escape hatch.

They didn't make it to the door before claws came out of the sky to grab them. Justin ducked in time and the knife-like talons raked through the skin beneath his shirt on his shoulder but didn't complete the grab. He was knocked to his knees.

Delores wasn't as lucky. The second gargoyle clamped onto her waist and as she screamed it lifted her from the roof.

Justin thought he was going to have to relive the horrible memory of when Laura had been taken, of her death, only with his friend this time.

He still had Delores' hand in his, reaching further up her arm for a firmer hold and throwing his weight into it, he pounded his free fist as violently as he could against the thing's flesh and, in the same instant, yanked her away from the gargoyle. At first he was afraid the creature wouldn't release her, but it did. He rolled with her in his arms, covering her body with his own; and pulling her to her feet, he helped her to the door and shoved her through it. He tumbled in after her.

As they rested, catching their breath, in the dark stairwell Justin could hear the dinosaurs' disgruntled screeches outside and their talons raking against the outside wood. They sounded as if they'd landed on the roof. Something heavy thumped against the door and Justin and Delores moved briskly down the stairs. Justin didn't believe the beasts could get in, get to them, but he wasn't taking any chances.

When they got to the top floor of the hotel, where there was light and strong walls, they slid down to the floor and leaned against them. Justin looked at Delores' injury. Blood was trickling down his back, he could feel it along with the pain, yet he only cared about how badly she was hurt.

"You need medical attention. Stitches," he told her after seeing the deep gashes around her waist. "We need to get you to a hospital." He had to give it to her, though, she wasn't weeping and wailing, though she had to be in a lot of pain. She was being incredibly brave.

She nodded her head and her voice sounded strained, weakening, when she spoke. Her words all spilled out in a tumble. "My benefactor…will take care of everything…all I have to do is call him. He'll make sure we get to hospital…where I'll get best of care. You, too…but left my phone…down there with…clowns."

"Call him." He pulled his cell phone from his

belt and handed it to her. There was blood on his hands and they were trembling. He was also fighting to remain conscious and propped his head against the wall. Either the rush of adrenalin was catching up with him or his injury was worse than he'd thought. Blood was pooling on the floor beneath them.

Delores didn't say much to whoever was on the other end of the line. Her message was cryptic, brief, but once she muttered they were hurt, the phone call ended immediately.

"They're on…way. Ambulance, too. They'll come and get us…told them where we were…what happened…don't worry about your luggage, samples…papers, Justin," she was struggling to finish what she wanted to tell him. "When we get there…someone will bring them…for you." She stopped talking but held his hand tightly as her eyes shut. He knew she was fighting to stay conscious, and he prayed help would come soon. The pool of blood was getting larger.

As they waited on the hallway floor by the elevator for the ambulance to arrive, no way they'd risk a helicopter ride after the gargoyle attack, a group of the scientists from the conference found them. But the paramedics arrived right after them so Justin didn't have much time to warn them or say much. "We were on the roof," he told them, "and were attacked by these flying dinosaurs. Two of them. Large. Hungry. They came out of the sky and tried to carry us away. I fought with one. We were lucky to get away. Tell everyone *not to go outside* without protection. Weapons. The dinosaurs are here. Inform the authorities and warn the other paleontologists of the danger. Don't wait."

He prayed they had listened to him.

But the level of concern in his colleagues reactions hadn't been strong enough for Justin, even when they saw the blood and knew Delores and he had been hurt. They'd acted as if they didn't believe his story of flying monsters attacking them because they weren't ready to see the severity of the threat. Not yet. Not in the fortified great city of New York. That didn't surprise him. It was easier for them to keep believing they were safe in the city surrounded by steel, concrete and men in uniforms with guns on their hips, and so far away from the real dinosaur outbreaks. Let them believe that for as long as they could. They'd learn differently soon enough.

The dinosaurs have come to the Big Apple, were Justin's fevered thoughts as he was put on a stretcher and carried away, *and it will only get worse. The gargoyles are merely preliminary invaders, an advance force. The rest of their army will soon follow. The people of New York had better be prepared or they'll suffer the same fate as Los Angeles. Invasion.* He wished he would have had more time to tell the scientists that, but he didn't because he passed out. Then, he supposed but didn't really know because he no longer had been awake, Delores and he were whisked away to the ambulance on the street far below. Later he had a vague memory of waking up in the ambulance, lights flashing and sirens blaring, as it sped through the streets and after that there was only pain and then darkness.

*****

The following morning Justin woke in a bed in a hospital room. He was alone. Attempting to see out the window, he couldn't, attached to tubes as he was he could barely move in the bed. He closed his eyes and listened. All he could hear was silence. The distinctive sounds of the city were absent. The smells were different as well. No car exhausts, the mingled scent of millions of people or the smell of dirty pavements.

He didn't think he was in New York any longer.

The room looked expensive with plush drapes at the windows and fancy furniture and little touches only money could provide.

A nurse came bustling in and chirped with a smile, "Ah, Doctor Maltin, awake at last. You're doing extremely well for the injury you had. You lost a great deal of blood. We had to give you some. But I just got the okay from your doctor to detach you from these tubes." She set about checking things nurses usually checked, and taking the tubes off him, as he grilled her with questions.

"Where am I and where is my associate Doctor Delores Taylor? Is she all right?"

"You're in a private hospital in D.C. St. Anthony's. Very exclusive. You have some powerfully rich friends, doctor. Oh, and Miss Taylor is doing well. She's in the room a door down and if you'd like to see her we can arrange to wheel you in there any time you feel like going. She's already asked about you."

Justin shifted slightly in the bed and his hand reached up to touch the bandage on his shoulder.

The pain wasn't too intense and though he was a bit weak, he didn't feel all that bad, either. He was relieved to be free of the tubes and needles. He hated needles.

"How long have I been here?"

"Two days."

Two days? And he'd slept all that time? No wonder why he felt rested.

The nurse finished what she had to do and inquired if he was hungry enough to eat.

"I could eat."

"They'll be bringing in your supper in a half hour. Roast beef tonight, mashed potatoes and apple dumpling for dessert. Take my word for it, it's all tasty. The food here is much better than most hospitals." That generic smile again.

Before she left the room she opened a drawer in the side table and took out a cell phone which she gave to him.

"This is for you. A gift from your benefactor, I was told." Then she was gone.

It was the most technically advanced and costly iPhone he'd ever had. Brand new, it gleamed in his hand.

He keyed in his father-in-law's number and was pleased when it went through on his first try.

"Henry," he spoke, "you're not going to believe what's happened here."

"Thank goodness you finally called, Justin, I was beginning to worry about you. It's been days. What's happened? And after you get done telling me, I'll catch you up on what we've been dealing with here."

When they were finished swapping tales, Justin spoke to Phoebe and a little to Timothy, who was too young to carry on much of a conversation. Yet it felt good to talk to his children, hear their voices, know they were okay. Justin hit the end button and lay there for a while, reviewing what Henry had confided. None of it had been good news. At Crater Lake the dinosaurs were awake in force and attacking, just like in New York. But Ann was doing better and his children were unharmed. Strange thing, though, about that mysterious dinosaur-at-the-window leading Henry and his men to that crash site. The helpful dinosaur's existence and its helping the humans was another enigma to add to the others.

His supper was brought in and he consumed it. As the nurse had promised, it was delicious.

He'd barely finished when Delores, in a wheelchair, was pushed into the room by the same nurse who'd attended to him earlier.

Delores grinned. "Well, about time you're awake and fed, I see. I only slept for the first day. I've been waiting for you. Soon as they informed me you were awake I rushed in to see you. How are you feeling?"

"Not too bad. My injury wasn't as severe as it could have been. And you?"

"I'm sore but healing. Like you, my wounds weren't as bad as I'd feared, but I lost a lot of blood. They say I nearly died because of it. That monster didn't have that good a grip on me, thank goodness." She stopped speaking and the look she gave him was tender. "I want to thank you for saving me. If you wouldn't have reacted as you did when you did I'd most likely be dinosaur poop. So thank you." She reached out and touched his hand gingerly and then withdrew it.

He almost laughed but she was serious, the subject was serious, so he didn't. "Anyone would have done what I did, believe me. And, after all, I've had plenty of experience dragging humans out of dinosaur talons, or jaws. But you're welcome."

She leaned in against the arm of the wheelchair and flashed him a deep smile. "So, Doctor Maltin, according to our doctor you've recovered enough to be released perhaps as early as tomorrow morning…are you ready to go to work?"

He nodded. "I'm ready. More than ready."

Her lips recreated her smile. Her hands slapped the wheelchair's arms. "So am I. We've wasted enough time. Tomorrow morning we fly out to that lab I told you about. The plane is waiting on the tarmac for us. All systems go. The other scientists are already there, as are your personal belongings, your research notes and your dinosaur samples. Everyone is waiting for you."

He caught something, some unexplained emotion below her smile, and pressed, "Besides dinosaurs taking over our world, what's wrong?"

"I might as well tell you. You'll find out soon enough. There's been more trouble in New York with our pesky primeval beasties since our rooftop adventure. There have been many reported assaults across the city in the last forty-eight hours. Mainly the gargoyles, as you called them, but other types as well. The authorities can't figure out how they're getting in but the people are beginning to panic. They have been fleeing the city in truckloads. There's been traffic congestion, extreme road rage, shootings, and overall pandemonium. It's been horrible. I've been seeing it all on television."

Justin had nothing to say to that. After the other night he'd more than expected it.

His decision was an easy one. "Can we fly out to that lab tonight? If the doctor has released me there's no reason for us to stay here. I can rest, sleep, just as well on a plane. If you're okay to go, too?"

"I am. I was officially released this morning but our boss agreed to let me stay until you were ready to go."

Justin carefully scooted to the edge of the bed because it made him a little dizzy to move, found his clothes in the second drawer of the side table and took them out. They weren't the blood-stained and ripped clothes he'd been wearing the night of the attack. They looked like the same clothes, identical, but weren't. They were brand new. His size. Even shoes. "By the way," he asked Delores, "who is this mysterious boss of ours?"

"You'll meet him when we get to the lab. I'm to call him when the airplane leaves and he'll join us there. He's anxious to meet you."

"I bet," his tone sarcastic. He was still having a hard time believing some billionaire was backing his theories and was going to give him everything he needed to prove them. He hadn't had many people in his life believe in him that way, except Laura, Ann and Henry. "Now if you roll yourself out of the room, I'll get dressed."

"Sure. I'll be out in the hallway waiting for you. Or if you'd like I'll roll back to my room and let you take a quick shower." She pointed at a door to his right. "Everything you need, towels, soap, shampoo, are in the bathroom there. If you need any help getting in and out of the shower, just call the nurse's station, the red button on the phone, and someone will be right in."

He looked down at the blood stains on his arms and nodded. "I think I need a shower. I think I can do it on my own, though, if I take it easy. I'll meet you in thirty minutes in your room. We'll go then."

"All righty. I'll let our boss know what's up so he can alert the airplane's pilot. See you." And Delores rolled herself out the door with a wave goodbye.

Dizzy though he was at times, Justin took his time, and didn't need help with his shower.

Two hours later they were flying to an unknown destination and, the pilot assured them, at an altitude high enough to avoid dinosaurs. *Yeah, sure, but those gargoyles can fly pretty darn high.* They were lucky and made it there without seeing any.

The lab was everything he had been told it would be and more.

He couldn't wait to begin the work.

*****

Justin was blown away at the gleaming facilities and state-of-the-art bio technology in the lab. It had everything he could ever possibly need to accomplish his final research. When he and Delores walked in, both still a little stiff and weak from their battle with the gargoyles, after seeing the lab itself, they were offered food and conversation in a meeting room with his new lab assistants.

He recognized Russell Gartner and Lucia Walters as fellow paleontologists who'd been at the New York conference. He'd spoken to both of them at different times about his virus theories and, unlike many other of his argumentative colleagues, they'd thought he might be on to something. They were both incredibly competent and he was grateful to have them on his team. The four of them, over a sumptuous meal provided by their new boss, discussed what they had to do and how. For the first time in years Justin felt a sense of hope they could find a way to fight and ultimately defeat their nemeses.

"You hand-picked these two, huh?" he murmured aside to Delores at one point.

"I did. I interviewed over twenty of our conference comrades and these two impressed me the most. They both had ideas similar to yours about how to kill the dinosaurs. Russell, especially, believed introducing a lethal virus or some kind of poison into their population could possibly eradicate them."

"Ah, and that's the final hurtle we'll have to solve. I know we can create a virus that would do the job but the big question is: How do we deliver it? The delivery method is still a mystery to me."

"We'll find a way, I have no doubt. I also have two other scientists, Stanley Louison and Courtney Waverly, on their way so soon we'll have a team of six. They aren't from the conference. I'd enlisted them months ago based on their own promising published research. You'll like both of them. They're smart, quick and creative."

"You've been busy, haven't you?"

"Someone had to be. This battle has been brewing for a very long time."

"You're telling me. I've been on the front lines most of it and I've paid the price over and over."

"I know." The look they shared assured Justin she understood what the fight had cost him in so many ways.

Food had been eaten and glasses of wine consumed. Justin was feeling the delayed effects of the last week and the wine. He was tired and his wound ached. He'd hoped to begin his work that night, he was so excited, but Delores had told him in no uncertain terms the morning would be soon enough. "You need, we need, to rest at least one more night. We've been through an ordeal."

For once Justin had to agree. "That's not such a bad idea. I am worn out."

"We can go to our rooms," she said, glancing at her wristwatch, "pretty soon. First, Justin, I'd like to introduce our benefactor to you. He should be here any minute. He wants to meet you."

"And I want to meet him so I can thank him."

"You'll soon have the opportunity."

Their benefactor, Jeff Smith, turned out to be a wiry, short man with curly black hair, calm eyes and a salt-and-pepper beard. He bustled in, all smiles, shook Justin's hand and sat down at the table. The other scientists had met him previously and seemed comfortable with him.

After talking to the man, Justin found he liked him. It kept nagging him as they spoke that the man seemed familiar and by the end of the meeting he knew why. Jeff Smith reminded him of an old friend, Dylan Greer, the FBI agent who'd helped hunt and kill the first dinosaur at Crater Lake years before. Dylan Greer who'd died saving all of them.

"Doctor Maltin," Smith said in a serious tone of voice, "I want to thank you for saving my sister's life."

"Your sister?"

"Delores. She's my sister. Well, my half-sister, but we were raised together and I consider her my sister. She's very dear to me. If not for you she'd be dead. The flying beasties would have had her for supper. So I owe you, friend. Big time."

Delores was smiling at Justin. "Yes, my brother is filthy rich. He's one of those Internet billionaires you hear about who started and grew his own web business in the early days of the technology revolution, oh, some twenty-years ago. He made a ton of money selling it. Now he wants to help the world."

"And just when the world needs it," Justin supplied.

"I just hope," Delores' brother asserted, "it isn't too late."

"You and me both."

Soon after the meet-and-greet party broke up Justin was shown to a room even nicer than the one at the hotel. He had no trouble falling asleep in the feathery bed. Tomorrow would be a busy day, a monumental day, and he'd need his rest and his wits about him. Tomorrow they'd begin the final leg of the journey to crack the code of how to destroy the dinosaurs once and for all.

Chapter 14

Ann felt better than she had in months, which was a good thing because, now of all times, her family needed her to be healthy, to be strong. The last clash had shown them the war had resumed and their defenses were lacking. It had cost them lives. That, her husband had vowed, could not be repeated.

Henry had been out the last week with the other men shoring up the gate and the barricades. They'd done everything they could think of to make it safer for everyone inside headquarters. They'd plunged more spikes into the earth on the outside and dug deeper pits in strategic places to trap any dinosaurs that wandered too near.

The soldiers went out on patrol every day in the tanks and engaged the enemy whenever and wherever they could find them, killing many, but the creatures kept on coming as if there was a dinosaur factory somewhere churning them out like chickens from eggs. The weather had warmed and the snow was melting below the rim of the caldera. The dinosaurs had become bolder, moving in closer to the humans. Her husband speculated they were so ravenous they were stalking the compound with desperate eyes, waiting for a chance to break down their defenses. No one dared leave the safety of headquarters without being heavily armed or protected. It was agreed upon the doctor couldn't leave to return to her hospital in Nampa on the original schedule. She'd wanted to stay a week and then go home; that was not to be. It was too dangerous and Henry couldn't spare the men to escort her. Not yet anyway. Doctor Emily had not been pleased about that development because she didn't want to abandon her Nampa patients, they depended on her, but she understood. She was smart enough to know, at this time, there was no way to guarantee her safe passage home or those with her. For now she was remaining at Crater Lake.

In some ways, other than abandoning her patients, Ann didn't sense staying longer would be much of an inconvenience for the doctor. The growing romance between her and Steven was easy for all to see. Steven rarely left her side and the two behaved like a couple already. The looks between them were those of lovers. Ann for one was happy to see Steven in love. It'd been many years since his wife had died and he'd been lonely long enough. In the world in which they now lived it was good to see people could still fall in love and find a little happiness. Dinosaurs or no dinosaurs, life and death, the world, humanity, carried on.

"Timothy. Timothy! No, don't pick the kitty up like that," Ann admonished, chuckling. The child held the cat around the neck as he hugged him and the look on the animal's face was priceless. Resigned acceptance. The cat loved the boy, loved all of them, so Ann was sure he wouldn't hurt him, but she wanted the child to learn how to be gentle with his pet so she was firm with him.

The cat escaped from the boy's grasp and high-tailed it to Phoebe, who'd been by the window conversing with Doctor Emily and Steven. The cat jumped into the girl's arms and Ann could hear him purring from ten feet away. The doctor had been in to check on Ann and, of course, Steven had been with her. Since the last round of violence Steven had kept close to Doctor Emily.

After watching the two lovebirds, Ann's eyes swept past the window and a shiver crept across her skin. *Wasn't there something there staring in at them? She thought she'd had a fleeting glimpse of something*...yet it wasn't there after she'd blinked and looked again. *Nah, it'd been her imagination, that's all.* After finding those left behind pieces of the crashed helicopter and the sign and confessing to Henry about what she'd seen before, she was always looking for something to appear behind the barred glass. Nothing had. So far.

"Ann," Doctor Emily had come to stand beside her, "I'll be in the conference room seeing patients until around three o'clock if you need me."

"I'll come with you," Ann said. "I need to get out of this room for a while. The walls are closing in on me." She'd been getting out of bed and leaving her prison more often the last week. She was feeling so much better.

The doctor smiled. "I know what you mean. I get that way sometimes. Cabin fever. Sometimes Steven walks with me around the compound just so I can get exercise. I'm not used to being shut in this much."

"Me, neither."

"Then come along," the doctor invited. "Your friends Zeke and Wilma are supposed to come in for a visit. Wilma hasn't been doing very well lately and Zeke hates to leave her bedside. I'm sure they'd like to see you. Zeke was truly worried when you were sick."

"I know he was." It'd be good to see both of her old friends. She left the children playing with the cat and trailed the doctor from the room.

And Zeke was happy to see her. Wilma, not so much. At first the old lady couldn't remember who she was. Eventually she remembered and gave Ann a hug. To Ann it seemed like another life…the day the behemoth tyrannosaurus had chased Zeke, Ellie, Wilma and her through the neighborhoods of Klamath Falls, almost catching and devouring them; they'd taken refuge in Skeeter Lockwood's cellar escaping certain death. One of many, many hair-raising close calls. But in the end, Ann thought morosely, a dinosaur had gotten Ellie anyway. She missed Ranger Ellie Stanton and wished she and Ranger Kiley had never died in the cabin the year before. Adding them up in her head, she realized she and Henry had lost too many friends.

Seeing Zeke and Wilma also reminded her of so many other better things like when she'd been a novice reporter for Zeke at his newspaper, her journalistic career and, later, when she bought and owned the newspaper, life in town, friends and family. Seeing them revived memories of her old normal, happy, life before the cancer and the dinosaurs. These were good memories she cherished. Now it seemed like another life. A carefree dream life.

"You look real spry today, Ann," Zeke declared. He gave her a hug. "You look like your old self almost."

"I feel like my old self. It's good to see you and Wilma."

"Well, we had to see the doctor here. I guess Henry's out with the soldiers keeping us safe?" Zeke spoke to her as Doctor Emily talked to the old woman and assessed her condition. Zeke had aged so much in the last few years Ann could barely recognize him. He was all skin, bones and white hair. Yet he was still one of the people she loved the most.

"That's where he is, out on patrol. They've been following a sizable pack of our enemies, trying to locate their lairs. He'll be back at nightfall."

When she'd been her sickest with pneumonia Zeke had stood outside her bedroom door each day and waited for the doctor to let him know how she was doing. At his age, with his and Wilma's frailties, he was better off staying away until she was better. When she'd recovered he visited her every day, until recently.

Zeke glanced over at Wilma. The doctor must have said something which made the old lady laugh.

"How's Wilma doing these days?" Ann kept her voice down. There were times when Wilma understood things and Ann didn't ever want to hurt the old woman's feelings. "She looks good."

Zeke had that look on his face she was familiar with. That expression of wise acceptance. "She does. All in all she's not doing too bad. Some days are better than others. She usually knows me, yet not always anyone else. Most of the time she's easy to handle, simply wants to sit and stare at things or talk about when she was a girl, but I'm glad the doctor is here to help keep an eye on her. The medicine she's been giving her has helped, too. It calms Wilma and lets her sleep on nights when she's anxious."

Wilma called for him and Zeke went to her. Ann observed the two old ones together. Zeke, taking her hand, was gentle with her and his voice was compassionate. Would she and Henry be like that someday? Would they both live long enough?

Steven entered the room and joined them. "I've heard some kind of a row outside. The soldiers and rangers are reporting to their battle stations. I saw it from the window. I was going to check on what was happening but thought I'd let you both know about it first."

The doctor nodded at him, showing she'd heard. She was still speaking with Wilma.

Steven was heading for the door when he hesitated. "Ann, you hear anything lately from Justin? How's he doing at that summit thingie? I talked to him days ago but after leaving messages he still hasn't gotten back to me. He must be really busy."

"He is. A lot has happened since you spoke to him. He called last night and talked to me and the kids. But the call was brief because he's in the middle of discovering something big to help us, he said. You know he and a colleague were attacked by gargoyles on the hotel's rooftop while they were in New York?" Ann had moved nearer to Steven. She didn't want Zeke or Wilma to hear what she was saying. Wilma was frightened enough.

"What! No, he didn't tell me about that. I guess when he talked to me last he hadn't got that far yet. He was at the summit and ranting about how ridiculous and petty some of his fellow paleontologists were behaving; complaining on how bad cell reception was, too. Are he and his friend okay?"

Ann quickly caught him up on the incident, that Justin and Delores were hurt but all right, and he was no longer at the New York conference. After, she threw in, "I don't know who this mysterious benefactor is, but Justin says he's at some secret location and the bio lab he's working at is unbelievable. There's a whole team of competent scientists working for him. He's making progress–though there are obstacles he has to overcome–on the virus he hopes will help deplete the dinosaur population if not destroy it."

"I hope so. When you talk to him next, ask him to call me. I have news to tell him."

Ann couldn't stop the grin from spreading across her face. She could guess what the news was. Steven was in love. "I'll tell him."

"And also keep me updated on his further adventures if you can," Steven ended the conversation and went out the door.

Now even Ann could hear the noises from outside: the sound of gunfire, men shouting and the tanks rolling out through the gates. She wondered what was going on. No doubt Steven would let them know soon enough.

Ann spent time with her old friends, ate an early supper with them, and later found herself in her and

Henry's room. Phoebe had taken Timothy off somewhere, probably to watch out the front windows at whatever was going on. Steven hadn't returned.

Outside it had fallen quiet. The sun was low in the sky. Henry would be home soon.

Ann was about to go in search of the kids to see what they were up to and make sure they had had something to eat when she heard a noise behind her. A scratching. She pivoted around. Again there was *something* at the window. At first her mind refused to accept what was there. It seemed impossible. Inside the fort and right outside her room. Again. There was a dinosaur, a small one, poised behind the bars and glass. It wasn't moving and its eyes barely blinked. This time she got a good look at it. It sat there and stared in at her as if she were the curiosity, cocked its strange looking head. It reminded her somewhat of a hybrid of a dinosaur and an ape. Could be it was of the same hybrid species as Henry had run into before. The simian breed. Strange looking beast. It did appear to be somewhat primordial but also somewhat…familiar.

It had something in its claws and Ann gasped when she saw what it was. It was an honest to goodness cat. A live cat. The feline was meowing and squirming in the creature's grasp but it didn't seem to be afraid. The dinosaur, cradling the animal delicately, continued to stare at her. It lifted the cat and pushed it gently against the outside glass as if it were offering it to her.

"Oh, it's Miss Kitty Cat! How–" It was Ellie Stanton's cat which had snuck out through the gates months ago and disappeared into the forest. Ann had given up on the feline and thought it had been long dead. After months out in the wilderness and cold how could it still be alive? But it was. "Oh Miss Kitty Cat," she sighed. Was the creature going to kill or gobble up the feline in front of her? Oh, no.

The dinosaur wasn't doing anything to show hostility. It bowed its head and kept the meowing cat against the window, waiting. The creature's movements, she thought, were so graceful.

Ann took a chance and later she'd be astounded she had the courage. She slowly inched towards the window and, as her husband had done the week before, slid her fingers cautiously between the bars and lifted the glass frame up a few inches. She kept expecting the dinosaur to grab at her but it didn't. It released the feline. The cat, seeing her so near, squeezed through the narrow opening and into her arms. It was as thin as a kitten, bedraggled and sick looking, shivering from the cold, but alive. The cat had never been a very large cat, Sasha was much bigger, but now it was so frail it looked like a baby rabbit. Ann couldn't understand how it had survived at all.

Ann hugged the cat to her and soothed it. She was so happy to see it she plastered its head with kisses. "I'm so happy you're home." When her eyes traveled up again the dinosaur-at-the-window was gone into the twilight.

Wait until she told Henry and Justin about this. One of those monkey dinosaurs actually brought back Miss Kitty Cat and hadn't eaten her. They won't believe it. But there was the cat in her arms as proof. Shaking her head in amazement, she went in search of food for the cat. Obviously starving, it was so emaciated she was afraid it would die in her arms before she could feed it.

One thing for sure, the children would be thrilled to have the cat back. They'd missed her. Ann was glad to have the cat back as well.

Sasha, meowing and rubbing around Ann's legs, was also happy to see Miss Kitty Cat. They'd been buddies. Ann lowered the returned kitty to the floor so she could nuzzle noses with Sasha. Ann hadn't heard Sasha purr as loud as he was in months.

"You can have her back, Sasha, after I get her some food and water." Ann took the cat and left the room.

What was it with that dinosaur-at-the-window? Why was it helping them and what did it want from them? More importantly, how on earth did it know the cat was their lost pet and if it was as hungry as the other dinosaurs in the woods were reported to be how had it not eaten the cat?

Questions Ann had no answers for. She was simply elated to have Miss Kitty Cat home again. Now Ellie's ghost should be happy, too, because Ellie had loved that cat.

*****

The doctor and her patients had already vacated the conference room when Ann got there. She wondered where everyone had gone but was too busy taking care of the cat to dwell on it.

Steven, carrying his guitar case, found her in the dining area of the room.

"Well," Ann asked, "what was all the uproar outside about?"

"Not much. The guard on duty at the north side of the stockade spied a gathering of those smaller monkey-like monsters who blitzed our gates last week. We thought they wanted a fight, deployed the troops and the tanks, but after a couple of minutes they scuttled away into the underbrush, running for their lives. They didn't want to engage us, I imagine, which was odd. It's all okay now."

Clever dinosaur-at-the-window, she thought. *It had arranged a distraction for its visit.*

"Another sticky situation avoided," he mumbled. "Henry and the others will be happy to hear it. They're due back any time from patrol. Now, at least, the coast will be clear and they can come in undisturbed.

"Where did you get the cat?" He set the guitar on the floor. "Oh, my goodness…it's Miss Kitty Cat. I thought she's been MIA for months. Where did she come from?" He knelt down and petted the skinny feline who'd finished its second bowl of canned cat food. The cat had always had a soft spot for the musician and was in his arms in seconds.

Ann told him.

"You're kidding, aren't you? Pulling my leg?" He was stroking the cat and it was purring.

"Nope. Every word is true. Miss Kitty Cat was saved and brought back to us by a friendly dinosaur. The same one who directed Henry to the helicopter crash site."

Steven shook his head. "I wish Justin was here to make some sense of this because I can't. This is too bizarre to understand for a simple troubadour like me."

"I'm with you." She took the cat, which had begun meowing pitifully and shivering uncontrollably, from Steven's arms. "But I'm so happy we have Miss Kitty Cat back. I can't believe she's still alive after months out in dinosaur frozen wonderland. She's one lucky cat."

"She really needs a bath, though. She's a mess."

"In time," Ann responded, gently cuddling the feline. "She's too weak right now to dump her in a sink of soapy water. If she makes it through the night I've give her a bath tomorrow."

"She'll make it through. Heck, she found her way back here and that's quite an accomplishment. Wow, she's a super puss!" He reached over and petted the cat again. "You are a very special kitty."

The cat meowed.

"What are you doing with your guitar?" Ann had made a make-shift bed, a cardboard box lined with soft towels, for Miss Kitty and put her in it. The cat was so feeble what it needed most, beside food and warmth, was rest.

"I thought I'd do a little practicing until Emily finishes her rounds. She's seeing to a soldier who's on duty on the fence and she'll meet me here when she's done. I wanted to work on a new song which has been on my mind lately. I knew this room was empty so I thought I'd sneak in and fill it with music."

"Don't let us stop you." Ann sat down at the table with the cat in the cardboard box in front of her. "If I remember correctly Miss Kitty likes your guitar strumming and caterwauling." She gave Steven a mischievous grin. "And so do I."

Ann hung around for a while, passing the time with Steven, listening to his new song and his guitar playing, cuddling Miss Kitty, and waiting for Henry to return. The children came in and she made them supper. They were overjoyed to see Miss Kitty again, especially Phoebe. In the girl's opinion, two cats were so much better than one; more to love. Locked up the way they were, it was comforting to have pets. The children fussed over the cat and watched Steven play. Phoebe even sang along. Ann was surprised to hear the child had a good voice. Music or no music, Timothy fell asleep in Ann's arms. The doctor joined them, other rangers wandered in to listen, and Steven put on an impromptu gig for everyone. Doctor Emily was impressed and smiling.

Ann was happier than she'd been in weeks. She was feeling better, she had the children, a new friend in Doctor Emily, and now Miss Kitty had shown up. She only wished Henry would return from patrol, which would make her happiness complete.

Twilight whispered in and that's when she began to worry. Soon after night settled in and her worry increased. The patrols were always back by dark. Where were Henry and the others? Were they safe?

Outside the night wasn't giving her any answers.

And her worry grew.

Chapter 15

Steven waited in the conference area for Ann to put the children to bed in her room. They both had cots there for the nights they stayed with her and Henry. That night was one of those nights.

While she was gone Ranger Williamson came in and updated him on Henry and his men's situation.

"They're running extremely late, but they're okay. Henry asked me to relay that message to his wife so she doesn't worry. They were on the other side of the rim searching for some of the dinosaurs' lairs and got boxed in by a herd of the monsters. They won the fight but it took time. They're heading in this direction now and should be here soon."

"Thanks, Williamson, I'll tell her. She'll be relieved to know Henry and the crew are safe and sound and coming home," Steven told the ranger. He'd laid his guitar in its case as everyone else had exited the room, except for Williamson and Emily.

Williamson got something to eat, a premade sandwich from the refrigerator and a glass of water. "I'm on guard duty tonight out on the fence," he said. "I figured I needed something to eat before I had to be out there."

"Keep your eyes open, friend," Steven sent him off with. "And I'll pray for you to have a quiet night."

"Don't we all? I hope the night's uneventful as well. I'm sick of fighting dinosaurs." Williamson left and the door closed behind him.

Emily had been standing at one of the windows looking out into the night. “I wish we could go outside for a walk,” she groused gently with a sigh, her fingers trailing down the wall beside the window. She turned around and joined Steven at the table. “I miss that. I miss being outside, smelling the fresh air and strolling through the town or woods. Going out at night to a movie or running out for fast food. I’d do almost anything for a McDonald’s Big Mac, shake and fries right now.”

“Almost anything?” Steven teased her. He took her hand. He wasn’t hiding it any longer. He was, miraculously and incredibly under the circumstances, in love with her. He’d fallen for her the first night, the first second, he’d met her and he still couldn’t believe it. After his wife, Julie, he’d thought he’d never love again. But looking at the doctor with her soft chestnut-colored hair caressing her pretty face, and the basic goodness in her eyes, he knew he had fallen beyond saving. With her he felt whole again. He was going to ask her to marry him and tonight, that moment, was it.

“Since we’re alone, rare enough lately with so many people around us all the time, I want to ask you something, Emily.”

Her eyes were sparkling. “What?”

“You don’t have to answer me right away. You can think about it.” His courage departed him but he forced himself to say the words. “Emily Macon, will you marry me?”

She shocked him by answering instantly without hesitation. “Yes, I’ll marry you, Steven James.” Her smile brightened the room and Steven found himself smiling, too. He pulled her close and kissed her. He was so happy he lost his words and could only hold her tightly.

Emily spoke first. “When?”

“As soon as we can. As soon as you’ll have me and we can find someone to marry us.”

Her face grew thoughtful and Steven thought he knew what she was thinking. “You’re worried about your hospital and patients in Nampa, aren’t you?”

“I’ve been here longer than I ever thought I would be already. What with the added dinosaur attacks I know I wasn’t going back anytime soon, too dangerous to travel…yet I always assumed I’d return when the hostilities settled down and the way was open again.”

Steven had mulled this over and he had a response ready for her. “I’ll go with you. I can live anywhere and have. Before this I was a traveling musician and can be again, if this crazy world allows me to be. This home we have here is only temporary. But none of that makes any difference…I will follow you anywhere, doctor.”

She was crying now, silent tears trickling down her face, but she was still beautiful. He hoped they were tears of joy.

“You’ve made me so happy,” she said. “I love you.”

“And I love you.”

They were still embraced when Ann walked into the room.

“Okay, you two, what is this?” She looked at him. “I’m gone a few minutes and you have Emily crying." Ann's expression changed to one of fear. "Has something happened? To Henry and his men?"

He was quick to reassure her. "No, no! In fact, Ranger Williamson just dropped by to inform us Henry and the others are on their way back to headquarters now. They had a little dinosaur trouble earlier but triumphed and they'll be here soon."

"Thank God." Ann plopped down beside Emily and presented her with a quizzical look. "So then what's wrong? Why are you crying?"

"Steven and I are getting married," was the reply.

Steven allowed Ann to give him a hug after she'd given one to Emily.

"I knew this was going to happen," Ann said smugly, grinning at them. "I knew it the night Emily arrived here. As sick as I was, I saw the instant connection between you two. Henry did as well. Oh, I'm so happy for both of you! When are you planning this great day?"

"As soon," Steven disclosed, "as we can arrange it."

The three discussed the wedding and what would come after. Steven wanted to inform Henry about the marriage himself so he and Emily waited with Ann for Henry to return.

"I'm going to try to contact Justin early tomorrow and give him the good news." Listening, Steven thought he could hear the tanks returning. There were noises, a deep rumble, outside in the night that could be nothing else. "I know he's really busy but I have to tell him."

Emily put her hand over his. “Perhaps you should hold off until he comes back from New York? It hasn’t been that long since….” Her eyes guiltily went to Ann.

“It’s okay. My daughter’s loss shouldn’t dampen your happiness with your coming marriage. You *should* be happy. It feels wonderful to have good news instead of bad and we’ve had more than enough bad since this dinosaur war began. I’m sure Justin will feel the same way. He’ll be excited and ecstatic for both of you, believe me. Tell him as soon as you can.”

“I’ll tell him tomorrow if I can get him on the phone,” Steven wrapped up. “Maybe he’ll have some good news for us as well. News that he’s created that virus we need to get our world back again or something like it. Suddenly,” he took Emily’s hand, “I want my, our, old life back. The one we all had before the dinosaurs showed up. I can finally say I’m tired of all this.” He waved his free hand around.

“Oh,” Ann inquired, “you’ve finally had enough of dinosaur hunting and fighting, huh?”

“I think so. There’s so much more to life than what we’ve had these last years. There’s been too much sorrow and way too many deaths.” He avoided Ann’s eyes.

“I agree. For me, I also dearly miss the comforts of civilization, not being able to travel without a tank escort, and I’m sick of being afraid all the time.” Ann must have heard the outside commotion because she stopped speaking and her eyes were on the door. She came to her feet.

Henry walked in and Ann was in his arms. "Henry, I'm so glad you're here. I was worried."

"Sorry, honey, it couldn't be helped." He collapsed into a chair and Steven brought him a cup of coffee which he gratefully took.

Henry's face was drawn, his eyes kept closing as if he were very tired. His skin was dirty and his uniform ripped. Obviously he'd had a hard day.

"What happened out there?" Steven directed the question to Henry.

"You mean what didn't happen out there?" Henry retorted, slumping in the chair. His fingers shook slightly as he held the cup.

"Well?" Steven urged.

"We discovered this cave below the other side of the rim, one of their lairs, and it was full of unhatched eggs. There must have been hundreds–or thousands. It shocked us at how many eggs there were. We didn't get too deep into the caverns before we were surprised by the parent residents. We weren't prepared for as many as came at us. As before they were working together, communicating, strategizing; we don't know how. The cave was too dangerous to stay in as they surrounded us. There was no room to fight, no place to go. So without destroying many of the eggs we had to flee. We barely made it out."

"You're returning there tomorrow to finish what you started?" Ann guessed.

"We have to. This time we'll be ready for whatever they throw at us and we'll take bombs for the caverns. Blow them up along with the eggs."

"And the war goes on," Ann muttered. She

glanced at Henry. "I have something really interesting to tell you. Our dinosaur-at-the-window was back tonight and it left us a present."

Henry perked up. "What?"

"Miss Kitty Cat. She's emaciated, weak and traumatized, but alive."

"Really? That cat is still alive? It's been missing for months." Henry cocked his head to the side, his expression baffled.

"Somehow it must have survived out in the wilderness and our little monkey-dinosaur friend knew the cat was precious to us. It found her and brought her back to us. Stuffed her in between the window bars so I could grab her and bring her inside. Then the dinosaur vanished into the woods."

"I must say I'm amazed. This shows not only empathetic intelligence…but compassion. I'll be darned. I'll have to let Justin know about this. Imagine that, we have our other cat back. I bet the children are thrilled."

"They are." Ann yawned around a smile. "The cat is sleeping in her own little bed next to the kids in our room. I'll give her a bath tomorrow if she makes it through the night."

"I hope she does. I always liked Miss Kitty Cat and she was Sasha's friend."

Steven caught Henry staring at him. "Okay, music man, what is up? You act as if you have a big secret. I can tell. You're smiling like a cat over a dish of cream. Doctor Emily, you have the same smile. What's up?"

Wrapping his arm around her, Steven took Emily's hand. "We're going to get married."

"Congratulations!" Henry rose from the chair and shook Steven's hand. "Ann, love psychic that she is, predicted this was going to happen. So she was right, and I'm so happy for both of you."

His gaze went to Emily. "Does this mean we're going to have a permanent doctor here at headquarters?"

"For a while until the immediate danger is over," the doctor replied. "I'll have to return to Nampa eventually. I have patients waiting there and they need me. I have my home there. It belonged to my grandparents and has been in the family for a hundred years. It's full of my treasures and everything my husband and I gathered and collected during our marriage. Everything I own. Memories. Steven's agreed to go with me."

Steven was aware of the disappointment in Henry's expression but the chief ranger hid it quickly. "That's all right. We're thankful for the time you've spent with us, the lives you've saved and the care you've given us. Truth is, if Justin finds a way to kill these dinosaurs we might all eventually get to go home and we'll have our lives back." He looked at Ann. "And we'll build a new cabin for us."

Ann nodded. "We will."

"Well." Henry stood up. "It's late and, I don't know about you all, but I am beat. I need sleep. Tomorrow is going to be a heck of a day with us having to clean out that cave. It won't be easy. The dinosaurs seem to be getting smarter every day."

"Chief Ranger." Steven was on his feet, too, still holding Emily's hand. "I'd like to come with you tomorrow if you'll let me?"

Steven didn't chance a glance at his bride-to-be. He didn't want to see her reaction.

"Are you sure?"

"I am. I've been sitting around here way too much and letting everyone else do the dangerous stuff. I need, I want, to help you blow that cave to kingdom come."

"If you want to go with us, as usual we leave in the morning when the sun comes up. Be at the main gate. Goodnight everyone.

"And again, Emily and Steven, congratulations to both of you on your upcoming nuptials. You make a great couple. I'm delighted for you." Henry and Ann left the room.

Steven was almost afraid to face Emily.

"You're a brave man, Steven James," was all she said with an encouraging smile. "I'm proud of you. Go get those monsters. Make our world safe again for us humans so we can have it back."

They kissed. Steven walked her to her living space and said goodnight after a few more kisses.

*****

As tired as he was, Henry was so content to be home and with Ann, the children and the cats, he couldn't go to bed until he gave them some attention. In the dimly lit room he tenderly observed his sleeping grandchildren and took time to pet Miss Kitty Cat and Sasha. He really hoped Miss Kitty Cat would survive the night and take her place in the family once more. The cat had always been a lovable feline.

After he got undressed, he and Ann sat in bed as

he ate sandwiches and an apple Ann had brought from the kitchen. He tried not to drop crumbs on the covers.

"I can't believe our *pet* dinosaur brought Miss Kitty Cat back to us. It's pretty weird," Henry murmured later as he was drifting into sleep. He dreaded the next day and what had to be done, but he didn't want to think about it when he was in Ann's arms. He'd learned to live in the moment. It was safer, and kept him saner, that way.

"Yeah, pretty weird. I wonder what it's going to bring us next?" Ann mouthed sleepily.

"That's a good question. I'd vote for a million dollars in a suitcase. Maybe a lump of raw diamond or something. Or, better yet, a way to kill off all the other bad dinosaurs."

Ann giggled. "But isn't it wonderful Steven and Doctor Emily are in love and getting married?"

"Hmmm, wonderful. Goodnight, sweetheart."

"Goodnight, honey."

And as they both claimed sleep, Ann whispered: *"I miss Laura so much...."*

But Henry was already in dreamland.

*****

Neither one of the adult sticks inside their cave knew they were being scrutinized from the window. The dinosaur on the outside listened and waited for a long time before it slunk off into the midnight woods. It wondered if the sticks had liked its gift of the furry tiny creature. It had almost eaten the ball of fur but didn't when it remembered how the female stick had made such funny noises while playing with the other furry creature. That noise had stirred something inside it and it wanted to feel that again. And it had when the female stick had taken the furry thing from its grasp and met its eyes. A warmth, an understanding, passed between them. It liked that feeling.

But it was still hungry so it went off in search of food. There wasn't much left in its territory and it had been going farther and farther into the forests to find something to eat; fighting with others of its kind over whatever it did find. All its brethren were starving, too. And it would get worse. It and its mate would soon have more offspring to feed. It had no idea where the food was going to be found as there was so little now. It bounded away through the trees, everything forgotten except the primal urge to hunt and feed. Feed and hunt. It barred its fangs and its tongue flicked in and out tasting the air, seeking the scents of prey. There was nothing.

It should have eaten the tiny furry creature and it wondered what it would have tasted like. Probably very tasty. It resolved right then and there if it found another one it would gobble it up. Yes, it would.

Chapter 16

Miss Kitty Cat was still breathing in her bed when Henry woke up before sunrise the next morning. Thank goodness. Ann and Phoebe were really attached to that cat and if it would have died in the night, neither one would have taken it well. When he caressed the cat's tangled fur it purred loudly and licked his hand. The feline peered up at him with clear eyes and began cleaning itself. Yep, the cat was going to make it. Henry dressed and making his way into the kitchen poured a bowl of milk for the cats and brought it back. Miss Kitty Cat was the first to partake. Sasha waited until she was done and helped himself. Sasha acted as if he was happy his friend was back. The male feline kept rubbing against the smaller cat and both were purring.

"Henry, is it time for you to go?" Ann's sleepy voice interrupted the sounds of purring. She sat up, rubbing her eyes. "Is it dawn already?"

"Almost. I'll be leaving here soon. Go back to sleep, sweetheart, it's so early. I can get my own breakfast."

Ann was up and out of the bed. "How's Miss Kitty Cat?" she whispered as she knelt down and leaned over the two cats lapping up the milk. She didn't want to wake the sleeping Phoebe and Timothy.

"She's doing well. I do believe the cat is going to live. I gave her some milk and she's reacquainting herself with Sasha."

Ann lifted Miss Kitty Cat into her arms. "Oh, she's so thin. All bones and fur. Like a ball of fluff in my hands." She nuzzled the cat. "We need to plump her up some." Ann, switching the cat to her one hand, took her robe off the end of the bed and put it on. "I'm going to get her some more food. Henry, don't leave until I come back, you hear?"

She and the cat were out the door.

Henry got his gear together for the day's mission and was about to head out when his wife reentered the room with a second bowl in her hand which she placed on the floor. Both cats padded up to it and began eating. The canned cat food supply, she'd told him earlier in the week, was getting low so they were supplementing it with table scraps. The bowl was full of them from the meal the night before.

"Appears our long lost feline has her appetite again, too," Ann noted. "She made it through the night so I think she's going to be fine."

Ann turned to Henry and hugged him. "You better be careful out there today, husband. You better come home in one piece tonight."

"I'll try real hard to do that, wife."

Ann, in her robe, accompanied him to the kitchen and watched him prepare a breakfast of oatmeal and gulp it down. The pre-light of the sun was shining into the windows.

"It's time to go." Henry preceded Ann through the awakening rooms of headquarters and they said their goodbyes at the door. She wanted to be with the children when they woke up.

*****

The sunlight was warming up the world, the snow melting away to water, as Henry strode towards the main gate and the rest of his crew. McDowell and her men had been in charge of the bombs they were going to need and she nodded in the affirmative when he arrived to stand beside her.

"We're ready to go whenever you are, Chief Ranger. The crew is inside the tank. The bombs are loaded."

"Then let's start this expedition and hit the road." Henry would have liked it if Patterson was with them but he was in Los Angeles fighting the good fight. What they had to do today was up to him, McDowell and their men. They were employing three tanks and a full crew in each. Steven was riding with Lieutenant Becker's crew, squeezed in with Becker and the others, in the third machine. After the rapacious crowd of primeval monsters they'd run into the day before they were being especially cautious.

The tanks never made it to the cave. It was as if the dinosaurs had been waiting to ambush them along the trail and stop them from getting near their eggs; as if they'd known the humans were returning to complete what they'd attempted and failed to do the day before.

Inside the lead Abrams, Henry, who was the driver for the day, brought the tank to an abrupt halt. There was a wall of dinosaurs in front of them. Most of them were of the breed *carcharodontosaurs*, the gigantic Cretaceous era meat-eaters, Justin believed were some of the ringleaders. Yet interspersed in the mob were the more voracious smaller *velociraptors*, the ones with the feathers, and what looked like other mutants of both species. It continued to amaze him how the creatures were adapting and evolving. He didn't see any of the monkey-dinos like the dinosaur-at-the-window and thought that strange. Then he noticed the Tyrannosaur Rexes in the background, unmoving.

"Oh, oh," Henry, in the hull of the machine, announced to the crew via his headset. "Looks like the fight has been brought to us. Are we ready?"

"Loader," McDowell commanded, "load in the artillery shells. Gunner, start firing on my order."

The dinosaurs were howling, stomping their feet and looking fierce, but they weren't advancing.

"Wait a minute," Henry shouted. "They're not attacking. They're only staring at us."

"So, what do we do?"

"Wait. Let's see what their next move is."

Everyone held their breath and the tanks sat. Minutes went by. The woods watched. No one moved, not a machine or a beast.

After ten minutes Henry said, "Let's try to go around them. We should fall back, regroup, and go another route to our destination. Fake them out and make them think we're giving up. Then find another way to the cave. I know a different route. Do I have permission to proceed?"

McDowell answered, "You do. All tanks reverse! Lieutenant Becker you go first. Sergeant Cassons next. Pull back until we can get ourselves in the lead again."

"Yes, Commander," Becker responded.

Cassons echoed the response, "Copy, Commander."

Henry waited until the other tanks had retreated and he reversed until he could pivot the machine around and retrace the way they'd come until a turn off which he planned to take. The other two tanks fell in behind him but the dinosaurs didn't follow and the woods were silent again.

What had all that been about? Henry fumed. The dinosaurs had showed up in force but let them escape without a fight? He didn't like it one bit. As he steered the tank deeper into the park down an alternate route to where they had to go, leading the others, he kept expecting to run into more prehistoric beasts. None appeared. Their path was unobstructed.

They made it to the cave and there were no dinosaurs to block their entering. The cave was waiting and open for them.

"I don't like this," Henry whispered aside to McDowell after they'd climbed out of the tanks and into the sunlight. "Where are the sentries? After confronting us yesterday, why would the dinosaurs leave their young unprotected?"

Steven and two of the soldiers from the other Abrams were with them. The soldiers, experts in explosives, would transport the bombs into the caves and set them to explode, giving the humans just enough time to escape.

"I don't like this, either," Steven concurred. "Where are all the dinosaurs? It doesn't make any sense, not after the way they've been behaving.

They're smarter than this…to leave their potential babies unprotected."

The bombs were unloaded and carried to the mouth of the cave.

"We all ready to do this?" McDowell asked, eyes scanning the mouth of the cavern, weapon poised before her; a flashlight illuminating their forward passage.

There was a soft chorus of: *Ready*.

And the team stepped into the darkness of the cave. Other flashlights were switched on. Men held their breath. Boots could be heard scraping against the cave floor.

For a moment Henry's memories of another cave, another time, came back to haunt him. A ghost of a memory about the underwater caves beneath the caldera where he, Agent Greer, Patterson, and Justin chased, fought, and killed the first Crater Lake dinosaur so many years before. He'd nearly died in that cave along with Greer and now he was in another cave. He didn't like caves much to begin with, too confining and eerie. Too dank. Dark. Too much of a trap. He had to keep his thoughts away from that long ago time or he would have felt even worse than he did.

"Keep as quiet as you can manage," McDowell advised.

But there was no need for silence or caution because the cave was totally empty.

"The eggs are gone," Henry exclaimed after they'd explored more of the cave and its passageways. They'd been searching for an hour and had gone down all the different cave passages they had seen eggs in the day before. There were no dinosaurs lurking around to protect the eggs because there were no eggs.

Steven laughed out loud. "Well, I'll be. The dinosaurs have relocated them. How in the world did they get all of them out of here overnight? It's mind-blowing. They knew we were coming, most likely what we were going to do, and moved them somewhere else for their safety. Now that is fiendishly cunning."

McDowell agreed. "So cunning it's troubling. I can't believe they anticipated what we were going to do and acted to prevent it." She was shaking her head. The cave around them was all of a sudden filled with the sounds of wings. Small wings. Bats, probably. One creature, apparently, the dinosaurs had yet to eat to extinction. Maybe they were tricky to catch, with their wings and all.

"Now I guess we know why and how the dinosaurs have reproduced so speedily and efficiently across the country. They know where to hide their eggs and keep them hidden. There's no telling how long they've been doing this. Moving them from one place to another."

"Justin thinks it's been decades," Henry supplied, "that they've been breeding in the back country of primitive wildernesses." The cave had worked its disquiet on him and he was more than ready to leave it. Once a few tunnels back, in a gloomy corner, he could have sworn he'd caught a glimpse of Agent Greer standing against the wall smiling at him. It creeped him out. He kept expecting to see him again around a corner or in a crevice. He didn't know why Greer had begun haunting so many of his thoughts lately, but he had. Was it a forewarning of something to come?

"Let's get out of here," Henry said what everyone was probably thinking.

"What now, Captain?" Steven had swung around in the narrow cave and requested of McDowell.

Henry caught her attention and offered up his plan, "We find other caves and keep looking for more eggs? The ones that were here might not be that far away. How far could the dinosaurs have taken them in one night? Not too far, I'd say. We have the explosives so why waste them?"

"Precisely what I was going to propose. Let's get out of here." McDowell trekked off and everyone followed.

They spent the remainder of the day in the vicinity going to any cave they could find hunting for dinosaur eggs. They didn't find any eggs but found signs there'd been recent dinosaur activity in some of the caves like dinosaur droppings, pieces of egg shells and abandoned nests.

By late afternoon, they had to accept surrender and reset their course towards headquarters. Henry felt the woods were far too serene which often meant something bad was about to happen. The fact they hadn't seen one dinosaur since morning made him uncomfortable. He knew they were out there…somewhere. He held his breath expecting an assault any moment. None came.

"We haven't seen any more dinosaurs since those brutes this morning blocking the roadway."

McDowell's voice came across Henry's headset with the same thoughts later that afternoon. "I don't like it."

"That's two of us, Captain." Henry could hear thunder outside of his little compartment inside the hull. Lightning ripped across the sky. "Captain, where to now?"

"I've been warned a severe storm's coming in, Chief Ranger. Night won't be far behind. So take us home. We'll continue our mission tomorrow."

"Copy, Commander. We're going–"

Something jumped up on the tank in front of Henry's window. It was one of those monkey-dinosaurs. Henry jerked in his seat. "What the–" The creature leaned over and stared in at him as if it knew he was the one driving. Which was a silly thought because how would a dinosaur know who was driving?

It waved at him and began wildly gesturing to something ahead Henry couldn't see. Its ugly little face with the shiny lizard eyes was pressed up against the bullet-proof glass.

The tank veered off the road and barely missed hitting a huge tree. Just in time Henry got it back on the road.

"Chief Ranger," McDowell's voice was interrupting, "what's going on? You forgot how to drive or what? Do you need a break or some more driving instructions?"

Henry was about to answer when the crazy beastie punched at the window with its claws, grinned at him and *pointed* ahead. Its claws went to both sides of its head and it shook it. It bounced up and down, clearly aggravated over something.

Oh, it could have been the *same* monkey-dinosaur Henry had seen at his window at headquarters; the same one who'd brought the news of where the helicopter had crashed and most likely the same one who had brought Miss Kitty Cat back. Henry wasn't sure, Ann was the one who'd seen the creature up really close not he, but he had a hunch it was.

Then the strange messenger was gone. It'd hopped off the tank and fled into the darkening forest. Thunder boomed and a wave of lightning lit the world around them.

And Henry thought he understood the message.

"Commander, we need to get back to headquarters now at top speed. Pronto. I think they're in trouble."

McDowell didn't question what he proposed. "Top speed, then, Chief Ranger. Take us home. I'll convey the info to the others."

Henry increased speed to the maximum and, as the rain pummeled the tanks and the day went black, they rushed back to base.

They arrived barely in time to rocket through the gates before the dinosaurs launched another full out assault.

As the last tank went through the entrance and the gates slammed shut, Henry thought: *Another ten minutes and they would have been trapped outside the base with the dinosaur army surrounding them. Another ten minutes.*

Henry was too busy defending headquarters after that to reflect on what had happened in the woods or to wonder why that weird little dinosaur kept helping them. But he knew when they finished repelling the latest attack he had to call Justin, if the scientist didn't call him soon as he'd said he would do, and if he could get through, and speak to him about the creature.

The battle didn't last long. The dinosaurs charged at the walls and the humans inside killed many of them. Then the storm exploded. It was a doozy. The rain was a vertical sheet of gray water and lightning fingered through the sky like an out of control forest fire. The storm scared the dinosaurs off. That's the only explanation Henry and the others with him had for their prehistoric aggressors suddenly turning tail and melting into the night woods and giving up the fight.

And no one behind the fence questioned why the dinosaurs withdrew, they were merely thankful they had.

That night after Ann and the children, who were still sleeping in the room with them because they were afraid of the storm, had fallen asleep, Henry stood a long time and waited at the window; stared out at the storm. His little friend never showed.

He must be going a little nuts himself, waiting for a dinosaur to visit. He must be losing it. As Ann before him, he wondered if he was imagining things. If he'd imagined the little helpful dinosaur bouncing around on the tank and by its timely warning possibly saving them. Or maybe the critter was also smart enough not to be out in the weather. He finally walked away from the window.

Henry had tried to reach Justin, when his son-in-law never called him as promised, but had only been allowed to leave messages. Sooner or later Justin would return the phone calls. He usually did.

Henry went to bed because these days he didn't know what sunrise would bring and no matter what he had to be rested and ready for anything. That was his life these days.

Chapter 17

Justin was running between labs when his cell phone rang again. Someone was persistently trying to reach him. Knowing he'd ignored the phone and incoming calls for the last day or so and he had to respond this time, he answered as he keyed himself into the main lab.

"Henry? Can I call you back in an hour? I have to do something very important first…but I will call back, I promise." He tapped the phone off and entered the room. Doctor Russell Gartner and Lucia Walters were busy at the lab station, hunched over their work, deep in concentration.

Justin strolled up to them. "Anything new to report?"

"I think you were right, Doctor Maltin, this particular combination might be the one." Russell Gartner looked up at Justin, his eyes behind his glasses a glittering blue. He was an average-looking short man, bald, but his mind was one of the sharpest Justin had ever known. He was brilliant in so many ways, but reserved with most people. Justin estimated his age at about fifty. He handed Justin a sheaf of papers.

Justin skimmed over the top ones. "Russell, you did a great job with this. It looks about right. This could be it."

"I think so, as well, and so does our colleague Lucia." He tossed a glance at the petite dark-haired woman working beside him. She was as pretty as

Russell was plain, as outgoing as he was shy. Justin suspected Russell liked her but would never dare tell her he did.

"Now, I suppose, we have to do live tests to prove this formula works? To prove it will actually kill live specimens?" Russell's voice was tentative. He was no dinosaur hunter and had been fortunate to have never had to face or fight one of them. He was a big city boy and until now the city had protected him. He despised the creatures but he was also terrified of them.

Knowing how scared Russell was of the creatures, Justin said, "We can try it out on a small one first, Russell. We'll take all precautions, I promise. The cages the soldiers have constructed for our lab animals are the strongest iron bars available. Don't worry, the dinosaurs won't escape. You and all of us will be perfectly safe."

"All right, I believe you. Live testing is the next step and we can't go on to the one after that until we see if this virus combination will work."

"You got it." Justin patted the man on the back. "And all will be well."

For the first time Lucia, who'd been listening intently to their conversation, spoke up. "Er, exactly how are we going to achieve these live tests? I gather we're going to test this on a *living, breathing* dinosaur here in the lab? Inject the virus into it? How are we going to do that? I'm not going near one of those monsters." She visibly shuddered.

"Leave that up to me," Justin told her. "I've been informed Mr. Smith's men will procure the test subjects, cage them and sedate them before we have to inject them."

"Well, it sounds as if you have a plan." She was smiling at Justin now. She smiled at him a lot. Perhaps she was just being friendly.

"Don't worry, Doctor Walters, I always have a plan." He winked at her and started to leave, the papers still in his hand. At the door, he tagged on, "Thank you again for all your hard work, both of you. I couldn't have done this without your help. Now onward and upward. I need to report to Smith what you've found. I'll keep you apprised as we go."

"Please do," Russell requested. "And you're welcome. If this works we'll all be heroes…and the world as we once knew and loved it might have a chance to return and the human race will survive."

"Why don't both of you meet us in the boardroom?" The boardroom was what they called the main lab where he and his team would meet and discuss developments over fancy catered in meals or for meetings.

"Soon as we clean things up here, Doctor Maltin, we'll be there," Russell said.

Once outside Justin stood at the doorway and inhaled deeply. Sure, they'd get the live test subjects…but how? Where? Now if he were at Crater Lake all he'd have to do was step outside the gates and take his pick of any of the wild dinosaurs that galloped by. Here, in a secret lab, on the outskirts of Boston, surrounded by thick fortifications and heavily armed soldiers it wouldn't be so easy a task. He'd have to talk to his benefactor and see how it could be done.

Justin marched briskly down the corridor towards the larger lab. Delores and the other two scientists were there waiting for him. The players were in place now. All he had to do was take the next step. But this step would be the most dangerous one.

They had to procure live dinosaurs for the tests.

Delores was waiting for him in the boardroom.

“What now, Doctor Maltin?” She got up from the table she’d been at with Doctors Louison and Waverly. “Have we cracked the code and found the final solution?”

“I believe we have.” All of them had worked around the clock on Justin’s basic viral hypothesis, building on it, perfecting and producing it. None of them had slept much the last week and it showed in their lined faces. But since the dinosaurs had invaded Los Angeles and were sneaking into other major cities like New York and St. Louis speed in finding a solution was crucial. So they’d worked nonstop since arriving at the facility.

Stanley Louison, a tall thin man around forty or so in a rumpled suit, with a serious face, and Courtney Waverly, an older bone-thin woman with gray hair in a boy’s short haircut, had turned out to be as smart as the two scientists Delores had hand-picked from the conference. The six of them had proven to be an efficient team and together they’d finally found the formula that could be lethal for the dinosaurs.

“Now what?” Stanley had stopped scribbling in his journal, which documented every minute of the man’s life.

"On to phase two. Live specimens to try the formula on and then if it works as well as I hope it will, on to phase three: finding a way of delivering it to the monsters everywhere until they are all dead."

"Isn't it ironic, Doctor Maltin, how scarcely a handful of years past we, paleontologists I mean, would have sacrificed anything to see a live dinosaur, much less have endless dinosaurs running around to study? It's been a hard pill to swallow, knowing we have to destroy them; that it's us or them." Stanley tapped his pencil on the table. There was a plate of Danish in the middle and Stanley, who apparently had the biggest sweet tooth Justin had ever seen, picked up a cherry one and bit into it. There was always food around and always the best of everything really. Justin loved being treated like a king but he never forgot the people he'd left behind at the lake weren't as fortunate. They were still probably rationing their food. It made him feel guilty.

"Stanley, you can call me Justin. We're all equals here. Anyway, I felt that way myself, at first, until they killed a friend of mine, and then another, and another, and they began multiplying like fleas and threatened the very existence of humanity." He didn't add Laura to that list. He couldn't bring himself to do that. "Now I don't care how rare or magnificent any of them are–I just want to get rid of them. I want humans to be safe. I want earth to be for humans." Justin helped himself to a strawberry pastry and munched along with his colleague as his brain continued to work. It was the best Danish he'd ever eaten and was flown in for them from some specialty bakery every morning. Delores' brother sure knew how to treat his people.

"What do we do now?" Delores wasn't eating for some reason that morning. A cup of coffee was the only thing she had before her.

"I need to speak with your brother," he said as Russell and Lucia came into the room and took their seats. Lucia poured herself some coffee from the pot beside the Danish, scooped in a spoonful of sugar and dribbled in cream.

"I'll give him a call and leave him a message," she replied. "He's somewhere in England right now at his U.K. office. He likes to visit his employees in person ever so often. I'm sure he'll get back with you one way or another as soon as he gets the message."

The meeting broke up a short time after that. Russell and Courtney went off to wrap up some last minute research while Delores and Stanley remained in the boardroom in discussion.

Justin retired to his room to take the shower he hadn't taken the day before. The room had all the comforts of home. His old home. The shower didn't help him wake up, though. He'd been going on perhaps two hours of sleep a night and it was catching up to him. He wanted to be awake when he spoke with Jeff so perhaps a short nap, as unusual as that would be for him at that time of day, wouldn't be such a bad idea.

Before he laid his head down on the plush pillow he put in that call to Henry. It'd been over an hour and he'd almost forgotten to call him back. If he was lucky he'd still catch him before he went out on patrol. They'd been missing each other's calls for days and Justin needed to know how his children, how all of them at Crater Lake, were doing.

He was lucky and Henry answered his phone on the fifth ring.

"Henry, this is Justin."

"At last. I've been worried about you, son. In fact, I stayed here a little later waiting for your call. I wanted to talk to you. How goes the research?"

"It's going well. We think we have what we need to start the purge. We'll be beginning tests on live dinosaurs as soon as we are provided with some."

Henry laughed. "I wish I could send you some of ours. We have plenty."

"I don't think my new boss will have to go that far to capture a couple of dinosaurs. They've infiltrated New York and we're not that far from there. We're somewhere outside Boston."

Justin went on to catch Henry up on what he'd been doing and what had happened since New York. He asked about Phoebe and Timothy, Ann and Steven, and was glad they were okay.

"They miss you, kiddo. Why don't you call Phoebe later tonight? She really wants to hear from you."

"I'll try, but things are progressing rapidly here now, even more so than last week. We're going into the live trials. If I don't get the time to talk to Phoebe and Timmy, please let them know I love and miss them and will try to get home as soon as I can."

"I'll do that. It sounds as if you've been having yourself some adventure," Henry proclaimed. "We've had some interesting adventures ourselves lately."

"Like what?"

Henry enlightened Justin about the strange helpful monkey-dinosaur and what it had done for them and how it had behaved. "I thought you'd want to know."

"It was jumping around on the tank?"

"Yep. It blew my mind how human the creature behaved and it was actually trying to warn me. Later, I understood what it might have been trying to tell me, that our compound was being attacked again. And thanks to it we made it back in time "

"I'm not surprised. I've seen this change coming for a while. It seems some of the individual species are becoming empathetic to our feelings and have the capacity for emotion. Most of it is destructive, aggressive emotion, but still. It's amazing. It's also frightening."

"Why?"

"Because it shows the rapid rise in their intelligence and sentience and if one of the larger and more aggressive of the breeds gains these attributes–if some haven't already–it could mean more trouble for us. Darn, I wish you could capture the little devil, ship it to me UPS, and let me study it."

"Justin, if there's any way I could do that I would, but the critter is as elusive as mist. It's gone almost before I realize it's been here. I've even thought it might be a trick of my imagination, though I know now that isn't true. Ann has had run ins with it as well. It brought us the cat. And then I saw it, too. It's real."

"Let me know if or when your little buddy makes another visit, would you? This is better than a fiction novel. In the midst of what is going on I need something whimsical to lighten my mood. The escapades of your dinosaur-at-the-window is perfect."

"Don't worry," Henry said, "you'll be the first one I call."

After the phone call Justin collapsed on the bed, shirtless but in his jeans, and hadn't fallen asleep when there was a knock on the door.

It was Delores. "I got a hold of my brother and, lucky us, he got back from England this morning and should be here, oh, any minute."

"Any minute?"

"Soon. He's meeting us in the boardroom. He's on a tight schedule and can only give us an hour. I'll meet you there."

So much for sleep, Justin thought. "I'll be there."

*****

"We need live dinosaurs to try our virus on," Justin stated as he sat across from their patron.

"Fantastic! So you're ready for final testing?" Jeff leveled his gaze at Justin and then Delores. There was excitement in his face as he rubbed his hands together. "I had faith in you, Doctor Maltin. My sister did, too. We were right."

"Thank you. But now we need to see if it'll

work and for that we have to have live subjects."

"Live dinosaurs, hmm." Jeff Smith pondered Justin's request. "That can be arranged. I'll deploy a team of retrieval specialists to bag a couple of the creatures. Any particular kind?"

"An assortment, if possible. We'll need a small specimen, like the velociraptor, and a larger specimen, like the mutated Tyrannosaurus Rex. Perhaps one in between."

Jeff leaned forward and his smile was wicked. "You mean you want me to capture a T-Rex and bring it here?"

"Or somewhere close where we can get to it for the tests. The T-Rex doesn't have to be full grown. A young one will do. It'd be easier to bag and handle."

Delores' stare was boring into him. "We're going to actually infect a live velociraptor, another one, and a Rex? Won't that be…dangerous?"

"Extremely," Justin voiced with a serious mien. "If they were out-in-the-wild, but they'll be sedated beforehand and during the experiments, of course. So the hardest part will be capturing them and getting them to us."

"And not the trials when we have to do the testing on them? Easy for you to say," Delores moaned. "From what you've told me you've been on the front lines fighting and killing the creatures for years. I don't have as much experience, other than with that scary flying reptile that nearly took me home to feed to its young. I didn't do too well with it. To me the dinosaurs seemed unreal until that night." She visibly shuddered. "And that was a nightmare I'll never get over, believe me. You make going out to round the monsters up and cage some so we can stick them with needles and experiment on them sound so…normal."

"Of course, it isn't. But it is necessary. It's the only way we can find out what we need to find out."

Jeff tapped the table with his fist. "Then absolutely we have to do it and we'll find a way. I'll get you your live dinosaurs, Doctor Maltin. The small, medium and the big. You can count on it."

"I could go with the retrieval squad and help round them up?" Justin felt compelled to offer. "I'm a seasoned dinosaur hunter."

"No, positively not," Jeff retorted firmly. "You're too valuable to our research, the trials and the solution we're desperately seeking to risk anything happening to you. You will remain here and I'll take care of obtaining what you need."

Justin didn't argue. He didn't really feel like putting on his dinosaur hunting hat and loading up his MP7 anyway. He had too much left to do before the live tests. He'd only offered because he thought he should. He was relieved Jeff had turned him down. "I will give your retrieval team a few important tips, though, on how to hunt and trap the creatures."

"And, I'm sure, they will be appreciated and heeded," Jeff said.

They talked about the increased dinosaur sightings and encounters around New York and Boston and Justin gave Jeff a rundown on his and his team's findings. Jeff claimed he didn't understand much of it but he was impressed they believed they had what they needed.

It was late afternoon before the meeting was over and Justin finally retired to his room to catch up on his sleep. He knew the next day would be a busy one, especially if the dinosaurs were brought in.

And it turned out he was right. His benefactor kept his word and early the next morning Delores knocked on his door, waking him up. When he opened it to her, she announced cheerfully, "Good morning, Justin. You might want to get dressed and come on down to the boardroom. Breakfast and the other scientists are waiting for you…and there will be three live dinosaurs coming in within the hour. There's been a containment area constructed behind our building here where the specimens will be released into. I thought you might want to be there when they are."

He stretched to push away the remnants of sleep. "I'll be there. And I hope that containment area is strongly fortified."

"Oh, don't worry, it is. Wait until you see it. The biggest, strongest monster in the universe couldn't get out of it."

He almost laughed at that. "You don't know our present day dinosaurs then. I wouldn't put anything past them. Tell your brother to make sure the locks are on the outside and somewhere the cage residents can't possibly get to them."

She left. He closed the door, got dressed and went down to join his team. He couldn't wait to see what Jeff's crack-shot dinosaur hunting posse had rounded up for them.

*****

"Oh my lord." Delores voice was a decibel below a wail. "That's the biggest nastiest creature I've ever seen. And I thought the flying nightmare who snatched me off the roof in New York was scary. This thing is worse."

Justin and his fellow paleontologists were out in the overcast day with their eyes on the three snarling, roaring creatures trapped behind iron cages. Three cages and three dinosaurs. Justin prayed the cages were strong enough to hold them. One cage held an unusually large velociraptor. It had to be six feet tall. Man size. The largest one Justin had seen so far. It crouched in the corner of the twelve by twelve foot enclosure and glared at them, its sleepy ebony eyes full of intelligent savagery and hunger. It hissed and spat at the humans beyond the bars. Delores stepped back a good ways.

"And well you should move back," Justin warned her. "What the velociraptor is spitting is something very much like acid. If it hits your skin it'll leave a nasty burn, or worse, eat away a deep hole in your flesh."

"Oh, lovely," Delores countered sarcastically. "It's bad enough they have fangs and needle-like claws, can jump like kangaroos, now they can toast our skin off, too." She visibly shivered, but moved even further away from the cage to watch the creature from a safer distance. Above the black-tipped clouds were gathering and closing in. There was the scent of rain in the air. Why, Justin thought, was there so much turbulent weather lately? It always seemed to be storming when he had to deal with the dinosaurs. Lucky him.

The second cage held an animal that could have been a gargoyle but it had no wings. A young one. It reminded Justin of their old friend Hugo but if it was one of those creatures it had mutated even further. Its skin was a different dark green leathery texture and it possessed an even longer tail which was now whipping back and forth angrily. The elongated narrow snout was crowded with more dagger-like fangs and the claws on its limbs were just as sharp. Every so often it let out a blood-curdling cry of defiance and stood ramrod straight and tall on its hind legs, making clicking noises or throwing itself against the bars; reopening the bloody wound on its chest. It hadn't come willingly.

The last prison held an immature Tyrannosaurus Rex or what passed as one these days. Practically a baby. It was not much bigger than a man, perhaps six and a half feet. It, too, was a well-developed mutant. Like the ones that had chased Justin at Crater Lake the year before, it had longer, stronger front limbs and would stand on all four as well as two. Its head was smaller enabling it to have better balance. Unlike the other captives it sat proudly in the middle of its cage and observed the humans milling around outside as if they were the prisoners and not it. Its tongue flicked out over and over and it glowered at its captors as if all it wanted to do was eat them. It probably did.

Jeff Smith appeared at Justin's side. "Just so you know, they've already been partially tranquilized so they'll be easier to deal with."

They didn't look tranquilized at all to Justin.

"Smart move. Wow, that was a speedy safari, Mr. Smith. Your men captured every specimen we needed and more in record time. Thank you." Justin gave the man an appreciative nod, not taking his eyes off the Tyrannosaurus Rex. Seeing one so near and not actually trying to eat him was fascinating. He could examine it without the usual terror. He studied it and it glared back at him. He would have done anything to have known what it was thinking. On the other hand, maybe he didn't want to know. The creature flashed him a horrifying look that chilled his blood. *If it could break out from those iron bars it would show him–them–who was the stronger. It would kill them all…if it was free. It would tear their flesh into bloody strips and gobble them up. That's probably what the look meant.*

"Well, my hunters are efficient. When they have a job to do, they get it done swiftly. A team of my best trackers went out last night into the woods about thirty miles from here because there'd been recent reports of dinosaur sightings and bagged these three fellows in no time. They can get us more if we need them because the woods were full of the creatures."

"We most likely will need more. The testing could require it. We have to be sure the poisoned virus can kill all the dinosaurs, not merely selected breeds. But these will do for a start. Thank you." In some ways he'd been hoping the retrieval crew would have bagged one of those peculiar simian beasts so he could have studied it. Since Henry had told him about his and Ann's experiences with the species he was interested in them. If he were at Crater Lake he'd be out actively hunting to trap one so he could study it.

Yet these dinosaurs before him were for testing. They were going to prove or disprove the potency of the virus he'd been thinking about or working on now for years, since Hugo had laid upon his examination table. His research was finally coming full circle.

The Rex had moved to the front of its cage, lowered shrewd eyes in Justin's direction, and the scientist had the unsettling notion the Rex knew what he was thinking; what he was planning to do to it. Doomed lab rat. It snarled at him, showing huge fangs, so much bigger than its size would warrant.

Justin turned to Delores. "We need one of these dinosaurs further and heavily sedated and brought into the main lab. Let's take the smallest one for now, which would be the wingless gargoyle. I can take a look at its wound at the same time. Could you get me one of those tranquilizer guns we had stocked in the lab?"

"I can. Be right back." She was striding towards the building as the clouds above began to trade thunder sounds. A storm was coming soon.

Great. Justin remembered how the dinosaurs hated storms and how they aggravated them.

The Rex began to scream and throw itself against the bars.

It knows what's coming, either the storm or what the scientists were going to do to it. It knows. Clever bastard.

Agitated as well, the other two dinosaurs hissed, screeched and also slammed themselves against their cages.

"Please hurry up, Delores! The inmates are getting restless."

"I'm hurrying," the words drifted to Justin from a distance, almost getting lost in the wind's renewed fury.

Delores wasn't gone long and within minutes Justin had his wingless gargoyle fully sedated and on its way from the cage to the lab. It took three men to load the unconscious beast onto a truck, and then into the building and its new prison.

"What has this thing been eating?" one of the transporters, a bearded lab assistant Justin had met once or twice before, asked, huffing and puffing, as he helped squeeze the sleeping dinosaur into the tight cage. "It's not that big, but it's as heavy as a gun safe." The cage was barely larger than the animal so they could inject the virus into it easier and follow the creature's reactions. Justin had no pity for it as he might have had once. Looking at it only reminded him of the day his wife was taken from him. He hated it. It deserved to die. All the dinosaurs did.

Justin didn't answer but looked at the creature differently. He had a hunch the monster might be a female and might be pregnant, which would account for its unusual heaviness. Female dinosaurs bulked up when they were ready to lay their eggs.

He thanked the men who'd transported the dinosaur and he and the other paleontologists began their work. Justin injected the virus into the slumbering creature and began taking notes which would detail and follow the experiment's progress. He was excited. He'd worked a long time on the serum and wanted to see if it would do what he'd designed it to do. He had perfected ten strains of the serum, hoping to increase their chances of success. One of them should work. He'd given the young gargoyle a shot of one of the final batches they'd produced. He could have gone in sequence but, at the last minute, he decided to try that strain.

"Now what do we do?" Delores was flanked by the other scientists as they stood around the cage, waiting and watching.

"We wait and see what happens. It could take a while." Justin walked away from the dinosaur in the cage and went out the door. Suddenly he had to get away, just for a few minutes. Being that near to a live young gargoyle had overwhelmed him with too many bad memories.

Delores joined him in the hallway. "Are you okay, Justin?" She placed a hand gently on his shoulder as he leaned against the wall, his head bowed. He hid his shaking hands behind his back.

He gazed up at her with bleak eyes. "I think so. Being so close again to a live one is hard. I'm so…weary of dinosaurs; of running, fighting, hiding from and of being afraid of them. It's taken too many years of my life. They're destroying the whole world, and my world in so many ways, not just my wife's death. If this doesn't work I don't know what I'll do."

"It'll work. You're a brilliant scientist and the poison cocktail will do its job. I know it." She seemed more sure of the results than he, but he couldn't help but smile at her belief in him. In that moment he missed his dead wife more than ever.

"I pray you're right. This is all I have. All I got. We need to be able to kill these creatures in larger numbers if we're to win the war."

She smiled back at him. A good friend. "We're going to win the war, don't worry. Mankind hasn't been the top of the food chain all these millennium for nothing. The dinosaurs might have developed brains and cunning in their reincarnation but our brains, our will to survive, are stronger. You'll see. We will triumph."

Nodding, Justin straightened to his full height, inhaling deeply. "We have to. If we don't then the world as we've always known it will cease to exist. That must *not* happen." He rubbed his face, fighting exhaustion and despondency. His night's sleep hadn't been enough to revive him. He wouldn't be getting much more, either, in the next few days. There was so much work to do.

"Tell you what," Delores' voice was soft, "I never ate the breakfast we were provided earlier because I was so busy gathering the last of the information we would be needing for the live trials. I don't think you ate much, either. With the way you're looking, downright peaked, I suggest we take a break and put something warm to eat in our stomachs while we can. It'll be a while before anything happens and one of our team will alert us when it does. You can't keep working this hard and not take better care of yourself. You'll keel over before we can complete the experiments and that won't help our cause. We need you."

That finally got through to Justin. "Then I better have breakfast. Both of us. Let's go."

They made their way to the cafeteria and had their meal, during which time Justin couldn't stop fretting about the dinosaurs in the outside cages, especially the T-Rex. There had been something extra strange about it. Not that there wasn't something odd about all of them these days, yet something about the way it had been glaring at him wouldn't stop bothering him. He'd have to check on the brute, still in the caged enclosure behind the lab, as soon as he had time.

"Let's go back now," he announced. "See what is happening to our patient."

They returned to the lab. The patient was dead.

"Why didn't you tell us the creature had died?" Excited, Justin demanded of Stanley, who was standing around and staring into the cage along with the others.

"It only happened seconds before you came in," Stanley protested in his defense. "Courtney was going to fetch you both. Then you walked in."

Justin opened the cage and with Stanley and Russell's help got the small gargoyle out of the cage and onto the examining table.

It moved a claw an inch. It blinked.

"It's not dead. Not yet." Justin was discouraged. "Why did you think it was?"

"It appeared dead. It ceased breathing." Stanley, with a confused expression on his face, was scrutinizing the dinosaur on the table from a safer distance feet away. "Well, perhaps it wasn't dead."

Justin's stomach lurched. *Or it had died and revived itself. Impossible. Right? Right.*

The monster on the table jerked. Its tail moved slightly.

"Let's do this again. Same strain. A stronger dose this time. Quickly." Justin was handed the syringe and he stabbed the young gargoyle expertly in its neck. It hissed and growled low in its throat, then stopped moving.

After they wrestled the creature into the cage he met Delores' eyes. "I want to get the velociraptor in here. Give it a sizable dose of the first strain. I've realized there's no reason to do one of them at a time."

"I concur. The sooner we get what we need and get it out into the dinosaur population the better. My brother told me earlier when we were outside by the cages there's been an alarming increase in the dinosaur attacks around New York and even here in the outlying woods the last week. My brother has beefed up our security with more guards outside the building, around the grounds and perimeter. The destruction, the human death toll in New York, is staggering. The terrified people are fleeing the city. Things are getting nightmarishly crazy."

"Now that sounds familiar. Dinosaurs attacking, killing, and scared people fleeing the towns and cities. Been there, done that. Can you ask for extra men to get the velociraptor contained and into the lab?"

"Already done. They'll meet us at the cages. But if we're going outside, I'd grab a raincoat, Justin. The storm's hitting now and it's a deluge out there."

Justin struggled into a raincoat and he and his team splashed out into the stormy day. He kept his eyes open as he grew near the cages, an uneasy feeling nagging at him more with every splash.

He heard the beasts long before he saw them.

Both captives were squawking and pressing themselves against the bars as the lightning flashed and the thunder boomed. The T-Rex had murder in its beady eyes. The velociraptor was howling like a mad banshee, spitting incessantly through the bars and its spittle mingled with the raindrops.

So much for them being tranquilized beforehand for transporting. They acted as if they'd had nothing given to them at all.

Of course getting the velociraptor out of its cage was never going to be easy but during a storm it was even trickier. Justin sent the dart into its hide. The thing hissed and fought the drugs until it quieted, dropped to the cage floor and grew still.

The T-Rex shrieked louder as if it was protesting the mistreatment of its prisoner buddy. The water drops fell and the thunder nearly, but not quite, covered the animal's cries.

They had the velociraptor strapped down on the bed of the truck and were on their way towards the building when the T-Rex broke out of its cage and, in a rage, came after them.

At first Justin didn't see the monster advancing through the rain until it rammed the rear of the truck and the vehicle rose, bumped and crashed back down on the earth.

"The Rex is loose and wants our blood," Delores shouted. She crouched inside the truck's bed and pulled the gun from her waist. No one went anywhere without some sort of weapon, without being prepared. She didn't have a chance to use the gun.

"No, don't shoot it with bullets! Give me a tranquilizer gun," Justin yelled and one of the men gave him one.

For a second time the T-Rex butted against the truck. The machine nearly turned over before the driver brought it under control.

That was too damn close. The T-Rex might be a young one but its teeth and claws could kill a man easily enough.

Justin aimed and shot at the creature; asked for and received another tranquilizer gun when he'd emptied the first one into the rogue dinosaur's thick hide. The creature wasn't stopping. It kept coming after them.

"Damn, it's riled up about something," Delores cried above the din. "Oh, oh, it's coming back for more!"

"I guess it doesn't like its buddy here," Justin shouted, "being drugged and taken away." He shot two more times and the T-Rex stumbled and slowly crumped to the ground behind them. The sedatives had finally taken hold.

The truck slowed, circled around and stopped beside the now prone T-Rex.

"We'll return for it as soon as we get this one to the lab." Justin stared down at the creature on the ground. "We'll take both of them there and give them a strong dose of the virus. Let's go. Make it fast. I don't think our friend here will stay down for long." The rain hadn't slowed. It was a curtain that softened all sounds. It made the day seem darkly eerie as if they'd gone far back in time to the primeval days when the original dinosaurs ruled the earth. Justin wouldn't have been surprised if a flock of gargoyles would have appeared in the gray sky and descended on them. The T-Rex, with its cries, had been communicating to something somewhere. They got inside as swiftly as they could.

They deposited the velociraptor in a cage in the lab and then retrieved the T-Rex.

It was a long night, but by morning the three lab dinosaurs had officially passed away. After triple doses of the final serum strain they were dead. Really dead.

The serum, in the end and with the correct strain and dose, worked.

For the next week they collected and injected a long list of dinosaurs all supplied by Smith's hunters. All of the dinosaurs eventually fell victims to the virus. Some took longer than others to die, but they did die.

Now all they had to do was find an efficient way of delivering the virus to dinosaurs everywhere. In some ways, Justin suspected, it would be the most difficult bridge to cross. How do you kill thousands of the predators and not hurt humans in the process? He didn't believe the virus would infect or harm humans, but he wasn't a hundred percent sure. Before they began feeding, injecting or spraying the virus on their prehistoric enemies he had to discover if it would hurt people. There had to be testing.

"Tomorrow," he told Delores and the rest of his

team, "we start human trials. See if we can safely use the virus without killing off the human race as well."

"How are we going to do that?" Lucia's pretty eyes were anxious.

"We test it on humans. We ask for volunteers."

"Let me be the first to volunteer then." Delores was before him and she was serious.

"No," Justin replied too quickly. "I need you–all of my assistants–more than ever from here on in. We have a lot to do. I can't risk any of you getting sick or of losing any of you."

Later, after everyone else had gone to bed, and he and Delores were sitting in the lab discussing what came next, he wasn't surprised when she asked point blank, "Are you worried this cure to our dinosaur troubles might actually be harmful to human beings?"

"Not really. I've already tested it on a human subject and there were no lethal side effects. In fact, there was only minimal side effects. Some diarrhea and dizziness for a couple days until the virus worked its way out of the human's system."

Delores stared at him. "You tried it on yourself, didn't you?"

"I did, though I was fairly sure it wouldn't–"

"Kill you?"

"Why yes. I created the virus to attack a *dinosaur's*, not a human's, nervous system; rendering them paralyzed until their breathing stops. I was pretty sure it would work."

"That was still immensely foolhardy to have used yourself as a lab rat, especially as you are so adamant that I–that any of us here–shouldn't take the virus."

"I admit it was a little foolish." His voice became a whisper. "But at the time I felt I had nothing else to lose. I'd lost enough. I didn't care what happened to me, only that I knew if it was safe for humans."

Delores must have seen into his heart for she laid a hand over his. "You have your children. You have family waiting at Crater Lake who are depending on you to help solve this crisis. You have friends." And here she smiled. "Lots of friends. Justin, you have so much to live for."

Justin thought about what she'd said. "I know you're right. I do have a lot to live for. But it's good to know the serum probably won't hurt human beings, though it needs more testing. I also have to work out what to do with the eggs that have been produced and will be hatching soon because of the coming warm weather. That's another conundrum I haven't addressed as of yet. It won't do us much good if we kill every last juvenile and adult dinosaur but new batches of eggs hatch this spring and repopulate the species. But we're one step closer to our goal. Now on to the next."

"One step closer," she echoed.

That night as Justin lay in bed, for the first time in a long time, he felt encouraged. He felt there might be a future for him, his family–and humanity. And he couldn't wait to begin the human trials.

Chapter 18

The monkey dinosaur was sad that morning and it had been sad now for a long time. It and its mate had had so many eggs ready to hatch and most of them had but the offspring inside were cold and wouldn't move. No matter how much it nudged at them, they refused to get up and walk, play or chase each other as little ones did. It wandered around the cool shadowy cave in and out of caverns that linked them together and mourned over the stillness of the nurseries. There were open and cracked eggs scattered everywhere. No babies or young ones anywhere. Its mate lay in another part of the cavern and refused to get up. Its mate was sad, as well, and wouldn't couple with it any longer.

Things were changing and it didn't understand what was behind it all. It was just one lone creature trying to survive.

The dinosaur exited the cave and bathed in the sunshine. It liked the warmth on its hide. All around, the grass and trees, the flowers, were pushing out of the warming earth with blades, leaves and blooms. It hadn't noticed all the green stuff much its first seasons of living, but noticed it now. It decided it liked the warm times better than the cold ones. The warm times made it want to prance, hop, run through the forest with joy–and hunt. The cold days with that shivery pale stuff on the ground made it want to sleep and do nothing.

When it was sad as it was this day it would

move through the woods and go towards the place where the sticks had their huge wooden cave. It would sneak up behind the cave and watch the sticks inside through holes in the walls with this hard see-through covering across them. It couldn't get in but it could watch. Their antics amused it. They were communicating among themselves by pushing out weird sounds from their mouths and making wavy movements with their limbs. The others of their kind seemed to understand it all, though. Good for them. Strange beings.

It enjoyed observing them and had nothing against them. They intrigued it. They lived in an interesting series of caves filled with all sorts of shiny, glowing objects of unusual colors and shapes. It wondered what some of those things were and why they needed them. It understood the large soft looking things–they took hibernation on them. What would it feel like to rest on one of them…covered with soft hides as they were? It was still trying to find a way to get inside and scamper across all of those objects, touch and try to eat some of them. And those tiny furry creatures that lived with the sticks? It was still wondering what they would taste like. It had a chance to eat one when it had brought it back to the female stick. It should have. It often did things it didn't understand. It knew it was different from the rest of its kind but wasn't sure why. It was curious. It didn't want to fight and kill others of its breed or the sticks. In that way it was more like the sticks than others of its species who only wanted to fight each other, kill and eat each other as well as any other creature in the forest. The sticks didn't eat each other or anyway it didn't think they did.

Ah, the sticks.

That's what it was doing. Going to see the sticks in their funny caves to warn them the big ones were again planning something terrible. It hated the big ones. They were forever squabbling and fighting among themselves. Throwing things at each other. They scared it. It didn't want the sticks to think it was like them. It only wanted to exist free in the forest, raise its young and be left in peace.

The sun felt good on its back as it bounded from tree to tree. For a while it forgot what it had set out to do and ended up swinging from the branches and hiding in the shadows when an angry horde of giant ones stampeded through the brush below it. It hid until they were gone.

It came across another miniature furry creature, not the same as the one it took to the female stick, because this one was a different shape and size. It had long attachments hanging from its head. It didn't make the same sounds as the other furry creature but it tasted delicious and almost filled its empty belly. The dinosaur became further distracted by searching for more of them and not finding any. Which was not surprising as food had disappeared lately from all the woodlands. It was hungry now all the time.

Finally the dinosaur made its way to the sticks' wooden cave and was perched on the ledge gazing in at them as the sun went off to sleep. There was many of the sticks inside and doing what it had no idea. It took note, though, of how they were gentle with each other. They didn't fight with or attempt to eat each other. Chattering at each other with their peculiar noises, they seemed to get along. Funny looking, tall and thin, no tails, pale hides, they sure were weird animals. The smaller sticks were playing with the tiny furry creatures and making sounds that made the dinosaur feel sort of good. Some of the sticks were eating something and the dinosaur's mouth fell open with the hunger it caused. It was so, so hungry!

How was it going to warn them of what was approaching? Then it had a thought. It waited until the tallest of the sticks inside the cave was near the opening–the one who seemed to be their leader–and the dinosaur raked its claws down the clear barrier. The stick looked up and stared at the dinosaur. The stick slowly moved closer.

The dinosaur didn't want to frighten the leader stick but it had to get across what it came there to warn them of. So it puffed itself up as big as it could in imitation of the big ones, put on a snarling vicious face and screamed as loud as it could, jumping up and down…lifting and moving its front limbs high and wide, and then pointing with one claw to something behind it. *They're coming! The big ones are coming to get you and your pack. To attack. Now! Be prepared! Danger! Danger!*

The leader stick jumped away from the opening, shock on its face.

The dinosaur tried one last time, repeated its wild gestures, the strident cry and again pointed into the darkening woods behind it. *They're coming! Be ready!*

Then the oddest thing happened. The leader stick wasn't afraid any longer. It came closer and reached out to the dinosaur on the other side and nodded its head.

Their eyes met and the stick mirrored the nod. *The stick understood. It understood.*

The dinosaur was content. Warning delivered. Then it turned and scampered into the black woods.

It had done its best. It hoped the stick and its companions would survive. It had grown quite fond of them all, even the tiny furry creatures.

Now it had to hunt and find food or it wouldn't survive, either.

Chapter 19

Henry abandoned the window and rejoined Ann in bed. The children were in the corner sleeping, he and Ann had put them down for the night. Miss Kitty Cat was napping between the children and Sasha, eyes at half mast, was purring beside Ann.

"The dinosaur-at-the-window is back again," he whispered to Ann so he wouldn't wake the children. "Or it was."

Ann sat up in bed. "Just now?"

"Yep, just now."

"Honey, you look worried. What is it?" Ann was in her pajamas, her hair tousled. It'd been a long day and she'd retired early. The children, as much as she loved them, did wear her out. She put out a hand and petted the cat, but her eyes never left Henry's face.

"I'm not sure…but I think it was trying again to warn me of something." He settled beside his wife and his fingers massaged his neck. Lately it always ached when he was stressed. She took over and rubbed his neck as he sighed in contentment.

"What do you think it was trying to warn you of?"

"Good question. It was waving its limbs around, gesturing in a way that seemed to describe larger dinosaurs perhaps. It kept pointing behind it." He suddenly realized what the message had been. "*That's it!* The larger dinosaurs are planning to attack again! It wanted to tell us so we would have time to get prepared. We have to be ready."

Henry got up from the bed and put the clothes on he'd taken off before his visitor at the window had interrupted his night.

Ann was slipping out of bed, too. "I guess I had better get up and dressed as well. Any idea when this new attack will come?"

"By the frantic way the dinosaur was behaving, jumping up and down, going nuts and all, I'd guess it must be real soon." Henry had finished dressing. "I'm going to wake the troops, get us organized and strategize as best we can for whatever is coming. Knowing an attack is imminent is a real stroke of luck for us."

Ann was standing by then. She put her arms around him and he kissed her on the lips. "Be careful, husband. We need you."

"I'm always careful, wife." He was heading for the door. The night world outside was silent and sleepy. So, so far, no dinosaurs were at the gates. Not yet anyway. How much time did they have? Not long.

"You can get dressed," he told her, "but you should lay down and try to get some rest while it's still calm outside. You might need it. Let the children sleep, too."

"Will you let me know when the assault begins?" Ann was dressing as she spoke. She kept looking at the windows.

"Oh, I think you'll know without me telling you, but I'll send a ranger in with the news when it starts. Stay away from the windows, though. If that monkey dinosaur can get inside the compound and to us, other less friendly dinosaurs may be able to also. Once the fighting begins I want you to get the children, arm yourself and Phoebe, and go out into the main room. Don't stay in here. There'll be soldiers and rangers to help protect you if worse comes to worse, but you know, in the end, the best protection is your own gun."

"I know that. Phoebe and I will be ready; our guns will be ready."

Henry went out the door, shutting it softly behind him so as not to wake the kids. Outside in the main room it was quiet and dim. Most of the rangers had turned in for the night. They rose early for guard or other duties and retired early. Many of the soldiers, men and women alike, had taken to sleeping outside in tents once more because the weather had warmed up. He found rangers and soldiers lingering in the kitchen area eating late night snacks, drinking coffee or talking.

"We need to get everyone up and ready to fight," Henry broadcasted to the men after he'd walked into the room. "The dinosaurs are about to hit us again. Any minute."

Steven was one of the men drinking coffee at the table. The music man glanced up. "Now, Henry? It's after ten thirty. It's dark out there."

"Now. I don't know exactly when the attack is going to occur but I would bet on first light. That's seven hours from now. We all have work to do. Get everyone up, armed and ready. This could be the biggest battle we've had so far."

"It's quiet outside and none of the guards have spied any unusual activity out there," Steven said.

"How do you know there's going to be an attack?"

The other men, two rangers and a soldier, also looked at Henry, waiting for the answer.

"Our friendly little dinosaur-at-the-window spy paid me a visit and let me know in its own unique miming way it's going to happen."

Steven and some of the other rangers had learned about Henry's dinosaur spy so they knew what he was speaking of. It was almost impossible to keep a secret in the fort with people living so closely together.

The soldier, a young private named Seth Richards, who hadn't heard about it, stared blankly at him. "Your friendly little dinosaur, Sir?"

Henry met Steven's amused gaze. "Do the honors, Steven. Tell him the fairytale while I take care of business and get everyone up and ready to fight."

As Henry left the room with his rangers following him, he could hear Steven telling the story and chuckled. Poor Private Richards. Maybe he'd believe Steven or maybe he wouldn't. Sometimes Henry couldn't even believe it. The dinosaur-at-the-window was an enigma Henry couldn't begin to explain or understand. Why was the little fellow or missy helping them? Weren't they the enemy after all?

The night sped by faster than Henry would have wanted. He hated rousing the sleeping rangers and soldiers so early in the night but he was determined to be ready when the strike came. Captain McDowell didn't ask many questions, she'd known about the dinosaur-at-the-window since it had first appeared to Ann. The difference between Henry's and McDowell's opinion on the helpful dinosaur was McDowell wasn't as sure as Henry that the creature's motives were always benign. She didn't trust the dinosaur.

"It's up to something nefarious, Chief Ranger," she'd say. "Be careful. It could be playing tricks on you. Leading you on until you trust it and then–wham–it sets you up for the big trap and springs it shut."

"Why? It takes a chance every time it sneaks inside our compound and shows itself. I could as easily shoot the damn thing as watch or listen to it. I think it knows that. No, for whatever strange reason, the creature wants to help. It must have some sort of empathy for us. It did find and bring Miss Kitty Cat back to us. It could have eaten the cat but it didn't. The dinosaur must have limited intelligence on some level. Justin maintains it could be a mutant offshoot of one of the dinosaur species that has advanced steps up the evolutionary ladder. I don't care. It's helped us now a couple of times and I'm grateful it has."

The raid came long before sunrise, which shocked Henry. It shocked everyone. The dinosaurs, as seen from the last battles, were no longer afraid of the night. In the dark and chilly pre-dawn the great dinosaurs battered at the stockade and the gates, roaring their fury. They were of the *carcharodontosaur, tyrannosaurus* and *Siats meekerorum* species and a collection of monsters Henry didn't recognize. More new species and all bigger and badder than their predecessors. When would the genetic transformations stop? In a terrifying moment Henry had the bizarre thought: *were these really creatures of the earth or were they from another planet or another solar system?* The idea was too ridiculous to even contemplate. *But where were they all coming from?* He knew why they were attacking…they were starving and had depleted the surrounding food supplies. All that was left on the menu was man.

The smaller primevals were climbing over the barbed wire, oblivious to the ripping of their hides, and trying to slink into the buildings while the larger ones butted the stockade fence and collapsed it in places at times. Keeping the fence up and the intruders out was top priority and the broken sections were propped up or repaired as soon as they went down. The rangers and soldiers fought the dinosaurs with everything they had. The explosion of gunfire, bombs and the dying screams of the creatures transformed the night into a slice of hell.

It was a huge attack force surrounding them. The biggest so far. Henry thought the dinosaurs would never stop coming. It was a miracle they'd had advance notice because the tanks McDowell had deployed on the outside, hidden in the woods and waiting for the attack, came in behind the dinosaur army as a surprise rear assault. It was probably the strategy that saved them. The tanks' guns cut through and killed from behind many of the invaders.

He owed that little monkey dinosaur friend of theirs a hell of a lot.

The battle lasted for three endless, grueling days. Wave after wave of dinosaurs kept coming intermittently and Henry, McDowell and their men kept repelling and slaughtering them. The breaks, sometimes as long as hours, between the assaults allowed the humans to regroup, rest and keep fighting. It was the longest three days of Henry's life and there'd been many other dangerous times to compare it with. At one point, a group of smaller velociraptors somehow got into one of the buildings and killed two rangers and a soldier before they were shot dead.

On the dawning of the fourth day Henry and the other humans in the compound stared out over the land outside the fence protecting them and saw the carcasses rotting in the ground mist. Hundreds and hundreds of dead dinosaurs. In the night some of the remains would disappear. The ones still alive were eating them. If they left the corpses out there long enough perhaps one morning they'd all be gone. No, there were far too many of them to leave them to rot. The humans would have to do yet another battlefield cleanup. Henry didn't look forward to that. He remembered the stench. Ugh.

The humans had lost fighters as well. In the end the death tally was three of Henry's rangers and five of McDowell's soldiers. There'd been twenty wounded. Steven had been one of the injured when a stray bullet, friendly fire, had accidently hit him instead of a dinosaur target. He'd be okay, though, the doctor promised after she'd dug the bullet out of his shoulder. He'd be sore for a while but he'd recover. Until then there'd be no guitar playing for him. The bullet had come a little too close to a major artery; he was lucky to be alive. But the humans had won–again–this time anyway.

This time.

Chapter 20

Scott Patterson was at a loss to explain how one day prehistoric terrors were overrunning the city of Los Angeles, butchering every human or animal they came across and consuming them, and the next day there were none to be seen anywhere. When he'd arrived the week before he expected to be there for a while but now since the invasion had mysteriously ceased he hoped his superiors would release him so he could return to his fiancé and Crater Lake. McDowell had told him they were in the midst of a new fierce battle and could use his expertise. But he had his orders and he couldn't leave until he was given permission.

So he patrolled the shadowed streets of Los Angeles with his men, helping those who needed help and searching for dinosaurs. They didn't find any. The clean-up crews were busy scraping up and carting out the dead carcasses to a place outside the city limits where they'd be burned. It was an on-going operation and would probably last for weeks or months as there were so many to dispose of.

They often found dead human bodies or partial corpses and it tore his heart out, especially when there were young survivors struggling to cope with the deaths or to live without parents or family. The dinosaur attacks had created so many homeless. The larger dinosaurs had not only stomped on or eaten many of the city's inhabitants but had left a huge swath of destruction in their paths. Whole sections of the city were in ruins with demolished buildings, homes, broken water pipes and destructive fires from gas pipe explosions. It reminded Patterson of some of the worst war zones he'd been in during his younger years as a soldier fighting America's overseas wars. It depressed and infuriated him…what the dinosaurs were doing to his world. He dispatched them with gusto whenever he came into contact with them. It wasn't enough. He wanted the earth freed of the monsters once and for all. He was weary of fighting them.

He'd been in contact with Justin off and on since he'd arrived in the city and was encouraged to hear of the scientist's possible success with his dinosaur-killing virus. Last he spoke with the paleontologist Justin had revealed the live trials on the creatures had worked better than he'd hoped for and he was now finishing up the human trials. It wouldn't be long now. The solution to their problems could be accessible within days. Not a minute too soon, either, in Patterson's opinion. Dinosaurs had besieged centers of high human population, charging out from their usual infestations in the backwoods and isolated wildernesses to go on killing sprees.

He and his team were entering a darkened neighborhood on the east side which had lost power days before during an early round of violence. He'd been sent as an answer to a frantic call for help from an assisted living apartment of stranded and frantic seniors who hadn't, for medical or economic reasons, been able to be evacuated when the first calls had gone out. The police and other National

Guard units were busy so Patterson had volunteered to do the rescue mission.

They'd traveled into the area in a convoy of over-sized military jeeps, flanked by tanks, so they could safely bring out the seniors. The streets were deserted, trash and abandoned vehicles were everywhere. Remnants left behind when the populace did their mass exodus weeks before. Their journey through that part of the empty city had been a little spooky because a city without people always was. Except for the noises the convoy made, there was silence. The day had been hot and muggy and so was the night. There was not even a sliver of moon to give them light. There was the scent of rain mingling with the heat but it wasn't supposed to start falling until later that night. He could see sheet lightning, though, flashing against the horizon in a spectacular burst of rainbow colors. Patterson wished the rain would come. Heavens knew, California needed it.

In the far distance against the velvet sky there were also flames and the smoke of yet another out-of-control forest fire a dinosaur skirmish had sparked five days before. It was spreading rapidly and threatened Los Angeles itself. As shorthanded of men to fight the fire as California found itself, with so many military, police and any other able-bodied men they could draft engaged in battling dinosaurs, they were doing their best. Everyone was.

Still…he wondered where their enemy had disappeared to. They couldn't have killed all of them, could they? The dinosaurs must be hiding.

Yet suddenly there were no live dinosaurs anywhere, just the dead ones littering the roads and blocking the alleyways. It was like a scene out of a science fiction or an apocalyptic horror novel. The end of the world–by dinosaurs. His and Henry's adventures fighting dinosaurs at Crater Lake hadn't been anywhere near as creepy as his experiences the last week had been in Los Angeles. Somehow fighting dinosaurs was so much more surreal in the city amidst the trappings of civilization and its shining technology. The creatures seemed almost at home in the deep woods wilderness but in the streets of Los Angeles they were a blasphemy.

"We're almost there, Sir," one of the men driving the jeep shouted out above the vehicle's rumbling and tire crunching. He was army and had been given the duty of squiring Patterson and his team around Los Angeles wherever they were needed.

A sudden wail of something unnatural echoed on the night air and faded slowly away.

"Did you hear that?" One of the other men in the jeep cried out. "Was it close?"

Another voice sent back, "I don't think so."

Another, "Sounds like it's behind us."

One more verbalized, "No…I think it was in front of us somewhere."

Patterson said nothing. He knew better than the others a dinosaur's call could sound as if it originated from one location and actually be coming from another. The monster could be merely feet away or miles. But he wasn't going to tell them that. They were nervous enough. All four of them had their weapons pressed against their chests and their eyes raked the shifting murkiness around them as the jeeps and tanks made their way through the lightless streets.

Once they arrived where they were going Patterson led his men into the dark hallways of the apartment building, flashlight beams showing them the way. They knocked on doors, some they broke open to bring out those handicapped, and ushered the residents from the building and into the waiting vehicles. These were people who hadn't been able to escape the city on their own; people who had no families or healthy friends to help them. Most of them would be transported to hospitals outside the city or nursing homes. They'd be made comfortable and they'd be cared for. There were more than Patterson had been prepared to rescue but they'd cram them all in somehow. No one would be left behind.

It took hours to get the residents out and into the jeeps. Three of the apartments held people who had died, without electricity to run the machines their lives had slipped away, and Patterson insisted on bringing the bodies with them so they could be properly buried.

Yet they saved many and Patterson felt good about the mission. He liked saving people. It was more fun than fighting dinosaurs. The old ones were grateful and thanked him and his men over and over.

Heat lightning was now illuminating the sky. Thunder followed, growing stronger as the minutes sped by. Drops of rain began to dance around them on the road. Patterson knew he had to get his people on their way and safe before the full storm hit. Dinosaurs attacked in the rain, too, and in the downpour were much harder to see coming.

During the operation, every so often, Patterson had thought he heard dinosaur cries haunting the night. As before some sounded far away and some near. He couldn't place what kind of dinosaurs they were because their calls were so distorted. By the final stages of the evacuation the cries had increased so much, seemingly everywhere, he became nervous. He wasn't sure but it sounded as if there were more and they were closer. They were coming.

"Let's hurry this up," he urged his team as the calls multiplied and grew louder.

But time ran out.

Patterson was leaving the building one last time, escorting an elderly lady with a bad hip from the main entrance of the apartment building, when the mob of velociraptors converged on them, blocking their path to the jeeps. There had to be twenty or more. They encircled the two humans and stood there, softly balancing on the balls of their feet, waiting, yet otherwise motionless. At first. Their heads cocked and their eyes glittered malevolently in the blackness around them. They clicked and hissed between themselves in what Patterson thought must be their unique language and made subtle gestures with their front claws. In the pitch-black street they were blurry shadows, small nightmares, but Patterson didn't need to see them clearly to know they were there. He'd seen enough of them in the past to freeze their image forever in his mind.

His men rallied to his aid but before they could get to him the velociraptors pounced.

The old woman screamed as the vicious diminutive monsters closed in on them. Three of them latched onto her, yanked her out of Patterson's arms, and literally tore her apart before his eyes as he raised his weapon and shot at them. They were too quick and he didn't believe many, if any, of his bullets hit dinosaur flesh. He kept firing, shouting for backup. The old woman's screams, mercifully, were brief. Then the dinosaurs dragged her pieces away into the gloom around and between the buildings. He could hear them munching in the shadows.

Patterson felt sick, but his training kicked in and he turned his AK-47 on the remaining raptors as more began to emerge from the darkness and rush the jeeps loaded with old people and his team. It was becoming a massacre. The dinosaurs were spilling over the vehicles grabbing and eating the live humans and the dead. There were so many of the raptors, hundreds, and soon the air was filled with gunfire, screaming, combat and the stink of fresh blood.

One of the larger raptors jumped at him and sent his weapon flying; another knocked him off his feet and he went to the ground. More raptors were closing in. Out of the corner of his eyes he saw some of his men trying to get to him. They were pulled down and torn apart by the dinosaurs.

He grabbed a brick from the street and used it to beat at the raptor biting into his arm. At the same time he kicked another of the dinosaurs that had scrambled over and attached itself to his leg. He cried out in pain.

As if in a nightmare he fought with everything he had. Anything his hands came across on the ground–stones, a pipe, more bricks–around him he used to bash his attackers as he crawled towards his AK-47. Keeping his head down to protect his face, he kept moving. If he didn't reclaim his weapon he'd be dead. He felt teeth in his arm, his leg and heard himself screaming in agony.

It can't end like this, his fevered mind cried. *I can't die like this! Sherman would be so heart-broken. They were going to get married...Henry and Ann would be so sad. He had so much more living to do. Sherman!–*

The night watched but there was nothing it could do. The man fought the dinosaurs and the dinosaurs were winning. It began to rain in earnest and the streets filled with blood flowing with the water.

Chapter 21

Ann was thankful the siege was over. It'd been an excruciating three days and nights with the screeching dinosaur cacophony seeping through the walls day and night and the stream of dead and wounded coming in. Thank goodness they had Emily to doctor the wounded. Without her many more men and women probably would have died. Ann had been by the doctor's side the whole time helping in any way she could by bandaging, or running and fetching things. She'd learned so much about treating the injured. Ann hoped her nurse daughter would have been proud of her. She found herself thinking of her a lot during her nursing of the wounded. Laura, if she would have still been alive, would have been right beside her and the doctor helping the injured, and how they could have used her help.

They'd made a make-shift infirmary in the rear of the main room and Ann spent most of her time there, when she wasn't with the children. It was primitive and they didn't have what they needed to treat the seriously injured. They'd lost three of their patients to death because they hadn't had what they'd needed to save them. It'd been hard but they'd done the best they could. It was strange how when the worst happened humans would rise to the challenge if it meant life or death.

"You should have been a nurse, Ann," Doctor Emily said countless times over the three days as

Ann helped her tend to their patients and Ann, because of Laura, had found her comments ironic.

"I'd thought about that once when I was younger, but I couldn't tolerate the sight of blood. It made me faint every time."

"You didn't faint once."

"I guess I've gotten used to blood being spilled the last seven years. I've seen a lot of it shed in these wars. Now I still get sick to my stomach but I keep myself off the floor."

They might have laughed over that but the wounded were around them moaning and in pain. Death had visited them that night and they were being respectful. Laughter wouldn't have been the acceptable response.

"My daughter was a nurse. A good one," Ann said to Doctor Emily in the makeshift hospital and then told her about Laura, her life and her death. It felt good to talk about her and it helped Ann to do so.

Ann was exhausted as she left the infirmary and made her way to her sanctuary. It was late. Emily had sent her to rest because Ann still hadn't regained all her strength. Her grandchildren were playing with the cats and looked up when she came in.

"Time for bed, you two." She petted the cats one at a time and after hugging the kids she helped them get ready for bed and slide in between the covers. The last days had been hard on them, too. They'd be asleep in minutes. She turned off most of the lights, leaving only one on near her and Henry's bed.

She got ready for sleep. Henry would be a while yet because he was in a meeting with his rangers and the soldiers trying to figure out what to do next, after the clean-up. He'd asked her not to wait up. As tired as she was, she had no trouble following that request.

The windows were inky rectangles crossed with bars and she thought about the mysterious monkey dinosaur and its warning. It had saved them, Henry had sworn. Hmm. But why was it helping them at all? It was after all a dinosaur. It made no sense. And was it still even alive?

She was in her bed and on the brink of sleep when the tapping began. At first she thought she was dreaming, but the taps came again. Louder. Louder. She opened her eyes and they followed the sound.

There was something at the window making the noises.

Her eyes had adjusted to the dim room and, leaving the bed, she went to the window.

A wizened monster face greeted her, peering at her through the glass and bars. It was their friendly dinosaur spy or she assumed it was. She hoped it was. They sort of all looked alike. This time it was staring right at her. It wasn't running away.

"What do you want?" she asked softly as if the creature could understand her. She must be dreaming or loopy, not enough sleep or something.

The thing continued to stare at her, tilting its head. Its eyes, glassy lizard eyes, widened. It was trying to tell her something…but what? Now that she saw it up close she realized it had, as she and

Henry had noted before, a somewhat monkey-looking face. The color of its skin, which looked a bit like fur, but wasn't, was a monkey color. Maybe it was the shape of its face? She wasn't sure. But it did look simian. And its expressions and manner seemed like an ape's as well. It wasn't very big. How big was hard to tell as it crouched on the ledge outside, crammed onto the narrow space. It began to make a faint noise deep in its throat. A sort of rumbling purr accompanied with a series of clicks. It was a sorrowful sound. It became louder.

One of the children moaned in their sleep and Ann glanced at their beds to see if they were watching, if they were awake. They weren't. Phoebe was dreaming again. She often did that. It reminded Ann of Laura. Laura always had such vivid dreams when she'd been a child and would often wake her or Henry up for comfort when they scared her. The child settled down and her breathing resumed its evenness. Good, she was asleep again.

Ann's attention returned to the window monster. It was making a strange face. She didn't have a clue what was it trying to express to her.

Again she asked, "What do you want? Why are you here?" *Oh, she must be losing her mind. It was an animal. It couldn't understand her as she couldn't understand it.*

In answer her visitor offered something to her it'd had in its claws. It shoved it against the window. Ann couldn't tell what it was. It looked like a tiny bundle of rags with white specks over it. The noise the little dinosaur had been making stopped. It put the small bundle on the ledge to its right and jumped off. It was gone.

What had it left behind on the outside windowsill for them? She'd have to wait until Henry returned and ask him to retrieve it because no matter how she tried to open the window and search her fingers out on the ledge for what had been left, she couldn't reach it. It was too far to the right.

She didn't have long to wait. She returned to bed but was too curious, too excited over the visitation and what had been left behind to sleep.

Twenty minutes or so later she was telling her husband about the monkey dinosaur's social call. He went to the window and tried to retrieve the object, yet it was also beyond his reach.

"What do you think it is?" Ann questioned as he was squinting at it.

"I have no idea. It's too dark outside to see." He grabbed a flashlight from the nightstand and let its light zero onto the item. "I still can't see it that well." But she thought he was lying. He probably had his suspicions and didn't want to say what they were to her. Not yet anyway.

"I'm going outside," he said. "I'll get it."

She was watching out the window when Henry appeared framed in it and claimed the article. His actions were hurried and she knew he didn't want to stay outside for long. If one dinosaur could sneak in so might others.

"Well," she stated when Henry was standing in front of her with it, wrapped in his jacket, in his arms. "What is it?"

"I think it's a baby dinosaur." They were both keeping their voices down so they wouldn't wake the children.

"Alive?" She looked at the jacket.

"No. It's dead. Cold stone dead."

He placed the bundle with its tender burden on the bed and opened the jacket. Ann couldn't help but stare at what was there. "Oh, my. It does look like a dead baby dinosaur. What are all those white things? Why, they look like egg shells."

"They are. This dinosaur was most likely dead on arrival." Henry covered the remains. "This was its egg. But there are other pieces of egg shell which don't belong to this particular dead one."

"What does that mean?" And then she got it. "Our dinosaur-at-the-window is trying to tell us something."

"Their young are being born dead," Henry replied somberly. "How interesting."

Ann was confused. "Why would it want us to know that?"

"Now *that* I don't know either. Maybe it has come to believe we're its friends or something. Maybe it wanted to share its grief. Or it's lonely. Who knows. It's very odd. I think Justin was right. Some of these dinosaurs are developing empathy and human traits and that is astonishing. This particular dinosaur has somehow bonded with us." He shrugged and tried to smile at her but the last few days had left its scars. His face was lined with exhaustion and sorrow. He'd lost men and friends and so had she. They were both tired and heartsick. The war had been going on for far too long.

He glanced down at the dead dinosaur wrapped in the jacket. "I'm going to call Justin before I go to bed and tell him what our little friend left us. See if he wants to have someone fly out and collect it so he can examine it. It might make more sense to him. Might even provide him with some of the answers he's been looking for. Something is going on in the dinosaur world, besides the war they're waging against us, and he would probably want to know about it. And I'll catch him up on what has been happening here. Let him know his children are safe and doing as well as the circumstances will let them."

"You do that. Call him, that is, and get it over with. Because afterwards we both need to get some rest."

"As soon as I speak to Justin I'll rest." Henry had lifted the dinosaur and the jacket off their bed and laid it on a table in the corner of the room. "You go on to bed, honey. I'll join you soon," he said. "I'm going into the meeting room to make the call so I don't disturb you or the children. I'll be back as soon as I'm done." He laid a kiss on her cheek and left the room.

Ann slipped into bed, leaving the night table lamp on so Henry could find his way when he came back, and pulled up the covers. Her eyes kept wandering to the jacket in the corner. She shivered as she had a strange premonition.

Something significant is going on in the dinosaur world. Something that might yet save the human race and end the dinosaur wars. And wouldn't it be truly wonderful if their troubles might finally be coming to an end–and if the world of humans were saved?

As she gazed at the bundle in the corner she prayed. *Please, please let this nightmare be over.*

*****

Henry tried to reach Justin three times and on the third attempt Justin answered.

"Henry! I'm so glad you've called. I've been trying to reach you for days. I was really getting worried. I was ready to send someone out there to see what was wrong," Justin claimed the second Henry came on the line.

"Sorry, son, but we've been pretty busy here fending off another big assault."

There was instant concern in the younger man's voice. "Is everyone all right? Are you and Ann, Phoebe and Timothy okay?"

"Yes, we're okay or as okay as we can be. It's been a hard couple of days. But it's over now and we won. This time again anyway."

Over the line Henry heard Justin release a sigh.

"But," Henry continued, "our friend Steven was wounded during the fight. No, no, he's fine other than a bullet to the shoulder–a bullet from a ranger's gun actually. Friendly fire unfortunately. Emily took care of him and he's recovering nicely. He fought bravely against the dinosaurs and slew a mess of them. He's turned out to be a great dinosaur fighter. You taught him well."

Then they talked about the battle Henry, his rangers and the soldiers had gone through. Henry spoke about their losses and their hard fought for victory, how the monkey dinosaur had forewarned them before the attack came and, lastly, the sad gift it had left that night. "I thought you might like to see the dead baby dinosaur so I haven't disposed of it."

"Yes," Justin's voice was excited, "I'd like to examine the remains and the egg shells. I'll see if I can get my benefactor, Mr. Smith, to fly someone in to you to pick it up. Hang on to it until that happens."

"I will do that."

"How is Ann feeling these days? She was still fairly weak when I left."

"She's been better lately and the doctor believes her cancer might be in remission. As soon as it's deemed safe enough she wants Ann to travel with her to the Nampa hospital for a full blood work-up and tests to see what stage the cancer is in now. But Ann seems more like her old self every day and I'm grateful for that. She claims she needs her energy to take care of the children. She's been home-schooling Phoebe as best she can when she can. The girl sure does like to read, doesn't she?"

"She does. I was the same way as a child. I loved reading. I could go anywhere, do anything in the world just by reading about it."

Henry caught his son-in-law up on what his children had been doing. "Timothy is really getting around these days. He carries Miss Kitty Cat with him everywhere. The cat loves him. They sleep together every night. And Phoebe, as always, has been a great help to her grandmother and to everyone here. Ann depends so much on her. They're great kids. They miss you. You should call Phoebe soon. She asks about you all the time."

"I'll call her. Tell her I miss her, Timothy, too,

and hopefully I'll see them soon."

"How is your dinosaur-killing vaccine coming?" Henry finally got around to asking.

"It's close to being ready. We know now it works. It kills across all the varieties, sizes and individual breeds. All we have to do is make sure they ingest, inhale or get it into their bloodstreams somehow. We're preparing the dispersion methods now," Justin explained. "That's been the difficult part."

"So how will you get it delivered to the dinosaurs?"

"We're looking at introducing it into the water supply where the dinosaurs have their heaviest populations such as Crater Lake and other state and federal parks and any other wilderness concentrations. We'll have crop-dusting aircraft dropping smog bombs of the killing agent over the cities that are infested like New York and Los Angeles. We're going to inject captured dinosaurs with it and reintroduce them into the population so they can infect others of their kind. Put out dead tainted carcasses where hungry dinosaurs will feed on them and therefore infect themselves. Anywhere there are dinosaurs we will get the virus to them.

"One of the greatest thing we've discovered is the virus won't affect or harm humans in any capacity. That was essential. I didn't want to exterminate half our human population along with the dinosaurs." Justin sounded weary but optimistic.

"You did it, son. I'm proud of you. I knew you could.

"You know, speaking of dinosaur carcasses, we

have an abundance of them here outside the walls, rotting away in the sun. We killed a massive number of our prehistoric nemeses the last three days and we haven't begun to clear them out yet. The surviving dinosaurs are already feasting on them so it would be a perfect opportunity to spread the virus in that manner here and now."

"That's an excellent idea. We've just turned out our first large batch of the liquid virus in handy hypodermics both for close combat and to load into tranquilizer guns. All you'll have to do is inject some of the dead carcasses. Ravenous dinosaurs will do the rest. I'll make sure you receive one of our first shipments."

"When would that be? Those dead beasts are being dragged away and devoured even as we speak. The live dinosaurs are hungry."

"Tomorrow," Justin said. "They can deliver the virus and pick up the dead baby dinosaur at the same time. I really am anxious to study that little fellow and see what's going on, if anything. You know, your friendly monkey-dino might not have had a logical reason to present it to you. It could have merely been an offering of some sort."

"Yeah, son, who knows the minds of these creatures or why they do some of the things they do. Nothing surprises me anymore with them. So you have any idea when you might be coming back here? The kids ask that every day and I'd like to be able to tell them something."

"I'm sorry, Henry. I don't know when I'll be back. There's so much work yet to do here. We have to keep producing the serum and get it shipped out across the globe. I'm coordinating with other scientists on how they can mass produce it. In the next few days I'm traveling to New York and then Los Angeles to help kick start the conveyor belt. I miss my children and all of you but you and I both know destroying these dinosaurs has got to be our top priority for now. Is it all right I'm not there? Do you need me to come home? If you do I'll turn over my findings to others and return."

"No, you are exactly where you should be. Don't worry about us. We have everything under control. The kids are fine. You do what you have to do, we'll do what we have to do, and then come back to us." Henry wasn't about to demand his son-in-law return when the world urgently needed saving and Justin had the answers.

They finished their conversation and said goodnight. Henry's body craved sleep and a bed and he was going to give it what it wanted.

He stopped in the restroom and cleaned up, took a quick shower. He, as everyone else at headquarters, used the large bathroom in the corner of the main building. Another feature he'd insisted on when headquarters had been rebuilt after the first dinosaur debacle years before was a bathroom of many stalls, basins and showers. Since they'd been living in the building he was so glad he'd had the foresight to have it built even though he'd had to fight Superintendent Sorrelson over it. The man had always been so tight with expenses, but that had been another time; another world.

Poor Sorrelson. The man had died the year before in a car accident while he'd been running from a dinosaur on a rainy mountain road. Henry almost missed him. The park hadn't had time to replace the man before the dinosaur problems had escalated again. He wondered if there would ever be another superintendent. Only if the world became sane again, he thought.

In their room Ann was sleeping so he carefully crawled in beside her.

And as his wife before him, his eyes went to the bundle in the corner holding the remains of a mystery. What had happened to the baby dinosaur and why had the monkey-dino brought it to them? More mysteries.

As usual, he slept restlessly, his senses alert to any strange noises in the night. If something happened he had to be able to leap out of bed, dress, arm himself and be out the door in minutes. They all did. Their lives depended on it.

Please, he vexed, no more dinosaur attacks. Not tonight. Not tomorrow. *They needed to rest for a while. They sorely needed it.*

*****

The dinosaur had revisited the opening into the sticks cave before the night was over. It had been there before but could no longer remember why. It continuously forgot what it had done before. That didn't bother it. There were always things to do and places to go to. But now it was dark inside their cave and it couldn't see them. Were they in there or had they moved to another part of their lair? It sat on the ledge peeking in for a long time. Waiting. It jumped down and ran around to another opening. That one was dark, too. The next one was as well.

Hmm, all the sticks must be hibernating. There was nothing to see here.

It was agitated so much of the time lately. Sometimes it ran through the trees until it dropped. The other beasts were behaving crazily, too, attacking each other or throwing themselves against large hard things or into deep pits in the earth. It would hear their cries at night.

It left the ledge and bounded into the woods, working its way to the food source it had been feasting on all night. Its food was others of its kind, but cold now; they no longer moved or hunted. So it was acceptable to eat them. For the first time in a long time its belly was full and it felt energy coursing through its body. It felt stronger.

The dinosaur observed others gorging, as it had done earlier, in the killing field. They'd been starving, yet this night they weren't. They'd feed under the cover of darkness until they were full and then they'd hide in the woods. Fight among themselves.

There was enough food outside the sticks cave to feed many of his brethren for a long time.

It ate until its belly was so extended it could barely move, much less run. It remembered its mate and tore off a hunk of cold meat to take home. It dragged it to its lair but its mate wasn't waiting.

The dinosaur searched the cave and found its mate, not breathing and cold.

It began to wail and did so until the sun rose.

Chapter 22

Justin gazed out over New York City as the airplane tipped its wing, circled around and began its approach to the airport. The shadows of evening, like lacy clouds, were drifting across the sky trying to catch up with the aircraft. Justin was dismayed at the destruction beneath him. The Big Apple had changed in the short time since Delores and he had left. There were barricades along the outskirts of the city jammed with soldiers and police, tanks and helicopters. He could actually see some of the skirmishes occurring below him in real time. It was frightening. Dinosaurs dashing between tall buildings and skyscrapers; hiding behind movie theaters and scurrying under bridges. There were soldiers fighting the monsters in the highways and men in uniforms shooting at dinosaurs from trucks and tanks. The Brooklyn Bridge was covered in stalled and wrecked vehicles and marauding primevals skulked along its span. The other bridges he could see weren't faring any better. The dinosaurs were everywhere. It was like watching a monster movie from ten-thousand feet.

The plane cruised over Central Park and Justin could barely believe his eyes. The park was alive with herds of prehistoric creatures prowling and hunting and being hunted. He could see the pond and it seemed to be full of swimming creatures. There were dinosaurs on the Central Park Bridge and converging around the conservatory. The carousel was overrun and the zoo appeared to be in chaos. Somehow the dinosaurs had gotten inside and he had little doubt most of the zoo's normal inhabitants had already become the larger predators' meals, a veritable buffet. In different sections of the park, from his great height above, he could see tiny animals fleeing from bigger ones. He shook his head. It looked all too familiar. The Big Apple had become Crater Lake.

New Yorkers were scared and had been fleeing the city for weeks as the dinosaurs encroached further and further into the land and took more of what didn't belong to them.

"I hope our plan works," Delores' voice reached him from the seat behind him. "The city below looks like a war zone. I can't believe it's gotten this bad. I feel as if I'm in one of those Jurassic Park movies. Remember that scene where the main characters are flying to the island in the helicopter and looking down on everything, before all the running, munching and squishing humans began?"

"Vaguely." It'd been a long time since Justin had seen the movies. "I'm afraid I don't need to watch movies about dinosaurs. My life has *been* those movies the last seven years."

Delores' chuckle was subdued. "This will be the second big city test area for your dinosaur serum. Let's pray it works. What I can see down below us is a mess. I can't imagine being a New Yorker on the ground trying to escape from those beasts. The people are probably terrified."

"They probably are." Justin couldn't take his eyes off the pandemonium below. Watching it he was bombarded with images of him and Henry, him and Laura, him and the rangers or soldiers, running from the beasts at Crater Lake in a car, a tank or a helicopter. He squirmed in his seat at the pictures in his mind. When the awful memory of the gargoyle snatching Laura into the sky came, he shoved it forcibly away. *Don't think about that now. You've got work to do. Keep your head. Don't cry.*

"They say Los Angeles is even worse off," Delores murmured as the plane begin to descend. "The city is in flames and whole neighborhoods have been abandoned. The fighting, my brother reported last time we spoke on the phone, is widespread and brutal."

"I have a friend who's out there fighting now. Scott Patterson. He's some sort of military consultant who used to work for the F.B.I. No one has heard anything from him in days. I hope he's okay."

"I'm sure he is. Communication is touch and go from that region right now. You'll hear from him soon, most likely. Did that batch of serum go out to Los Angeles this morning?"

"I made sure of it. They said the planes were ready to disperse it so," Justin glanced at his wristwatch, "I imagine by now it's been dropped over the city wherever it was needed. Your brother promised me he'd let us know how well it worked as soon as the reports come in. They're keeping him posted."

"He'll let us know. I haven't heard from him in a couple of hours myself but I expect to see him when we arrive at his New York office. He'll catch us up then."

"I can't wait," Justin said. "What the serum does in Los Angeles and here in New York will tell the tale, so to speak."

He and his team had strenuously tested the serum on human volunteers–some who had been paid handsomely to go through the trials and some who had lost family members to the dinosaur scourge and only wanted to help in any way they could–and Justin had been overjoyed when none, not one, of the test subjects fell ill, except for the minimal side-effects like he had suffered. He would have liked to extend the testing but since time was of the essence the testing continued but Justin moved forward with dispatching the vaccine. People were dying every minute, towns and cities were being destroyed, and there was no time left for niceties such as prolonged testing.

He'd had a consignment of the vaccine flown to Henry and in return had received a tiny dinosaur corpse in a Tupperware. He'd studied the lifeless creature and had tentatively sleuthed out what might have caused its demise. It was the same contamination he'd seen years before in the dinosaur pit when they'd rescued Ellie Stanton from the gargoyles. He'd often questioned why he hadn't seen other signs of the illness in the last year. So he wasn't surprised when he dissected the dead baby dinosaur and discovered some of the same infectious signposts as back then. It was a convenient discovery. It meant besides the serum they would use to decimate the dinosaur population perhaps nature would be helping to get rid of the creatures as well. They could use all the help they could get.

He'd spoken with Henry earlier in the afternoon and told him what he thought. "They were possibly born alive with the toxicity but died soon after. Otherwise, they couldn't have hatched."

"That's encouraging news. Let's hope the toxicity, as you call it, is widespread and affects more of the newborns. If fewer are born that would help us, too.

"And I'm happy to inform you," Henry reported, "it appears the tainted carcasses here are doing their job. We've seen dinosaurs feeding on the dead around headquarters and later on patrol found them expired across the park. Your dinosaur-killing virus seems to be working. For the first time in a long time, son, I feel encouraged. I think we've turned the corner and soon our world will again belong to us. I'm so proud of you…and grateful. You've worked so hard for so long and I hope the world appreciates what you've done and what you've sacrificed for it."

"What we have all sacrificed," Justin reminded him. "I haven't done any of this alone. What I learned from you and the people back at Crater Lake has been put to good use. And my team of scientists here were instrumental in producing and perfecting the final serum and helping to perfect the dispersal methods."

"Now what?" Henry had asked.

"Later today my team and I are flying to New York where we'll establish another lab and when ready the military will begin crop-dusting the fog version of the solution onto the dinosaur herds loose in the city. Packs of them have been sighted outside and now they're sneaking in. We perfected the serum just in time."

And here he was, flying into New York. Below him he continued watching the dinosaurs milling around on and in the city's limits and pointed them out to his colleagues sitting around him. Half of the group, Russell, Stanley and Delores, had volunteered to accompany him and help. He'd need every one and more to do what had to be done. The other paleontologists he had left behind to continue producing what they'd need and making sure it was shipped off to the locations that needed it.

"There's so many of them. The dinosaurs, I mean. I knew they were advancing on the city but can't believe how many there are and that they're already inside. Those poor people." Delores was watching out the window, her head inclined against the glass. She turned and looked at Justin. "Are we safe up here?"

"I don't think anywhere is safe any longer. The flying ones, the gargoyles, have been sighted over many of the major cities and, as we both know well, they're in New York, too."

Delores face was a white oval in the faint light. "So we're flying on a wing and a prayer, hey? Any minute something huge with wings and teeth could swoop in on us and knock us out of the sky?"

"It's a chance we as well as others who fly these days have to take. Our pilot was warned to keep his eyes open for anything…unusual in the skies around us, and take evasive action if attacked. From what I understand he was military and has flown in combat situations so he knows how to handle the plane if we're threatened."

"Let's hope that will be enough," Delores retorted, her eyes anxious. "The way I see it is if a flock of normal sized birds can bring down an airplane, what would a flock of those flying nightmares do to one?"

Justin didn't answer her because he didn't want to scare her more than she was. He'd seen up close what gargoyles could do to an aircraft. Many times. If one or more came after them then only a prayer would save them–and perhaps not even that.

They were fortunate, they landed without incident and were escorted to another one of Delores' brother's buildings, defended by armed guards and surrounded by tall metal fences topped with sharp electrified spikes. Any dinosaur attempting to climb in would have a field of daggers to crawl over and a hot butt. Of course, there were still the airborne varieties and no fences could keep them out.

"How much real estate does your brother own anyway?" Justin was impressed at the accommodations they were given and the security they'd been provided as they were ushered into the lush steel and glass building. Everything was first class. Expensive. Shiny desk tops, stone floors and elegant furniture. The smell of money was everywhere.

Justin was simply happy to be out of the sky and somewhere safe or as safe as anywhere could be these days.

The lab they were taken to was as lavishly equipped as the one outside Boston. Better. They had everything–and more–they needed. Delores' brother had even had the generous foresight to have a catered lunch ready for them. The man thought of everything.

Justin and his crew were introduced to a collective of top scientists and people who would be aiding them in preparing the serum to ship around the world and then afterwards he was too busy to think any further about anything but the job at hand.

Much later that night as he was settling into the plush room he'd been given, he was joined by Delores and her brother. The other scientists had retired, but Justin had wanted to do a final check on some of the equipment that had been delivered so he arrived at his room late. It was after one in the morning and his body felt every hour he'd been awake. He collapsed on the bed, clothes and all, then someone knocked. This waking him up just as he was about to get some sleep was becoming an annoying habit.

He opened the door and Delores and her brother, Jeff Smith, were behind it.

"I know it's late, Doctor Maltin, but I just flew in and I have to leave again early so I thought I'd drop by and let you know what's been going on."

Justin perked up. If Jeff knew, he was eager to hear about how the serum had worked in Los Angeles.

"Sure, boss, come on in. I wasn't sleeping…yet. Hi again Delores. Didn't I just see you?"

"Very funny."

He offered a smile to his colleague as she moved past him into the room. They'd become closer friends since the incident with the gargoyle last time they'd been in New York and their work together. There were times he had the suspicion it could be more than that someday. Someday. He suspected Delores was falling in love with him, again, but this time for him it was too soon. His heart was still full of Laura. But friends were always welcome and she'd become a good one.

"What's up?" He directed the question to Jeff.

"I thought you'd like to know Mission Los Angeles so far seems to be a huge success." The man appeared happy and relieved. "They've been spraying the vaccine over the city now for hours and are beginning to see results. Dinosaurs are dropping all over. The military is moving in now to start clearing them out. The mayor is so grateful to us, to you and your scientists for what you've done. He told me to thank you again for him and the people of Los Angeles."

Justin was so excited all thought of sleep fled. "That's great news."

"You were concerned, even after the tests, it wouldn't work, weren't you?" Delores, as usual, could almost read his mind. Her eyes were soft. She had to be tired, too, yet she was still going. She sat down at the table the suite provided. Her body wilted in the chair but she kept smiling at him.

He caught the knowing smile Smith was giving both of them. He probably thought they were involved. Well, nothing he could do about that even if it wasn't true. Let the man think what he wanted to. Delores would set him straight.

"The helicopters are docking as we speak, ready to take on their precious cargo. Some of the choppers are on the roof and more are on the grounds around us. Are we ready to load them up for dousing New York?" Smith asked, lowering himself into a chair beside his sister. As always, he was dressed in an expensive suit and looked rested. The man never seemed to tire, though, as far as Justin could see, he was always on the go and flying somewhere.

"First thing tomorrow morning. We're still waiting for the final shipment of vaccine from home base. It should come in as soon as it's light." It was too dangerous to fly the vaccine at night with gargoyles and other airborne dinosaurs haunting the skies. They couldn't afford to lose any of it in an airplane crash; that wouldn't efficiently disperse it.

"How's your father-in-law doing with the shipment you sent him to Crater Lake?" Jeff locked eyes with him.

"It's working beautifully he says. The live dinosaurs are coming in to feed on the deceased ones left after the last battle and it's effectively poisoning them. They're finding corpses littered all over the park on their recent tank reconnaissances. My father-in-law will keep us apprised as they carry on their patrols."

"Excellent!" Jeff shook his fist in the air, his eyes shining. "I was hoping we'd have these favorable results. I can't wait until we begin fumigating New York and other endangered cities after that. It can't come too soon."

"We're producing the serum as fast as we can," Delores interjected. "Our scientist friends in England, China and India have set up similar labs and we've given them the formulas to duplicate. They should be delivering their treatments within a week or so."

"How is the situation worldwide then?" Justin asked. Patterson had kept him appraised of the dinosaur epidemic over the globe the last year but he hadn't heard from the man in days, which wasn't like him. The ex-agent must be too busy fighting dinosaurs in Los Angeles to stay in contact. Justin made a mental note that next time he talked to Henry to ask him if he'd heard from Patterson lately.

"This is no surprise, it's gotten worse. We have had reports from almost every country of either sightings or infestations. Some worse than others. World leaders, after hearing of your vaccine are clamoring for its formulas. We're sending them out now as fast as we can, Doctor Maltin. When this is all over, you'll probably be given the Noble Peace Prize for saving the planet. You'll be famous and your future will be secured."

"I don't care about that," Justin's voice was flat, "I just want to make the planet safe for humans again. I've lost too many people I care about and loved to these prehistoric anachronisms and I don't want any more people to go through what I've gone through if I can help them. I couldn't care less about fame and fortune." And he meant it.

Delores flashed him an approving look. "But I'd be proud of you if you won a Noble Peace Prize. I could brag about you to everyone."

"Hey, wait a minute, esteemed colleague, you'd be getting your own Noble Peace Prize; you and the rest of our team. I couldn't have done this without all of you. And your brother."

Jeff grinned.

"Ah, you're only being modest." She smiled that gentle smile he was beginning to look for again at him. "You are the one who was out in the field, took the losses and faced the dangers, knew what was needed, and created the serum. We only helped you finish it and work on the distribution channels."

"Doesn't matter." Justin was firm. "If I get accolades, cash and prizes, we all do."

"Not only is he an incredibly smart genius, brother," Delores stated, "he's a humble one. Which is extremely rare in our egotistical profession and in the world."

"On that I agree." Jeff was beaming at both of them.

"Oh," Justin ignored the compliments, and addressed his next words to Delores' brother, "and another recent development, and I hope a very optimistic one for humanity, is my father-in-law claims he believes some or all new dinosaur hatchlings are expiring soon after birth. The eggs hatch and the baby dinosaurs, for some unknown reason, though I've seen the infection causing it before, don't make it."

"More great news. We're going to beat this plague of dinosaurs yet." Jeff was already on his feet, ready to sprint out the door. Justin had never seen a man more on the move than he was. He was like a laser beam, here one moment and gone the next.

"I can't stay," Jeff excused himself. "I'm sure you understand. My plane is waiting for me on the tarmac. I have a summit meeting in Iceland tomorrow. Mainly business stuff but there will be opportunities for me to push your vaccine. So much to do. So little time. Oh, and I'm been meeting with authorities from other U.S. cities. Have you heard about the attack on St. Louis?"

"No." Now Justin sat down, a sinking feeling in his stomach, and looked up at Smith. "What happened?" The gloom in Delores' face, though, told him before he had the answer.

"Dinosaurs rioted through downtown St. Louis, stomping everything in sight, crushing cars and humans. It must have taken people by surprise because they were unprepared, as most cities being attacked, and there were a lot of injuries and deaths. Heck, some of the larger bastards like the Carcharodontosaurus and tyrannosaurs species shoved against the St. Louis Arch and nearly brought it down. If the army wouldn't have moved in when they did, the Arch would have been knocked over into the Mississippi River in pieces. They nicked and battered it up pretty good, though."

Justin didn't know what to say. Dinosaurs in the big cities were still shocking to him. For a moment as Smith described the attack he had this vivid image of a mob of rabid dinosaurs rampaging through the wide streets of the city past Union Station and the Old Courthouse; tossing people, cars and SUVs wildly into the air. It was a mind picture which almost made him laugh…but it was no laughing matter. People were dying. Property was being bulldozed and trampled by dinosaur feet. Justin realized at his inappropriate reaction his heart and soul must be slightly damaged. He'd been fighting monsters for too long.

Finally, knowing he had to say something, he pulled himself together. "That's terrible. I've been to St. Louis many times for conferences. And I had a friend I often visited who lived there. He had an apartment on the riverfront. We could see the Arch and Laclede's Landing from his living room windows. The Arch is a remarkable structure. It's shiny silver in the sun, hauntingly beautiful in the morning mist and it glows in the golden sunsets. I hope the damage to it and the city isn't too bad."

"Bad enough. We have enough serum to send them?" Jeff was now standing by the door.

"Not yet."

"We need to make more pronto. St. Louis isn't the only city the monsters are rapidly advancing into. Las Vegas is being invaded, as well. And others."

"We'll work as quickly as we can. I promise you."

"That's all I can ask, Doctor Maltin. If you need anything Delores can track me down anywhere. She has my itinerary. I'll say goodnight and goodbye now."

"Goodnight, Sir."

The two men shook hands and after giving his sister a perfunctory hug when she stood up, their benefactor slipped out of the room.

"Now St. Louis and Las Vegas." Delores was shaking her head. "Where the hell are they *all* coming from, Justin? If I didn't know my brother so well I would say he was pulling our legs. But he never kids about serious matters, or not to me anyway. Why are the dinosaurs attacking so many places all at once? The cities? If they've been hiding and breeding for decades, as you believe, why the major offensive now?"

"I've been wondering the same thing since Henry and I first tracked Godzilla down on the lake. I have some scientific hypotheses and explanations but beneath all that I have nothing. It's just another mystery."

"You ever think it's God's way of telling us we've failed…that humans have messed up His beautiful planet beyond forgiveness and this is our cataclysmic event? The human race will be wiped out and the dinosaurs will finally inherit the earth if we can't rise up, work together, and find a way to stop them?"

"Not if I–we–can help it. Don't count humans out yet. We've triumphed over millennia of adversity and I'm positive we will overcome this tribulation as well. The earth will always be ours. God willing." Justin gave her a brave grin.

"All right, you optimistic person you, on that note I will take my leave and let you get some sleep. You look like you need it."

"I do."

But Justin was taken off guard when Delores walked over and placed a gentle kiss on his cheek.

"What was that for?"

"No," she shook her head, "don't read anything in that other than I think you're an amazing man and I'm happy to be your friend. You've been working so hard I thought you needed a kiss. That's all. Now get some rest."

The door closed behind her and Justin, still wondering about the kiss, collapsed on the bed and was asleep within minutes.

Chapter 23

"You're going out on patrol again today?" Ann asked as she watched him sling his AK-47 over his shoulder.

"Yep. I think we're going to travel up to and around the rim today; check on the Lodge and see how Norma and Jimmy are doing. But I'm going to get some breakfast first. McDowell and Steven are meeting me in the main conference room at eight."

"Good, the kids are almost ready so we'll come along and have breakfast with you."

"That would be nice." Henry suddenly had a small bundle of energy in his arms.

"Gampa!" the boy shrieked, a goofy smile on his lips and laughter in his childish eyes. He was grandpa's boy and followed Henry everywhere when he was in the building and the child was awake. Henry's shadow, Ann called him. The child couldn't quite pronounce the word grandpa yet, so it came out as *gampa*. It made Henry smile every time he said it. Yet he was secretly tickled the youngster loved him so much. A child's love was strong medicine for almost any ill. Henry put the boy down on the ground and the child hobbled towards Ann, who the child also loved.

Timothy was walking, albeit unsteadily. He had to hold on to tables and chairs and anything else his little hands could grasp so he could stay upright. But he was learning and growing, as Henry's father used to say, like a watered weed. He was Laura's son in so many ways. Curious, generous and with boundless energy. He had her expressive blue eyes but the boy had Justin's fine blond hair.

Phoebe was growing and in her features Henry could see the woman she would someday become. She'd be tall like her mother. Her brown eyes were so different than her half-brother's because they reflected a wisdom far more than her young years. But then she'd seen too much in her short life filled with dinosaurs and the death of people she'd loved; it had left scars and most could not be seen. She loved to read, sing and draw. Henry thought she was extremely talented, but then he was somewhat prejudiced being her grandfather and all. She'd had Ann cut her long hair the week before saying it was easier to care for now she had a little brother who was into everything. At any time of the day she could be seen chasing after the boy and laughing at his antics. She'd taken her mother's death so hard but with every passing day and the love Henry, Ann and everyone else at headquarters, rangers and soldiers alike, lavished upon her and Timothy, she seemed to be getting better. She smiled more often that was for sure. Yet she hadn't forgotten her mother.

"Phoebe still cries at night in bed sometimes when she thinks we're asleep. I've heard her. It breaks my heart," Ann had confided to Henry recently. "We speak about her mother, though, whenever she wants to and I tell her about Laura as a girl and what she was like. It seems to soothe her. She loves to hear the stories of young Laura."

"We all miss Laura," Henry had responded

trying not to let the grief overtake him again. "I think about her all the time. I bet she's up in heaven rooting for us. Looking down and smiling at the way we're fighting the dinosaurs and how we never give up."

"I think about her all the time, too," Ann had whispered in return as they lay in bed one night the week before. "All the time. You know sometimes, especially when I'm with the children, I swear I feel her presence around us."

"I do, too, sometimes. I also like to think she's watching over us."

"Sometimes," Ann had murmured, "I hear her voice. Where is she, I ask myself. What has happened to her? Why isn't she here with us, the ones who love and need her? I just can't take it in…that she's *gone*." And she had begun to cry.

Henry had taken his wife into his arms and together they'd fought off, as they had for weeks, the greatest loss they'd ever suffered.

Phoebe and Timothy in tow, Ann went out the door in front of Henry. The kids were hungry.

Henry was in a fairly good mood that morning. He'd been on patrol now two days in a row and this would be the third. The poisoned dead meat scattered around headquarters and dropped everywhere they'd traveled in the park, had done its job better than he had ever hoped. They'd postponed the clean up because the self-serve extermination was working so well. Dinosaurs would sneak in and tear at, consume, the decomposing beasts and sign their own death warrants. During the patrols Henry and his men rode through the park and counted the carcasses that were everywhere. Then other dinosaurs would eat those and themselves die. It was an accumulative process. Justin's vaccine truly worked and Henry had never been so relieved. He was ecstatic. The turning point had at long last come. Victory was within humanity's reach. The dinosaurs were going *down. Hallelujah!* He'd telephoned Justin the night before and had given him the good news. Justin had been jubilant as well.

Henry walked into the conference room. Captain McDowell, Steven and Doctor Emily were there eating. Oatmeal for Steven and Emily and cold bran cereal with raisins for McDowell.

The kids headed for the cold cereal–which Ann informed him was reaching a low supply and soon he'd have to go on a restocking run for more–and Henry grabbed a bowl of oatmeal.

Sitting down beside Captain McDowell, he had to ask as he'd done almost every day for the last week, "Have you heard from your better half lately?"

McDowell's face changed ever so subtly. He knew her well enough to recognize her troubled expression even if she tried to hide it. "No, not for days and that's not like him. No matter how sensitive his operation is, he always finds a way to contact me. I'm getting concerned. I gather you haven't heard from him this week either?"

"I'm sorry to say, no. And like you I'm uneasy about it. I assume he's still fighting our enemy in Los Angeles somewhere. Justin said last night when I spoke to him the military has deployed his serum in fog form over the city and the dinosaurs are dying everywhere. So we should be hearing from Patterson soon, I would think."

"Justin hasn't heard from him, has he?" Finishing her breakfast, she shoved it away. She'd clean the bowl and spoon up before she'd go, she always did. No one wanted Ann to be stuck with washing dishes all day.

"I asked him last night and, as with us, Patterson hasn't contacted him, either, and he was expecting to hear from him. Patterson, being the reason Justin was picked for and sent to the New York Conference, liked to keep in touch with Justin to see how his work was progressing. Justin said he was eager to convey to Patterson the fog planes carrying the cure had been dispatched to Los Angeles and the initial results were proving to be highly effective. Wherever it was sprayed it was killing dinosaurs. But he hasn't been able as yet to pass that information along."

"I don't like this," McDowell grumbled. "Something's wrong."

Doctor Emily had been getting a cup of coffee but came over and settled down beside Steven. She was usually a quiet woman who mainly listened and spoke little. At the moment, though, there was sympathy in her eyes. She knew what it was to have someone she loved missing. The year before, as she'd told Ann and Ann had then told him, her husband had been missing for days before his body, or what was left of it, had been found. It had been anguishing for her.

Steven, who'd been listening to the

conversation, joined in. "From what I know of Patterson, Captain McDowell, I bet he's somewhere hunkered down, busy fighting. Incommunicado for some reason, perhaps by orders, for now. I'm sure you'll hear from him soon. After all the stories I've heard of him from Henry and Justin, I believe the man is immortal."

Captain McDowell actually smiled at Steven. "Let's hope you're correct and he has either been in the thick of it, or silent by orders, and hasn't had the opportunity to contact any of us. Yet."

"Yeah, he'll call one of you soon." Steven's smile for McDowell was compassionate. He liked, admired, the woman soldier as all of them did.

The people at the table finished their breakfast, took time to talk to, play with and interact a little with the children as they always did, and prepared to begin their day.

A short while later, Henry, glancing at McDowell and Steven, had announced, "We ready to go?" when Zeke came running into the room, looking as if he'd just fallen out of bed. His hair was sticking out every which way and his clothes looked hastily put on. He made straight for Henry.

"Henry, Wilma's gone! You have to help me find her. Crazy woman is probably trying to get back to her house again." The old man's eyes were red-rimmed and wild with worry.

"Slow down, Zeke." Henry caught the old man's arm and ended up supporting him, Zeke was shaking so badly. "How long has she been missing?" Henry sent an oh-boy-here-we-go-again-look at Ann and she sent him the same back. She was already at Zeke's side comforting him and she made him sit down before he collapsed. Ann had become extra protective of Zeke the last few years because, as Wilma, he was often forgetful and his physical condition continued to decline.

"I don't know! I woke up and she was gone." Zeke was visibly upset and shaking his head.

"Have you looked everywhere in the compound for her?" Henry asked him.

"Yes, well, everywhere I could get to. Inside and outside. I can't find her nowhere." Zeke groaned. "Where is that woman!"

Henry and those in the room with him wasted no time and went out to search for Wilma. Henry wanted Zeke to remain behind because he was such a wreck, but the old man refused to and limped out behind them.

They ran out into the bright summer sunlight and began looking for the escapee.

It didn't take long to find her. There she was, in an inside corner tucked in by the main gate, crouched down as small as she could get in the dirt…and poised above her, blood dripping from its jaws and claws, was a mutant velociraptor. Mutant because it wasn't the everyday velociraptor shown in the old dinosaur books or even like the ones Henry and the others were now familiar with. It was different. This one had more bulk than the ones before it, had powerful hind legs and enormous fangs. It had eyes that were almost human.

Henry and the rangers and soldiers who'd come running when the news about Wilma's absence spread had their weapons out and aimed at the monster.

"No, don't shoot it! It's too near Wilma," Henry yelled. "We have to get it away from her."

There were bloody scratches down Wilma's left side and she was cowering beneath the dinosaur's shadow. It turned its glittering eyes on the humans now around it and hissed, swaying as if it were drunk or sick. It edged closer to Wilma, hovering over her, barring its fangs and rising to its full height, which was as tall as a man. It glared alternately at the old woman and the crowd around her. Indignant and ferocious, it was defending its prey. Snarling and swaying it let out a blood-curdling screech to the sky and appeared to be in some sort of distress.

Wilma stole a look up at Henry, terror frozen in her eyes, her mouth trembling. *Help me*, she mouthed silently. *Help me*. She was in her pajamas, her face smeared with blood. She began to cry.

Zeke was frantic. "How did *it* get in here? How did it get inside the gate without anyone seeing it?"

"It jumped over the fence," McDowell deduced, her weapon at the ready in her arms. "It's so strong it cleared the barbed wire and all. These creatures never cease to amaze me. They just keep adapting and evolving." She raised her weapon and took aim.

"Shoot it!" Zeke cried. "Kill it! Look, it's hurt Wilma. Do something!" He pleaded with Henry and McDowell.

McDowell was standing in front of the old man to keep him from rushing the dinosaur and Ann was helping to hold him back.

The creature swung around and seemed to lurch

towards Wilma. It stumbled and righted itself. Now it was almost on top of the old lady.

"Shoot it!" Zeke yelled again about the same time Henry shouted the same words.

"I'm taking the shot," McDowell cried out.

But before she could, the dinosaur crumpled to the earth inches from Wilma and lay still. Wilma sprung up and ran into Zeke's waiting arms.

"What happened?" McDowell lowered her weapon. "I didn't shoot it. It just fell."

Henry moved closer to the dinosaur on the ground. The thing didn't move.

"Watch out, it could be pretending to be dead," Ann warned. "Remember, they're good at that."

Henry was standing above the creature and prodded it with his boot. It twitched and then stopped moving again. "I don't think it's pretending to be dead. I think it is dead." He squatted down on the balls of his feet and, leaning in closer, examined the thing's body. "It has a lot of blood on its mouth and claws. I don't think the blood is all Wilma's. I'd bet you this dinosaur was feeding on one of those dead carcasses outside before it got in here…and what it ate killed it, but it took a few minutes."

"Justin's serum killed it, huh?" Ann was at Henry's side and gazing down at the dead dinosaur. There was a satisfied look on her face.

"I believe it did." Henry's lips formed a grin. "And darned if it didn't save Wilma's life. Otherwise, the velociraptor would have made short work of her long before we found them."

"Thank the lord the creature fed at the poisoned dinosaur buffet before it snuck in." Ann was looking towards the gates. Then, with a smile, she said to Henry, “The tide has finally turned I do believe. We are witnessing the end of the dinosaurs. Justin’s vaccine might actually rid us of them everywhere. Forever.”

Henry gave her a quick hug. “I sure hope so.”

Doctor Emily, who had come out with Steven when the confrontation began, stepped up and took control. “We need to get Wilma into the infirmary. Those wounds needs tending to.”

Zeke, Emily, Steven and Ann hustled the injured woman into the building, leaving Henry and McDowell to dispose of the dead velociraptor. With some of the soldiers help they drug the corpse out through the gates and left it with the other stinking remains so it could infect others.

“Okay,” Henry said to McDowell when they were done, “let’s go on patrol. Let’s see what’s out there today.”

“My men and I are ready to saddle up if you are, Chief Ranger.”

They took out two tanks that morning. In the first tank Henry, driving, with Steven, Sergeant Gilbert manning the guns if they needed them and McDowell commanding. Lieutenant Becker was with his soldiers in the second tank.

For the first time in over a year Henry couldn’t wait to get out in the park and see what was going on with the dinosaur population.

Driving through and around the dinosaur bodies outside the stockade Henry reveled in the knowledge that for the first time in a very long time the humans were winning the war. He was actually cheerful and joked with the soldiers riding with him as they rumbled through the woods and up to the rim.

They found dead dinosaurs everywhere and no live ones.

The tanks circled around the rim and Henry scrutinized the lake, looking for creatures swimming below or above the waterline. There were no ripples, no dinosaur fins or heads poking up out of the water, but there were decaying dinosaur bodies everywhere decomposing in the sun. More were scattered along the shore and floating in the water. It was strange to see so many of them, all dead, but it made Henry's heart sing.

Over the radio, Henry heard Becker's crew cheering every time they discovered another dinosaur graveyard. There were a lot of them.

When they were done with checking the rim and celebrating Henry announced, "Let's go by the Lodge. I need to see how Norma and her boss, Jimmy, are doing. Tell them the good news that the age of the unwanted dinosaurs may be over. They can go outside again. Reopen the Lodge as soon as we know we're all safe and we reopen the park."

"Go ahead take us there, Chief Ranger," McDowell replied. "Lieutenant Becker you follow us."

McDowell's tank turned around and Becker's fell in behind it.

Rolling into the Lodge's parking lot the place didn't look much different than the last time Henry had been there, except he still wasn't used to seeing it so empty. No cars on the lot and no boisterous visitors milling around. Eerie silence reigned. The building itself looked lonely as it rose in all its historic glory over the lake.

Henry, Steven and McDowell exited the tank and walked up to the entrance. That's when Henry realized something wasn't right. The front door was smashed and splintered. Inside there were other signs of a fight. The main room had been trashed and it made him sad because he remembered how beautiful it had been after the last renovation when it had been transformed into a 1920's looking chalet.

"Dinosaurs," Henry breathed, taking in the destruction, and his heart sunk. There were still live dinosaurs around, or were there?

But as they roamed through the main dining room and past the cold fireplace nothing came charging out at them; nothing attacked them. There was no sign of living dinosaurs anywhere.

"Must have been an old fight. But there're no dinosaurs here now," Henry said. His words echoed in the empty rooms. "But where are Norma and Jimmy?" he asked after they'd completed a tour of the central rooms.

Henry hadn't wanted the two old people to stay in the Lodge last fall during the worst of the dinosaur troubles but they'd adamantly insisted. He could have forcibly escorted them off the property and out of the park but both of them had had nowhere else to go. Norma had lived in the Lodge for over forty years. Jimmy, besides being the owner, took care of the plumbing and electrical and if no one was there to keep the pipes from freezing in the winter the Lodge could have sustained extensive damage. They needed to remain to protect and care for the place, as they put it. So, against his better judgement, he'd left them weapons and let them stay because the place was strong enough, he believed, to protect them behind its walls. Over the last year he'd kept an eye on them, though, except when the deepest snow had kept him away.

"Norma! Jimmy! Are you here," he shouted as he and his companions explored the building. No one answered. "Let's check Norma's room."

Norma had a tiny room on the first floor. Henry knew about it, where it approximately was, but he'd never been there before so he had to knock loudly on every door in the rear of the first floor. It paid off. After he'd pounded on a door in the east wing, he heard a voice behind it. "Is that you, Chief Ranger?"

"It's me, Norma. Are you all right?"

The door burst open and there was Norma. The woman's face was one big grin. She rushed at Henry and hugged him. "Thank goodness you came. I've been hiding in here for days and I'm about starved to death. You got any water or any sort of food on you, Chief Ranger?"

"Not on me, but you'll have both real soon. Does that broken in front door have something to do with your hiding?"

"It sure does. We were overrun by those monster lizards, oh, about three days ago. They came at us in a slobbering rabble of teeth and claws and battered down the door. Jimmy tried to fight them, but there were too many, so we both skedaddled in different directions to confuse them and to hide until they were gone. Thing is there was no way for us to know when they were gone. So I've been holed up ever since. We tried calling headquarters but the stupid phones are down, too. Even our cell phones wouldn't let us get through."

"Well, the dinosaurs are gone. We searched the whole place. You're safe now."

"Good," Norma huffed. "And good riddance to evil dinosaurs."

"Uh, where's Jimmy then?" Henry was shocked at how ragged Norma looked. She was a scarecrow, her hair, usually short, dyed and permed, was dirty and showed gray roots; her green eyes were bloodshot. There was twice as many wrinkles on her face than the last time he'd seen her. But, at least, she was alive, and seemed happy to be.

"Now that's a mystery. I lost track of him. We were surprised in the beginning and he ran off somewhere when the attack came to get more ammunition or some such thing, he said, and I haven't seen him since. But I haven't left that room, too scared, so he could be anywhere. I sure pray he's alive. Those critters were wicked and vicious. They were demented, too." She was rocking her head back and forth. "Whew, I was lucky to even get away. I crawled under tables and behind chairs until I could get to my room. Let me tell you, it was no fun. A couple of times I thought I was a dead woman."

So they continued the search for Jimmy and eventually found him in one of the supply rooms, fat and sassy because he'd had plenty of canned food to eat. He had tripped running away from the dinosaurs, he told them, and done something wonky to his back. "I could barely walk, much less flee from those prehistoric bastards so once I made it into this room here, I stayed. I knew someone would come looking for us sooner or later. Most likely you, Henry. I was right."

Jimmy was overjoyed to see Norma was okay. "Lordy, Norma, I thought the dinosaurs had caught and eaten you. I heard you screaming. That's why I didn't come looking for you. I thought you were a goner."

"Oh great," she snapped, "you thought I was dinosaur chow and wrote me off. Thanks a lot. As you can see, boss, I survived."

"All right, you two. I want both of you to come back with us to headquarters so Doctor Emily can examine you. We'll fatten you up Norma and the doctor will look at that wonky back of yours Jimmy."

"I guess we can go for a while," Norma reluctantly agreed. "But I ain't staying. This is my home. Someone has to protect, stay and take care of it."

"You won't have to stay long with us, Norma. We think the park might be safe now." And he told both of them the good news about Justin's vaccine, the hatchlings mysteriously perishing, and how the dinosaurs were dying off. "We've been scouring the park all day and for the first time in over a year haven't see one breathing dinosaur."

"Hallelujah," Norma exclaimed using the same word Henry had used earlier that day, her eyes lighting up. "It's a miracle. Does that mean the park will be reopening soon and we can–at long last–have our old calm lives back and the visitors will return to fill this place up again?"

"That's what we're all praying for. Now, let's get out of here." And Henry led them through the building and out to the tanks. Each tank took one of the survivors and headed back to headquarters.

On the way, to Henry's elated relief, there were still only dead dinosaurs to be seen; not one breathing one.

"This could be it," Steven said to him in an awed voice, as they had helped load Norma and Jimmy into their rides. "The dinosaur wars are over and we've won. Humanity has won."

Henry smiled up at the sky, so blue and full of fluffy clouds, as he looked around at his beloved park, and nodded. *And they could have their lives back again. Finally.* He was almost too afraid to say it out loud, but he did anyway. "I also think the days of the dinosaurs are over. We've won." And knew as the words came out that it was true. It was just a feeling he had. The dinosaurs were gone forever or soon would be.

"Let's go home," he said over the radio to everyone in the tanks.

And the machines continued through the woods, now empty of live prehistoric beasts for the first time in many years, and rolled back through the gates.

Chapter 24

It thought it knew what was happening to its comrades. They were all dying. The large angry ones were feeding on their own dead and then they also ceased moving and breathing. It thought it was something the sticks were doing, but it couldn't be sure. Perhaps it was just the natural way of things to live and then die.

But after that first time it had feasted on the food outside the sticks' cave it had stopped eating them. For when it had returned for more after the next sunrise the food smelled…funny. It had a taint to it. A foul smell. So it hadn't eaten any more. Others of its kind hadn't seemed to notice or care the food was tainted. They ate it and then they stopped breathing and another one ate that one, ceased breathing and moving, and another ate that one and so on and so on. Now there were others like it not moving anymore everywhere.

That's why it was leaving. It couldn't take the chance any of its remaining family would make the same mistake and devour the bad food. Its mate, now motionless and cold, and the hatchlings weren't going with it, though. There hadn't been any new offspring for a while and it didn't understand why. Still it and its family were going.

So the unmoving cold ones of its kind were everywhere and it was no longer safe in the woods near the sticks. It would take its family and burrow deeper into the forest to hide and where nothing could touch them. It didn't want to leave the amusing sticks and their entertaining furry tiny creatures in their big cave behind but it had to do what was best for its family. So as the sun came up it gathered them together, what was left of them anyway, and they scurried deeper into the woods. They didn't look back.

In time it would forget all the cold dead ones…and it would forget the sticks. That was its way.

Chapter 25

“How’s Wilma doing?” Henry asked Ann as soon as he walked in. Steven had taken off to be with Emily and McDowell was still with her men doing whatever soldiers did between patrols. Norma and Jimmy were also with Doctor Emily getting checked out, fed and cared for and would join them later.

Ann gave him a warm embrace. “Wilma’s doing poorly, the wounds were deep, but Emily thinks she’ll be all right, physically anyway. If she wants to be.”

“If she wants to be?”

“Emily is afraid Wilma, in some way, realizes she’s losing her mind, dementia or Alzheimer’s most likely, and her will to live is almost nonexistent. Wilma told Emily she wanted to die, it was time.”

“I’m sorry to hear that. The poor woman.” Henry sat down and Timothy climbed into his lap. The child was sleepy and laid his head against grandpa’s chest. Phoebe was bustling around the kitchen helping Ann put dinner out. She grinned at him and gave him a kiss on his cheek. She was listening to what he and Ann were saying but Henry didn’t feel the need to hide anything from her. The girl had gone through a lot, was growing up, and she wanted to know what was going on.

They were in the conference room where he’d found Ann making supper, canned ham sandwiches, canned green beans and apricots, for the children.

The two cats were slinking around begging for scraps. Outside the sun was going down, but it had been a wonderful day and Henry felt better than he had in a very long time. For the fifth consecutive day they hadn't found one living dinosaur, just legions of dead ones. Somehow the dinosaurs that fed on the poisoned ones sometimes lived long enough to travel and expire somewhere else. Then other dinosaurs fed on their lifeless bodies and they, in turn, traveled and the cycle continued. The serum was working even better than any of them had anticipated. Its never ending benefits were like falling dominos. Wait until he told Justin.

"About Wilma? You know as well as I do no one can make a person want to live. It has to be up to them. Wilma is well over eighty years old, she's seen a lot in her life and she's lived it. We'll be here for her, Zeke will be here for her, but what else can we do?"

"I don't know." Ann finished serving the children their food and put down a plate for Henry and herself as well.

Henry brightened up. "But hey, I have a bit of news that might cheer her up some and perhaps even make her want to live again."

"What's that?"

Phoebe was listening attentively as she ate her canned ham.

"The good news actually is for all of us."

Everyone at the table was waiting for him to finish.

"Yes?" Ann asked. She'd taken Timothy into her lap and was forking mashed green beans into his mouth. He'd begun eating solid food a few weeks before and loved green beans. He'd eat them until he got sick so she had to be careful how much she let him have. His chubby fingers closed around hers holding the fork and she smiled at him. He was such a sweet child. So much like his mother everyone couldn't help but love him.

"I really believe," Henry said slowly, building up the suspense, "that our dinosaur troubles are over. We didn't see *one* breathing, living dinosaur *anywhere* in the park the last five days. All we saw were dead ones. Oh, Ann…I think it's really over." He leaned over and kissed her on the lips and let his happiness explode on his face. "I think we are going to have our old lives back again very soon."

"Thank God!" Ann exhaled softly. "And we can reopen the park, rebuild our cabin and no longer live in fear of these monsters? Klamath Falls can be rebuilt as well and Zeke and Wilma can return to their houses if they're still there?"

"I think so. If, and I say if because it also depends on one other thing, the vaccine is working all over the world as well as it is here, then humans will have their world once again."

"And we will have our lives back again," Ann murmured. Henry saw true uncontained joy in her expression for the first time in years. "Oh, Henry!" She put Timothy into a smiling Phoebe's waiting arms and, after he came to his feet, embraced him, tears trickling down her cheeks.

"That's what I prayed for, Ann. And we're going to do all those things you wanted to do. I might keep working or I might not. I've been thinking about it. If I officially retire we can buy that RV you've always wanted and we can travel…all over the country. We can see all those other places you have on your bucket list and always wanted to visit. We can enjoy what life we have left."

"That sounds so good," she said, hugging him tighter, her face against his chest. "I can't believe it's really over but I'm more than ready to start a new chapter. I'm ready to be happy again."

The rest of the evening everyone gathered in the mess hall and the mood was festive. They broke out some of the rare whiskey and soda they'd been hoarding for just such an occasion. Norma and Jimmy joined them. Zeke came in later after being with Wilma, who had finally fallen asleep in their cubicle.

Everyone heard the good news and was hopeful and happy. They laughed and talked of the future and what they'd all do. Henry and Ann, of course, would remain in the park helping to get everything running smoothly. Steven spoke of staying around to see that happen and then settling down with Doctor Emily, and the two of them exchanged shy smiles. Zeke thought he'd return to his house in Klamath Falls and take care of Wilma. McDowell said she'd keep serving her country…and waiting for Patterson to return from Los Angeles. No one had heard from him for over a week and all were worried. They all waited for news.

It was strange, Henry mulled it over, to once more optimistically be looking towards the future, but it felt so good. He smiled the whole evening.

Outside the summer night was quiet and peaceful. There were no dinosaur cries, no sounds of battle and no gunshots.

The world, Henry believed, once again finally belonged to the humans and the heavy burdens he'd been carrying for the last seven years slowly began to slide off his shoulders.

McDowell took him aside later. "You know, Chief Ranger, as much as we'd like to believe the dinosaurs are dead or dying all over the planet we have to be absolutely sure. Only time will tell."

"I know, Captain. I'm going to touch base with Justin tonight by phone and see what's going on in the rest of the world. He'll have a more complete picture of the situation than we do."

"Let me know what he says, would you?"

"I will."

Before she left the room, Henry had to reassure her as he did every night, "Patterson will show up sooner or later, I know it. He's done this disappearing act many times since I've known him. And he always returns. So much of what he does is top secret and sometimes he can't emerge from his mission until he's allowed to. He must be doing something truly important. But he'll show up."

McDowell nodded and always the staunch soldier, said nothing else.

He watched her leave and felt sorry for her. Ann had told him days ago McDowell had confided she and Patterson were going to get married as soon as he came back from Los Angeles. He couldn't stop thinking about that. It reminded him too vividly of Rangers Stanton and Kiley. The dinosaurs had ruined their marriage plans, too. *Please don't let McDowell's and Patterson's story end that way.*

*****

When the others had vacated the room and retired to their beds, Ann taking the children to tuck them in, Henry telephoned Justin and was delighted to reach him on the first try.

"Hi Justin," Henry initiated the conversation and went on to fill the paleontologist in on what he'd been observing in the park, that the dinosaurs had died in record numbers and he and his teams hadn't seen a live dinosaur in days, only dead ones.

"Is it possible we've won? Are the dinosaur wars really over?"

"I sure as hell hope so, Henry. In the last week the reports are flowing in from Los Angeles, New York, St. Louis and other major populated areas of the earth and, thank heaven, the results are even more promising than we had hoped for. The serum, in all forms, is decimating the dinosaurs and, like at Crater Lake, the carcasses are being fed on by other dinosaurs and they in turn are dying, too. Compounded by the hatchlings mysteriously dying across the world before they reach maturity, it's been a perfect storm. Dinosaurs everywhere are disappearing. The vaporous vaccine we've been dropping over the infected cities and what we've put into the water systems are working the same way. If it doesn't get rid of every dinosaur then the poisoned meat finishes the rest.

"We've put it in the water, the ponds and lakes where the creatures drink at, and it takes longer to kill them but in the end it does. Direct injection works almost instantly, but it's harder to achieve. You have to get dangerously close to the beasts and sometimes that's impossible. But it has its uses at times, as well."

"That's wonderful! You're saying everything I want to hear." Henry leaned back in his chair, totally relaxed for the first time in years. He wasn't listening for the sounds of attack or on edge because he feared at any moment he'd be snatching up his MP7 and running outside to track down and destroy more prehistoric predators threatening visitors or his men. He was looking forward to rebuilding his and Ann's home where the old shell stood…if that was what they would do. He wasn't sure. Not yet anyway. They were talking about other options. After that, who knew? The future was wide open.

Then he remembered. "By the way, have you heard anything about Patterson or from him? He hasn't been in touch with any of us for a long time, not even McDowell, and we're all worried."

Justin didn't answer at first and then muttered, "No, I haven't heard from him, either. Though I was told the fighting in Los Angeles was brutal before we sprayed the city. There were so many human fatalities. I've asked them to look for him yet so far he hasn't been found. I'm so sorry. I'll let you know if I hear anything. I promise."

"Thanks Justin." Henry looked up at the clock on the wall. It was late and he was tired.

"How are my kids doing? I miss them so much. I can't wait to hug them, see you, Ann and everyone." Justin sounded as tired as Henry felt, which was one breath away from sleep.

"Your children are fine. Phoebe can't wait until you come home, she asks about you every day, and Timothy, well, he doesn't say much." Henry laughed. "But he'll also be happy, I'm sure. I know he misses you. Every child needs their father." The reference made Henry melancholy because of his own loss, but he covered it up. Justin, all of them, should be happy. They'd accomplished a great victory.

"When do you think you'll be home, son?"

"Good news on that front. I've asked for a brief but necessary leave of absence to see my family," Justin disclosed. "I'm flying in tomorrow sometime for a visit. Probably late afternoon. I told Jeff Smith I had to see my kids or I'd have a nervous breakdown." He chuckled. "I won't be home to stay yet, there's still so much work to do here, but soon I will be home for good."

"So we'll see you tomorrow sometime?" The news produced more happiness for Henry. Ann and the children, everyone, would be so thrilled to have Justin back with them, even for a visit, and it would help morale so much. Everyone could ask all the questions they'd been wanting to ask Justin about the progress of the cure. They'd like that.

"Tomorrow sometime. I can't promise an exact time of arrival. But, thanks to Jeff Smith, I'm flying in with a load of special supplies. Fresh meat, fruits and goodies. He wanted to give me a gift and that's what I asked for. Food for you guys back there. I know you've been on tight rations for a long time. No longer, though. Tell Ann I'm bringing chocolate for everyone."

"Oh, she'll love you for that. We ran out of chocolate weeks ago. You know how she loves it."

"I do. I'm bringing a big box of Russell Stover just for her."

"And did you say fresh meat, too?"

"Steaks. Lots of them."

"Bless you." Henry laughed.

The phone call didn't last much longer, Justin had things to do and Henry wanted to spend time with Ann before he slept.

After they'd hung up, Henry looked up at the black window. The room was dancing with shadows. He enjoyed the silence and the peace for a few minutes, thinking of the monkey dinosaur who'd helped them so many times. He wondered where the little bugger was. For a second he thought he saw it framed in the dark window…but it wasn't really there. Perhaps it was dead now with all the others. Pity. That was the only dinosaur he'd ever not hated.

Sighing, Henry got up, switched off the lights and left the room.

All he could think about was: Soon life could go back to normal and soon he would have his park back. Oh, and there'd be steaks for supper tomorrow night. He was so happy he could have done a gig in the hallway, but he didn't. His rangers, if any saw him, would think he'd finally lost his mind.

*****

The following morning Henry and his rangers, McDowell and her soldiers, drove out on patrol as usual. Henry knew they'd have to continue patrols for weeks, perhaps months, before they could inform the new Park Superintendent–a man named Don Pelley–that the park was truly safe to reopen and they could begin cleaning up the destruction the dinosaurs had left behind.

But the mood with the humans in the tanks was light-hearted as they toured the park and didn't encounter one living dinosaur the whole day. There were lots of dead ones found, but not one alive.

They roared through headquarters' gates as the sun cast evening fingers over the land. Summer was in full swing and the park Henry had loved for so many years was coming alive again, as well. Small native animals, birds and squirrels, were returning. Henry was a happy man.

McDowell, over his headset, was the one to tip Henry off there was a military helicopter arriving out front as they drove up and Henry scrambled out of the tank and ran excitedly to meet its debarking occupants. Justin had come home.

*****

Ann was in the mess hall cleaning up the supper she'd just helped serve the children, Zeke, Wilma and Doctor Emily. She'd been feeling so much better and attributed it in part to the end of the dinosaur troubles. Her spirit and stress level were lighter and she found herself singing an old Beatles song under her breath as she did the dishes. She was looking forward to Justin coming home.

She heard the helicopter and, with Timothy in her arms, and Phoebe trailing along behind, she made a dash out the front door. As she came out of the gates, which were open, her heart lightened even more at what she saw.

There outside the gates by the helicopter was McDowell hugging Patterson. Everyone was standing around clapping and chattering away. Justin was looking on with a mischievous half grin.

Ann rushed up to him and the scientist held out his arms and took Timothy from her. The child threw his arms around his father, his innocent face happy. Phoebe was next and hugged Justin, too. Then Ann hugged him. "I'm so glad you're back," she said, her eyes then going to Patterson and McDowell.

Justin picked up on her thoughts. "Patterson? He showed up this morning in New York and hitched a ride here. I thought you'd all like to know he was okay so I brought him along."

"Where has he been?" Ann asked as they moved closer to the happy couple and Henry met her half way, taking her hand. He was smiling, too, watching the reunion unfold before them.

"Why don't you ask him," Justin told her.

As soon as Patterson and McDowell separated, Patterson turned to face Ann and Henry, his arm around a beaming McDowell.

It was Henry who asked though. "It's good to see you, Scott! We've been so worried. You didn't call, you didn't write." A small laugh. "Where have you been?"

That's when Ann noticed the deep cuts across Patterson's face. The way he moved slowly and carefully. The sling on his right arm. The cast without a shoe on it sticking out on his right foot below his slacks. He looked thirty pounds lighter.

His face narrow and gaunt. He was nearly unrecognizable as the Patterson who had left their company weeks before. But he was alive.

"I've been fighting prehistoric devils, you know that, Chief Ranger and Mrs. Chief Ranger." Patterson grinned. "I got caught in a vicious ground fight and had to be rescued. It took a while. Los Angeles, before the airplanes dropped the poisoned fog and saved us all," he shot an appreciative glance at Justin, "was a dinosaur battleground. I was extremely lucky to get out of there alive."

Before Henry, Ann or anyone could comment on what he'd said, Patterson looked down at McDowell. "That's why I'm retiring from the agency, effective as soon as they can process me out. The wounds I took in Los Angeles will make that easier. I was in a coma for days afterward. They didn't think I'd wake up, but I showed them. There was something really important I had to do. I couldn't die until I did it."

Now his eyes were only on his companion as he paused dramatically and gravely asked, "Sherman McDowell, will you please marry me?"

McDowell's eyes widened and everyone held their breath for a long moment until she answered, "Yes, I'll marry you."

Everyone cheered and Ann felt her happiness grow another leap.

"When do you want to do this?" McDowell's smile was the biggest one Ann had ever seen on her face.

"As soon as possible. What happened to me made me reassess my life–nothing like almost dying to do that–and now that it seems the dinosaur war is most likely over I don't want to waste another day without you. I want our new life to begin together."

"How about next Sunday?" McDowell was gazing at Patterson as any woman in love would look at the man she adored.

Patterson turned to Henry and Justin. "Can you two be my best men?"

Both replied *yes* at the same time.

"Two best men?" Henry remarked, amused.

"Two. I can't decide, so it's both of you."

McDowell asked Ann, "And will you be my maid of honor?"

"Of course." Ann gave the woman a hug and whispered in her ear, "It's about time, you two. We've all been waiting forever for this."

"Me, too," McDowell whispered back, and Ann laughed.

Steven and Emily had been watching all this take place and by the impishness on their faces, the way they tightly squeezed each other's hands, Ann guessed they wouldn't be far behind in the marriage department. But Emily was the kind of woman not to be hurried. Ann hoped it wouldn't be too long, though. Nothing like a wedding to bring peoples' spirits up. And two weddings were always better than one.

"Let's get inside," Justin spoke loudly. "I've brought presents for everyone, supplies, and I think we should have a feast to celebrate Patterson's miraculous return and their coming marriage."

"And to celebrate your victory, Justin, in defeating the dinosaurs!" Henry tossed in and everyone seconded both statements with more cheers. "Because of you we have our world, our lives back…and our futures."

"Ah, shucks, you're making me blush. But I didn't do it alone. I had plenty of help," Justin declared, yet Ann could see how pleased and proud he was.

Oh, if only Laura could see him now. Then she thought, *well, maybe she does see him.*

And they moved inside to celebrate Patterson's and Justin's return.

*****

Henry couldn't sleep, he was too excited over the end of their troubles and his stomach was full of steak and the other treats Justin had brought them. It was after two in the morning but his mind kept replaying the night's festivities and he couldn't stop thinking about the future as he sat alone in the conference room. Earlier he'd discussed everything with McDowell, Patterson and Justin and hoped within the next few weeks they could leave headquarters behind and start the park's reconstruction. He and Ann could live normal lives again.

Patterson, with Justin agreeing, had warned him to be cautious. "Take your time, Henry. There are still dinosaurs hiding out there and it could take a while before we've completely eradicated all of them. Some are smart enough to go into hiding and we'll have to rout them out."

"What's a couple of weeks or so?" Henry had acceded, gazing around the mess hall as they'd lingered over dinner. People were smiling and enjoying themselves, eating and drinking. It was a real party. He liked hearing Ann's laughter. "I feel like we've been here forever."

But soon, soon they could leave.

Henry wasn't surprised when first Justin wandered in, blurry-eyed and yawning, and after him Patterson. He'd had a hunch Patterson would want to talk privately at some point about what had happened to him in Los Angeles. Henry only had to look into Patterson's eyes to see the scars went deep, much deeper than his physical wounds.

The three friends sat down in the dim room and talked about their recent experiences.

"We were really worried about you, Scott." Henry studied his friend's face. The man looked so different than when he'd gone to Los Angeles and he seemed to still be in pain.

"Heck, I was worried about me, too."

"What happened to you in Los Angeles? Can you talk about it? Only if you want to." Henry was aware Justin was listening closely, as well.

"I don't mind. Could be it would help if I did talk about it. I've had enough nightmares about that night. It constantly haunts me." With a slight shudder, Patterson began his story and had gotten to the part where the crazed velociraptors had torn the old woman to pieces in front of his eyes and then had surrounded him.

"The velociraptors came at me and I was sure I was a dead man," his voice was shaky as he spoke. "There were so damn many of them and they were rabid. The pain when they tore into my arm and my leg was excruciating and I had to fight like hell to remain conscious. I was dragged down a backstreet and that's when the velociraptors trying to eat me started fighting over me among themselves. I don't know why they suddenly left me, bleeding and going in and out of consciousness, but they did. The last thing I remember–before I woke up in a hospital bed days later–was seeing the bastards running off as if something had chased them away. I didn't see what it was, but I believe now it was a larger predator they were afraid of and they took off running when it arrived on the scene. It was the only thing that saved me, I'm sure of it. But the larger dinosaur, whatever it had been, didn't come after me. I was so lucky I didn't bleed to death and my surviving men found me.

"Then I was lucky again later when I got to keep my leg here." He tapped the leg with the cast on it. "The doctors thought at first I'd lose it."

Henry put a hand on the man's shoulder. "I'm so happy you didn't lose your leg and you're still alive."

Justin's mien of sympathy seconded that.

"Is this why you're retiring, Scott?" Henry asked. "What you went through there?"

"Partly. The truth is I think I...*died* in that backstreet." Patterson hesitated, looking embarrassed.

"Died?" Justin was staring at their friend now, entranced.

Patterson released a pensive sigh and his eyes seemed to be looking at something far away. "And don't laugh at me, but I believe I had a near-death experience. The white tunnel, the bright light, all my old friends and some of my deceased family members welcoming me…the whole shebang."

"What happened? Obviously you didn't die because you're here." Henry was also fascinated with Patterson's story. He always was with near-death stories.

Patterson lowered his head and his words were awed. "I did die. I died, I was half way on the journey to the other side and then I saw Dylan Greer…and George Redcrow. I saw and spoke to them."

Justin was silent, waiting for whatever Patterson would say next. Henry knew Justin wasn't a believer. His scientific mind wouldn't let him believe in such things as white tunnels and the afterlife. But Henry was a believer.

"And what did they say?"

"Greer told me it wasn't my time yet. That I had other things I had to do before I joined them. He laughed that weird sarcastic laugh of his. He seemed blissful. Younger than I ever remember him."

"And what did George Redcrow say to you?" Henry felt a shiver ripple through his body. Redcrow had been one of the first of his rangers to die in the dinosaur wars seven years ago because he'd protected Ann during an attack and saved her life. Redcrow had been his friend, too, and Henry thought of the man often even after all this time.

"I'm not really sure…he spoke in his native Indian tongue. Though I'm familiar with and can speak many languages, I couldn't understand a word of it but I *understood* what he was telling me.

He was saying the same thing Greer told me. It wasn't my time. There was something else I had to do. The world needed me.

"After the two turned me around and sent me back through the tunnel I glanced behind me and Greer and Redcrow were waving at me. Smiling. And I felt such an enormous sense of peace. Happiness. Redcrow had also told me not to worry, I wouldn't lose my leg, and Greer told me to marry Sherman right away; that we'd have children together and one of them would someday do something incredible. Then both of them and all my deceased relatives simply dissolved into the white light and the tunnel closed up. I woke up in the hospital bed and here I am."

"Whew, that's a hell of a story." Henry's demeanor was thoughtful. He was not as much of a skeptic as Justin because he, too, had seen and heard things from the other side. He'd heard Greer's and Redcrow's voice in his head many times since they'd died.

"And you believe you really died?" Justin questioned in a respectful way, his eyes sleepy.

"I do."

Patterson turned to Henry. "Do you believe me?"

"I don't know, but I don't disbelieve. There are so many things in life and after that are mysteries even to me. I think if you believe you died, traveled the tunnel and spoke to dead people, that's all that matters. And if you want to change your life because of a close call with death as you went through, more power to you. It's like with Ann and her cancer. The last bout she had with it made her decide, like you, to reinvent her life. Her cancer has made her realize our time here on earth is short. That's why she's not going back to work and that's why neither am I."

That declaration woke Justin up. "You're not going to remain as Chief Park Ranger here? You're retiring as well?"

Henry hadn't wanted to announce his plans so soon but somehow after Patterson's heartfelt confession he couldn't help himself. He hadn't even run his decision past Ann yet but soon he would.

And suddenly Henry knew what he'd said was exactly what he was going to do, what he wanted to do. "I'm retiring as soon as the park begins to get back on its feet, so to speak, and the park service can find my replacement. Not more than six months is what I'll be telling Superintendent Pelley. Ann and I want to travel. We want to live. Free and unfettered by anything else."

"How about rebuilding your cabin?" Justin wanted to know.

Henry shrugged. "We'll build one somewhere else. Start all over. Ann was saving money for a long time just for such a scenario. When she revealed to me how much she'd saved before this crisis began, I was flabbergasted. Of course, living here and fighting dinosaurs we never touched any of it. Now we will. Along with my retirement money, our savings and the money she'll get from the destruction of her newspaper building from insurance, we'll be fine. We will live a simple life. We'll be happy."

"You know where you'll settle down?" Justin was looking at him, waiting.

"Around here somewhere. This area is our home after all."

"My, my," Patterson commented. "It looks like all of us are moving on. I hope we can stay in touch."

"Oh, I'm sure we will." Henry stretched in his chair and his fingers rubbed his weary eyes. His bed was calling.

"How about you, Doctor Maltin?" Patterson pushed himself up from the table. "What are your peacetime plans?"

"Well, I've been offered a big fancy job with Jeff Smith's worldwide conglomerate, but it'll be a long time before I'll be free to take it. There's still so much to do now wrapping up the dinosaur extermination. Just because most of the dinosaurs have been killed off here in the park doesn't mean it's that way all over the world. I still have work ahead of me…and so does my team. After that, who knows? My plans are still in flux."

"On that note," Henry remarked as he, too, stood up. "I say we go get some rest. There will be so much to do tomorrow. More patrols and the beginning of the final cleanup. In the near future, I'll also be taking Doctor Emily back to Nampa to see if her hospital and her patients are still there. The doctor wants to take Ann with us and run tests on her to see where her cancer problem stands."

"Good idea," Justin seconded. "Though I noticed Ann is looking and acting so much better."

"She is. But the doctor wants to give her the full

treatment in a hospital so we'll know for sure."

Patterson said his goodnights and left the room.

As Henry and Justin walked out together Justin divulged, "I made a really good friend in New York, her name is Delores Taylor. We went to college together ages ago and met up again at the conference and then we were colleagues on the dinosaur team. She also happens to be Jeff Smith's half-sister."

"Ah, I recall you mentioning her a few times. She's the paleontologist you've raved about so much. The brilliant one."

"The same. She'd like to come and visit when it's convenient. Meet you, Ann and the kids. See the park. I've told her so many stories of all our adventures here at Crater Lake she just has to see it."

Henry tossed his son-in-law a strange look. "Just a friend, huh?"

"Just a friend."

"You know, son, Laura wouldn't want you to be unhappy and lonely. She was my daughter and I loved her, but Ann and I love you, too. We'd want you to be happy so–"

"Just a friend," Justin repeated, but he smiled.

"Just saying."

"I know, I know."

And the two men turned off the lights and left the room.

Chapter 26

Epilogue

A Year Later.

"The park looks wonderful," Ann exclaimed to Henry as they drove up along the rim. "It's all green again and…safe." The day was ending and the fading light, a million diamonds, played on the water below them. It'd been a cool day for August with a lovely breeze which swirled about them. All around were sky, fragrant trees, grass and sparkling water. Birds fluttered in the air and many of the native animals the dinosaurs had nearly consumed to extinction were repopulating. He had seen squirrels in the trees and elk and deer on their ride. And not one dinosaur anywhere.

They'd left their RV on the ranger headquarters' parking lot and were in their new 2014 Ram Dodge, in the blue color Ann had loved so much, driving around the park they'd once called home and had fought for for so long. The wooden stockade around headquarters had been dismantled months before and the outer and main building had been spruced up for the visitors that were coming back in droves. "It's as if the time of the dinosaurs had never happened."

"Oh, it happened," Henry mumbled, twisting the steering wheel so he wouldn't drive them off into the lake. He was happy to be back in his park, but months away had changed things for him, for Ann, for everyone. They'd remained in the park for the six months he'd promised the new superintendent he would and then he'd given the reins over to Ranger Collins or now Chief Ranger Collins. Henry knew the veteran ranger with his many years on the job and experience would be an excellent Chief. He'd wished him well. Laura's death had been one of the reasons Henry had retired. He couldn't stay in the place that had taken his daughter from them. He couldn't just go back to his old job as if the last eight years hadn't happened. It was time to move on and have a different life. Wipe the slate clean and begin again. So they had.

Henry and Ann had been on the road in their RV for months but had felt the need to revisit their old home. Not the cabin, that was long gone, razed to the ground along with the other damaged structures the dinosaurs had left behind, but the park itself. The lake. The rangers. Friends.

Henry halted the truck on the shoulder of the rim road and the two of them sat and admired the lake. For a moment he thought he could see Godzilla swimming through the waves, the Deep Rover skimming along behind it trying to catch it, and above in the skies a flock of gargoyles flying with their brethren. Out of the corner of his eyes along the rim road he thought he spied a herd of phantom velociraptors scampering away into the tall grass. On the air in the distance came the sounds of a mutant T-Rex's defiant cry. But the images and the sounds were just in his mind and only fading memories.

The dinosaurs were dead; dead in all the forests, mountains, towns and cities of America and across the world. They were still hunted and sought and dispatched of when found, yet those rogue beasts were becoming rarer every day. Justin's serum had worked far better than anyone had dreamed it could and it had freed the planet of its primordial scourge.

Patterson and McDowell had married not long after his near-death experience in Los Angeles. After Patterson retired he spent his days being a contented house husband, doing home improvements and writing his memoirs. Now that book would be one Henry would have to read. McDowell was still in uniform but wouldn't be for long because she was pregnant. She'd be leaving the military and the working world soon, as well. Between the two of them they'd amassed enough money in investments and savings to keep them comfortable, if they were careful, the rest of their lives. They lived on the edge of Klamath Falls down the country road from where Henry and Ann were getting ready to build their new cabin.

Their friends being there was one of the reasons Henry and Ann had returned to the Crater Lake, Klamath Falls area; that and it was home and always would be. Klamath Falls was in the midst of reconstruction, too. Most of it had been demolished by the dinosaurs and everywhere the citizens who'd stayed were rebuilding as the townies who'd fled were moving back in. Soon the town would be as it once had been, or even better.

Henry and Ann's traveling would be taking an hiatus as they oversaw construction of their own new domicile and filled it with furniture and comforts. Ann had designed the new cabin herself, the plans were in the glove compartment, and Henry had drawn in extras like a roomy garage and a sunroom in the rear. It wouldn't be like their old cabin because nothing could be like it had been, but it'd be comfortably cozy. Their port in a storm, their home base, when their traveling slowed down or was done.

Steven had moved to Nampa with Doctor Emily and they were planning on a September wedding. Emily had gone back to her hospital, resumed her duties and seemed pleased about it. Steven had moved in with her and after a few months had gone back to his troubadour ways, though mostly accepting singing gigs close by. He'd told Henry the week before during one of their weekly phone chats he'd decided to put off writing that book about his dinosaur adventures. "It's still too real for me to relive it. Maybe in another year or two I will sit down and write that novel, complete with all those photos I took. Right now I'm spending time helping Emily at the hospital–turns out I'm a pretty good nurse's aide, all around repair man and sometimes janitor–and getting back into my music. There's so much to be done at the hospital Emily needs all the help she can get. She has more patients now than ever. So many people didn't have doctors to go to this last year.

"You and Ann are coming to the wedding, aren't you?"

"We wouldn't miss it. September 10, huh?"

"Yep, the tenth. One o'clock. Don't be late. You know Justin, Delores and the children are coming, too?"

"I know. They'll be staying at Patterson and Sherman's house. It's arranged. All of us plan to spend a lot of time together. We'll travel down to the church in our RV and use it instead of a hotel. It's big enough."

"Splendid. We'll see you on the tenth."

"You can count on it."

Henry sometimes missed all of them, his family and friends from the dinosaur days, as he'd begun to call them, but it was nice being alone with Ann and seeing the places they'd dreamed of; even if some of them, the parks and national monuments, were still cleaning up from the dinosaur devastations. The country, the world, would need a long time to heal its wounds but it was on its way and chugging along nicely.

There'd been less happy news in the last year as well. Zeke had passed away in the winter of a heart attack and Wilma's dementia had gotten worse. She was now living in a nursing home. It was a nice one, with flower gardens and a caring staff, that Zeke had lovingly picked out for her before he'd died. It was as if he'd had a premonition he would go before she and wanted her to be taken care of. Ann dropped in to see her often and made sure she was as content as she could be. Sometimes the old woman even remembered who she was. Sometimes she remembered there had been a Zeke, as well, but less and less as time went by.

And the family, the Winters, who'd in their own way had helped find the cure that saved the world, hadn't made it intact. Henry and McDowell had taken a trip back to their glass mansion and discovered the dinosaurs had finally attacked them, protected bubble or not. The house, the front half, had been partially destroyed. Winters' wife had died fighting the creatures, but Noah Winters and his son, Brant, had survived and still lived in what was left of their home. Like many humans, they'd had to grieve and then start over.

But Ann–Henry caught his wife's gaze and smiled–Ann was okay. Her cancer had gone into full remission. Doctor Emily had run every test on her over the year and had found no signs of cancer anywhere. It wasn't a complete cure, but it was close. It'd be five years of remission before they could call it a total cure. Henry was grateful, though. She was with him and they were happy, journeying all over the country and seeing the things they'd always dreamt of seeing. The Grand Canyon. Yellowstone National Park. Bar Harbor. Mackinac Island. Before cold weather came they wanted to go to on a New England fall leaf trip and see the autumn colors. Ann's request.

Henry still made sure he kept weapons close by as they traveled…just in case they ran into one of the last remaining rare dinosaurs. It didn't happen often these days, but Henry wanted to always be prepared. But he hadn't seen one, of any kind, now in almost a year; few people had. Justin's poisoned virus had worked far better than anyone could have hoped.

Justin had taken that great job with Jeff Smith's worldwide conglomerate heading a team of scientists continuing to study the dinosaurs that had once almost taken over the earth. There was still so many questions to be answered. And he and Delores were finally openly dating. He'd waited a long time after Laura's death to even think about falling in love again. He lived in New York in a plush apartment supplied by Jeff Smith's company with Phoebe and Timothy and he had a very competent nanny to take care of them. Henry and Ann visited them often and had just spent three weeks there seeing the sights and being treated like royalty. Ann had loved being with the kids again and had hated to leave. When Timothy got a little older he and Phoebe would be able to travel with them in the summer when Phoebe was out of school. Justin had also agreed they could spend weeks with them in Klamath Falls over the main holidays or Henry and Ann would spend them with Justin and family in New York. Ann liked New York at the holidays, especially Christmas when the city could be so stunningly beautiful with the snow, decorated trees everywhere, and the colored lights.

"It feels like the old park again, doesn't it Henry?" Ann laid her hand on his arm as he started the truck again and drove with his free hand. "Peaceful, beautiful and wild."

"Just like I remember it," Henry whispered as Ann kissed his cheek.

"You ready to head to town?" Henry asked his wife. They'd park the RV, a 28 footer, on their property and go have supper with Patterson and McDowell who were waiting for them. Sasha, who had been traveling in the camper, would get to be free in Patterson's house for a while after being cooped up for weeks. She'd like that. Miss Kitty

Cat now lived with Phoebe, Justin and Timothy in New York because the cat loved the young boy so much and they couldn't be parted.

"I'm ready."

And they drove to headquarters, spent a little time with Henry's old ranger friends, hooked up their trailer and pulled it through the park and into Klamath Falls as the sun was slowly going down around them.

Leaving one life behind to begin another.

****

**If you would be so kind, please leave a brief but honest review on this book at Amazon and Goodreads. I would really appreciate it. Thank you, the author Kathryn Meyer Griffith rdgriff@htc.net*

About **Kathryn Meyer Griffith**…

Since childhood I've been an artist and worked as a graphic designer in the corporate world and for newspapers for twenty-three years before I quit to write full time. But I'd already begun writing novels at 21, over forty-four years ago now, and have had twenty-two (ten romantic horror, two horror novels, two romantic SF horror, one romantic suspense, one romantic time travel, one historical romance, two thrillers, and four murder mysteries) previous novels, two novellas and twelve short stories published from Zebra Books, Leisure Books, Avalon Books, The Wild Rose Press, Damnation Books/Eternal Press. But I've gone into self-publishing in a big way since 2012; and upon getting all my 22 books' full rights back for the first time in 33 years, have self-published all of them. My Dinosaur Lake novels and Spookie Town Mysteries (Scraps of Paper, All Things Slip Away and Ghosts Beneath Us) are my best-sellers.

I've been married to Russell for thirty-eight years; have a son and two grandchildren and I live in a small quaint town in Illinois. We have a quirky cat, Sasha, and the three of us live happily in an old house in the heart of town. Though I've been an artist, and a folk/classic rock singer in my youth with my brother Jim, writing has always been my greatest passion, my butterfly stage, and I'll probably write stories until the day I die…or until my memory goes.

2012 EPIC EBOOK AWARDS *Finalist* for her horror novel **The Last Vampire** ~ 2014 EPIC EBOOK AWARDS * Finalist * for her thriller novel **Dinosaur Lake**.

***All Kathryn Meyer Griffith's books can be found here:** http://tinyurl.com/ld4jlow

***All her Audible.com audio books here:** http://tinyurl.com/oz7c4or

Novels and short stories from
Kathryn Meyer Griffith:

*Evil Stalks the Night, The Heart of the Rose, Blood Forged, Vampire Blood, The Last Vampire (*2012 EPIC EBOOK AWARDS*Finalist* in their Horror category), *Witches, The Nameless One erotic horror short story, The Calling, Scraps of Paper (The First Spookie Town Murder Mystery), All Things Slip Away (The Second Spookie Town Murder Mystery), Ghosts Beneath Us (The Third Spookie Town Murder Mystery), Egyptian Heart, Winter's Journey, The Ice Bridge, Don't Look Back, Agnes, A Time of Demons and Angels, The Woman in Crimson, Human No Longer, Four Spooky Short Stories Collection, Forever and Always Romantic Novella, Night Carnival Short Story, Dinosaur Lake (2014 EPIC EBOOK AWARDS*Finalist* in their Thriller/Adventure category), Dinosaur Lake II: Dinosaurs Arising and Dinosaur Lake III: Infestation.*

Her Websites:

Twitter: https://twitter.com/KathrynG64
My Blog: https://kathrynmeyergriffith.wordpress.com/
https://www.facebook.com/pages/Kathryn-Meyer-Griffith/579206748758534
http://www.authorsden.com/kathrynmeyergriffith
https://www.goodreads.com/author/show/889499.Kathryn_Meyer_Griffith
http://en.gravatar.com/kathrynmeyergriffith
http://www.amazon.com/-/e/B001KHIXNS

CPSIA information can be obtained
at www.ICGtesting.com
Printed in the USA
LVOW10s1130301217
561326LV00029B/933/P

9 781537 667362